CW01149913

THE WHITELAND NOVELS

Whiteland
Karliquai
Memento Mori

ROSIE CRANIE-HIGGS

MEMENTO MORI

A WHITELAND NOVEL

bhc press

Livonia, Michigan

MEMENTO MORI
Copyright © 2023 Rosie Cranie-Higgs

All rights reserved. No part of this publication may be reproduced, distributed, or transmitted in any form or by any means, including photocopying, recording, or other electronic or mechanical methods, without the prior written permission of the publisher, except in the case of brief quotations embodied in critical reviews and certain other noncommercial uses permitted by copyright law. For permission requests, please write to the publisher.

This book is a work of fiction. The characters, incidents, and dialogue are drawn from the author's imagination and are not to be construed as real. Any resemblance to actual events or persons, living or dead, is entirely coincidental.

Published by BHC Press

Library of Congress Control Number: 2022941263

ISBN: 978-1-64397-337-1 (Hardcover)
ISBN: 978-1-64397-338-8 (Softcover)
ISBN: 978-1-64397-339-5 (Ebook)

For information, write:
BHC Press
885 Penniman #5505
Plymouth, MI 48170

Visit the publisher:
www.bhcpress.com

For Emily, my oldest friend

'Comes in like a Lion, goes out like a Lamb.'
Gnomologia: Adagies and Proverbs;
Wise Sentences and Witty Sayings,
Ancient and Modern, Foreign and British

Thomas Fuller (1732)

MEMENTO MORI

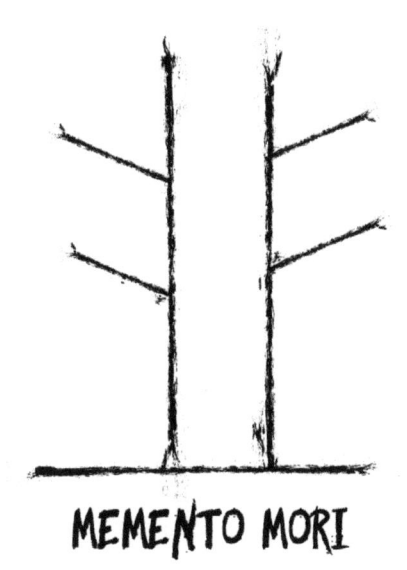

Prologue

They say that if you step out onto the air, at just the right place, you can walk to the other side.

They say that it would be transcendental, a journey akin to enlightenment; breaching the emptiness, belittling the winds.

They say that, and standing here, chained in her mind and trapped in her body, she hopes to the skies, to Ørenna, to the worlds she's split at the seams, that it's true.

The edge is immaterial beneath her dreamer's feet. The smallest sigh of air brushes her face. Her toes curl, oh so faintly. Would that she were actually dreaming; she'd force herself to wake up, but here, now, with her body not her own, she's helpless. Hapless. Hopeless.

Stop.

Arms by her sides, no ceremony. Her boots scrape against the rock. Her calves tighten, bracing. *Stop*, she whimpers again, at the wall of resolve building in her head. Her toes curl tighter. Her eyes fix firm on the trees across the gorge. Caught in the wind, in the chaos, she sways.

The far-off pines sway with her. Misted in the blue dusk, they echo with madness and swarm with the dead. She shivers, more inside than out, and tries, yet again, to sew the wisps of herself together. She was here to make a statement. She wasn't here to die.

The other voice is shaken, bleak. *Then you should have hidden.*

It stretches her lungs with a tremolo breath. Cold pine chills her nose, the scent of smoke and damp. The wall stops building. She teeters on the top.

The curtain falls. It's the moment you sense that everything's final: a snap, a click, a pinched-out candle. Her eyes widen in horror.

Talie. Her whimper becomes a scream, and she plucks at the name, at the other girl's fraying sense of self. *Talie, stop. Stop, stop, stop, STOP—*

They say that if you step out onto the air, at just the right place, you can walk to the other side.

Arms by her sides, no ceremony. Her dreamer's feet step out, and her dreamer's body falls.

1

In paradise

Kira sits on the edge of the rock and stares. The gorge is full of bluish clouds, the hazy evening falling; they say that if you step out onto the air, at just the right place, you can walk to the other side. If she drowns much more, she might try it.

Here and now, though, she simply lets her eyes unfocus. She stares past the last trees leaning into nothing, across the gorge to the rest of Atikur, shrouded in mist and far, far away. It's an atmospheric, heavy quiet. Beside her, Freya shifts.

'You need to stop acting like you know what you're doing.' Freya nudges a loosened shard of rock. Detaching with a deadened crack, it tumbles out of sight, the low clouds eating up the sound as it flees. 'Because you don't. Okay? You don't.'

It would be preferable to ignore her. Sometimes, this is tolerable; most times, it's not. But Kira's never been good at blatant rudeness, and Freya clearly has a point.

'Carry on.' Kira focuses her eyes. They fall upon a pine slightly taller than the others, directly across the gorge. If she walked across, she'd end up at its base. Half-heartedly, she squints. From here, it looks mystical, like woodland sprites would call it home, but that's Atikur. That's Whiteland. No doubt she'd be faced with a new band of horrors, each one merrily worse than the last.

Except she'd never walk across because it's just a story. A story for children, for lovers of wonder. A long time has passed since those graces let her fall.

'You also need to stop this melancholy.' Freya kicks another shard. It trickles into white and blue. 'It's maudlin. I can see the pity party taking place inside your head.' Freya trots two rigid fingers smartly down her leg. 'Miserable thought after miserable thought. March, march, march. They don't even get a fanfare, do they? Just a funeral song. A wail. A lament.'

Kira stares at her blankly. 'And that's not maudlin?'

'No.' Freya fixes her with a full expression that says, *Get over yourself*. 'It's not.'

Kira looks away again. Her sight is blurred and watery from the time she's sat here, brooding, staring. It was still the bright of morning when she brushed a spot clear of snow. Here, that doesn't mean much, but she must have been here hours.

And then Freya sat down. If Kira were more like Romy, she'd have threatened to push her over the edge. Romy might have even done it.

'Hello? I know that party's a riot, but leave.'

Kira feels Freya's icy stare land on her cheek. 'You don't have the right to complain.' Kira rubs her dry lips and then makes herself stop.

'I'm not.' Freya leans back on her hands. 'Get Yvette to give you some beesleaf.' She nods at Kira. 'For your mouth.'

Yvette hates me, Kira thinks but doesn't say. She'd only get slapped with *maudlin*.

'And I'm honest-to-all-Ørenna not complaining.' Freya burrows into her huge woollen coat. It belonged to a dead man, something that would sicken them both had it not been so bitter. Kira twists her fingers in her scratchy cuffs. At least hers belonged to Erik.

'Then what are you doing?' Kira asks.

Freya dips her chin. 'I'm saying that sadness gets you nowhere. What are you gaining by staring at clouds?'

The wool itches Kira's nail beds. She's picked her fingers raw. 'Does it matter?' Gripping her cuffs, Kira narrows her eyes. High above the treeline, far across the gorge, a thin black bird flies up and circles, a steady, graceful ballet. 'You said to stop acting like I know everything. Does it not suit your purpose if I'm sat doing nothing?'

Freya laughs. Short and sardonic; it's the slamming of a door. '"Does it not suit your purpose"?' She shakes her head, her mouth a sneer. 'You're better than this, Kira.' She nods at the black flutter, gliding up and hovering. 'And that's a Hyrcinian bird.'

'I know.' The words snap out of Kira's mouth. 'This isn't my first time in paradise, remember.'

Freya's surprise glances off her cheek. Setting her jaw, Kira watches the bird. Small and soundless, another joins it, tiny sparks in the gathering dusk. They dip and rise and tug at her. In a matter of breaths, they sigh away.

'You didn't say why you cared.' Kira sweeps a hand around the gorge, at the creeping, blue mist-cloud. 'About anything. Everything.' She kicks her heel against the rock. 'Up and at 'em. You're free to leave.'

Freya is silent for a moment, two. 'You know why.'

Kira looks across at her. Freya's mouth is twisting, her eyes on the snow. Kira wills with the spiritless force of her brain: pick up the damn gauntlet. They've repeated and rehashed it fifty thousand times, but she's wallowed all day. She needs the bite.

'The answer's no, by the way,' Freya says, sitting up to cross her legs. 'If we're being pompous, it doesn't suit my purpose to have you a despondent pit.'

Kira gives a dark huff. 'I'm not a pit.'

'No.' Freya swivels on the frosted rock. 'You're a chasm. I don't want you to be a chasm any more than I want you to kill us with what you're doing. Forgive me for repeating myself, oh worldly outsider'—she waves her hand in an odd royal gesture—'but you don't *know* what you're doing. Getting involved with witches is not a happy-go-lucky activity. Assuming, of course, we find someone who'll admit to being one.'

Kira ignores her.

'Which is the great-grandfather of all assumptions.'

Kira ignores her.

Freya sighs. 'I'd even say great, great, great.'

Lifting her chin, Kira tilts it away. Ingrid said Hyrcinians are rare, and seeing one out in the open, let alone two before dark, is a wonder, but that doesn't stop her from combing the sky. Last time she saw them, she was with Callum.

'I'll just keep talking,' Freya says, casual and shrugging. 'A lifetime of exile arms you pretty well for being ignored.' She shuffles her crossed legs closer to Kira. 'Do you have any idea—*any idea*—how hard a task you're setting yourself? Witches aren't as common as crows or even as common as huldra.' She brushes her palm across the powder, spraying it into the canyon. 'They make Hyrcinians look like snow.'

Kira watches the white disperse and fall. 'Fascinating.'

'Oh, my—' Freya shakes her head, breathing sharply through her nose. 'Kira. The Kyo had to kidnap a seventeen-year-old, who may or may not have been a witch. The *Kyo*. Doesn't that tell you something?'

'Probably.' Kira shoves her stiff, numbing limbs upright. The mist is snaking up to her perch, and its tendrils on her dangling ankles are clammy, leering perversions. She could have chosen boots over moccasins, but the flat hide is more or less warm and more or less silent on snow.

With a sound of frustration, Freya stands. 'You're so very lucky I'm human now.' Tipping her head back, she exhales a cloudy plume. 'If I wasn't, you'd be dead.'

'Yes, you've told me this before.' Curtly, Kira turns to the forest. 'The number of times you've resisted murder and the languishing huldra inside you.' Bored, she waves a hand. Kira heads away from the forest's drop. Behind her, snow and rock scrape.

Freya falls into step with a shiver and a skip. 'You know what, never mind.' Her voice slows and thickens like molasses. 'Kira, you have to understand how serious—'

'I *know*.' Hunching her shoulders, Kira lets the dusk-dark trees enfold her. 'It's not like I'm after genocide.'

'I don't know what that means.'

Kira veers left of the old jay's nest. 'I'd be a hypocrite to follow Taika too closely. No one needs to worry; I just want the four of us to leave and stay gone.' Her throat clogs up. *The four of us*. Angrily, she swallows. 'That's what the Whispers were trying to do. They should give me a round of applause.'

'Kira, it's not *about* the Whispers.' Freya rams her hands in her oversized pockets. 'Not at all. You just don't…' She makes an indistinct noise. 'You have no idea. Magic isn't the same as on the outside; it's not romantic or sweet or even talked about, and it's *definitely*—the word echoes from the trees—'not made light of. This way.'

Kira follows her through two whispering birches, whippet-thin and patchy. 'I'm not making light.'

'I mean the outside in general.' Freya's voice is as thin as the birches. 'You, all of you—with your pointed hats and story books and turning into animals— you have no idea. Waving a stick and getting things done, or visiting mysterious women in caves, who smile enigmatically and hold out a candle. Magic is dark here, and what we do'—she gestures to herself, at the forest, and beyond—'the

Huldra, the Leshy, the human weavers; none of it even comes close. Real magic is heathen, and it makes your skin crawl. You taste metal. Your spirit feels metal. I'm hardly even being dramatic.'

'Mmhmm.' Kira casts her a look that doesn't need words. All of this is dramatic. *And the doll? When it squeezed Kira's mind between finger and thumb, before it took them to Urnäsch, the air tasted—* She slams the memory shut. Even the thought of remembering makes it hard to breathe. 'You spent a long time with Taika, to say magic feels like metal.' Kira softens her footsteps further. In here, more than magic is dark; she should have brought an enigmatic candle of her own. The trees have their own version of night, where your eyes feel covered by a sharp-lined velvet. She rediscovered that fast. 'Or does nothing count when it's you?' Freya's eye roll is almost audible. How many times in the last day alone has Freya called her trying? Kira's started to feel like Romy must have for nearly seventeen years.

'I stayed away from the magic part.' Freya sticks close to her, the Tweedledum to her Tweedledee, as they pass to the left of a storm-struck tree. Freya may be trying, but she learns in no time; it's oh-so-tempting to get her lost.

Kira could do it. She could suddenly sprint, so the forest would shift, and Freya would be too slow. With any luck, Freya would get caught halfway; she'd find her way back, but not for hours. If the forest found her plight amusing, it could twist her around here for days.

An ex-huldra, stranded by her, an outsider. Kira shakes off the fantasy. God, she needs some fun.

'…and the magic I did see,' Freya is saying. 'I didn't ask about.' Stepping ahead of Kira with a juvenile burst, she runs her fingers through a hand of branches, cracked and dripping snow. 'I helped Taika because I was meant to get out, and I didn't think I'd be here, without her protection, to face the consequences.' Freya waves sarcastically around. 'Joy of joys. If you join with a witch, you're as cast out as she is. Double if you're already huldra.'

Kira rubs at her lips. 'You poor, poor thing.' She meets Freya's eyes with a point, a glint. 'At least you're still alive.'

Freya's gaze holds steel of its own. 'Trekking through the wilds with the spawn of a devil. The greatest huldra of anyone's time, whose light burns bright within you!' Freya steps on a tree-root tail, perfectly poised to trip them up. Both hands are sarcastic now. 'And to think, my love, I could have had it all.'

'Absolutely.' Kira rolls her eyes. Stopping, she hesitates, getting her bearings. Her eyes have adjusted, but the velvet stays sharp. 'How do you know about outside magic? You were there for like two days.'

Impatient, Freya taps her arm, nodding at a slope in the snow. On the right, the spruces muscle together. In the day, they glitter with frost.

Shrugging her off, Kira tramps toward it. Her moccasins barely squeak. 'You do know magic's not real on the outside, right? It's just for stories.'

'Yes.' Freya crunches back beside her. 'I'm well aware it's make-believe, but it's also everywhere. I had to get clothes and eat and travel, so I saw a lot of things. A *lot*'—she jogs up the slope—'of things. Images on walls, people on squares that move and talk to you. Even outsiders saying things like, "It's like magic!"'

She jiggles her hands, briefly buoyant. Kira almost laughs, jazz hands. Freya would have no clue what that means.

'Okay, you get my point.' Freya drops her hands to her thighs, stopping them just before they slap. 'In my few days'—she throws Kira a meaningful look that Kira pointedly misses—'I took a lot in. People are obsessed with this one story. That's where I got the hats.'

Kira nods. '*Harry Potter*,' she says as her chest pulls tight, like amateurs trying to sew. Here and now, and especially *here*, it rings a discordant bell. All her life, *Harry Potter* gave her all of her magic. *Harry Potter* and Neil Gaiman and a crush on Damon Salvatore. For the outside world, that's all magic is: a safe imagining, devoured on beds, by electric living room fires. It's so out of step with *now*, like a too-clean, bright-lit dream.

Bitterly, Kira blinks it away.

'The point is,' Freya continues, 'that magic—'

'Is treated like a big, giddy joke because out there, it isn't real.' Kira slaps her palm to a rowan trunk. 'You've laboured it to death. But unless there's a better way, and unless we find it soon, I need a witch.'

In the near distance, golden lights flicker into life. The rich aroma of bee syrup honeys the air, mixed with resin and a sharpening knife. Glittering gold, Freya stops. 'Okay.'

'I could be too late already,' Kira says. Curling her fingers into fists, she coils her toes tight. 'I can't sit here, staring at clouds. I'm… I'm dancing. In the dark.' A tormented expression rumples her face, but she smooths the whorls away. She has to stay together; she's the only one left. 'If you're human, you'll understand. We have this thing called empathy.'

Freya regards her evenly. 'I said okay, Kira.' Eyeing her, she shoulders past, crunching toward the lights. 'We'll go tomorrow. Right now, I'm hungry, and I'm smelling a roast.'

For a second, two seconds, three seconds, four, Kira watches her go. She's a pale-haired spectre; they both are. They're shadows. Shadows shunted into hiding, scorned and threatened like scum. Talk about dancing in the dark; she feels like she's barely whistling.

Wrapping her arms around herself, Kira sets off after Freya. There's warmth, food, distrustful shelter. Light and life and women who knew her mother. Berry wine that sticks to her throat. A world in the trees.

Tomorrow. Kira clings to this as she squints at the firelight, flinching at the far-off howl of a wolf. They'll go tomorrow.

If it's not too late.

2

The shock of life

Several days earlier

Kira doesn't truly register she's being pulled away, and by the time she does, it doesn't matter. In actuality, it might help.

The first thing to fade back is sound. The detached sound of boots on snow, the sound of heavy breaths made quiet. The sound of arms in coats against sides.

The second thing is feeling. A raw, raised slit in her lip, where she must have chewed it through. It throbs in the cold, and so do her ears, poorly covered by her frostbitten hair. Her legs barely stumble. Her feet are just pain.

The third thing is sight. Her vision is blurry, greyish and grainy, swollen and slitted from tears. Everything is white and green: the thin, featureless towers of trees, erupting from the snow. The bright sky, matte and flat. The woodchip path through the bracken.

There is a thud in her chest like a fist on glass. The body behind her urges her on, to the path's squelchy give. It's a different angle, and she took it on the darkest, heaviest, most smothering night she'd known, but if someone's leading her along it…it's presumably one and the same. The path to the road, that leads to the clearing, that leads her out of Whiteland.

They must have been walking for ages. Kira lets the dull shock settle, cooling and turning rationally numb. At least her outsides aren't numb too; she'd be an ice queen who'd never thaw.

If anything, she's overly warm. She feels each eyeball as she casts them down. Why—

Nostalgic déjà vu jolts her, merciless and wired. A giant coat enfolds her. Its thick, woolly pockets rasp her wrists, its hem swimming round her thighs. The smell of the wild is cloying, as familiar as if she was here a week ago, waking up in the snow hole with it bunched around her neck.

Waking up with Callum. The familiarity turns to clay, fires hard, and sets. Callum. Romy. Jay.

A muffled curse sounds to the left. Kira sweeps her eyes, misshapen in their sockets.

'Jesus Christ,' she croaks, with a second jolt. The huldra they named Fiona is everywhere. Is she haunting her now? A grinning token of all that's gone wrong? Of how Kira wronged her and will pay forevermore?

Kira's gained her own personal ghost—or Kyo as they call them here. Great.

Fiona looks up. 'Look, the catatonic princess.' She focuses dourly back on her feet. 'I'm glad my tripping woke you.'

The catatonic princess. Kira frowns, foggy, slow. She must have been the walking dead, vortexed by shock, somehow moving her mechanical legs. A solid body props her up. Her sluggish mind slogs: Erik. Holding her around the waist, he steers her by the shoulder, his breathing laboured on her hair. He smells of woodsmoke and grizzled older men.

'Kira?' he says, but her heart clenches. She'd been on the verge of finding him comforting, like the smell of her father's work shirts: their reliable mix of aftershave, laundry detergent, and sweat before it grows too strong.

No. Kira pictures glass and then herself. She needs to stay together; she needs to find a plan. What *happened*?

'Kira,' Erik repeats, on the edge of her hearing. Kira hauls her heavy memory back. One: Talie told them—she and Romy and Callum and Jay—that the Chlause would protect them. Two: they—she and Romy and Callum and Jay—set blithely off for Urnäsch. Three: the Chlause turned out to be aligned with Hades, for all the hell they wreaked. Four: the four of them ran, and then…

And then. Five: Urnäsch slammed shut. The others were trapped. Kira glasses this over the most. What about the Whispers? The Kyo? The witch? Anna? Mathew? She's left with half the tale and none of the hows and whys.

Like why the huldra's next to her, with no intent to murder.

'Wait.' Kira stops walking. Behind her, Erik emits a soft 'oof.' 'Why are we still alive?' Her voice is cutting in the winter chill.

Fiona stops, too. 'I think'—one eyebrow arcs—'you'll have to be more specific.'

Kira's thoughts are sludge. 'You.' She pulls a hand from her woolly pocket. Her nails are clogged with dirt. 'Why haven't you killed—' she glances back at Erik—'me. Us. Anyone?'

The huldra's expression cools. 'A lot has happened since our last encounter, oh charming princess of mine.' Fiona folds her arms, looking like a frozen ice-queen herself with her Swedish skin tinged purple. Even her hair, as blonde as Anna's, looks brittle and bitter and ready to break. 'Right now, I'm a glorified guard dog who isn't allowed to guard.' Fiona eyes Erik.

'You were a huldra,' he says, his rough voice terse. 'You don't change overnight.'

Fiona's expression flares and curls. 'What am I going to do?' she snaps. 'Have my way with her? I should. It might make her look less dead.'

'You look fairly dead yourself,' Kira says quietly. She meets the huldra's red-rimmed eyes. 'Do you like being human?'

The frosty air crackles. The trees lean in. Erik puts a broad hand on the small of Kira's back. 'I think, Freya—'

'It's fine.' With a silent snarl, the huldra turns. 'She can say what she likes. I'm not going to touch her. There's no way I'm screwing up getting back out.'

'Her name is Freya?' Kira asks. 'We were calling her Fiona.'

'Close enough.' Freya strides off, then stops. 'In fact'—Freya spins on the sucking woodchip path—'it's not me you should be watching. *I've* never hurt her. *She* caused this'—Freya gestures to the red, angry welt on her cheek—'and dumped me back here to die.'

Freya's face contorts. Kira doesn't correct her. Every snapped-off syllable drains her, as if she wasn't already dry. 'Okay,' she manages dumbly.

The huldra stares. The corners of Freya's eyes flicker with something unreadable. 'Okay.' Freya laughs. Short and harsh and ugly; it echoes. 'Okay.'

Jerkily, Freya sets off again. Erik presses the small of Kira's back. 'We should follow her,' he says. 'Atikur may pale in comparison to Urnäsch, but it's less than safe.' He pushes Kira gently. 'I'd prefer to be home by night.'

Guilt throbs beneath Kira's resolve. Offering Erik a limpid smile, she stamps on its beating heart. 'You don't have to come the rest of the way.'

To prove it, Kira starts to walk. Her stiff legs stumble on the path, and Erik catches her arm. 'I'll see you to the outside.' His gruff voice is firm. 'Until a few days ago, Freya was a predator. She's human now'—he urges her on—'but humans are predators too.'

Kira forces herself to focus on Freya. Stalking down the path, it's easy to picture. Even in outsider clothes, her aura is sharp, like if you come close, you die. She watches the huldra slap a snowy branch blocking the way.

Letting the branch spring back, Freya snorts. She hesitates, half looking over her shoulder. 'And believe it or not, my intentions are honourable.'

Kira ducks beneath the bowing branch. The trees bristle like brambles here, clinging and clawing and cloying and cold. Milky-white icicles hang above boulders, almost scraping a frozen stream. It looks like the road to nowhere. 'Why?'

Freya snorts again. 'I'm a wonderful person.' She waves a hand as the path swerves past a crossroads of animal tracks, craggy-edged and deep. 'No. I haven't killed anyone, as you put it, because it's no longer in my interest. If you deign to hurry up, so we can hurry out, I'll deign to tell you the rest.'

Kira considers her and then the sky. It's not growing dark, but the light is changing, the way of days in the heart of winter when the afternoon atmosphere turns. At once, colour is bright and dim, sharp and stark and textured. Soon, the crowded forest will wake. 'Erik…'

'No, Kira.' Erik's whiskered eyebrows furrow as he scans the stirring trees, his glove still gripping her arm. 'I'll come as far as I can. It's not far.'

Succumbing to numbness is a war when her emotions rule as general. Kira bites the ulcer blistering her cheek. In the place of guilt throbs gratitude. It's the kind that makes her want to cry, but God, she's sick of tears. On her knees in the snow, and held against Erik, she cried enough for death. For life.

'Thank you.' Biting until it hurts, Kira swallows for composure. 'Again. The way you keep…' She sniffs, hard. Glass. Ice. Nothing. 'I'm sorry. When I first saw you, I was awful. I acted like an…I don't know, like an animal.' She balls her fists in her pockets. 'You didn't deserve it. And I lost your coat.'

She sweeps her swollen eyes down her new one. Below it, Carol's boots peek out, scuffed and scraped and wary. Her fists ball tight enough to strain.

Erik's beard twitches with a hint of a smile. 'It came back to me,' he says, as the forest starts to thin. Pine in the air, ice on the breeze. The trees inch away from their neighbours, haughty, tall, and cold. 'I was travelling back from trading, and our boat ran aground.' He bends beneath a hand of branches. Powder dusts his hat like a cake. 'I say ran, but it was pulled, very gently. Everything I gave you was waiting in an inlet, and once I took it, the ground let us go.'

Kira hints at a smile, a hint of a glimmer of wonder. 'How?'

The woodchip path narrows to a winding trickle. Erik stops to let her go first, bowing his grizzled head. 'I assume the shapeshifter had a part to play. As for acting like an animal—'

'This hurrying up isn't going very well.' Scratching past a wayward thicket, Freya taps her leg and looks back. 'Come *on*.'

Kira meets Erik's eye. His coarse beard twitches. 'As for acting like an animal,' he says, 'I would say your reason was sound. All I know is what Freya has said, which is sparse, but enough.'

He stops walking, shading his eyes. Through two weedy saplings, lacing their knotty fingers over it, the woodchip path ends. The forest ends. The thorny part of Whiteland ends. Kira's chest twists and thumps. Last year's endless road begins.

Stark beneath the blinding sky, it's a blinding, tree-lined white. The only thing marring it is Freya, stopping in the middle and turning. 'Come on!' Freya marches off again.

Slowly, Kira pushes through the saplings, stopping on the edge of the woodchip path. You don't see how much you remember until you're suddenly back: everything here, on this road, reminds her of Callum: muttering about a bear hunt, scaring her with stories of lynx. Callum, when she barely knew him and no one's life was screwed.

'I'm sorry,' Erik says gruffly, 'for whoever you left behind.'

Romy. Callum. Jay. Kira stares through the snow until her memories are thinly iced.

'Thank you.' She slides her glassy gaze up. 'Not for that, just…everything. One day, I'll pay you back.' She forces another pale smile.

'Don't.' Erik meets her smile with almost a growl. She blinks. A frown creases his weather-worn forehead. 'If you do, it means you have returned here.' His eyes are shrewd and sharp. Watching. 'You're brave, Kira. Don't ruin it.'

Kira keeps her face as smooth as she can. 'I don't feel brave.' She looks away. It's not a lie, but still. 'I feel like I need to get as far away as possible.'

Also not a lie, but it feels like one. Kira shoots Erik's silence a sidelong glance. Still watchful, still discerning. His blue pouched eyes pierce further by the second.

'Do that,' he says. With his creased frown lingering, he readjusts the snowshoes crossing his back and steps out onto the road. Thankfully, the wooden window doesn't drag its feet. The window she found with Callum. The window that shows a fork in the road.

The window that, a year ago, let them into Whiteland.

'This is as far as I'm able to go,' Erik says, as they catch up to Freya. The huldra is walking around the window, a hard little smile on her face. 'I can watch you down the road, but I can't move further.'

Erik stops just shy of the Whiteland side. Freya rolls her eyes. 'Guard dog,' she mutters. Tracing the too-familiar tree, scratched in one spliced corner of the wood, she backs toward the outside world. 'Catch me now.' She smirks. 'Oh, wait.'

Kira fights the urge to kick her. 'Thank you.' Impulsively, she puts an arm around Erik's waist, a bulky, unsure hug. 'Again. And again. And again.'

Pulling back, Kira fiddles with the toggles of her coat. He stops her gently. 'Keep it.'

The words are a low grumble. Swallowing, Kira lets him move her hands. 'Are...are you sure?'

'Yes.' Somehow, he looks softened, the lines on his face not covered by hair more fatherly than brusque. 'Even out of Whiteland, if it's winter, you'll freeze.' Erik straightens, squinting into the distance. 'From the look of the road, it is.'

Refastening the coat against the thin, breathy air, Kira tracks his gaze. 'The road changes?'

'It does.' Erik inclines his head, twisted with irony. 'Some come and watch. With the right eyes, you see the road become grey and everything around it green. I've heard the sky changes too, but that's more likely the watcher's longing to escape. A perfect world beyond this one, where the colours of the sky are always bright, and everyone has hope.'

He gives a slow headshake. Kira's mind drifts to Devon, often dull with rain, or the typical Whiteland white. Urnäsch, where the landscape was vivid and garish, the brightest of them all. Her mouth knits tight. 'No world is perfect.'

Halfway down the road, Kira looks back. Erik stands as he promised, watching from the window, and she lifts a lingering hand. When she looks again, with the same pang as at his woody, smoky smell, both he and the window have gone.

Remember, he said again. *You're brave.*

The words run on a reel through Kira's head. She's going to let him down.

Meekly, a sole bird starts to chirp. A robin joins in with its spinning-coin trill, and a jay with a rakish *wrehhk*. Ahead of Kira, Freya lifts her arms.

You're brave. Kira walks on.

The birds fall soft as the sky grows dark. If you looked from the window, you might see it change; quicker even than Urnäsch, the sky smudges from early evening pinks to late evening purples to night-time indigo and black. Moon-haze haloes the tops of the trees. Stars wink in, then Sirius, Mars.

At an owl's hoot, Kira starts. A jilted, feral bark bites off the hollow sound. Lit with lamps by wooden huts, the car park curves into sight.

Slapping the metal with a jarring clang, Freya vaults the barrier. Kira watches her land, sleek and lithe in the snow. Her own limbs feel lumpy by comparison, but that shouldn't be surprising; this is the woman, creature, thing who leapt from a window, chased Romy and Callum through Montreux, and came to Callum's house with the belief that she could kill him. Either the huldra are naturally strong, or living in the heart of Whiteland, shunned and abhorred, which means you have to be too.

'You can't take it away this time!' Freya pivots wildly, arms out, as Kira tramps past the barrier. Her grin is wicked, but the sound is flat, not muffled by the claustrophobic night or the baby's blanket of snow or the closed atmosphere; it's broken only by the buzz of overhead wires—just flat. Flat, void, blank. It rings like a stilted child, forced to act in a play.

'Just accept it,' Kira mutters. Brushing none-too-gently past Freya, she steps onto the tarmac, stomping snow from Carol's boots. Ice sheens the car park, but she only walks faster. 'You have feelings now. You're not an evil, cackling overlord, or whatever that's meant to be.'

Kira flicks her wrist, glancing back. Freya is still for the barest of moments, but the moment is enough; in the creaking lamplight, her face glows lost.

Good. Kira carries on, toward the road through the village.

At the bottom of the sledge hill, the huldra catches up. 'Where are you going to go?' she asks. 'Now you're as alone as me.' She huffs. 'It's refreshing. For once, I'm not the one being hunted.'

She grates like nails on ice. Kira walks faster. 'Go away.'

Freya quickens with her. 'But have you thought about that?' She sounds oddly caught between mocking and morose. 'What you'll do next to stay hidden? To live?'

Grating, grating. The ice splinters. 'It doesn't matter what I've thought about,' Kira says, as clipped as wings.

'And yet, I'm intrigued.' A pause. 'So have you?'

'If you think I'll sail into the sunrise with you, you need to find a bike to get on.' Kira wheels in the road to face her, flaring hot and black. 'Start your new life as far from me as possible. Figure out on your own how to travel, how to make money, how to live in society without skidding straight back to outcast. How to live with what you've done now that you're human. I hope you're miserable.'

Kira spins to stamp up the road again, tears clotting her throat. *Stop it.* She swallows so roughly the sound is a snap. *Fucking stop.*

'Your mother lived with what she did,' Freya calls behind her.

Kira's breath hops from her mouth to her stomach. Billowing, skipping, it blows past her lungs.

'Very well, from what I've heard. A husband, children. A compact life.'

'My mother's monster stopped in Whiteland.' Kira doesn't turn. Her voice aches, becomes almost a tremor. 'Your monster had barely started.'

⁂

Slowly, slowly, Freya comes to a stop. Kira's rigid back retreats up the road, rounding the tree-lined corner. Kira's words felt truer than they should have. She *felt* them more than she should have. As slowly as she stopped, Freya starts up the road again, the night air nipping her cold-stiff joints.

The two of them have changed far more than they should have in such a short space of time. Their roles have tilted, blurring at the edges: Freya's lost her malicious whirl of energy, giddy and drunk on freedom, and Kira's not the bright-faced girl she drank beer with, fresh from her reunion with Callum. Kira's hard-edged and bitter, as wild as any of the women whose men were killed by huldra. Black, pinched circles beneath her eyes, a pungent Whiteland coat.

She's also right. Freya's exactly what Kira said she was: lesser, trying to recapture herself as she was when she first got free. Human, already. Weak, already. Empty without the Kyo telling her what to do. Freya was small without her talents, gone without a trace. Worried about the outside.

Freya keeps seeing faces. Callum: *you're pretty, for a monster.* Talie, fighting to look calm, speaking a tongue already unknown. Clocking at once who Freya was.

One of Kira's friends, who was so surprised when Freya slunk in that terror never struck. The second friend, who didn't have time to squeak, let alone scream, before she died. The third friend, whose neck Freya snapped.

And then the men. Nameless, luckless, lifeless.

Stop. Kicking the faces away, she bloodies them, blackening their eyes so they don't crawl back. That part of her existence is over. Gone. As over as ghosts and magic, as gone as Urnäsch and Whiteland. If she doesn't let it be over and gone, she'll end up like Anneliese.

Not Anneliese in a good way, the kids-and-nice-life way; that would be fine. The curious way, the lured-back-and-banished way; that's what she doesn't need. Until recently, Freya scoffed and scorned, but after the last couple of days, if the kids-and-nice-life way crooked its finger, she'd follow it into its room.

Freya speeds up, skirting a patch of black ice. Briefly, Kira comes into view. Freya slows down until a dark bend swallows her. A little car hums past. Freya doesn't dodge it. The shadows have gone; towering lamps illuminate the dark places with their light. The old hotel where Talie lives, frosty cars, homes. Up ahead, Kira crosses the train line.

Slowing further, Freya twists her face. Oh, *dear*. Glumly, Kira turns toward stepping-stone stairs, bowing her head at the bottom. That's sure to go well: showing up at Callum's house in the middle of the night, lacking both Callum and his brother. Kira's braver than she looks.

Then again, she has nowhere else to go. Freya skims over her sneaking guilt. How depressing: to survive the Chlause, return to your world, and then be stuck with your boyfriend's mother. Not only that, but your boyfriend's mother will probably send you packing.

At least it makes Freya's own pickle seem not quite so bad.

One stepping-stone. Two stepping-stones. Kira's coat disappears through the powdered arch after the fifth stepping-stone. Her footsteps crunch the snow.

Done. Freya releases her bated breath, lifting her arms for the drama. She walked a whole road more than she had to; what a great human she'll make.

And now for a night in the desolate barn, and her first unbothered sleep. Crossing the tilted tracks, Freya heads for the field, greeting the empty road like a friend. No women in her head, plotting and cackling. No lordly men she can't even see. She'll dance. She'll build a fire. She'll sit on the edge of the open hayloft and look out over the lake. She'll dazzle herself with the glittering lights, grapple for her elation, and deal with the morning when the morning comes.

Free. A smile shapes Freya's face, gratifying and strange. This time, freedom couldn't have been easier: take girl, leave Whiteland. Accompany girl to Callum's house. At least Kira hadn't kept up the hysterics from when she had first left Urnäsch.

This is a satisfying thought until it's not. By the gate to the moonlit field, Freya stops.

Kira had been hysterical. Crying, yelling, primal, wild, adamant she had to go back for the others. But when she saw that she was leaving Whiteland, she said nothing. Nothing at all.

Ørenna.

No. No, no, no. Freya's lungs freeze and shatter, driving ice through her chest.

There was a reason Kira said nothing, and it was not a change of heart.

Kira wouldn't trade guilt for gratitude. She wouldn't think it was enough, the fact that she's alive. She wouldn't want to give up on the others, even if it was justified, because Kira cares for everything so damn much.

Kira wouldn't want to give up, so she wouldn't.

Ørenna. Freya turns and runs.

3

The dying flame

Stupid. Stupid, stupid, stupid. How can any one person, at any one time, be so out-of-the-worlds *stupid?*

Freya pelts down the white road, skidding, arms out. Perhaps Freya's wrong. Maybe Kira did go to Callum's house, to face the wrath or despair of his mother. Maybe they'll plan a future in mutually despondent, grieving peace.

Really?

Not a chance.

'Kira!' Freya shouts, leaping up the black-iced stepping-stones. '*Argh!*'

Freya slips. Pain smashes through her knee. She growls, as guttural and coarse as a brute, grabbing for the arctic hedge.

'Kira!' Freya hauls herself up with a yell. The frozen thorns raze her hands, and she limps up the garden. 'Kira, come down or I'll…'

Pause. Heave. Breathe. Nothing. '*Kira!*'

Kira! Ra! Ra! The midnight mountains echo.

Freya stops, bends, and breathes like a beast, exhaling into her thighs. This garden is so much steeper than before. Skies, Kira had better be in there.

'Kira!' Freya's words are more wheeze than shout. She straightens up, squeezing her lungs to project. 'Kira!'

Pause. Heave. Breathe. Nothing. Squatting, she scoops a handful of snow, shakes her head, and aims for the chalet. Save us all. Freya's throwing snowballs.

The snowball splatters with the thud of an axe. She squats for more snowballs, one for each hand. 'You can't ignore me!' Freya shouts. 'I'll break in. I'll rip you from your bed and drag you to the barn.' Screwing up her face, Freya aims for a window. Snow thuds once, twice, dull on the dark chalet. 'If someone hits me again, I swear—'

Light blooms behind an upstairs shutter. Finally, *finally*, someone's alive. Freya pushes back her white-blonde hair and holds it away from her neck. It's the first time she's ever really sweated.

Half a minute later, the door ghosts open. A small, round face appears in the gap, bleary-eyed and rosy. Freya frowns at it. There's a child?

The girl at the door yawns, loud and unselfconscious. 'Who'—she yawns again. Smacking her lips with a *tuh, tuh,* she swallows her sleep—'are you?'

'Is Kira here?' Freya bobs on the balls of her jittery feet and scans the upstairs windows. Behind a bare pane appears a second glow of light. 'I need to see her. She would have come in just now.'

Rubbing her bare arms, the chubby girl shakes her head. Her lurid nightdress is far too short. 'I haven't seen her since…since'—she pouts. The girl's lilting voice is peculiar, not all one sound and not all another—'since she went somewhere for lunch.'

Fat lot of good that is. A muffled query calls from the depths of the chalet, and as the girl jumps, turning, plucking at her lip, Freya drops her hair and wheels around. Kira's not here.

Which means Kira had a plan. Which means…

Throwing out her arms, Freya skids down the garden. *Stupid. Stupid, stupid, stupid.*

'Julia?' a woman calls behind her, echoing in the night. 'Did you hear something as—oh.'

The *oh* is a puff. Freya doesn't look back; she'd rather not see the hurting face of the woman whose sons—

'Romy? Is that you?'

Freya's body stalls. One hand stretched for the frosted arch; she can't will herself to move.

'Romy,' the woman repeats. Her voice cracks like hoarfrost. 'Talk to me.'

'Carol?' the girl whispers. 'I don't think that's—'

'Go back to bed.' The woman clears her splintered throat. With an unhappy huff, the door creaks open further. 'Romy, please. Did you all get out? Where's Jay? And Callum?'

'I'm not Romy.' Freya turns in a jerk, her face open to the air, to the moon and a thousand stars. A tallish, lumpy silhouette, the woman is wrapped in something warm. 'If Jay…' The words get stuck in Freya's throat. Averting her eyes, Freya takes a breath and exhales once from her nose. The woman's a mother. A *mother*.

'If Jay's the boy,' Freya manages, staring through a barren rowan, 'he's still with Callum and Romy in Urnäsch. I got Kira out, but the door shut on the others. I think Kira—oh, I need to *go*.'

Freya spins on the glinting snow, ducking through the arch, throwing herself down the slope by the stepping-stones. Her knee twinges at every bend. How did she get distracted? Waylaid? If Kira's not here, she's doubled back, and at this time of night, in such a sleepy, isolated pit of a place, there's nowhere to go but—

'Wait.' The woman's voice follows Freya, high with desperation. She sounds like Callum. 'Who are you, then?'

You're pretty, for a monster.

Tripping onto the road, Freya wavers. 'Freya,' she calls. The mountains echo, *Freya! Ya! Ya!* Once upon a time, she would have lied.

Go.

This road is beyond monotonous. Freya sprints past the lamps, past the dark, poky chalets, and over the squat, shadowed bridge. One of these days, she'll be done with pines and never see snow again. The sun will scorch her skin to blisters. The sky will have colour. The land will have colour. She'll find seasons, the kind that stories love, stories both of the outside and of Whiteland's hidden nooks. The river people, festering in Taika's spiteful recollections, seem to live a picturesque life; maybe she'll find a balmy river and work the rest out later.

Or she'll find a man who thinks her innocent, take his heart, and give him hers.

Freya's lip crooks like a fishhook. She's not that human yet.

Faster. Freya's feet burn. Her legs are infernos, her raging chest and wounded knee throwing dead wood on the flames, but fixing her sights on stories and sun, she flies across the car park.

Kira must have joined the wind; she's not even in sight. Her tracks are, though. Tracks, like an animal. On the edge of the field, Freya staggers to a stop, off-balance from the force of her sprint. Boot prints blunder away through the snow, shin-deep, blunt, and drunk. Freya grips her shuddering knees. Sweaty, panting, heat steams off her. It's not too late to give this up; Freya could head back to the barn, sleep through the cold in a mouldy-hay corner, and let the blithering idiot make her own bloody mistakes.

Not my circus. Freya gasps at the greying slush of the car park. She heard it in one of these faceless towns, tall and bland and grey. *Not my circus, not my monkeys.*

The crotchety answer was stern: *It may not be your circus, but they may become your monkeys.* Freya gathered what it meant. Kira was not her problem and won't become her problem. And yet…

And yet. Blotting the battle-ready forest from her view, Freya shoves off her knees and plunges into the snow after Kira. Her head could float away on a string. Her legs…what are legs? What's *food?* Right now, she'd eat the basest outside muck.

And she's never running again. With her lungs around her ears, Freya stumbles and flails. Past an odd contraption, like a car on skis. Past another, huge and silver, soaring silent up the mountain, through a treacherous gap in the trees. Her feet sink deep. Icy snow trickles down inside her boots, grating at her ankles. Up a gentle slope, and then—

Kira. There, whole, by Karliquai; she found the Chlause chalet.

There, as a light falls down.

※

Kira doesn't turn. The sound of snow and laboured lungs flounder up behind her, but the light is already drifting. The star she dreamt. The gold she painted. The glow that brings the Chlause.

Clouds bruise the edges of the greying night. Slowly, in silence, the light tumbles down as she balls her hands in her pockets. Zombie-esque and breathing hard, she's here. Kira's legs felt like pylons as she fled down the road, severed from her brain, but they had to be. Everything has to be severed, lobotomized. If she thinks, or feels, she'll fall.

Rooting her trembling legs, Kira focuses on the light. Ploughing through the snow made her headache snarl, from a throb to a rushing, spiking heat, but she's here. Here to act, somehow. Here to find the others. Here as the boiling clouds pull in, as the wind stirs up. Here as a tint of metal starts to taint the winter air.

Freya shouts.

Kira lifts her heavy chin. Softly, softly, the light drifts. It is folktales and promises, ruffling her numbness. It whispers of Sleeping Beauty and faeries, of Snow White and the prince; even her old Scandinavian stories, where elves dance at midnight and careless girls lose their hearts in forest pools. Barring the metal tint, there's not a hint of what it leads to.

Of course there isn't. Kira swallows, pressing her lips together, tensing every muscle. Even no longer drenched in ignorance, the blue-white, cutting enchantment draws her. Why would the Chlause want anything else? If the road to Hell was paved with fire, no one would ever walk it.

Steadily, Kira makes herself breathe. In, metal. Out, blood where she's gnawed her lip to flaps of skin. She needs to keep her mind. Even now, with hindsight and all, she can feel the throb of numbness, of the Chlause taking hold.

Wrong kind of numbness. No, no, no. Kira watches the light, filling her mind with endless flitting thoughts. Bone-cold terror writhes, like snakes trapped behind her ribs. But no. No, no, that can't get in either. If it does…

It won't. Kira focuses on her breathing. In, metal. Out, blood. Endless thoughts, flit, flit, flit: tiny bopping pugs. Macaroni and cheese. The smell of fresh canvas. Christmas gifts from Romy that come in February, like teasing Valentines. Early spring mornings. Wood pigeons calling. The crash of the sea. Sun-smell on her limbs, the only time she knows what her own skin smells like. Kissing Callum in the park.

Settling on the snow, the gentle light snuffs out. A shadow moves out of the trees.

'No, no, no, absolutely *not*.' Freya's full weight hits her hard.

'Hey!' Kira yelps, lurching forwards. 'What the hell?'

'What the *hell*?' The huldra jerks them both upright. 'What do you mean, what the hell? I did not pull you from Urnäsch, not to mention act as your spat-on keeper, for you to throw yourself back in.' She wrestles with Kira's arms. 'Are you legitimately—ah—stupid, or do you just like acting it?'

Yanking Kira's arms behind her, Freya wrenches them in place. They click, and Kira yells, 'Freya!'

'No.' Freya wrenches Kira's arms again, hissing by her ear. 'You don't get to do this.'

Kira's mind shuts down. 'Neither do you.'

Stamping on the huldra's foot, she snaps her skull back. Her head cracks into Freya's.

'Bitch!' With a gasp, Freya reels back, clutching at her face.

'No.' Kira shoves her away and whips around, searching for the light and the shadow by the chalet. 'I'm just refusing to let you make my decisions.'

'*What?*' Wiping the blood from her nose, Freya lurches to her feet. Her expression is ugly, raging, and warped. 'I'm not choosing you a husband, Kira. I'm stopping you from being a martyr.'

Kira laughs. It feels nasty. 'Yeah, I've heard that before.'

Kira looks back to Karliquai. The shadow's approach is slow, ghosting steadily from the trees. The murky night masks its shape, but its mantle is long, bumpy, and black. Its mask flashes snatches of red. Kira tenses her shoulders, and steps toward it. The doll, the Ugly, the fire man that stole Callum's face. Is she doing this?

'*You are not going back.*' Freya grabs Kira by the shoulders, wrenching her away. 'All it will gain you is torture. What can you do? You have no abilities, nothing special that means you can help or fight. You'll be killing yourself.'

'The Chlause don't kill.' Kira yanks herself free. The Chlause is still approaching, its hands over its crotch. A calm step, and he's swallowed by the shadow of Karliquai.

'Kira!' Freya's fingers grasp at Kira's coat.

With a cry, Kira spins out of reach. 'Just stop!' She flies around to face the huldra, throwing out her arms. 'Leave! Take the freedom you have killed for! This is not your fight, and I am not your responsibility. I never have been.'

'Yeah, I know.' Freya wipes viciously at her scarlet-smeared nose. 'Not my circus, not my monkeys. Considering how it feels like you broke my face, I should leave you. But I won't.'

Kira casts a wild glance at Karliquai. Her numb control is thawing, and the snakes are slipping out. 'Why not?' Her voice is as bitter as the air. 'It seems exactly like something you'd do.'

Freya's mouth sneers in her too-white face. 'You don't know anything about me, Kira.' She steps forward.

Kira flinches back. 'Don't I?' she cries, gesticulating widely with one harsh hand. 'What is there to know? You killed my friends. You tried to kill Callum. You're a monster. You had a tail, and, and…' She cuts a quick look at the Chlause. He's almost at the point where the doll took over, probing their dusty minds. 'And you're all the same. You're all monsters.' Kira jerks her chin at Freya. 'I was chased by a mob with burning torches because they thought I was one of you. Isn't that enough?'

If Freya weren't human, the violence on her face would make Kira run for her life. 'Not to beat the dead horse, Kira'—Freya takes three rapid steps forward—'but are you throwing your mother in with that?'

'Absolutely not.'

'No?' Freya grabs Kira's shoulders. Her furious fingers are unforgiving, the hatred of the unforgiven. 'Because I knew her when I was little, before she escaped, and okay, maybe she was a monster. She started young and loved it. It's in our nature to, but most of us fight. Did you know that? No.'

The huldra shakes Kira, brusque and snapping. Kira stares. Suddenly, she feels slow and cold. 'You knew my mother?'

Freya lets her go. 'Really?' She shakes her head, open mouthed. 'That's what you take from this? You won't even'—she clenches the air in her fist, her face scrunching—'you won't listen. You're judging when you don't know a damn thing, and you won't even listen. But hey, that's people!' Freya throws up her hands. 'Point and incriminate and ask questions later if you deign to ask them at all.'

In a jerk, she pushes Kira backward. Kira's head swoops, and she falls, landing hard in the crusty snow. Anger flares, but it's muted.

'I'm no different than your mother,' Freya spits, before Kira can think to speak. 'We did everything we could to leave a place that was choking us. We didn't want to be what we were born to be, and you're judging that?' Her voice jags up to a ragged shout. 'I want to forget my life and Whiteland and the pretty little road it sets out for us. So did Anneliese.' Freya shakes her head, hard-lipped and vicious. Her cheeks work, and she shuts her eyes.

Kira watches her, wide-eyed. The snow soaks through her clothes.

Freya juts out her chin. Her voice is hoarse but lower. 'Anneliese. Anna. You know the mother you loved for what, seventeen years? The mother I bet you never suspected of not being what you knew her to be. The mother the Whispers brought back from the desert to help *save* you, who was so terrified you'd be trapped that she was nearly crying, on her knees. I saw her. I talked to her.' Freya steps back in soft disgust. 'There wasn't a trace of a monster.' Her eyes shift over Kira's head. 'Well'—Freya lets out a laugh, short and sharp and unpleasant—'at least I did what I came for.'

It takes Kira a whirling moment for Freya's words to click. Anna? Freya? The Whispers?

'No!' Kira scrabbles off her elbows, sending snow skidding. The night dripping over Karliquai is empty: just shadows and powder gusting off the roof. No drifting glow. No metal taint. No red-masked, shrouded Chlause.

'No! I have to—' Kira pitches forward, spinning around. The cutting enchantment has glittered away; now the winter's night is wild, brushed with rising wind and grey, heavy-bellied snow clouds. Kira's spirit sinks into Carol's old boots. 'No,' she protests feebly. Listless, her hand lifts to her hair and drops. 'He has to come back.'

'It won't.' Freya is definite, biting. 'You've missed the boat. Poor you. Thank me when you remember you're alive and not insane.' Freya's eyes are flat.

Kira's heart flutes in her chest. Everything gutters, like a dying flame. 'You had no right,' she tries, but her whisper catches. Her face sags. 'God.' Her hand lifts, and again, it drops. 'What do I even do now? *God.*' Kira rubs her eyes, her papery cheeks, her lips, the back of her neck. 'It's not safe on the outside,' she chokes. 'Not with the manhunt you started. I can't get back to the others, and my dad…' Kira flounders, moving her mouth like a bird without a song. 'That was all I…'

※

Freya recoils as Kira tips back her head and screams. It's a racking sound, like it's shredding her throat, and balking. Kira screams again, and again, scratching up her face to tug at her hair. At the belly, she buckles.

Freya's skin crawls like spiders from the Tomi desert caves. She saved Kira's sanity. She saved Kira's life. This is better than Urnäsch. It is.

But as Kira smacks her hands to her face, heaving great, hoarse gasps, Freya's guilt slithers in like a beast to her bed. Yes, Kira's infuriating, with her righteousness and dogged lack of self-preservation. Yes, she's riddled with prejudice. She was right that Freya never had to help her, and yes, she should be just another human to Freya, with no idea how lucky she was born; but Kira's here, alone, unsafe, because of a plot Freya was part of, and she's in tatters.

Kira was right about something else too. Freya had nothing to lose from this and hadn't cared that others might. But becoming human, as she's swiftly finding, involves far more than a spiderweb, leaf-frail form. And she has an idea.

'Come with me back to Whiteland.' Freya's words blurt out before she'd made the choice.

Breathing into her shaking hands, Kira stills.

A lynx barks from the forest. The wind gusts and groans. Freya lets her snarled hair whip her face as slowly, Kira unbends.

Kira's fevered eyes meet her own. The building, deadening snow clouds hang. The quiet is a pressure between them, throbbing in the wind. 'What?' Kira whispers, dishevelled and red. She looks like a child, and it makes Freya hurt.

'Ahh.' Sighing long and resigned, Freya shakes her head. It's done now, an anchor dropped through the waves. 'We'll go back to Whiteland and do it that way.'

Kira doesn't seem to be breathing. Unblinking, she stares at Freya. 'Do what?'

Freya holds her gaze. 'Get to the others.' She takes a grim step toward Kira. Incredulity doesn't cover it: this is madness. 'You're Anneliese's daughter, and you need help. I don't know if we'll manage it'—she sets her jaw—'but we'll damn well try.'

Ørenna. This is madness.

'Once more unto the breach.' Freya turns. 'Let's go.'

4

The waking mind

'What now?' Mathew has to spear the loose dirt with his heels to keep from colliding with Vasi. The path is as steep as it is narrow.

Vasi has stopped midway down the pebble-strewn, fern-lush path. 'Surely not.' He looks up. 'Did you feel it?' The leshy turns in a half-moon, his broad, buckled face tilting up the wooded slope. 'The shift?'

Mathew's head thuds from tension. Kira here, Kira gone. Anna somewhere. A gruesome part of his life lost. 'What shift?' He sighs. He feels as old as the forest's bones.

Vasi's brow wrinkles. 'The door was open again, but now'—he keeps his face tilted, far off and listening—'it's gone.'

Head shaking like a pendulum, Vasi turns back to the path. His staff prods the uneven dirt.

Mathew's mouth opens. 'What?' Clumsily, he jerks after Vasi. Pebbles skid beneath his feet, plinking off boulders as they bounce down the slope. 'What do you mean the door was open? Does that mean Kira's back?'

'No.' Vasi brushes through a lover's tryst of ferns. 'But your other girl is.'

Following Vasi down the steep, narrow path is like trying to walk down a street blind drunk. '*What?*' Mathew splutters. His parroting makes him feel and sound like a child. 'Romy's back? Here?'

'Here is what "back" implies.' Vasi's tone is almost amused.

Mathew's annoyance shifts up a gear. 'I'm sorry, but what about this is funny?'

Shrouded by the ferns, Vasi glances back. The two of them are caught in a tunnel of green, heady and fresh and alive. Running water tinkles in the background. 'Nothing. I apologise.' He bows his head and carries on. A cloud of metallic bugs buzzes up in his wake.

'Thank you,' Mathew says, swatting at the bugs. 'Can you…' he frowns. It fuses his hot temples. 'Can you tell where Romy is?'

'I can tell you nothing,' Vasi says, 'barring the fact that she's here.' He bends toward a sprawling, ruffled fungus, sprouting from a yellow-green aspen. 'I can't tell you where. I only know she's here at all because she's connected to you. The feeling was'—he lifts a hand as if sampling the air—'fleeting. An impression. A spark that lit and was snuffed before it took.'

Mathew ducks beneath a juvenile branch, lifting his it over his head. The slender wood seems to thrum. 'That sounds like she's dead,' he says. His throat thrums, too. He swallows, and it burns.

'She is not dead.' The leshy stops, angling his head to the side. 'Again, I apologise. It was a badly worded image.' Vasi prods the dirt with his staff. It thuds like a pair of clapping hands trying to sound through gloves. 'Flowing, yet careless. My impression of her was the spark, not her life.'

This should help, but it doesn't. Kira here, Kira gone. Romy here, Romy… lost?

'In that she probably doesn't know where she is yet.' Vasi moves off, tracking the flight of a large, red bird as it flits between two oaks. It looks like a barn-owl-sized red cardinal. 'And neither do we, seeing as we know no more. However, if she came through that door'—he jabs the staff as if the door is here, among the heady flora—'she's better off here than there. Urnäsch…'

'Is the Whiteland equivalent of Hell.' Mathew's voice is tired, so tired. The woods are oppressive. 'We established that earlier. Is there really no way you can—'

'I find Hell a most fascinating concept.' Vasi cuts him off mildly enough, but in a way that says, firmly, *no*. 'We have no fabricated equivalent. Urnäsch provides the atmosphere, the damnation, and the fire, but it's real and certainly not a form of punishment after death. We have enough options there without involving the Chlause.'

Mathew carefully navigates a rut in the track, crumbled with rock and earth and cascading down to the right. He rubs his jaw, hot and prickly. 'Vasi…'

'Urnäsch is, however, closest to your Hell.' Vasi turns his head toward a second cardinal, following the first with a *chaaaaah*. 'From what I can discern, it's unequalled in the outside. Is that why your idea of Hell was constructed? Because there's no place for punishment, to warn against atrocities?'

'Enough.' Mathew's voice is half-rasp, half-gasp. His feet falter, and he stumbles to a standstill, one hand grasping for a weedy trunk. 'Christ. Just stop. You tell me what happened a year ago, some garbled confusion about what's just happened, and now this, but instead of slowing to let me process it, you waltz into a one-sided existential analysis of Hell.' He laughs, a dead, disbelieving puff. 'Christ almighty.'

Mathew wipes his forehead with his knuckles. They come away wet. He lets his bundled coat slip to the forest floor. Oaks upon rocks upon ferns upon bracken, vivid and dense and abundant, so rich his girls would love them. Or at least, Kira would. Romy would have, too, as a girl, scaling stones and leaping from tuffets, the grass squeaking from rain beneath her Wellingtons. Not now. Although it has been a year. *A year.*

It's too much. He wipes his forehead again, and this time his knuckles are not only wet but shaking. He should be at work, tinkering with a new-old motorbike. He should be at home, with a beer or a book on seagrass meadows or a cup of weak coffee and a cheese-and-pickle sandwich, because who knows what time of day it is, let alone the day itself. Whiteland never changes its hue but changes its form on personified whims. It makes men of giants.

Mathew shouldn't be here.

'They are not personified whims.' Vasi carries on, down and around an oddly cambered curve in the track, Mathew's thoughts apparently plain to him. 'The landscape changes according to those within it. Those like me, if we're strong enough, though it is usually accidental.'

'With all due respect.' Mathew cuts in again, weary and clipped. 'This is not the time for culture or legend or whatever it is you're giving me.' He crouches to retrieve his coat and moves just far enough around the bend that Vasi comes into view. The leshy is studying something on the ground, next to a tangle of brambles. 'Why do I have to say it twice? Slow down, let me breathe, assimilate, explode. Or, if you have to blather, explain some more of this.' Mathew steps forward. A pile of twigs cracks beneath his boot.

The thing at Vasi's feet gives a squawk. Vasi slides his knotted fingers under it. 'No.' He lifts, soft and smooth, until the shapeless, angular form is level with his chest.

Mathew takes another step, bewilderment rather than will moving his feet. 'What do you mean, "no"?'

Vasi extends his hand. 'If you stopped asking me what I meant and started accepting things as they are, maybe I would stop blathering. Look.' Slow and minute, he inclines his head in the direction of his palm.

Mathew feels his chin dip, and his eyes along with it. The angular shape is a bird.

'Yes.' Vasi holds it still. The turquoise bird is blinking, opening and closing its beak, tousled and squatting and out of it. 'And no, I won't use it as a teaching point.'

He meets Mathew's eye, his own crinkled and alight. Mathew straightens, annoyance rolling in. Christ almighty, forever and a day; is his head not his own? Is anything? 'Then why did you want me to look?' he says tightly.

'Because it has fallen from a nest. It is here in front of you, yet your mind is full of ocean creatures.' Vasi lifts his arm above his head. Dwarfed by his palm, the bird squawks in alarm, but he slips it onto a lichen-covered branch, flashing its scarlet belly. 'Why not others? Now, by way of warning, this is a teaching point.'

A scrabble sounds from the branch. A flash of scarlet down, a silver-tinged beak, and the bird disappears into the canopy. Mathew grits his teeth for patience. 'A teaching point for what?'

'For action.' Vasi returns to the path. 'You're letting everything overwhelm you, and you're missing what's here, what's happening now. It's an astonishingly human thing to do. My advice is simple: don't.' He jabs the air with the staff: onward. 'I don't have to spell out all that you're experiencing, but instead of doubting and worrying and mourning the life you no longer have, if indeed you're no longer to have it, do something. Leave your boxed-in mind and act.'

It's the closest Vasi's tone has come to sharp. Everything he said on the mountaintop, of cars and homes and static land, can be summarised by those seven words: leave your boxed-in mind and act.

His mind isn't boxed-in, or maybe it is, but from its horror-swamped fog, something struggles up. Mathew breathes out slowly. 'I have to find Romy.'

5

You've started wars

'The Whispers aren't as clever as they think they are.' The pale woman cocks her head.

'It's not about being clever.' Taika shivers and quails in the blue-fire heat. Dragging her knees to her chest, she rings them with her thin arms and pulls them even tighter.

'Then what is it about?'

A shudder knocks and rattles, clattering through Taika's bones. 'Knowledge.'

'Yes?' Enny tilts her head further. The Kyo do this to intimidate, to ice you with fear, and while it tremors through Taika's chest, she's seen it enough to prepare herself for the moment Enny's neck will snap. 'Are knowledge and intelligence not the same?'

Tilting, tilting.

Taika swallows her nausea. It's mostly recovery making her weak—who wouldn't be weak after opening Urnäsch, meeting death at the hands of the Whispers, then opening Urnäsch again—but the woman might take it as fear. The Kyo don't need to feel she's less than them.

'Not in this case,' Taika says, forcing her voice above a whisper. 'They killed me. They just don't know…' Another shiver rattles through her. Taika swallows and breathes. 'They don't know it didn't work.'

Enny's head tilts, tilts. Her fixed black eyes are unblinking. 'No,' she says sadly. 'In a way, we would have liked if it had. We saw your shadow, by the wall.'

Taika keeps herself still. For a flicker of a moment, she was the shadow; she saw, in the sharp dimness, the granite walls and the cavernous ceiling, the rippling surface of the pool. She saw the glinting gems above her, iridescent colours. She saw her rotten future, whirling into madness with the wraiths who turned to stare. Taika saw the reason she stretched her magic to never become like them.

'You,' Enny says, 'are as clever as you think you are.'

With a final bend, her pale neck snaps.

Taika flinches.

'You won against death.' Enny smiles, thoughtful. Were it not warped by her crooked neck, it would have been charming. 'When we were alive, we could never achieve victory against death.'

Taika closes her eyes. Focusing on the fire at her back, she gives it the tiniest of pushes. At once, it warms.

Taika breaks her focus. Not too much; not yet. She should have waited before reopening the door, but it would have been too late; the Chlause were greedy, and the fire was burning. Taika expected that, and so did the Kyo, but still…she should have waited.

Nausea sweeps through her, curdling like sheep's milk. Taika scrapes her nails across the snow. 'I won only once,' she manages, digging the bone of her chin into the bruised bones of her knees. She needs to stay grounded, focused, awake. Her light braids graze her arms. The firm snow is warm beneath her fingers. The fire flickers blue, the only light in the hollow. Furs, Taika's last resort, line the wall behind the woman. 'I'm not immortal.'

'You could be.' Enny rights her neck with a drawn-out click. It's almost as jarring as the break.

'It would…' Taika digs her chin in harder. 'It would take too much.' She swallows. 'I can't do everything.'

Enny smiles. It's almost sane and close to beauty. 'Ullrych did.'

'He's the only human to become immortal.' In her mind, Taika throws up her hands. In reality, she's frail, and cold. 'And we have different ideas of immortality.'

Idly, Enny trails her fingers along the snowy wall. The tips pass through. 'How old are you?'

Taika looks away. 'Seventeen,' she says. *Ørenna, please let this be over.* 'You know that.' Her focus is slipping. Sleep, and those furs. Her vision judders and blurs. By rights, she should be dead.

'Seventeen.' Enny continues tracing, less corporeal than air. 'Wouldn't you like to stay alive forever?'

Carefully, Taika shakes her head. Nausea churns but doesn't surge. 'Not like Ullrych.' *And not like you.* 'I wouldn't join the Whispers, even if they'd let me. When I die, I die.'

'Yet you kept yourself alive.' Enny widens her eyes. Matte and black, they're unnatural.

Taika focuses on her kneecaps. The hollow is dark, but still too bright, glittering and detached. 'Like you said,' she mumbles, her voice watery, 'I'm seventeen. I'm too young.'

Turning her thoughtful gaze on Taika, Enny sighs. 'A pity.'

Taika squeezes her eyes shut. The Kyo want her alive. They want her to join them. They want her immortal. They want her to die. Ørenna. Gripping her knees, Taika opens her eyes. She could force the woman out of the hollow, but without the Kyo, the Whispers might as well have succeeded.

'Let me recover,' Taika says into her legs. The firelight flits up the wall, and she winces. 'I'll be useless if you don't. Let me build myself up.'

Enny's eyes don't leave Taika's. Her mouth quirks into a leer. 'You've started wars, little witch.'

Taika shifts back toward the fire. The words scald her. 'I haven't.'

'But you have.' Enny's leer becomes pointed, knowing. 'You've started a war, and you've picked your side. Where will you go now you've nowhere to hide?'

Sing-song, lilting, Enny flickers out. Taika's temples unclamp.

The blue flames flare. The hollow warms. Breathing, holding her legs, Taika waits. When the woman doesn't try to come back, Taika crawls across the snow to the furs and curls up.

Where will you go now that you've nowhere to hide?

6

And names are funny things

It's a dream where you can't breathe. The air is thick and full of fog, or it's snowing up a storm, or you're trapped underground with dirt for oxygen and sixteen tons of earth on your chest. You can't breathe, but if you force yourself awake, up and up...

His eyes fly open. It wasn't a dream.

Cold water rushes in. His eyes pop, straining wide. The water is a wash of light blue fabric, the front of his skull just straining through, and he opens his mouth to let out an instinctive shout—

The water rushes there too. Snorting up his nose, it gags him, flooding the gaps between his teeth and pouring down his throat. He coughs, retches, flailing his arms. The taste is sweet, mountain-fresh, of snowflakes and panic.

Oh, God. Kicking his legs, he chokes it out, swathed in blue and hot and sick and overrun by water. His lungs are water. His brain is water. A maelstrom of thrashing limbs, his sight swoons black.

The crown of his head breaks the surface. Air, daylight, heat, *air.* Heaving a salty breath, he flounders. His bare toes scrabble for purchase in the shallows, slipping on stones laced with cool, clammy algae. Too smooth. Too round. With a gargling cry, he crashes back under, grazing his knuckles on the ground. Another gulp of water washes into his mouth. No, he just got *out* of this, and he splutters, gasping, choking, snorting, his mind a kaleidoscopic of panic lost in a dream of fire.

'Good grief!' Muffled by water, the voice is rich. A hand hoists him up by the back of his shirt. 'What's wrong with you?' The grip tightens his sopping collar, squashing his Adam's apple. He gags. 'Eh? Don't go near the water if you don't know how to swim.'

The fierce hand shakes him, drags him, and drops him. He lands on his chest with a bubbling puff. The last of the water balloons his shirt, billowing beneath him and cushioning the fall. Still spluttering, he heaves.

'Get up.' The voice and hand have gained a body, bleary in his vision. His eyes feel sandpapered. 'You're blocking the jetty. The fishers need in.'

Brown-skirted and heavyset, the woman wades away, through the shallows to a sandy, rocky road. 'Idiot,' she mutters. Shaking droplets from her fingers, she shakes her broad head.

The water pools around his chin. Spitting away the dribbles, he pulls together a frown. 'I'm not...' He narrows his eyes to a squint. The light is glassy, sparkling, bright. 'I'm not an idiot.'

His voice is a croak the dying would envy. On the low, stony bank, the woman stops.

It's a moment before she moves. Slowly, like clockwork winding down, she turns. 'I didn't say you were.'

She steps into the water again, sending ripples toward his mouth.

He coughs. 'You did. I—'

'No.' She frowns with sunken eyes. Her lullaby voice is honeyed and strange; she looks like a buffalo and glares like a beast. Her dark hair has rolled itself sternly by her ears. Each cheek is bigger than his head. 'I didn't *say*,' she repeats, frowning deeper, 'anything.'

A buffalo. A beast. 'I'm sorry.' Clearing his scratchy throat, he pushes up to his knees. His arms tremble, plastered with rough brown sleeves. His legs quake, and his fingers are white, crinkled. 'Maybe my hearing's messed up or full of water. All of me's full of water.'

It is. Swilling in his left ear, running from his nose, caught in the belly of his baggy brown shirt. His hair is slathered to his scalp. She did call him an idiot, though.

She also stopped him from drowning. If she hadn't yanked him out, he may well have stayed there, flapping in the shallows and far less fluid than any fresh-caught fish.

The woman speaks just long enough to stop the staring from being awkward. 'Okay.' She flicks her wrists again, although the heat is so cut and dry that any drops have fled. 'You're welcome, by the way.'

He almost misses the honeyed barb. Building and buzzing like a swarm of locusts, something inside him is wrong. He blinks and shakes his head. 'Sorry. Thank you.'

'Mm.' Eyeing him, she turns away, splashing back out of the shallows. 'Tell your mother to teach you to swim, or your father, if you're desperate. By your age, it's a grievance that you can't.'

She hauls her bulk up the bank. He watches her hit the busy road.

Then his senses explode.

It wasn't a swarm of locusts; it was the sea and a tsunami, and now, it's crashing down. Gritting his teeth until they squeak, he crushes his thighs with his palms. They squelch in the water lapping at his waist. Heat. Noise.

Madness. Colours blare, and he swallows, giddy. The endless sky is bluer than beads. Purple-mottled shells prod his aching kneecaps, stones shot with red banking up to the road. The road itself, adrift with dust, backs onto multi-coloured buildings, from here to the left and here to the right until alders sever the view. Boats. People.

So many people. He grips his thighs tighter, like a python or a noose. Men carting hefty sacks and women carting baskets, travelling by horse or foot or water. Ropes slung, jetties groaning. Tramping feet and pattering feet, sunny skirts and dull skirts, the smell of ripe bodies, of fish, of dung, of a thousand different foods.

And the *noise*.

Shouting, laughing, whistling, orders. Deals made, contented trade, arguments, and children's games. A goat's bleat, ramping up and repeated. The unloading of bigger, wooden boats, of something weighty escaping. A roll, a thump, a *plunk*, and an oath, followed by slapping sandals. Clipping, clopping horses' hooves. Creaking wheels. A distant cockerel. A tenor voice, singing a lilting chaos with too many notes for the mind to hold.

And it can't. His mind. He can't hold it, any of it. Panic jolts inside him, a burst close to tears, and he slaps his wet hands over his ears. The sigh of relief is ready in his lungs, but no.

No.

Different voices filter in, like flat, cardboard whispers.

…Jurnado should come and do it themselves. I'm not their…

…knew it was too heavy, and now the whole thing's gone…

...Arnaud go? Last time he was by Nikoli's, but he won't go there again because the healer...

...Karine's waiting...

...agh! She promised...

...invite him to watch the ellepiger...

Staring at the sand, he removes his hands from his ears. The noise soars back like a slap: the oaths getting filthier, blaming someone else, the water churning as a long, loaded barge rocks away. He covers his ears again with a whimper. His temples spike and throb.

...Ørenna, Ørenna, Ørenna, let them come back safer than...

...did not call that boy an idiot...

His eyes fly wide of their own accord. His heart stutters, fluttering, beating frantic hummingbird wings against his brittle ribs. The rushing sea roars up in his ears, drowning out everything else. Something's wrong. Something's really, really wrong. He shouldn't be feeling this, hearing this, doing this. He shouldn't be here.

His throat clamps shut. He shouldn't be here, but he should be...where?

He erupts from the water in a lurching trance. Slipping on the slick stones, he scrabbles up the bank, blundering onto the wide, dusty road. Sand and grit stick to his feet. Breathing feels like breaking iron. Has time slowed down?

No. He sways, heart booming. He's just bursting, bursting, bursting at the seams, black blooming across his vision from standing up too fast, too weak. He sways again, throwing out his arms. Are people staring?

No one's staring. Barrels to the left of him, cages to the right, holding disgruntled, chinchilla-type things. This place is too busy to see him. As long as he's not in the way, he's just a barefoot boy, drying off quickly and not so different from the other kids weaving their way through the throng. He rights himself on a barrel. *Breathe.*

He *can't* breathe. His stomach sloshes with swallowed water. He needs the toilet; he needs to vomit; he needs to stop the cardboard voices, flat inside his head. He needs to work out where he is.

Pushing off the barrel, he staggers away. A horse nickers. A horn blows. The noise ricochets through his head, and he teeters, catching himself on a wall.

That'll do. Winching up his throbbing head, he squints. Between this tired building and the next, a shadowed gap and a tumble of rocks shelter from the port. Briefly, he shuts his eyes. One. Two. Three.

Move. Dragging himself around the corner, his legs less solid than the water he woke in, he drops to the dusty ground. The rockslide hulks, rife with crevices. Crawling toward a boy-sized gap, he wriggles around and squeezes back. There, with his knees to his chest, he's hidden, protected. The shade is cool. His clothes are dark. Filing by the mouth of the alley, not a soul will see.

Breathing deeply, he shuts his eyes. White noise crackles through his mind, and slowly, the throbbing and rushing and booming and panic and hot horror starts to ease.

Leon.

His eyes flick open; he stares. He could sink into the rocks; it's not a voice. It's knowledge. It's *him.*

Hugging his damp trousers, he blocks the white noise, people both cardboard and real. Leon. Leon, a name, a funny thing, a sense, a presence, a life. Settling in between his lungs, it unpacks.

And there it stops. The sense, the presence, the life stops short of adding homely touches, sitting down, and folding its arms. There's an element missing, a dimension. He's cardboard. Flat.

A fresh surge of panic boils up from his belly. Where is he? No idea. How did he get here? No idea. Why did he wake up in the water? Refer to questions one and two. The panic claws up his throat, and picturing a fist, he rams it down. It won't help. He's alone, wedged in a rockslide, with a hundred other people in his head. There's so little room for things that won't help.

'Leon,' he says aloud. His voice is less of a croak than before, but rusted, parched by the onslaught of salty water. It makes him feel less like an autumn leaf, or a boy made of paper. 'I'm...'

His thoughts sneak back to the voices, a greyish layer separate from the noise by the water. Heard as if *through* the water, muffled but clear. It doesn't make sense.

Because waking up in unknown water does. Because having amnesia does. Because knowing that what you have is amnesia, but not knowing how you know that, does. Leon stares through his knees. Frayed, faded, indigo knees, leading to solid ankles. What does he *look* like?

Hysteria is panic by a different name. He rams this down, too, frantically scratching his head. Thick hair, brown and in the way. Okay. He shoves it back. A scratching brown shirt, too loose and airy. He lifts his hands. His knotty fingers are clean, but the nails are clogged with dust. Red dust.

He can't have been in the water long. Leon fixes on this, steamrolling the sneaking, snaking thought that the dust here isn't red. He runs his tongue over his teeth. A cock-eyed canine. He pokes his face, but it just feels round. No image of himself emerges. He's a round-faced boy with prominent bones, too much hair for this heat, wonky toes, no known age, and—

A hell of a hunger in his belly. The rumble starts at the back, ricochets around like thunder in the mountains, and drops to a growl that shakes his whole shape. Maybe the rest of this can wait to be figured out. The round-faced boy needs food.

Palms on the cool rocks, Leon stands stiffly. Weak, yes. Weary, yes, but not quite collapsing. Thirsty for water that won't make him choke. Starving and ready to follow his nose. Humming the chaotic tune, he braces himself for people and heat and steps from the shadows to the street.

No one so much as spares him a glance. He looks like them and dresses like them; dark skin, light skin; clothes like his of different colours; women in white tunics and girls with vivid headscarves, barefoot; dusty boys running with bundled, smoky stolen food.

Food. Leon cracks his mind open, just a little, just to see.

...to hope he didn't notice. Too late anyway. It'll be gone once we...

Leon slides the tune back over the top. Stolen food is no better than panic.

In the middle of the road, he stops.

'Skies!' A woman trips and veers around him, swinging skeins of reeking pelts. Dumbly, Leon stares at her. He's going to have to steal. With no money, or any idea of money, he doesn't have a choice.

Leon swings his gaze behind him, tries to listen more to the boys, but the dusty thieves have vanished, guzzled by the bustle of the crowd. He's on his own.

Leon is a round-faced boy, with no known age, and now he knows this: he's not a thief.

Not yet. Vaguely trailing the stoat-like pelt-woman, Leon starts to walk. Men sell cloth and passage on boats. Women sell fruit, great doughy dumplings, and sizzling unfamiliar fritters that smell of aniseed, lemon, and toast. He barely needs to hum to distract himself; his belly is yowling chaos.

Trundling into more of a market, the harbour becomes no less of a rush. The water is an endless stretch. The people are an endless river, hectic, fast, and loud. Bright homes hide among belligerent boulders, jostling ramshackle shops. A brook trickles under a short, low bridge. No signs mark streets.

No signs mark anything. Leon walks straight on, through the sprawling town as it pushes back the hills. Sweat sticks his hair to his neck. Wooden figures crowd makeshift stalls with lights that seem to move on their own and flighty, gossamer toys. The smell of chicken bores holes into his stomach. Rowdy laughter echoes down a backstreet, coupled with twanging music. The cloudless sky deepens to the shades of his trousers and the shells in the harbour. No sun.

It takes a few seconds, but Leon stops, swivelling to face the horizon. *No sun?* Shouldn't there always be sun?

So he's never been a thief, and he needs the sun. That should tell him something about who he is, or where he's come from, but it doesn't. None of this does.

Tugged by unease, Leon turns away, shoving his hands in his pockets. His mind sneaks back to those other voices: if he cracked his mind, he could help himself. He could get a bigger picture.

He could find some way to eat.

He's sold. The shock of hearing people's thoughts has dimmed, if not died, settling down and unpacking its bags beside his sense of self. If anything, it's more Leon than anything else. It puts out roots. It waters them. It quickly starts to grow. Whatever he's forgotten, this is what he does.

Acceptance feels stranger than the thing he's accepting, so he strides past it, walks on, and slowly lowers his walls.

The gloomy man with a one-wheeled cart is meant to be collecting flint. The couple with faces stained with flour are both concerned for their daughters, hoping the girls will get home in the light.

Neither of which is helpful. Leon shifts his attention elsewhere. A tall, pale woman is drawing attention, some thinking *huldra* and steering away from her. A boy tossing olives for his mouth to catch looks over, thinking—

Cold rockets through Leon's body. Thinking, *Well, you're a stranger.*

Quickly, Leon looks away. So much for blending in; the last thing he needs right now is attention. Weaving through the crowd, he dips down a side street, glancing over his shoulder. Nothing.

Good. The high walls ring with the music's twang. Shaken, he makes for the growing shadows.

Rapid footsteps pad behind him. A hand takes hold of his arm.

7

In labyrinths

Coming back to Whiteland feels like losing, winning, and a staccato, beating dread. Not the maniacal verge Kira was teetering on when she hit the field before Karliquai but the full force of association, of memory. As much as it's a cliché, it feels like where she should be.

No, it doesn't. Kira stamps this down as she and Freya walk in silence, the sharp air shifting and letting them in. It feels inevitable but not because of who she is or what Anna was; that really would be cliché. This was where it all began, so this is where it ends. Whatever that end will be.

Currently, it's walking with an ex-huldra, wrapped in night, with no idea where they're going. Kira can't even muster fear. A year ago, she would have been holding her breath. She would have been bracing for the unknown, wary of lynx and the mist and men, but now it's dark, the forest is watchful shades of grey, and Kira doesn't care.

A year ago, Kira had Callum. Callum, calling her William Wallace, making light of their every move. A year ago, she had a linear goal, of finding her family and bringing them home. A year ago, everyone was alive.

A year ago, she was naïve enough to think they'd stay that way.

'You're brooding.' Freya's voice breaks the hush. Somehow, her English has a hint of French. 'I didn't suggest this so you can curl up like a dead leaf and lament your silent sorrows.' She pauses. 'At least brood out loud.'

A gust of wind rushes over the treetops. Inside the forest, the air stays still. Kira tips her head back. At a squint, she can just see the shaded pine tips, swaying against the clouds. 'I don't want to brood out loud,' she says, and settles back into silence. She'd rather not brood at all.

'For the skies, woman, is that it?' Freya teeters into exasperation. 'Speak!' She lifts her arms. 'I know you hate me or think I'm the spawn of something monstrous, and probably both, but what rescue mission is a miserable one?'

Kira glances back through the gloom. The thinning trees are starker here, more ominous, more Grimm; more darkly, hungrily Whiteland. Somewhere nearby is the cabin with the birds. She skirts a thicket. Frozen berries cling to the tips, brambles clawing for her legs. 'You're free to leave,' Kira murmurs, returning her eyes to the snow. 'It was your idea, but you don't have to stick to it. I'll figure out what to do.'

And I'd rather do it without you, Kira adds silently. Hello, naïveté. She keeps her mouth shut. 'Like you figured out returning to Urnäsch?' Freya makes a noise that can't decide if it's laughing, mocking, or struck by despair. 'Because that would have gone so well.'

Kira stops. For a moment, there's the silence of words that should have stayed indoors. The distant wind sighs. The dark trees lean in. Kira's dull brooding kindles and starts to burn. If she had hackles, they'd be up; if blood could boil, hers would bubble through her skin.

'Okay, I'm sorry.' Freya holds up her small, rose-white hands. Turning to Kira, she fashions her rose-white face close to contrition. 'I'm used to being—'

'Forget it.' Kira rams her hands in her scratchy pockets. 'I don't need your condescension. Thanks for the new plan, but you're done.' She waves a sour hand dismissively. 'I release you.'

Brushing past Freya, Kira stamps away. Every direction is the same, but that's fine. Powder-laden branches, frosted thorns, the grainy, glittering grey of the night. It's fine. Dandy. After the Havsrå took Callum, Kira managed on her own; she can manage again now. All she has to do is hole up until dawn.

'If I wanted to be released, I'd do it myself.' Freya crunches the crisp snow as she ghosts into Kira's peripheral vision, stepping over a fallen log. 'You need me.'

Kira doesn't look directly at her. 'I don't.'

'You do.' Freya grasps her arm. Kira tries to shrug her off, but the huldra's grip is cold and metal. 'Can you hunt? Do you know how to get around? Do you know the people or the creatures or the'—she gestures fluidly around them, at the deep silence, the cavernous shadows, the lines upon lines of trees—'the dangers?'

Kira huffs. 'I've done dangers. Dangerous people too.' She yanks her arm away. 'Remember the mob with burning torches?'

'Which you were rescued from by the Kyo.' Freya curls her mouth. 'If you can call it a rescue. The point is you needed saving.'

'I will not be your atonement.' Kira loads her voice with vinegar and veers around a tree, through a tangle of bushes, and out of Freya's sight. 'I've given you a sock, Dobby. Shoo.'

This was a mutter, but after a short, trudging silence, Freya calls out, 'What?'

The word echoes for a second before the trees absorb it, swallowing the syllable whole. Kira burrows into Erik's coat. Let the huldra leave it at that; let her realise this is a hopeless case, turn around, and claim her sunset. Her freedom. Kira tramps faster, kicking at the snow. A small clearing opens, trailed with animal tracks, and she hugs the murky edge. She can manage on her own…if nothing sees her.

Kira plunges back into the trees, through an arch of branches. Freya had a point about the Kyo. She had a point about many things, but she killed Macy, Eva, and Veronica. She tried to kill Callum, and she lured the four of them into Urnäsch, where Kira lost them all. A rescue may be Freya's atonement, but for Kira, she's the living, constant effigy of everything that's burned.

When her chest starts to hitch like a stalling car, Kira stops. Her breath puffs white. The night is silent—no soft footfalls following her, no breathing, laboured or otherwise. It's the kind of quiet that makes your skin want to crawl because it's far too still. Unnatural.

Freya must have taken the hint. Chilled surprise drips through her, and in a slow circle, she turns. The black-grey forest stretches away. It feels like a rocking endlessness, as if she's the only one alive.

Kira got what she wanted. Wrapping her arms around herself, she hugs her torso tight. She's finally, truly alone, but instead of relief, the feeling is hollow. She's *alone*. In a forest. At night. Kira's mind *thunks*. Her gut *thunks* with it; the heavy click where you realise what's done is done. And maybe, just maybe, you shouldn't have done it.

I'm stopping you from being a martyr.

Too late. One leg at a time, Kira makes herself walk. The forest's presence hangs in the air, pressing like a metal-grey rain cloud. It wants to turn to mist. It wants to settle and fog her mind, freezing her body to creaking ice.

It wants to, but it won't. Kira shakes her head, sharp and brisk. Air so cold, it makes her ache. Pine so strong it's *part* of the air, coating every breath. Legs that haven't recovered from Urnäsch, so every muscle feels like rope. The forest won't win. That, at least, she can beat.

'If I…' she whispers, but falters. Kira feels stupid, singing to herself, such a small person in such a vast land, a sparking star in space. She used to do it all the time on the way home at night. Talking would only bring her fears to life as she'd wind up rambling about *why* she was talking, but singing doesn't give you that option. Here, though, she's David, and Goliath plays tricks.

David still won. Kira almost smiles, a tiny inward quirk. A sparking star in space.

'If I…' she whispers again. Clearing her throat with a click, she lifts her chin. 'If I took my eyes and tore them out, would you let me look into your soul and shout I miss you…'

It helps. It's a distraction, a safety measure, and a battle against loneliness, and it helps. Kira walks until fatigue drags her through the snow, until her throat is dry, and her lips feel strange. Until, finally, a scraggy, scrabbling web of undergrowth holds promise.

It's no snow hole. Kira stops, but her legs could carry on without her. It's no olive tree, either, but she hasn't even *rested* since the olive tree. Until dawn decides to break, it'll do.

Dropping her umpteenth song, Kira glances around, stoops, and parts the unhappy, knotted branches. The shyest of gaps untangles itself, and she sighs. If she was more awake, maybe she'd think twice about sheltering here, but bowing her head, she scrapes her body through. Thorns snag her coat. Roots bump her boots. Twigs scour her scalp, rasping through her hair, but with the dogged determination of the weary, she drags herself on.

The space she emerges in is barely an opening, let alone a hollow. Straightening, Kira manoeuvres around. Her back comes to rest against a cool, thick trunk. The labyrinth of undergrowth blocks her other sides. Her head doesn't reach the top, and even if she was as thin as a bramble, there's no way an attacker could fit, so by all accounts, it's perfect. Kira slides down the tree to the base. There.

Powder fluffs the roots. Lifting into a squat, she brushes them off. *There.* Hidden, and sheltered, if not warm. Would a fire be counterproductive? She could end up setting the labyrinth alight. Or does frozen wood not burn?

Who knows. If it doesn't burn, she's lost nothing, and warmed herself up in the process. If it burns too much, she'll pile snow on top. Win-win.

Scoring a dip in the powder, Kira combs the debris for twigs, leaves, pine cones, anything. How do you actually *light* a fire? From scratch, with no matches? She was never an outdoors girl. Theirs was never an outdoors family, taking tents to farmers' fields or campsites in the Pennines. She never joined Brownies, or Guides, although Romy was a Rainbow before she realised what it meant. Once she got home, Romy marched up the hall, stamped her five-year-old foot, and declared she was never, *ever* going back if she had to do arts and crafts.

Dropping her dry debris, Kira thumps her head back against the tree. Do Brownies even go hiking? Do Guides go camping? Are wilderness skills reserved for the Boy Scouts? For all she knows, the Scouts might no longer exist. Political correctness might have banished them, ruling them sexist and out of date.

Either way, she's useless. Kira blows out her lips into her hands for warmth. Sure, she did DofE, but they had matches, and for health and safety reasons, the children couldn't light the fires themselves. All Kira knows is not to eat the snow.

Come on. Kira eyes her dejected kindling, rubbing her hands together. Making fire is something like creating friction with sticks or grinding a stick on a stone. She can do that.

Kicking the snow with the heel of her boot, she hacks at her shallow dip. Again. Again. A—

Slowly, she winds down. It's useless; all of it's useless. The snow is compact, knotted with roots, and she has neither two solid sticks nor a solid stick and a stone. No matches. No candle. No water. No food. All she has, stashed out of habit in the pocket of her jeans, is Callum's futile phone.

Suddenly, she's hyperaware of it, excavating her thigh. It's not futile. With a breathy, aching flutter of hope, she digs it out. If it's alive, it gives her light and wards off the night.

Holding down the button, Kira swallows the pangs that collide and regroup and explode. Callum's phone, the one they read at the kitchen table, drinking his cinnamon coffee concoction while trying to force a plan. The phone he forgot on the same kitchen table, that she scooped up and never returned. It's another cliché, the clichés she hated so much that Anna teased her with, but everything happened so fast.

The phone lights up, and Kira's heart hiccups, sweet and sad and full. Shading her eyes, she taps the torch on, shines the sheet-white light around— nothing lurking on the far side of the labyrinth, nothing perched in the branches above her head, nothing hovering in the sky, bird or ghost or worse—before tapping it off. Forty-nine percent battery. Whether or not the phone will continue to work, is unknown. She'll conserve its life while it does.

With the briefest hesitation, Kira opens Callum's photos. Yes, they're private, but if he had her phone, she'd want him to use it to keep himself sane. And besides, by now, she's unshockable.

Flicking the screen from side to side, Kira stares through it. She could take photos of her own. What mementos they'd be for later in her life; what a travel diary.

What a terrible plan. Kira shivers, wriggling against the bark for warmth. One: it's so ridiculously trivial. Two: it would only make her sadder and more at odds with the outside. Three: if the forest, the Whispers, whatever, noticed and worked out what she was doing, she'd likely incur some unholy wrath and be eviscerated. At the very least, they'd kick her to the tree-lined curb.

No one needs to think about that. Quickly, Kira focuses back on the phone, cupping its glow like a candle. The photos date back only a year; its predecessor must have been the phone she left in the boat.

Kira bites her lip, hard. Callum clearly isn't one for photography, but what is there ties knots in her throat and prickles hot in her eyes. Summertime mountains, patterned with narcissus flowers. Carol, laughing, a belt attaching her to the fridge. *Keep women in the kitchen.* Callum would wink, smirking to get a reaction. A sunset over Lake Geneva, framing three beers; Diego neck-deep in snow, with last year's lumbering beast; a colourful concert, and another, and another; blurry shots from a party, blurry shots from a cable car; and then…

Three photos that hurt so much the pain becomes physical, lodging in Kira's chest like a gallstone. One: Callum, grinning a cheek-splitting grin, standing with a man she vaguely recognises from a band she doesn't like. Callum, his hair a rough tangle, in a Montreux Jazz Festival lanyard and a black T-shirt that says *Staff*.

Two: Jay looking grouchy in the living room. Julia, red in the face, arranges Rudolph antlers on his head while Karl giggles behind his own hand and decorates Jay with tinsel.

Three: the last photo this phone ever took. Kira sniffs and looks away, laying her cheek on her knee. Everything inside her aches, pushing through her chest. The last photo is Callum. Standing by the bottom of the stairs; he hugs her, grinning at something he probably said. She looks like she's shaking her head at his chest.

'You could be easier to find.'

Kira starts, shot with swooping shock. Violently, the Samsung jumps from her hand, slapping the snow face down. Electronic colour lights up the white.

'You know,' the voice continues, 'if you tried.'

Freya starts to rustle her way through the gap. Kira blinks, blinded by sparkling afterglow, a hologram of her and Callum, bright before her eyes. Hurriedly, she scoops the phone up again. 'What?'

'I mean, you could try harder.' Freya's fingers claw through the branches, followed by the rest of her.

On instinct, Kira backs into the tree. It's something from a horror film, where the ditzy heroine has locked the doors, crouched in a corner, and quakes as the undead scratch their squealing way through the wood.

Ice chills Kira's chest. What an unhelpful thing to think.

'The light from that'—Freya nods at the phone—'and your Kira-sized scene of destruction weren't enough. Next time, do a rain dance.' The branches release her grudgingly. Planting a hand on the tree, she wobbles. 'Preferably while singing your little human heart out.'

Swallowing a swoon of idiocy, Kira shoves the phone in her pocket. 'I was, before.' She clears her throat, wiping at her cheeks. She hadn't thought the glow would travel; anything could have been lured through the dark. 'To keep myself sane.'

With an artful twirl, Freya slides down the tree trunk. Her boots crush Kira's hopeful firepit. There's nowhere near enough room for them both.

'Shame you stopped.' Freya leans back. 'I'd have gotten here so much quicker.'

She settles her frosted gaze on Kira. Freya's tired skin is dark-circled and tight, but her sarcasm has gentled.

Kira watches her until she looks away. 'Next time, do a rain dance.'

Jostling the thorns for space, Freya huffs. 'I'm not sure that makes sense, but thanks.' She snaps off a hand of lecherous twigs. 'And don't worry about your mind.'

Kira lifts her eyebrows.

'You know.' Freya nods at the phone-lump in Kira's jeans. 'The reason you shouted, "Take me!" to the world. The longer you stay here, the less you're a novelty. Soon you'll be as boring as me.'

She shifts. The labyrinth encroaches in, a spiny, jabbing wall. 'Who is it?' Kira asks. Freya's appearance has made her lightheaded, just one pirouette too many. 'Or what? The thing that does its own little dance in your head.'

Freya shrugs, almost airily. 'Sometimes the Kyo. Sometimes the Whispers if they've nothing better to do. Sometimes it's multitalented spirits.' She rolls her head across the tree, looking at Kira sideways. 'Whoever it is, they'll get bored.' She smirks. 'You're no longer a delicacy.'

Kira rolls her eyes but says nothing. The snow is always whiter on the other side of solitude; now, she longs for loneliness, for Callum's phone and quiet. Kira sighs. 'And yet you came back.'

The dancing humour stills its feet, packs its shoes, and leaves. Freya's mouth winces. 'Agh.' She shuts her eyes and rubs them. 'I never actually left. I couldn't.'

Kira watches her and frowns. 'Why not?'

'Because I never intended to.' Freya's voice is raw suddenly, her head whipping round. Her eyes are wide and wild. 'I know you think I'm atoning, but that's not all. I'm…'

The war on her face is obvious, the wrestling to understand. It's there in her tightening forehead, in the pursing and relaxing of the corners of her mouth, in the flicking of her eyes from the thorns to her hands, to her battered combat boots.

'Normal,' Kira says. 'Soon you'll be as boring as me.'

Freya looks up from her scuffed black jeans. For a second, there's almost a moment. Freya snorts. 'Well, we'll see how long that lasts. Come on.' Bracing her knees, she slides up the trunk. 'No more melancholy, no more soul-searching, and certainly no more sitting around.'

Kira yawns. 'Meaning what?'

'Meaning'—Freya ducks her head—'that I've made an executive decision.' Crackling through the brambles, she squeezes out with a grunt. 'Get up. We're going to the huldra.'

8

The hopeful skies

Of all the things Kira might have thought of doing, this would not have been one of them. Trekking deeper into the forest, tired beyond her bones, following Freya's invisible crumbs to the heart where the huldra live. Kira wouldn't be overly surprised if she wakes up in her scraggly shelter, Callum's phone slack in her lap, to find it was all an illusion. Enough have tricked her before.

She's pretty sure it isn't, though. If Kira was being tricked, she'd be tricked by something better than a woman she dislikes and a nerve-snapping walk. She'd be tricked by her sister, suddenly safe, or a dream that none of this happened. *That* would make her happy; this just makes her grouse that, again, Freya was right.

No more melancholy. No more soul-searching. Certainly no more sitting around. If Kira thought she was wrecked before, she was wrong, but at least she's moving. Acting. Let Freya help if she's so damn set on it. Feeling foolish and fooled and narked with company is better than feeling deadened alone.

This is what she tells herself; this is what must be true.

'How do you know where you're going?' Kira asks, for probably the twenty-third time. The sky is starting to lighten, from night shades of grey to the grainy dream of sunlight, but Freya found her way in the dark. A hand around a pine cone would take them left and slipping between two close-bowed trunks would lead to a new, impossible rise. This is how Whiteland works, and this is how you work it.

Freya palms the bark of a giant-esque tree, too broad to hug. 'Magic.'

Magic. Well, that's better than last time; all night, Freya's given her answers like *ghosts* and *wheedling* and *wiles*. 'Is it science, or is it magic?' Kira says beneath her breath.

'It's magic.'

Kira blinks. 'I—you know what, never mind.' Skipping a step, she walks closer to Freya, all too aware of being left behind. 'I don't want to sound like a meddlesome child, but is it something you learned growing up? Like riding a bike?'

Freya glances at her, almost tripping in the snow. Here, it's up to their knees. 'Three things. No'—she lifts a finger—'four. One, I don't know what a bike is, but it doesn't sound like I want to. Two, yes, it is, through instinct and sensation. Three'—she strokes the spine of a gargantuan pine—'a meddlesome child is better than being a miserable one, and four, stop talking in outsider riddles. Or at the very least, explain them.'

Sweeping through a weeping-willow web of branches, sprinkled with snow that glints in the dawn, Kira stops. The world has opened.

One step behind Freya, Kira's lips part. A sunless sunrise lifts above a gorge, either masked by the weeping willow or not, there until it was. Sensation. Instinct. Magic. She stares. The sheer edge splits the forest for a metre, maybe two, misted with pinkish, golden, garnet clouds, and as Kira watches, as dawn lights the sky, something puffs inside her that's a lot like hope.

'For some reason, it never turns blue.' Freya watches the colours blend and breathe, soft chaos in the echoing space. On the far side, the trees continue, toy-town tiny silhouettes. Clouds lap the rock's edge like sea-foam swell. 'It does this, then goes back to white. Night is the reverse. Out of interest for you'—she points to the right, along the tree-line and out of sight—'Taika's burrow is off down there.'

Taika. Freya talked about her while they walked, but what might have sparked a desire for vindication is swallowed by the sunrise, lost in the view. 'It's beautiful,' Kira murmurs.

Freya nods. 'Nova Vanca.' She nods again. 'This spot, I mean. It has its own legends.' She turns from the edge, fingers brushing Kira's arm as she moves back to the forest. 'Come on. It'll still be here at sunset, but unless we reach the huldra, I won't. I need a year's worth of sleep.'

Kira tears herself away from the gorge like a dreamer waking up. The sky is vivacious. Something else bothers her. 'Are you sure the huldra will let us in?'

Avoiding a snowdrift, she steps up beside Freya, unsteady in the deep, hard snow. 'Considering…well'—she twists her mouth—'everything.'

Freya gives them both a once-over. In not dissimilar outside clothes, they could be human sisters. 'We'll do,' she says, in a shrugging voice an inch or two too light. 'Especially seeing as they sheltered Taika.'

Somewhere distant, snow *whumps*, followed by a crackle of twigs and thorns. 'Why did they shelter her?' Kira asks. Thankfully, the crashing fades. Whatever it was sounded big.

'Largely for their own amusement,' Freya says. 'With a dash of vengeance. Vengeance against the Whispers and Whiteland as a whole.'

Kira sidesteps a protruding root. 'But I'm an outsider.'

'And?' Freya casts her a beady, probing look. 'Are you trying to tear the worlds apart?'

Kira's stomach moans. She glances down, scuffing the snow with Carol's boot. She's done with it already. 'Not yet.'

'Or…' Freya wrinkles her face. The dancing humour is toe-stepping back, one little twirl at a time. 'Making dangerous deals with the Chlause?'

'Not if I can help it.'

'Making even more dangerous deals with the Kyo?'

'No.' The word is vehement, so much that Kira blinks. 'I mean…'

Freya's humour dances back in force. 'Then they'll spit on you, curse your dullness, and throw you out in disgust.' She winks. 'They might even give you a tail.'

Kira thins her eyes, suppressing a hint of a smile. 'They can't do that.'

'Can't they?' Freya spreads her arms and turns to walk backward. 'You'll find out soon enough. We're here.'

Kira's chest jolts, cools, and heats again, in a swoop of giddy shock. Before she can speak, Freya swings to the left, and voilà: in a clearing a short way ahead, there's a village.

Words don't come close to matching all that's in her head. Worry, but no, it's apprehension. No, it's relief, it's dread, it's unreality, blurred like a Monet sunset. They've been walking for eons, but still, all she wants to squeak is *already*?

'You thought there'd be a build-up.' Freya's face is worthy of Munch. Curiosity, amusement, uncertainty, hope. 'What did you expect, exactly?'

Kira opens her mouth and shuts it. 'I…' she says in an odd little garble. What *did* she expect? A sense of the forest growing furtive, more darkly enigmatic? A still, misty atmosphere, from old, bloody tales? 'I don't know.' She folds her arms tight. 'Something more than this, more than thick bushes and giant trees.'

Freya huffs. 'I imagine most people would, but I can't exactly say. This is the first time my new friend hasn't been mute.'

Kira looks at her. 'That makes me feel so much better.'

'Bah.' Freya flicks her wrist, but her eyes have lost their dance. 'Anyway. The huldra don't need a build-up or mystery or secrets. Nobody comes here. If they do, they don't leave.' She waggles her eyebrows.

Despite themselves, Kira's lips find a smile. 'Are you being a stereotype on purpose?'

'That depends on if it's working.'

Kira's eyes slide to the waiting village. In the dawn light, it's empty, and that makes it worse. No gates. No guard. No walls. No life. Scratching her arm, she shifts and swallows. Breathing feels nothing like a natural act. 'Do you not hide from anything?'

Freya runs a hand over her buzzy, knotted hair. 'Not really.' With a grimace, she lifts a tangle. 'Nothing tends to bother with us. They think we're more like them than we are like people.' Thoughtfully, she cocks her head. 'I'm never sure if that's sad or thrilling.'

This is a lion's den. A vipers' nest. A snickering coven of witches. Kira's eyes slide to the side again, like moths to a flame. 'Thrilling when you're in a sly mood and sad when you're not.'

Freya flashes her eyebrows. 'Exactly. Now'—she claps her hands softly—'I can see you're not, but are you ready?'

A snickering coven of witches with tails. Glamour, seduction, and tails. If they're all like Freya was when she—

'Kira.' Freya clicks her fingers, close to Kira's eyes. Kira blinks. 'Let's go. Sooner or later, they'll spot us lurking, and I'd rather walk in like a beast than a babe.'

In like a lion, out like a lamb. Hung, drawn, and—

'Okay.' Kira rubs her forehead. 'I'm just—okay. It's been the longest of days. Of weeks. Okay.' She reminds her lungs of deep, cold breaths, and stands up stiffer, straighter. Maybe it'll toughen her mind. 'Let's go.'

After what the Kyo made her see, she would have expected cabins. Not a conscious expectation but one rooted enough to blink and look twice: rather than a cluster of witches' huts straight from *Hansel and Gretel*, the village isn't much of a village at all. Dotted around the clearing sit tree stumps. The cinders of a fire smoulder in the centre. Beyond that, quite literally, the huldra go to ground.

The bases of the crowding trees have hollows, and the hollows are as massive as the trees themselves. Kira's chest expands with the similarities: Romy, found in a clearing like this. Romy, found in the hollow of a tree, bordering a clearing like this. It pinches her blood vessels, throbbing in her head. More Kyo manipulations. Oh, how *clever*. They probably loved their tricksy subtlety. They probably believed no one else would get the joke.

Kira slows, falling behind Freya's advice not to lurk. Romy's clearing was tricksy in itself, and the hollow was haunting; these are alive. Ashes gather beside each gnarled knot of roots. She slows further, openly staring. It's easy to see in the lifting light: dim and cave-like, the hollows are doors.

At least, they're entryways. Leading a few feet into the trees, earthen tracks slope down and round. Soft glows light them, faint where they fade from underground, and every door has some kind of smell or sound. Rhythmic clattering. Mingled murmurs. Hot vanilla. The tang of blood.

Kira steers away at once. Glancing back, Freya snorts. 'It's not what you think it is.'

Kira hardly hears her. 'Is it not?' she murmurs, distracted again. Around the trees sits anything and everything: carvings, candles, pinned-up pelts. From strings of beads to frozen fancies and from frozen fancies to bones.

Bones.

'Those are for humorous effect,' Freya says. Her mouth slides into a smirk.

'They *what*?' Kira's widened eyes widen. Blood and bones. Oh, God. She's dead.

'Flushing out the prejudice, Kira. Come on.' Freya winks. 'If we don't laugh at our plight, who will?'

It looks like someone else's plight was somewhat more severe. Kira's eyes scurry around the clearing. Some bones are scattered. Some are arranged artfully into the shape of the symbol. Some are stuck in the snow like warnings of ritualistic death.

Kira feels like pinching herself. 'Um.'

'Yes, well'—Freya waves a hand, as if to say, *what can you do?*—'as you see, not everyone's that sarcastic. I thought it was funny.' She shrugs. 'But you've got pine cones and berries and austerity too. Also'—she flicks her fingers above them, tilting back her head—'look up.'

Kira's eyes become moons, supernovas, white dwarves. Below the ground looks impressive enough, but up…up is enchanted, mystical, magical, an eerie spectacle lit by the sunrise. Up is the stuff of stories.

'Oh.' Kira's sigh is barely a breath. High in the trees is a kingdom of shelters, tightly woven from branches. Woven with strings of berries, they're threaded with unfamiliar plants, wreathed with feathers that glint in the light and packed with gossamer moss. Kira tips her head back farther. Linking the shelters are thick-branched walkways, lashed in place by hefty rope. They're bigger than the cabin the Kyo showed her and smaller than the beach huts back at home. They're everything in between. They're a dream.

'Younger girls prefer them.' Freya nudges Kira with an elbow to the flesh of her upper arm. 'Up there, you don't feel quite so trapped, though the underground is cosy. Is madam overwhelmed?'

Robotic, Kira nods. 'Madam is.' She shakes her head, open-mouthed. 'Madam definitely is. It's an elf kingdom.' She drags her eyes back to earth. The kingdom stays on her retinas, imprinted like afterglow. 'If a man with pointy ears appeared, I'd shake his hand and say "sure."'

Freya arches an eyebrow. 'We spoke about this. No talking in riddles. And while you're suitably amazed'—she swings a look around the clearing, crossed with frosted footprints—'I'll go and greet someone. Again, we don't want to lurk, and you don't want to be a stuttering wreck.' She gestures vaguely. 'As you were.'

Perfectly robotically, Kira obeys; it's a thousand, thousand glittering times better than sliding back to dread. She's a minpin, tiny in her woodland world; she's a city girl, used to knees and bins and being as tall as a bus seat, overawed by the giant-esque newness of nature. All Kira's ever seen in the forest has been danger. All she's ever heard has been disbelief from others that she survived and warnings not to go back. She never thought there might be more.

This, though. *This.* Bony ladders scale the trees. Icicles hang from branches. Kira shakes her head, at the wreaths of feathers, the hanging, interwoven garlands, the smell of snow and smoke and cooking, something sweet and spicy. *Life.* This is more, so much more.

And she found it with the monsters.

'Get ready.' Freya's voice and a nudge shake Kira gently awake.

Slowly, Kira drifts to the ground. 'What?' Her vision sparkles. Her neck aches. She blinks, hard, and turns to Freya. She could have stared for hours.

'I said, get ready.' Freya nods over Kira's shoulder. Leaning in to whisper, Freya's unusually close. 'She's usually the first up and sleeps near the air, so I went to get her before she can get us. Remember, beasts over babes.'

Kira blinks again, and frowns. 'That doesn't—'

'Freya.' The word is stunned yet flat.

Kira stills and stiffens. Her eyes grow wide. *Turn around. Don't turn around. Turn. Don't.*

With a mind of its own, her body turns. A woman has appeared in one of the hollows. Somewhere shy of grandmother age, she parts the split in the thicket outside and steps into the snow.

A huldra. Kira's dread blooms, flaps its wings, and starts to moan. A full huldra. Her lined skin looks tough and coarse. Her rusty, rustic, sleeveless dress scrapes the trampled snow. What happens if it rises up?

'Freya and Kira.' Freya puts a hand on Kira's shoulder. 'We'll be here for a while. I wanted to see you first, so one of the others doesn't, you know.' She squeezes Kira's shoulder.

Kira shrugs her hand away. No beating around any bushes, then; no asking, or hedging, or explaining. Maybe they find explanations dull.

The woman folds her arms. 'I know.' She flicks her violet eyes between them. Her paling hair is braided, looped, and pinned where her collarbone meets her neck. She lifts her sharpened chin. On the outside, she'd be elegant, the perfect picture of growing old. Here, she's… 'You'—almost holding weight, her eyes fix on Kira—'you're only half-human.'

The woman's focus shivers through Kira's mind. Her first thought is, *What an odd way to put it.* Her second is, *You can tell?*

'She's Anneliese's daughter,' Freya says, as if she's introducing a friend. 'One of them, at least.'

'Anneliese.' The word is flat again but flinty.

Freya almost seems to recoil. 'Yes.'

The woman's face hardens, sinking into danger, a live wire where Freya's burned out. 'Ørenna,' she says. It sounds like a curse. 'We gathered that things weren't rosy, but they must have sunk to the depths of Skarrig if you've brought us the girls you were hunting.' She casts her shrill eyes around the clearing. 'Or half of them. Does she speak?'

'She does.' Kira's mouth acts before her brain. By some rare miracle, her voice doesn't catch. 'Things aren't rosy. They went wrong for all of us.' Pettiness flares, and she glances at Freya. 'But I did get her knocked out and dragged back to Whiteland.'

Fractionally, Freya's eyes widen. 'At least I didn't go for suicide by sacrifice.'

If they were in a desert, there'd be tumbleweed. As it is, there's silence and the dead weight of snow. Kira shifts. The woman regards them. Two seconds, three, four, five. Kira shifts again. Those electric, violet eyes. They see her, cut her, shrink her; perhaps cajoling Freya, in the heart of the huldra, was not the wisest of plans.

Eventually, the woman looks away. 'What happened to Taika?' she asks. 'Have you simply replaced one stray with another?'

Freya tenses in Kira's side vision. Freya's face is the level of even that has to be fought and strained for. 'I think,' the huldra says carefully, 'Taika died. Because of the Whispers.'

The woman considers Freya. 'Then take Kira to her skydd and go to yours.' She retreats through the thicket, back into the hollow, and yells over her shoulder, 'You both look atrocious. Take a sleep and come out in the afternoon. Preferably closer to evening.'

Freya brushes a flake of snow from her forehead. Another takes its place, and she frowns. 'Any particular reason?'

Cutting a look behind her, the woman dims her voice. 'Because, by that point, you'll have been here hours. You and I can *say* that you've been here hours and are therefore not the victims of a manhunt.' Her words turn dry, and she almost smiles. 'Then, we let it unfold.'

Ducking out of the drifting snow, she winds down into the gloom. She could be descending into her tomb, a vampire raised before night.

Kira twists her mouth and looks away. 'That doesn't sound—'

'Like the best of plans.' Freya steps back, spreads her arms, and lets them clap to her sides. 'Older isn't always wiser. But Solveig is respected, and she'll make sure you don't die.'

Kira looks at her. The silent snow is starting to flurry, delicate and soft. 'You mean "we."'

'No.' Freya's face flashes wicked. 'I mean you.' With a beckoning finger, she walks away, past the cinders to a bone-scattered tree. Patting the trunk, she grins. 'Sleep tight.'

9

The jittering

The oliveless olive boy's hands fly up as Leon's fists fly out.

'Whoa!' The startled boy reels back. 'Hey! Calm down!'

Leon punches. It's an automatic reaction, clumsy but defiant; he may be a foreign amnesiac, but Leon's not a foolish foreign amnesiac, and he'd rather not be a dead one.

'Calm *down*!' The boy skips out of the way. 'I just didn't want you to disa—hey!'

He bats at Leon's second punch. Leon stumbles, jumps back, and jerks his fists up, poised in front of his face. His heart hammers, bang-bang-bang. It doesn't feel like he's ever been in a fight. His body doesn't know how to move.

But then the boy's words register, after the fact, as words are wont to do.

Leon pauses. The pause expands, and in the quiet, the boy's thoughts slip through.

...*Whoa mad bad idea. Nikoli might not—Nikoli would.* It's a muddled, wary rush, coupled with the raised hands and teetering stance, like a lion tamer ready to bolt.

...*Should have let it go. Stupid now this alley thought he might need—wrong, yes, maybe I...*

'Okay.' Forcing his fists down, Leon makes himself uncoil. His heart is more of a drum than a hammer, but he confiscates the drumsticks and meets the boy's eyes. 'You didn't mean to scare me, and I don't want to hit you.' He steps back anyway, just in case. 'So why'd you follow me?'

Something to do with a man called Nikoli. A smile stirs behind Leon's breastbone. It's like having the scales of justice in his head.

The boy shifts from foot to foot. Rubs a large mole on his faintly fluffy jaw. Turns a small ring in his nose. Shifts again, his uneasy gaze darting around the alley. Quickly, Leon appraises him. The boy's spirals of hair have been shorn short. His baggy vest is moss green, and where Leon feels more or less in proportion, the boy seems to need to grow into his feet. Leon's stirring smile snuffs out. It's all very well having justice in his head, but some other things, too, would be great. Like knowing how old he is, so he can guess if this boy is younger.

'You,' the boy says at last, rubbing his hands together. The paler palms glitter with sweat. 'You looked new, I guess. Like you didn't have a clue. And there's something else.' He looks Leon up and down, as skittish as a mouse.

Leon's stomach ticks and thumps. 'Like what?'

'I don't know.' With a slow shrug, the boy digs his hands in his pockets. 'I thought Nikoli might, though, or might want to.'

The truth, then. Leon's fingers twitch. 'Who's Nikoli?'

Filtered around a corner behind him, the music ends and blends with applause. Approving, bawdy shouts ring out. The sizzling fritter smell wafts over, lemon and toast, and oh, so good.

The boy looks up from under his lashes. 'Is there something else?'

Another song winds into life. The jumping, jaunty instrument is as jittery as Leon. 'Why do you think there is?' he asks.

The boy shrugs again. 'I get a feeling,' he says. 'Not a very good one yet but something. Nikoli told me it should get better.'

Frustration licks and flickers. 'Who's Nikoli?' Leon's hands ball into fists. The boy stares at them. 'If he might be interested in me, then I want to know why. I can't skip off with you and your dad like we're, I don't know'—he scans the darkening alley. The lowering night is a purple bruise—'the best of friends or brothers. You could be bait. This could be a trick.'

'I'm not bait.' The boy's face jumps almost to defence. 'And Nikoli is *not* my father.'

Leon blinks.

'He's my instructor.' The boy straightens. 'A healer. Don't you know him?'

Leon just stares at him.

'Okay, you don't.' Standing even straighter, the boy taps his nose ring. 'This is part of it. And this.' He extends his arm. From his wrist to the crook of his elbow runs a thin, black tattoo, a vine full of leaves and thorns.

Leon rubs his forehead. His fingers turn sweaty. The dusk has wrapped the heat into a stifling, stuffy package, and it's making him feel oppressed. 'Okay?'

Retracting his arm, the boy blinks. 'You really are new.' He considers Leon as if only just seeing him. 'You don't have a clue.'

The words grate. 'Well done.' Leon snaps more than he meant to. 'Thanks for rubbing it in. Now that we've gone round in a circle, are you going to—' He bites off *take me to your leader*. Arriving unbidden, it doesn't make sense.

The boy folds his arms. 'Take you to Nikoli?' He narrows his eyes. 'Are you done with demands?'

Leon bristles again. The boy clearly thinks he's gained the upper hand, the biggest and bravest of men. His chest is practically puffed, and whatever he's trying to do with his face, it just makes him look like a pig. Head tilted. Nostrils flared. Leon sighs.

'Questions aren't demands,' he says and turns his attention to his nails. The red dust is still a puzzle.

The music jitters to a jangly end. Down the alley, someone whistles. An animal barks. Doors shut. Wheels creak, and back toward the river, something splashes.

Eventually, the boy huffs. 'Okay, whatever. Let's go.'

10

The fireflies

Ella.

Made up of fireflies, of sparklers, and dancing lights. She lifts a finger to trace them. Each letter is a constellation, far in the darkness above her head. E, L, L, A.

And then they fade away.

The dancing lights are still there, though, bright and pierced but foreign. They're peace. An endless landscape of silence, space, and peace, of clarity and floating. Oh, how she's floating.

E, L, L, A. Ella. A smile smooths her face, as dreamy as the lights. She's Ella. She's floated here forever and will float forever more, with warmth on her skin and soft, soft air, as soothing as whispers in her hair. Surrounded by it, grounded by it.

Suddenly, it stops.

Or rather, it's added to. Ella floats a little less, and it feels like pulled threads. There's sound: whispers, real whispers, hotter than the air around them. Like *Ella* in the lights, they repeat the same things, and now, she's starting to move.

No, no. The threads pull more, tearing her seams. No. They're tugging her down, and she might be moaning, but she might not have a mouth. She's moving. She's being moved. The dancing lights are moving, too, dancing with fever rather than grace.

No. No, no. The threads can't take her clarity. Not the space or the silence or the peace or the dark, being a bodiless body. They can't.

They can. She's starting to feel things, with her non-bodiless bones. She's falling, down, down, down, and the whispers are close to words, and the words are close to—

'Are you okay?'

Dark ghosts over the light. A shadow like a nightmare, but also like a cloud. Then the sounds, the words, come again. 'Are you okay?'

Ella hums. She's moving again, or being moved. The shadow has gone, but the words are closer. Instead of the softness of before at her back, there's something warm and solid and breathing. She can *hear* the breathing, too, now, catch a smell distinct from the flowery, heady night. Ella hums again. She needs to find the constellation, to trace it, to pinch it between finger and thumb before it fades away.

'That's not a yes or a no.' The whisper sinks quieter, even though it's near enough to rustle through her hair. 'What are you doing out here? Did something happen?' A touch chirrs down Ella's legs, up her belly, down her arms, around her head. 'You feel okay. Have you been attacked?'

Ella rolls her head around softly. The lights, the dancing lights. Where did the shadow put the dancing lights? In their places are different shades of darkness, swaying grass and swaying leaves on swaying trees. Not a forest but an openness, swells and shadows and dips and shadows and hedgerows and—there they are. The dancing lights. The stars.

Ella's smile unfurls. She keeps her head tipped back on the shadow's thick shoulder.

She hums a third time, a long, low note, and the hum becomes a song. 'Papillon of winter light—'

The body sat behind her starts. 'Shh,' is the whisper, and then, when she doesn't, the smell and taste of dust and dirt become fingers over her mouth. 'You could bring anything to us. Shh.'

The fingers press tighter. Ella's lips are confined. She slips back into a drifting hum.

'Thank you,' the whisper sighs. 'Can you tell me who you are? Or where you've come from?' Another sigh. It flutters away like her papillon, like the wistful words of her song. 'Anything?'

No, no. E, L, L, A. 'El,' she murmurs, light and floating. 'Ella.'

Finger by finger, her mouth is released. 'Sorry.' The whisper tickles her ear. 'Can you say that again?'

It tastes like snow and tingles like magic. 'Ella.'

The shadow nods. Its covered chin scratches her ear. 'Ella. Okay, Ella. I'm Asgeir. Where did you come from? It's really not—'

'Asgeir,' Ella breathes. It's not spelled out above her, to be plucked from the stars, but she can see it. The shadow has a name.

'Yes,' Asgeir says. There's a bite behind it now. 'And where you're lying isn't safe. Do you know how to get home? Is it somewhere I can take you? Actually, no.'

Yet again, she's moving. The warm body leaves her back. The dirt-dust fingers take her wrists, and then she's swooping upwards, rocking, rocking. *Standing*.

The fingers unlace. Ella holds out her arms and smiles, smiles. The air surrounds her. She's floating.

'We'll go back to my camp.' The fingers return to tug on her own. 'The rest will have to wait. Your lack of a ward makes me feel ill.' Gently, Asgeir pulls her forward. 'If you could walk a bit faster.'

Beneath Ella's feet, the grass is down. The arid breeze is strengthening, flitting through her strands of hair like summer wind through wheat. Sun-bleached wheat, waiting for the gust to pass before alighting by her ribs. Her dress billows about her legs. In the starlight, her skin is a phantom, and she watches it glow, unsteady as Asgeir tugs her on.

Down a hill, across a field. Ruts and tuffets and copses, small clusters of bushes and trees, fetid smells of animal droppings and unforgiving boulders. Once, she's pulled through a cool, clean creek, the burble splashing on as they leave it to the night. Somewhere, something screeches. At once, something smaller screams. A white bird swoops low.

And then the world starts to drift.

It stops as soon as it starts, like a paper boat caught in the current, but instantly snatched from the brook. Asgeir stops too. 'Did you feel that?'

Ella sways and nods. Yes, yes, she did, and it was magnetising, tugging her toward the sky to collide.

'We need to go faster.' Asgeir, still a shadow, not glowing like a ghost, grips her hand tight. 'I'm okay, but this is why you need a ward.' He jerks on her arm, and she stumbles. 'Move, Ella! Did you hear me?'

She did, but running? It's unnatural for her legs. She could tell him this if the letters were more than lines behind her eyes. She drifts, and she floats; she doesn't throw herself through tilting fields. She watches the stars burst. She doesn't stagger faster and ignore them, and oh, she's never seen so many burn and spray. She's never seen so much—

Fire. Ella's legs stall. She *has*, once, all around her, but—

'Ella,' Asgeir hisses, and the fire is gone. Over his shoulder, his eyes flash dark, and he pulls her faster, faster. 'If you had any idea what was coming, you'd be sprinting instead of that shuffle.' He starts up a low hill, faster, faster. 'In the state you're in, you won't understand. But please'—he skids down the other side—'at least try to speed up.'

The hill becomes yellow clutches of flowers, peppered with trees both living and fallen. Grass, tufty-dark and downy-light, swishing up to Ella's knees. A different scent, now, herby. White flowers bordering the yellow, and through a thick patch of breaking trees, up another slope, life nestling quiet in the night, they emerge in a valley that rolls.

'Ørenna,' Asgeir sighs through his teeth. Wrenching Ella a short way forward, he lets out a bigger, giant, colossal sigh, before releasing her and throwing himself to the ground. 'Sit.'

Ella obeys. Cross-legged like him, she arranges her fingers on her knees like him, and watches him like she watched the sky. 'Pretty.'

It's not a thought before it's out of her mouth. Russet hair straggles to Asgeir's collarbone, his russet beard almost as long, and oh; oh, he's strong.

'What's pretty?' Asgeir lifts his hands briefly, his large palms up. His chest heaves in great, hard gasps. Ella touches her own chest; it's trembling, quaking like Christmas excitement, but all she feels is a dizzier kind of drift. 'Ella?' Asgeir lifts his hands again. Bulky knuckles. Dirty nails. 'Are you going to explain anything? Or thank me?'

'Will you shut up?' A head slides through a flap. Ella tilts her own toward it, slow and dreamy. She hadn't realised there was a tent; three tents, in fact, and six horses and more bulging sacks than it's fun to count. A charred mess of a fire, surrounded by stones. She sees the head register her and bob. 'Who's that?'

Asgeir eyes the night. The grass bank rising above them, the still-burning stars. 'I don't know.' He turns to the head. A more boyish, beardless version of his, it gawps. 'She says she's called Ella.'

The head waits. 'And that's all I'm getting?' It adds a pair of hands, supporting itself on the trampled grass. 'She looks like the Night Hunter.'

Asgeir is silent. If she feels like the stars, his face is the endless darkness behind them, beautiful but grave enough to swallow you and lose you in the night.

'She could be a rebel?' the head continues, as though everyone is a fool. 'She could have been planted where someone would find her, and any minute now, we'll be set upon. You know that happens, right? She could be bait, and because you'—one of the hands clicks at Asgeir—'have a saviour complex, the bait will have worked.'

Ella twines a tall blade of grass around her finger. Purple bell-shaped blooms brush her knee. Something tufty and pink butts her elbow.

'…back to the village, we'll get ripped apart.' The head is still speaking. Its words are as thick and throaty as Asgeir's but eons more alive. 'If we don't get ripped apart by rebels before then, or Dad when he wakes up. I mean, *look* at her. She's so obviously bait.'

Ella starts to hum. The vibration thrums in her throat, lulling, spreading from her body to the shivering grass. Out to the otherworldly air, to the night, a visible, shimmering line of sound rippling over the earth. The head and hands jump.

Asgeir looks up. 'Don't start singing,' he warns.

Ella twists the grass until it squeaks, then lets it spring back, in shorter, supple curls. She doesn't want to sing; she wants to hum until the world vibrates. She wants her papillon.

The head looks between them. 'What are you doing?' It asks her, angling itself toward Asgeir. 'What is she doing? She's literally leading the rebels to us. And if Dad wakes up—'

'He won't.' Asgeir rocks onto his knees, leans forward, and presses a finger to Ella's lips. 'Stop,' he says. His dark, dark eyes soar into hers. 'It's dangerous. Do you understand? And if you don't stop, *he* won't, which will be worse for all of us.' Nodding his chin at the head, he sits back.

The hum shivers to a whisper, then nothing. Ella stares and smiles. Those *eyes*.

'Oh, now I feel great.' The head throws up a hand, almost overbalances, and replaces it. 'The most words that come out of you go to the bait. And are also making fun of me? Someone needs to take you in hand, Asgeir, and introduce you to people skills.' The head scowls at Ella. 'She looks like a huldra.' Its scowl widens again. 'Skies. She could be an alder tree girl.'

Asgeir sighs the sigh of the bone-weary traveller. 'She's not. I checked. Go back to sleep.'

'But if she is—'

'Then it'll be me that has to worry.' Asgeir gets shortly to his feet, bends for Ella's hands, and pulls her up. She ascends on a whoosh of air and a sigh. 'I've told you before, the alder folk sense preference, not gender. Watch for the men and you'll be fine.'

The head scrunches into thought as Asgeir moves past, leading Ella to a peaceful tent. 'That also sounds like you're making fun.'

'I'm not.' Parting the tent flap, rough and heavy and smelling of beast, Asgeir motions for Ella to enter. 'Someone should take you in hand, Iolo, and introduce you to the world we live in.'

Asgeir nudges Ella forward. She wavers, swaying. Space and dark, if not silence and peace; the air and stars are so much more than a tiny human space.

'Come on.' Asgeir nudges her again, one large hand on her spine. 'We need to sleep.'

This time, rocking on her toes, she obeys. The air will be there tomorrow. The stars will be there forever.

Asgeir stoops to enter behind her. 'Lie down wherever.' Nodding at the crowded ground, he lowers himself to a nest of furs, resting his head on one arm. 'You're not from here,' he says, watching her carefully copy him. His voice is the whisper that tugged at her threads. 'Are you?'

Ella tucks her hands under her head. No words appear in the cloying space, no letters to pull from the air. She can't sing. She can't hum. Opening her mouth, she shuts it again. 'Ella,' she says.

That's wrong. That's not what he wants. Drawing her legs to her chest on the furs, scratchy, itchy, far too warm, Ella swallows. Licks her lips and forces out the words like bubbles. 'F…rom. From where?'

Asgeir moves his jaw in what might be a smile. It's not the dark that makes it hard to tell. 'Whiteland.'

Whiteland.

The letters pirouette before her eyes. They're less graceful, less willowy than her name, and dimly, she shunts them away. Their claws are sheathed, and their smiles mask fangs.

'I don't…know,' she manages, all a-tangle. 'I don't'—she rolls the idea around, but it gets stuck—'know anything. I don't think I know anything.'

Too many words. Too small. Too warm. Ella presses her palms together and her thighs and her lips and her naked feet.

'Except your name.' Asgeir shields a yawn with his knuckles. A pause. 'Is it your name?'

No. No, no. Ella shuts her eyes. She should have stayed outside, with the air and the stars, even though they burst like fire. The world is pushing her, down, down, down. Before, it felt so light. Light and free, light and bright, a lightness she could capture, like a dainty white plume moth. Now, the world is iron on her skull, and the words she forces are blurred. 'I don't *know*.'

Beast-smell stops her breath. Her mouth feels wrong. Ella curls herself tighter. Maybe she'll fold small enough to fold away or disintegrate like space dust.

'Maybe not.' A *thump*. Asgeir shifts on the furs. His boots scrape her legs, and she flinches. Electric skin. She's on *fire*. 'But someone somewhere has to. You won't have appeared for no reason, and appear is what you did. I saw you.'

I saw you.

Appear.

Whiteland.

Heavy on her head, her torso, her legs. Ella lets out a whimper or maybe a moan. Sick. Fire.

Nothing. The world falls down, the sky falls in. Ella's mind becomes a shroud and takes her far away.

11

Where stars dance and hidden glaciers sing

Climbing the ladder lashed to the tree worsened Kira's aches, her pains, and her vertigo.

While they may look magical, reaching Taika's skydd was a small form of torture. It was the chairlift with Callum all over again, although this time, at least, she had control.

Perhaps Kira could have argued; perhaps she should have. For one thing, she knew it would be a small form of torture. For two, she also knew it left her exposed, and for the cataclysmic third, she abhors the idea of sleeping in the bed of a dead witch. A dead witch, no less, who's not only to blame for her being here, but for stirring up three worlds' worth of Hell.

She could have argued. She should have. But at the mention of rest, and the blissful thought, Kira's reservations stashed themselves away. She clung onto the wood, climbed the ladder, and made her swooning nausea become a swooning sleep.

A sleep that's broken by an argument battleground. Kira cracks her gummy eyes open. The skydd smells of metal, smoke, and pine, and she wrinkles her nose. Sleep swishes away like a cloak. A stench *and* an argument; welcome to the Huldra.

Down below, the voices pitch. Ice pierces through her chest. The huldra arguing about her; they must be. Solveig's told them, or Freya has surfaced, and they're readying the pitchforks and fiery logs. Any minute now, they'll be up her tree…

And the world does not revolve around her. Kira lies for a second, groggy and blinking, before pushing up to her elbows. Straining her ears, she thaws and sags. The fight isn't over her. Not at all.

'You shouldn't have left him so close to us.' Solid, livid, and bullish, the first voice shouts up a storm. 'Ørenna, you've invited a revenge attack. When are you going to grow up or start thinking?'

'When you realise you're wrong.' A second voice slings back, young, reedy, but just as raging. 'There won't be an attack, come on. You say this every single time, and every single time, nothing happens. They've always known where we are, but they're scared.'

'Leaving corpses like trophies will make them angry, not scared.'

The young voice laughs, high and grim. 'Then they can be angry. If enough of them come after me, maybe I'll wind up free.'

Kira rubs her knuckles into her eyes, into her ears, and sits up. That's more than enough of that.

And…back to me. It's a line from a batty English sitcom, light years away in both space and time, but it's apt: what is she meant to do now? Wait until the fighting's over, the battle either lost or won.

Wrapping her woollen blanket tight, Kira hunkers down like a wise man. Taika's skydd is fairly bare: no childhood mementos whining little-girl-lost or voodoo dolls with pins. White dappled light illuminates the blankets, a faded pile of clothes, colourful stones shaped like birds, and nothing else. When you're a witch intent on magical destruction, there's probably not much time for hobbies, and certainly not for knickknacks.

Kira brushes her fingertips over the stones. Her stomach plummets.

Heat swarms from her chest to her hairline, and she yanks her hand back. Okay, okay, no touching. She eyes the crimson-cinnamon-jade as if the birds might take flight and strike. Taika could have done anything to them; maybe that was her hobby.

'Oh, my—this is all we need.'

Outside, two more voices join the bitter, brawling fray. Tearing her eyes from the uneasy stones, Kira gives in to intrigue, pulls her blanket tight, and peeks through the moss-woven branches.

All she sees is light. Light and a sense of green and snow, of a cocoon in the treetops while a hurricane roars. The powdered branches are a creaking curtain.

The ones connecting the skydds create ethereal, elf-like, fairy-tale paths through the forest's canopy, enough to almost forget how high—

The voices jolt her rudely back. Kira's eyes sink closed as her heart sinks low. One of them is Freya.

Oh, dear.

'Why in the skies are you back?' the reedy girl exclaims, incredulous. 'We felt something happen yesterday, but'—Kira pictures her throwing up her hands, flummoxed, flabbergasted, lost—'why are you *back*?'

'I missed your hospitality and the romance of exclusion.' Freya's tone is dry enough to be desert and more than a touch impatient. 'Now seriously, stop squalling. You might not bring humans, but you could bring other things. And you're annoying. Both of you.'

'Did you hear what she's done?' the third voice cuts in. 'She needs to be—'

'Chastised with a harsh tongue and a good dose of manners. Told not to play so much with her food.' Freya sounds like an eye roll. 'I know.'

The bullish woman's anger shudders. 'She needs far more than that.'

'Either way, you're appealing to the wrong person.' The eye roll turns dismissive. 'I just came out to get you to be quiet. Some of us'—she pauses, long and hanging—'are trying to sleep.'

Silence. Unease pools in Kira's belly. She can imagine three heads tilting up, following Freya's meaningful look, but no. Surely not.

'That's Taika's skydd,' the third voice says, less suspicious than unsure. 'Did Taika come back with you?'

Damn you, Freya. Kira closes her eyes.

'No,' Freya says, and now, it's a smile. Kira grits her teeth so hard they squeak. *Damn you, damn you, damn you.* Now they'll really fetch the pitchforks or the sacrificial knives. *Why?*

Why? Kira opens her eyes again. Why should be obvious; Freya can't feel bound to help if the helpless human's dead.

'Then what are you getting at?' a new voice asks. In her mind's eye, the women group around the fire, interested parties peeling away to join their massing ranks. Heads tipped back, one by one, staring at her shelter.

Her very exposed, very vulnerable, very precarious shelter. Kira balls her fists in her lumpy blanket. Damn it, she should have argued.

'Freya's brought someone with her.' The reedy girl's fury has bled into intrigue. 'And she's hidden them up there. Is it a larder?'

Someone laughs. Someone else tuts. Kira wants to hit them or at least hit Freya.

'Ingrid, be more of a stereotype.' Freya's tone suggests that she finds it more amusing than anything else. 'Someone could have uprooted you from a patch of earth marked "Huldra."'

The bullish voice is still barbed, nails and rusty wire. 'That's the problem.'

Kira breathes in, breathes out, and unclenches both her jaw and her fists. Perhaps she should be more afraid. Perhaps she should be curling into foetal terror, but as the women spar and bicker and laugh, something inside her grows and steels. They sound like girls anywhere, and women anywhere, at work, outside school, at a restaurant for someone's birthday. Only the subject hints at the monster.

And what did not-Callum say, back in the church in Urnäsch? *I'm so sick of everything happening to us, like we're nothing and probably worse.* He may have been, in real-Callum terms, a fire pervert, but he had a point. Kira's not corn waiting to be harvested, or a chicken waiting to be plucked. She can act.

Taika's skydd will not be a larder.

Shrugging the blanket from her shoulders, Kira wriggles into Erik's coat. Not knowing whether she'd have to flee, she'd kept her boots on, and good. The space is tiny. Struggling like a child who can't tie her laces might well have swallowed her nerve.

Moving the branch-woven door aside, Kira ducks out into the treetops. The huldra women are talking, still; they didn't see her leave. Breaths in, breaths out; Kira swallows the giddy nausea that trails her down the ladder. Still talking. Still talking. Still talking.

As quietly as she can, Kira creaks to the ground. Even now, the women haven't seen her; the skydd faces the wrong way, and the titan of a tree masks the cackling ladder. Whatever skills the huldra have, one of them isn't sensing humans.

Not from this distance, at least. With her feet safely on the snow, Kira lifts her chin. A Romy-esque bravado is snaking through her mind, a gift from the last few days: she's half-human, yes, but also half-huldra. It's time to make an entrance. It's time to cause a scene.

'The mystery's over.' Forcing away her usual worry, Kira rounds the tree in a burst of movement. 'I'm Anneliese's daughter.'

By the burnt-out fire, the huldra women turn. Kira crosses the clearing with her head held high. If she *were* Romy, she'd have mimed a mic drop, regardless of whether they'd understand. If she were Romy, or even Freya, she'd be spewing a steady stream of snark.

She couldn't do that if she tried. Fixing her eyes on the growing group, Kira folds her fingers in her oversized sleeves and fights the nerves from her face.

Freya looks as though she's had her lollipop stolen, but the others could be *The Last Supper*. Astonishment on wizened cheeks, walnut-crinkled with glassy blue eyes. Something close to horror on a woman Anna's age, sprigs of pine and berries threaded through her endless hair. A teenage girl with her hip popped, her mouth half-open in sharp delight…and, beneath her obsidian dress, the tufted tip of a tail.

Kira stops walking, her eyes going wide. With everything else, she'd forgotten this: tails. *Tails.* Her mind swoons. It doesn't seem real.

The short-haired, knife-edge girl looks down. 'Well, fancy that.' From under her lashes, she offers Kira a sly, slippery smile. 'Anneliese's daughter never saw Anneliese, in her true, radiant form.' She cocks her head and tsks. 'I guess you were always good as a girl.'

'Ingrid,' the berry woman snaps. 'Shut up.'

Ingrid, the reed-voiced daredevil, laughs. 'Only if someone else eats her.'

Not corn to be harvested, or a chicken to be plucked. With another fiery burst, Kira drags her eyes up—she has to get used to these women, tails and all, and fast—but their expressions are no better. Suddenly, she feels like the mouse with the vipers. This was the worst of plans.

'Kira?' Freya spreads her startled hands. 'Care to tell me what in human hell you're doing?'

Kira looks at her as levelly as possible. 'No.'

Ingrid snorts. Someone laughs. Someone whispers. Someone coughs. Freya's face settles into stone.

'You're going to tell someone,' a low voice says. Kira glances round. A curvy woman appraises her, her arms folded tight. A scar puckers her left cheek, scouring her skin from one mangled ear to the bridge of her nose. 'You're an outsider.'

'Of course she is.' Freya's lips are thin. 'If she's Anneliese's daughter.'

The woman's eyes narrow. Spiky and mistrustful, they take in Carol's snow boots, Erik's coat, Kira's dirty black jeans and chopped, bleached, unnatural hair. 'And why is she here?'

'I let her in.' Pushing through the bushes outside of her hollow, Solveig is strong and unfazed. The scarred woman arches an eyebrow, so reminiscent of Romy that Kira's chest pangs. God, this is madness. All of this is madness. 'I let them both in, her and Freya. They came to me this morning, wanting to stay.'

The scar stretches and tightens. 'That wasn't your executive decision to make.'

Straight-backed, Solveig is still implacable. 'Which is why the decision was for now,' she says, elegantly moving toward them. More huldra filter over, moment by moment, from the hollows or the ladders or the woods. 'I didn't want to refuse them the instant they got here, so I told them to sleep.' Hands clasped in front of her, she surveys the women, gathering from the hollows and the ladders and the woods. 'Now they're awake, and we all can decide.'

Kira's stomach plummets, like when she touched Taika's birds. That's nowhere near as positive as earlier. It's barely positive at all.

'Freya.' Solveig turns, as mild as springtime. 'Entertain yourself. Show your half-human chickie the forest or how to hunt or whatever your brief outsider time thinks will keep her amused.'

Freya's words don't tally with her still, blank face. 'She's been in Atikur before. I think she's seen enough of it for fifty-seven lifetimes.'

Solveig's smile doesn't tally with her still, cool eyes. 'Then tell her a bedtime story. You used to be full of scare tales.' She glances at Ingrid. The girl smirks, her lips pale. 'They caused Ingrid fifty-seven lifetimes of sleepless nights.'

Whether these are taunts, and who they might be taunting, Kira doesn't know. Either way, the air is shifting. An unruly tension whispers through the huldra. Kira swallows the rock in her throat. 'We'll go.' Kira directs this quickly to Solveig, and then, to Freya, 'Come on.'

For a heartbeat, Freya looks ready for war. For a heartbeat, the clearing feels like danger, like something ill and untamed.

'Fine.' Brushing past Kira, Freya strides away. 'Nothing like hospitality and the romance of exclusion.'

Kira doesn't speak for a tense, long while. Nothing crunches but their boots. Nothing breathes but them. Nothing moves through the trees, and finally, with the clearing far behind, she relaxes. At least it no longer feels as though they're tipping off a cliff.

Quietly, she steps up beside Freya. Stamping in silence, Freya's been more or less retracing their steps. 'Where are we going?' she asks. 'Or'—she rubs her dry, peeling lips—'where is there to go?'

Freya trails her nails around a years-wide tree, the opposite to this morning. 'Nowhere.'

Kira twists her mouth. Somewhere she read that if you fake an emotion for the first four minutes of something, the emotion becomes real. She's missed the four-minute mark, but it might be worth a try. Anything to stop her sinking back to despair.

'Well, we should find somewhere.' Kira skips forward, through the gap between two branches. She remembers them from earlier; they look like skaters, touching fingers on the ice. 'You're meant to be amusing me. Watching the baby while the adults talk.'

Freya follows her through the branches. 'Yeah.' She snorts a laugh. 'Actually, yeah. It does seem like that. They want me out of the way as well, though.' Lithely, Freya slips in front, weaving around a bush hung with delicate shards of ice. 'Where does baby want to go?'

Kira turns in a circle. 'Somewhere magical.' She holds out her arms. 'Where stars dance and hidden glaciers sing.'

Glancing back, Freya stands on tiptoe, stroking a gnarl in a trunk. 'And really?'

Kira finds herself close to a smile. 'And really, baby wants to go to Nova Vanca, where she wants you'—she quick-steps to catch up—'to tell her how to live in the forest.' The almost-smile becomes a cloud. Physically deflating, Kira sighs. 'And then, she wants to work out how to open that door.'

*

The day has bled to hasty night by the time Freya deems it safe. At least, it's time to find out if it's safe. Having found neither stars that dance nor hidden, singing ice, Kira slipped into a mournful quiet. The kind of quiet that spreads like ash; it almost makes Freya sad.

Not even the sky shook her out of it. The sunset was one for the ages, leaving the world a dreamlike violet, but it wasn't enough. Kira sat like this, and Freya watched.

Freya watches still. One leg drawn into Erik's coat, Kira stares across the gorge. Her skin is brushed with grime and the remnants of a reddish dust, a bruised lack of proper rest deep beneath her eyes. Gingerly, Freya touches the sore line on her cheek. She must look much the same but without the soft haunting. That settled on Kira when she failed to find a plan.

Maybe she thought it would be easy. Freya flicks a pine cone into the gorge. Maybe suggesting breaking through from here was a mistake; maybe it gave the impression that there actually was a way, or a path to follow to find one. Maybe Kira thought her a fountain of knowledge, ready with tricks of the Whiteland trade that'll lead them all back home.

Wrong. Freya sends a spray of pine needles after the cone. Most of her Whiteland tricks are irrelevant and don't scratch the surface of the Chlause. All she has are scare tales. Now, Kira has them too.

They probably did more harm than good. On the outside, she got Kira's hopes up; here, at Nova Vanca, the hazy place of stories, she watched them topple and perish.

Better that than what some little half-Chlause said: *they drive you mad, they torture you, and make you one of them.*

'Get up, chickie.' Freya clambers off her numbing rear, nudging Kira with her boot. 'By now, they should have squabbled their way to a majority.' Stretching out her back, Freya grimaces. 'Oof. Even if they haven't, I want clean clothes and a clean body, if not a clean mind.' Her old wickedness cracks a smile, which makes her smile more. 'Or at least some real food. Your stomach must be rotten from all that outsider muck.'

Rather my stomach than my soul, Kira could say, or something like *at least I'm not a murderer*, but getting to her feet, she merely stretches. 'Food and getting clean sounds amazing.' Her voice falls short of alive. 'If they're not going to throw us out.'

'They won't. Here.' Freya points out the old jay's nest. 'And then here.' They pass left of a burnt-out trunk. 'We're good at putting people on edge, giving everything a sense of drama. You're dramatic yourself, so you should relate.'

A ghost of a smile lights Kira's lips.

'Believe me,' Freya says when that's the end of the reaction, 'they'll help. It'll be in their own way, sure, but you're as much of an outcast as they are. Also, you're shiny and new.'

And yet. Freya steps in front of Kira, enough to hide her face. She saw the looks on the women's faces when they realised she'd returned. Some, like Ingrid, were surprised, but others were glazed with dismay, distaste, and even, like Yvette, full-on disgust. She was one of them but shed her skin to become something else.

Will you be a butterfly? Bo asked, before she left. The innocent rancour was worse than if it had steamed on the surface, like shit.

You know that snakes leave their membranes, said Ciri, *but never change.*

That was better. More hostile. But is she a snake, a butterfly, or a bastard in-between?

'Here.' Freya points out the hand of branches, running her fingers through the twigs. Damn, the scrape in her skull won't *stop*: snake, butterfly, bastard. Traitor. Unwanted, human-stained imposter.

Before, she moved as part of them. Yes, many loathed what she was doing, the fact she was harbouring a witch and the taint of death and magic that was sticking to her. But she was a huldra. Now, her freedom has backfired, her plan has backfired, her humanity has backfired, and she's left crawling back to wheedle for protection. Not huldra. Not human. She might as well be Chlause.

She might as well gouge out her eyes, for all the good this'll do. Sharply, Freya clicks back to herself. Kira's moody fretting has grown contagious; not being huldra, or part of this world, was the whole damn idea. If she doesn't fit in, well…good.

Around the next corner, the fire crackles into view. Smoky warmth fans out toward them, even from a distance, and Freya straightens her spine. Her concrete memories of Anneliese are scant, but the night before she left, she said something that stuck: *don't try to recreate the past.* The context was something else entirely, a minor crisis unrelated to them, but the sentiment clung like a spirit to a tree. Don't try to recreate the past.

The evening's cold nips around the heat. A shiver skims her skin, and Freya glances at Kira, unreadable in the dusk. Whatever spirit clings to her, it had better not come free.

12

The fire

Flames. Tall and fast and almost violet, on a backdrop of dark trees twisted with vines. Thick with unconsciousness, Callum blinks. A red-stone wall lurks beyond, and above…

His mind clears and hones to dread. Above him, the sky pulses, sweeping and dipping, curtains of green, rose, gold in the black. Flames lick its edges. He didn't get out.

Red stone. The Northern Lights. Deep in Callum's chest, a tsunami starts to build. He's in the labyrinth, where the fire pervert impersonated him, tried to seduce Kira, took her to a church, and turned on her. The tsunami teeters on the crest of the wave. He didn't get out, and the Kyo didn't take him. He's still in Urnäsch.

Boom. The ocean of crashing, crushing horror overflows. All that's left is fire.

Callum tries to jerk up, but his limbs won't move. His head swoons, hot and black. Sleep paralysis. Real paralysis? He wrenches his chin to the side, but nothing. Flexes his fingers; nothing. Another ocean weighs him down, and his horror rages, scorching his lungs. Have the Chlause done it already? Is he trapped in a shell? Have they made him one of them?

No. Callum shuts his eyes and tries to breathe. He still has his mind. If they'd already dragged him through the fire, his sanity would be shot. The Chlause drive you mad, they torture you, and make you one of them. They wouldn't let him off so lightly; not when they torture even their own.

That should have been more comforting. Callum's horror roars into nausea, and he squeezes his eyelids tight. He can't see his body, but it must be his own. If he concentrates, he can sense himself, in the afterglow of the violent flames. The tension in his cheeks from keeping his eyes shut, the hot pressure on his eyeballs. The waist of his jeans, digging into his pelvis from this dumped, skewed position. The lay of his teeth against his lips and his lips against each other. His hair, getting far too long, pricking below his ear. The way one boot chafes his ankle. The stinging of his palm, scraped on the wall when he ran to get to Jay.

Jay. A third ocean quenches his breath, and his eyes fly open again. If they've touched him, if they've even *tried*…he'll take them tooth and nail. Fire twists his mouth, knotting his muscles. He had qualms about hitting Freya, the huldra woman, with a poker, but that was protecting himself; in defence of Jay, he wouldn't hesitate at all.

That means that he needs to *find* Jay.

Callum tries to jerk up again. Again, nothing happens. Goddamn. His pulse starts to scurry in his temples. God*damn*. It's hot, too hot. He yanks at his limbs, straining his neck, but he can't even open his mouth. He can swallow, grit his teeth, and that's it.

He strains again, breathing harder. His tongue is too thick, the air too full, smoky, musty, dense. Callum's lips parch. His chest works overtime. His eyes flicker with the exertion, the effort of trying to move. Trembling without trembling, he breathes, breathes, breathes, the air stuffy in his nose until there isn't any—

Panic. Callum's vision blurs black. This is panic, and panic won't help, but he can't move. *He can't move.* Can't move, can't move, can't move; his mind starts to scream, a dark, terrified holler. He strains again, grunting, sweating, blurring. His teeth are ready to burst through his jaw, his eyes to spurt from their sockets. His breath is hot and dry and fast, and nothing works. He's going mad—

Stop it, you imbecile, a faint voice shouts, in a drowning part of his mind. *Stop, or you will go mad.*

Jesus, though. Callum strains and wrenches, wrenches and strains, but all he gets is a throbbing giddiness. His heart bangs. This is it; this is the madness. This is the torture they put you through, so you'll welcome it when they tear you apart. Can you panic so much that you die?

Shut up. Callum thinks it with a heaving ferocity, yelling, bellowing, straining. *Shut up, shut the fuck, shut the fucking fuck up.*

The words ring through his head.

His body snaps free.

'Fuck!' Callum slumps to the floor with a thump and a gasp. Limbs spasming, he shudders in the dust. His pulse gallops. Every inch of skin is dewed with sweat, but he lifts himself up on one elbow.

For a heartbeat, he thought he got free on his own. For a heartbeat, he thought he might be able to run. No. Callum's panting relief shrivels and faints, sickening to dread. Beside him, beside the dry tree trunk against which he'd been propped, is a man made of fire.

He smiles. *Good morning, Callum.*

Everything in Callum shrinks. It's not a true smile, and he's not true fire; the man is cruder, crueller, his mouth a slash, stretched unnaturally wide. His charred black lips are cut at the corners. A feathered mask grows angrily into his skin, a cloak of leaping scarlet blending with the flames.

The pervert. The imposter. The head of the Chlause. Kira didn't do the man justice, not at all.

Callum wobbles on his elbow, gritting his teeth. Some people feel like condescension. Some feel like frightened rabbits. Some feel like fake happiness, but this man, this *thing*, he feels like he would scorch through your skin and eat your heart.

Yes, the fire man says. His voice is soft and dead. *I am the phoenix. The Pretty. Are you ready?*

Fresh horror surges. Callum stamps it down. 'Ready for what?' He spits, grasping for his sarcasm. His arms tremble, but he clenches his fists, forcing himself up to sitting. 'Where are the others? Or'—breathless, he sags into the tree—'are you still playing party games?'

The phoenix bows his head. The violet fire casts shadows through his smile. *We have never played games*, he says. The smile splits and stretches, to the Joker, the Cheshire Cat, a leering Chelsea Smile. *We've prepared. You are far from perfect, but we expected to lose you to the Kyo.*

Callum forces his mouth to twist and snarl. 'I wish you had.'

The phoenix steps closer. Charred and black in the gloom before the flames, his eyes burn Callum's skin. *I would not speak like that*, he says. *You and your escaped friend were uncouth.*

The burning increases. Callum's whole body winces. White-hot waves wire through his arms, leaving them red and sore. He grits his teeth, breathing through spit. Not just sore, burned.

You do not want to be any more uncouth. The phoenix speaks in the way of the mild man who is anything but. *Considering how your saviours held us back, we may well be vicious.*

Callum almost laughs. 'What?' he exclaims. 'You—oh, this is *bull*shit.' He *thunks* his head back against the tree. It's cold, as papery as a stage prop. He's still so goddamn *weak*. 'Everything you're saying, it's pompous bullshit. Where's my brother?' He swallows through the ripple of pain in his arms. Every vein, sinew, bone is on fire. 'And where's Romy?'

The phoenix looks away. Callum almost gasps as the burning stops, but clenching his fists, he holds it in. *Over there.*

Callum's head turns round so far, and so fast, that it clicks and twinges his neck. Slumped against a wrinkled tree behind him is Romy. With a thick vine curling over her shoulder, her body looks almost relaxed: one knee is bent, one leg outstretched, and her careless hands lie in her lap; but her eyes…

Callum's aching breath comes harder. Silent tears slide over Romy's lower lids, streaking her dusty, rust-coloured cheeks. Her eyes themselves are wide and fixed, glassy and insane. Callum's terror bleeds out for her again, a not-so-distant echo. She's not insane, but she must think she is; it's a stain on her unmoving face, a spiral into roiling darkness, sweaty and fevered and screaming inside.

'Romy,' Callum says. Gripping the cold, dead roots, he shunts himself awkwardly around the tree. It shudders through his hot, heavy head. 'Listen. You're not—'

No. Something thrusts him back against the trunk, hitting every knob of his spine. *All of you are alone.*

His head is jerked back to the phoenix's gaze. The burning lances his skin, and he grunts, biting back a groan. 'Romy—'

No. The phoenix takes a step, two, back beyond the fire. *But don't worry.* The words are like bated breaths. *Soon, you will care about nothing.*

Callum aims a kick at him. 'Fuck you,' he tries to shout, but his throat is arid and smoke-hoarse. 'Fuck,' his boot falls short, '*you*. You can do what you like, but it won't work. We're human.'

The phoenix links his blackened hands. He's retreated so far beyond the flames that he's almost one of them. *Are you sure?*

'Oh, yes.' Slapping his hands against the tree, Callum scrapes up the trunk to standing. His gut churns. His legs buck, and he braces against the bark. 'Oh-ho, yes. Call me uncouth all you want, but I don't tear people apart for fun.

Now where the hell'—he cuts his frenzied gaze around to Romy, the fire, the throbbing sky, the red, dusty walls through the thick, sadistic glade—'is my brother? I know he didn't get out with Kira.'

The phoenix smiles like a burning razor. *Are you sure?*

Madness. Callum breathes through his nose, grounding himself, trying not to float from his mind to the lights. The Chlause want to drive him mad. They want to, but they won't. 'Yes,' he manages, through lips too thin and dry. 'Yes, I'm sure. I had hold of him when you knocked us out and brought us to your murder shack.'

The razors burn cold. *Careful,* the phoenix says, in a murmur as soft as suffocation. He's close to gone, retreating through the trees, a shadow in the parting flames. *All you're achieving is a more bitter torment.*

Behind Callum comes a gasp and a *thump*. Relief flutters numbly in his chest.

For you, the phoenix says, *and Rosemarie. Jay will not change yet.*

The words are a punch in the solar plexus, a fist laced with ice. 'What?' Callum's brain sharpens. 'What do you mean, he won't change yet? Where is he?'

Quiet. Slowly, smoothly, the phoenix melds with the shadows. Callum's jaw clamps shut. *You will see him before long.* The phoenix pauses, savouring, slick. *He is going to watch.*

Callum's mind greys to a buzz. No. Oh, Jesus, God, no. The thought of the fire is bad enough; even more horrific is the thought of Jay watching, knowing that someday, that'll be him. Do the Chlause children grow up knowing too? Do they have to watch? Are they so smothered by their closed, crazy lives that they see it as a coming of age?

'Callum,' Romy whispers. Her voice is faint, still heaving from paralysis. 'Callum, we have to get out.'

It's the break through the grey that he needs. 'I know.' He makes to turn his head, but it stalls. Up, down, to the left…but not right. Not toward Romy. 'Oh, my'—he sinks back against the tree again, frustration surging scarlet—'I can't turn round.'

All of you are alone.

'I can't come to you either.' From Romy's direction comes a scuffle, a straining, and a huff. 'It's a wonder they let us talk.' Another scuffle, a sliding shuffle. '*Damn* it.'

'No harm in talking when we can't go anywhere.' Callum hardens his jaw, flexes his fingers. Fist. Harmless. Fist. What's happened to Jay? What's happening to Kira?

Romy says nothing. Her breathing is deep and slow, with the caprice that comes when you're fighting for calm. Callum stares stolidly through the branches, up at the Northern Lights. His heart is thudding hard, too hard to copy Romy, but he can drift. Distract himself. He used to see the Northern Lights when they still lived in Shetland; huddled on the doorstep in the bitter depths of winter, woken by his mother in the peak of night, he'd freeze and shiver and marvel and grin. Their camera never captured it as iridescent, as sentient and mystical and smooth as it was, so they got up again and again and again, at every hint of the coloured life that rippled round the island.

They watched a blood moon like that too. Callum settles into the memory, as though he's back in his days of insomnia, lulling himself to sleep. It was cold. It was hazy. It was four in the morning, and they startled the milkman, out on his quiet rounds.

Callum fades back to himself. The huge, bloody moon becomes hot, bloody flame, the winter chill the heat of a sauna. You'd think that memories as bright as those, even through a dim, little-boy-mind and dark, sleepy nights, would count for something, but still, he's ended up here. Staring into the sky's charade, he's as helpless as if he were dead.

'There must be something we can do,' Romy whispers. A pause, then, 'Callum?'

Callum drags his eyes down to the fire. Something stirs inside him, something stubborn and roaring and righteous. He's not helpless. He's not helpless, he's not dead, and she's right. 'Climb the tree,' he says abruptly. Romy stops speaking, but he hadn't heard her, anyway. 'It probably won't work, but you're right. We can't just wait here.' He swivels in place. 'We have to get out.'

Spinning was a mistake. Callum's head swoons, dizzy and sick. The desert heat dries his lungs, the sweet, swelling smoke curdling his senses, but pressing his palms to the tree, he breathes. Parched grass beneath his boots. The bark's strange texture. The weight on his bladder that might be from fear.

Beyond his tree, out of sight, bark scrapes. Feet shuffle. 'How will this help?' Romy asks, with an inarticulate noise in her throat. 'Climbing trees?'

She's taken his advice, and he's hardly moved. Dragging his arms through sap, Callum reaches up. 'Remember Kira's fun-filled tale?' he says, fixing both hands on a branch. Kicking the trunk for footholds, he hoists his quavering body up. 'About the labyrinth?'

A grunt, a sigh from the other tree. Limbs and leaves block their view, but at least they're moving. They're not helpless or dead.

'She was under'—Romy gasps—'a sky. Big sky. Colourful sky. Like this one.' The words are punctuated by a creak of wood, a *thud*, the branch's groan. 'God, I wish I'd been good at PE. I feel like I'm made of matchsticks. What's that sport with a pole and a high bar?'

Straightening his legs, Callum grabs the trunk, juddering far too much. 'Pole. Pole-vaulting.'

'That.' Romy's branch groans again, accompanied by a scrabbling. 'Got it. I thought'—kick, scrabble—'Kira was being melodramatic, but no. No, no, no.'

Callum heaves up to a higher, beefy branch. 'Nothing here,' he says through his teeth, 'is in any way melodramatic.'

'Yes.' Romy rustles through needles and breathes in gulps. 'I see that now. Kira tried to push her arm through the sky, didn't she, but nothing was there.'

'Half true.' Callum swings heavily up to another branch. Every muscle trembles, taut. Matchsticks? He's made of splinters. 'You and Jay were there, but she couldn't see you. Her hand might have been a trick for you, and this sky might be a trick, too, but if we don't try…'

The sentence doesn't need finishing. Callum climbs higher, higher, shaky, slow. Sap and splinters and thinning branches, Christ, they must be nearly there. Below him, Romy's breathing is ragged. They can't keep this up.

'Pretty sure I'm dying,' Romy mutters. Her gasping packs no punches, and Callum glances down. He still can't see her, and he's lost the fire, entombed in the tree like a cramped, gloomy womb. He looks up again. Through waxy, odourless leaves, the sky is a dash of colour, and he muffles an ache of unease. Most of him expected to fail by now, to be yanked down to the ruddy glade like an old-style Woody with his string caught.

'Maybe they'll get the door open again,' Romy says from around his level.

Callum blinks and coalesces. He hadn't realised he'd stopped. 'What?'

'The Whispers.' Romy doesn't sound hopeful. He can't turn his head to see her through the trees. 'I guess, anyway. Right?'

Grimly, Callum starts climbing. 'Right.'

'Actually, no.' Twigs snap. 'Shit. Ow.' Scraping, the sound of Romy's jeans on bark. 'I mean—ow—actually, I don't care if it's the Whispers who opened the door. It could be the Kyo, or some batshit group we've never heard of. The Penguin People, the Ice Jews, I don't know.'

Face contorting, Callum stretches. His fingertips strain for the branch above. 'The Ice Jews?'

'Humour hit, Callum.' Romy growls in her throat. Her tree creaks. 'We're screwed whether I joke or not, and you get my point. I never thought I'd say it'—grunt, creak—'but I'd rather be anywhere in Whiteland than here.'

Callum's fingers grapple for the branch. 'Same.' The wood beneath his feet complains, and hurriedly, he levers himself off it. 'And I fully remember being there. This place is like a circus gone wrong.' He looks up. 'Oh, praise the Lord.'

Above him, the tree opens. Callum sags against the trunk. Only two weedy branches remain, and standing, weedy and frail himself, he rests his arms along their lengths.

Below him, Romy mumbles something. Callum's hearing burbles. His vision blurs, and he ducks his head, breathing through the black. Dizzy. Shuddering. Faint.

Get out.

Behind his eyes, the sky dances and sighs. If he blocked out everything else, and craned his neck back, he could be on his doorstep, awed and open-mouthed. Awed, open-mouthed, and crackling with life.

Get out.

When he looks up again, he's fuelled and firing. *Get Jay, get Kira, and get the Hell out.* Get back to the outside, and its human mess. Someday, they'll see the real Northern Lights, and marvel in the magic that snagged him as a child.

'I'—fitfully, Romy struggles up and stops. He can almost, *almost* see her, in the corner of his eye—'need…' She gulps scratchy gallons of air. 'To rest. I can't. I…'

A branch creaks oddly. Callum doesn't try to turn. 'We can't,' he says, in barely a sigh.

'But I'm shaking'—Romy's mumble is muffled by the wood. The branch creaks again.—'so much. Can we wait a minute? If I move, I'll fall.'

'We don't have a minute,' Callum says tersely. He's stopped too long already. Just look at where they are. 'We won't be left alone for long.'

Drawn-out and shuddering, Romy sighs. 'But I don't—'

'You said we had to get out.' Closing his eyes to brace himself, Callum flicks them open at once. What a godawful plan at the top of a tree. 'You're right, Romy. We can't stay here. You know what they're going to do.'

Wrapping an arm around the trunk's thin tip, he sets his mouth severely. *One.* He huffs once, through his nose. *Two. Three. Go.*

Swinging his leg up, he hooks it over the last branch. The treetop sways. With both grimy arms, he hugs the trunk harder, clutching it like the lifeline it is. Breathing?

No. His lungs have shrunk. Holding so tightly the bark bites his skin, Callum lifts his other foot. Leaving the safety of the wood is madness, but he works his leg up, his boot scraping the branch, until, until, until…

13

The phoenix

He's up. Callum's heart does the *Danse Macabre*, but sitting forward inch by inch, his heavy legs hanging in the thick, murky air, he's balanced. Ish.

'Callum?' Exhausted trepidation rings flat in Romy's words. 'I can't see. What did you just do?'

Slowly, Callum straightens, loosening his grip as much as he dares. The hair on his scalp and arms feels electric; if he slips even a little…

'I'—he clears his throat, and swallows—'I sat on the top of the tree.' He exhales, long and cautious, shaking, strangely loose. 'If you do it really—'

'No.' Panic sparks through the flatness. 'I can't. Seriously, Callum. I'm shaking so much, and my head…' Romy breathes in heaving silence. 'I—no. Just no.'

The wood *criiiiks* as she shifts. Callum's chest flips. 'Romy, if you fall, I'll kill you.'

Just do it, he pleads internally. *Get it over with*. Kira would have. She'd gripe, and have many litters of kittens, but she'd do it. She always does.

Christ. Kira. He grits his teeth. He misses her griping, guilty drama like an ache goring his bones.

There isn't time for this. Tightening his grip on the tree, Callum slowly lifts his feet. Maybe if he moves, it'll kick Romy into action.

Unless he's wrong. In that case, it's immaterial.

'Callum,' Romy protests weakly as, inch by inch, he reels in his legs. 'Believe me, I—'

'I believe you.' His concentration strains every fibre, every atom, and with his feet as secure as they can be, Callum rises to a crouch. Everything trembles. The bumpy bark skins his white-knuckled hand. 'But you need to force yourself through it. Apart from anything else, you can't pass out here.'

Inch by inch. Inch by inch. Callum straightens up, lifting his arms without loosening his grip. His breathing is clunky, spasmodic. Screw this stifling, dust-red air.

Inch by inch. Inch by inch. Finally, he's almost standing, stooped so the tree-tip ends at his hip. He doesn't look up. He doesn't look down. The only thing left is letting go.

Christ. Shit. Fuck, fuck, fuck. One hand clenched around the treetop, Callum slowly reaches up, up, up.

'Callum,' Romy protests.

'Shut up.'

Callum's legs judder. He can't deal with her right now. He can't deal with anything, beyond keeping his balance. He's never moved so slowly, and it seems to take an age, but up, creeping, inch by inch. Up, to the Northern Lights.

He must look like he's catching stars. The image permeates his brain, sparking through his focus. Reaching for the stars, climbing every mountain. Steps? S Club?

It doesn't fucking matter, but the Chlause worked their magic, and now he's gone doolally, insane.

'*Callum.*' Romy's voice turns shrill.

No. Gripping the notched, papery tree, Callum swipes his mind clean. He has to concentrate; if he falls, he'll literally die. He won't catch stars, no matter how he reaches, and the phoenix could return at any time.

Up. Lifting onto his quaking toes, he stretches, stretches, strains, forcing his eyes up without moving his head. Let Kira be wrong. Let Romy be right. He passes his hand to the left, to the right. His fingers don't vanish; they're shaded violet, a greenish-gold, but—

In the indigo, they hit something solid.

A thrill shoots through Callum's chest, hot and cold and drunk. 'Romy,' he murmurs.

At once, Romy shuts up her worrying. 'What?'

Callum draws his arm away and back. The solid thing meets his hand again, a rock, or a sanded ledge. He stretches further, barely pinching the tree. 'I think...'

His fingers slide over the wedge top, and he stops. It's rough and warm and invisible, like feeling forged air, but it's *there*.

'You think what?' Romy asks. Less shrill than before, she speaks in a hiccup. 'You think what, Callum? Is there something there or not?'

There is. Callum fumbles. Hot stone, sandy. The ledge carries on beyond his reach, and with another heady thrill, he knows. It rattles through him. It whacks him with terror, a jump-scare to beat them all. It's either this, or face the Chlause.

Fat chance.

'Yes,' he forces out. 'Yes, there is.'

Digging his fingers into the rock, Callum lets go of the tree.

Christ. Shit. Fuck, fuck, fuck. Swooning, swooping, his heart cartwheels, his free arm swinging in space. His giddy mind bellows, and he's falling.

He's not. Scrabbling for purchase, his fingers latch onto the ledge. Sweat trickles down his spine, toward the waistband of his jeans, and he grits his teeth so hard they squeak. God, if he could stop. God, if he could *breathe*, but he can't. He's leaning out, teetering, away from the tree, his toes sliding, losing traction, his armpit cramping—

Before his feet can slip completely, he gulps a gulp he wouldn't admit to, shuts his dizzy eyes, kicks off from the branch, and swings his legs to meet his hands.

His gut plunges like freefall. He missed. There's only air, just blue and colour, ready to swallow his sweaty hands as his fingers start to slip—

One boot jars the ledge, and he thrusts it up and over. A half-shout, half-growl explodes from his throat, and pushing down with his bending fingers, Callum heaves.

His torso lands on sturdy rock. 'Fuck!' He gasps, scrabbling fast, hauling himself forward with his leg, his nails. When one foot is all that hangs over the edge; he flips over, bends at the middle, and replaces it with his hand. 'Romy?'

Romy's voice comes back muffled, and what she says disappears. Callum rubs his eyes with his knuckles, vicious. The space below him is already darkening, fading out like the end of a scene. The flames flicker up through the thinning pines, licking where they didn't before. If Romy gets trapped...

She won't. Writhing onto his stomach, Callum lowers both arms to the treetops.

Romy. Staring at his hands with her eyes white and wet; she's wild, smeared with makeup, her mouth half open. And all the while, her scene fades.

'Romy, listen to me.' Callum wriggles forward, stretching lower. Jesus, she's too far down; why could she not find it in her to climb? 'You need to hurry. Jump for my hands.'

He beckons with unsteady fingers, clammy and grimy with dust.

She can hear him. 'Yes, Romy.' Callum beckons again, gritting his teeth, straining lower still. His balance is slowly tipping. 'If you don't, you'll be stuck there. Do you want to climb back down?'

Do you want to be trapped like an on-screen shade, watching the blackness pen you in before the nothing swallows you whole? Do you?

Closing his eyes, Callum breathes through his teeth. 'Romy—'

It's a rushed, clumsy thing. Suddenly, there's a creaking, a sob, the sound of feeble, outraged branches, and Callum's arms jerk down at the sockets.

'*Gah.*' His eyes fly open. His body thinks fast, before he can panic, before Romy's weight can drag him down. His toes bend in his boots, anchoring him to the stone. His hips drive into the ground, and gripping Romy's sweaty hands, he yanks her up through the sky.

His arms scream. Romy screams with them, as Callum wrenches back, scraping his knees up under him. They shake. His kneecap almost buckles. Romy screams again, slipping from his grasp, and with all his painful, giddy strength, Callum shouts, propels himself back, and heaves her up on top of him.

Callum's head knocks stone, rushing hot and dark. Romy lands on his chest and clings to his T-shirt, gasping into his neck. Her feverish breath is hot on his skin. Her smoky hair coats his chin, catching in his mouth, and slowly, shaking, his muscles like water, he wraps her in his arms. He got them out.

The relief is a tidal wave. He holds Romy tighter, breathing deep, uneven under all her weight. A stupid grin struggles onto his face. *Fuck you, you bastards.* He got them out. He wants to laugh. He wants to cry, to punch something, to have Kira on top of him instead of her sister. Instead, he stares up at the sky. *Fuck you.*

His grin freezes. Everything stops. The sky.

A swooning déjà vu hits harder than the relief. No. No, no, no, no, no. Hugging Romy's trembling body, Callum lurches up to sitting. Her hair falls from his face, but the smell of smoke remains. Above them, the Northern Lights dance and sway, and with dread rising from his belly like bile, he slowly lowers his eyes.

'Oh, God.' His arms go slack. His mind flies up and spaces out.

In his lap, Romy awkwardly turns. 'What?' she asks, hoarse and scraped. She shifts again and flinches. 'Shit!'

Shit. Callum floats somewhere above himself. Patchy grass and trees enclose them, leading back to the red-stone walls. A crimson fire flares feet away, and around it...

Shit. Shit, shit, *shit.* Callum slams back into his body, and suddenly, everything is far too bright. Around it are the Chlause.

Well done. The phoenix steps from the dirty shadows. His dead, dusty voice is amused. *If you'd fallen, the game would have ended. How fortunate it did not.* He bows his head, his broken leer glinting in the gloom. *We do so love to play.*

From the tall, murky trees emerge two silhouettes. 'No!' Callum shouts, but too late, too slow; a shadow hewn from jagged holly seizes him by the arms. 'Get *off!*' He strains against the holly's hands. Beads of pain prick his skin, hot and welling. It only fuels his anger, his horror. He didn't get them out after all.

Now, Callum. The phoenix lifts his burning eyes. They make the blood in Callum's arms bubble. *Are you ready?*

The holly Chlause yanks Callum harshly upright. 'Ready?' he growls, clenching his jaw. The pain is seventy needling pins. 'Ready for what?'

The angry fire rages higher. The phoenix extends a hand to it. *You know*, he says softly. He extends the other hand to Romy, dragged, kicking and cursing, away toward the flames. *Are you ready, Callum, to watch her burn?*

Terror punches him in the gut, bloody and blacker than ice. Shit. Shit, shit, shit, shit, shit, shit—

'No!' Callum bellows. It was all a trick, another *game.* 'You fuckers! Leave her alone!'

'Callum!' Romy yells from the edge of the flames, higher than a voice should go. 'What's he—ah!'

The bulky Chlause holding her drops her. Cracking to her knees, her hands clap to her sides, her body snapping in place.

'Stop!' Callum strains against the figure behind him. The thorns puncture his arms. 'You can't do this to us, goddamnit!'

He strains harder. His eyes and muscles pop, but the holly will scar him before it lets go.

Romy's chin jerks up. Her spine straightens. She's trembling, breathing her way to hysteria, her face a rubber band of exertion. The fire bloodies her damp, grey skin.

The phoenix turns to her. *Rosemarie.*

Shuddering, Romy watches him, approaching through the murk. Callum breathes like a bellows. God, Romy, *move*. She should be running; nothing's holding her. She should be fighting, kicking and screaming, as violent as she gets in Kira's defence. She shouldn't be shaking, on her knees, speckled with searing firefly sparks. She shouldn't be waiting to burn.

Horror rushes through Callum. Paralysis.

Just when you think it can't get worse. A hot flush sweats across Callum's skin. Romy will go into the fire paralysed, so she won't be able to fight. The absolute fear will smack her backward, that uncontrolled, dehumanised terror, when you try to move and feel nothing. Nothing, a dark, dizzying nothing, meshed in the flames with spirit-rending pain. Excruciating. Mad.

'Romy!' Callum's horror surges to mania. Spit flies from his lips as he wrenches, but the holly doesn't give. 'I'll…'

What? Do what? His voice becomes a series of pants, and he watches, helpless, raging, as the phoenix lays a hand on Romy's cheek.

Bowing his head, the phoenix stills. The fire pales. *Become.*

The word shivers through the grove like a murmuring crowd. The flames surge to life again, yelling, bruised, and sore. Romy's wide eyes flick up. 'Go,' she hisses, 'to Hell.' Her face blazes wild beyond terror, alive. 'I hope the Kyo destroy you.'

A disembodied laugh drifts out of the trees. *They won't*, a shadowed voice says, soft and amused. *The door is closed. We rule ourselves. They no longer so much as see.*

A fresh surge of fury kicks through Callum: the uncanny, muted, brutal doll. God, if he had a poker to take to their skulls, their sadistic brains would be mush.

What I see, though, the doll says, thoughtful, musing, light, *is treasure. Rosemarie, your mind is a trove.*

It's ignorant. The phoenix beckons. Behind the doll, shadows shift, lit in hellish red. *Ignorant and curious, even through its fear.*

Romy glowers, jutting out her jaw. She shakes like electrocution. 'And?'

The phoenix retreats from the fire. *Not all of the Chlause resemble us.*

Unease sits slick in Callum's gut. The flickering figures are ghosting closer, one large, one small and solid. No footsteps sound. The fire roars like hot wind. His nose is full of metal.

The majority, the phoenix continues, *are creatures without their shells. Partially human in a spectral form, and akin to us in mind. We choose the elite.* He smiles again, gory in the flames. *The rest only exist.*

Christ, you batshit, screwed-up twats. Callum sags in the holly's arms, his vision swirling black. Romy's never been more right: damn them. Damn them all to Hell, the Kyo, both. Why create monsters that only exist?

Why not? A different voice creeps in. Low and drenched in monotony, it sickens Callum's stomach. *It's inherent.*

'Like hell it is.' Romy spits at the ground. 'You—' Her mouth snaps shut with a clack of teeth. Violently, she flinches.

You'll understand, the phoenix says. He spreads his charred hands. *Jay.*

The figures step into the firelight. Dizziness, shocked and shooting, washes out Callum's fatigue. In front of the wicker-masked Ugly, whose gaze caused an ache inside, is Jay.

Callum's throat constricts. 'Jay!' he shouts, in a tearing garble. Jay is cut from marble, his glazed eyes on the fire. 'Don't watch. Please. Close your eyes.' He pulls against the thorny hands with a meagre burst of life. 'Look away, at the ground, at—I don't know, tune out.' He pulls again, and slumps. '*Anything.*'

I'm sorry, stay alive, get out, get out. Callum's vision glitters, like midday sunlight reflecting off water, breaking into shards of glass. He watches Jay watch the flames like stone. God knows what they've done already, but God, Jay, please be okay. Callum swallows. Pine-smoke. Metal. Dust. Jay's more intelligent than anyone else, than the rest of them put together. If Talie's parents got out, then he—

Romy screams. In an eye blink, her head snaps back, and she's kneeling in the centre of the fire.

Callum's breath stutters and stops. She wasn't—she was next to Jay, paler than death, trapped inside—

She screams again. The fire deepens to violet, to the richest blue of the northern sky. Callum's legs quaver, slip, and drop, leaving him hanging in the holly's grasp. His mind roars. He shuts his eyes. There must be something, something left, something he can do.

Watch.

Callum's eyelids are pried apart. Giddily, they focus, and fix on Romy. She's not on fire, but her arms are out, shaking as if she's possessed. Her eyes are wide enough to burst. Callum's faintness blooms like a bruise.

He can't move. He can't turn his head, can't look away.

Romy's chin cracks forward, hitting her clavicle. The grove blurs. Romy's jaw slackens.

Callum strains, but he can't close his eyes again.

In unnatural, chilling slow-motion, her mouth stretches into a scream.

Oh, Christ. Callum sags further, a ragdoll beneath his staring head. The Chlause are silent. The blue fire blares. There's no Jay; there's just colour, madness, Romy, waxy and feral as her face distorts. She's becoming one of them; they're tearing her apart.

Acid bile crawls up his throat. He's watching the destruction of a person, oh, *Christ*. 'Kira,' he says, in a weak, sick whisper, 'I'm sorry, I couldn't stop it. I tried.'

A racking, animal shriek roars raw from Romy's throat. Her head droops. Her back convulses.

The bloody, metal fire dies.

The thorny hands let go. Callum collapses, landing on his front in the dry, sparse grass. All sound stops. Not a whisper in his mind, not a popping spark, not a single gasp of pain. Weak and shaking, he lifts his head.

The firepit is empty, blackened, and cold. In the centre, Romy sprawls unconscious. Callum squints, but his eyes are too faint to focus. Beside her stands the dark-skinned, braided girl, the one who warned them to run. In the shadows, the Chlause are still.

'Monsters,' the girl mutters. It comes to him through a windy tunnel. The smell of metal is stronger than ever, and taking a long, deep breath, the girl meets his eyes. 'Hello.'

14

The lion

The present

Tomorrow can't come soon enough. Kira lies awake, far from sleep, even though this may be the last night for a while that she'll have a bed. That damn dead bird.

They had returned to the Huldra, finding them in uproar. Kira stopped behind Freya, shot with cold, suddenly, acutely alert. While the clearing was silent, the underground was alight: noise drifted up from the hollows in the trees, like the clamour of a distant war. It was eerie, the ghostly, arguing traces of historical chaos, but by the fire waited something worse.

Kira's skin broke out in goosebumps. After all her talks with Freya of witches, the shivering pinpricks swept over her body, rendering everything less than real. A branch had been stuck in the snow, etched in charcoal in front of the flames, and impaled on the splintered end was a bird. Instinctively, Kira drew herself in. The bird was raven-like, but larger, its broken body mangled. Its head lolled, waiting for rigor mortis. Horror-movie dread crept through her, blossoming black in her belly. It could only just have died.

The thought was nonsensical. Kira should have been struck with something dramatic, akin to *portent* or *warning* or *God*, but it made no sense until Freya grabbed her.

'Good thing we're leaving.' Freya nodded at the raven. Her forced blank look was back, far too studied and far too still. 'The collective might have accepted us, but someone's not content.'

Age of the understatement. Kira lifted the back of her glove to her nose. The dread was rising up her throat, like Stephen King's erupting blood. The raven smelt of sulphur and rot. 'What does it mean?' she asked, her mouth pressed to the wool. 'Anything?'

Swallowing, Kira made herself focus on Freya. The bird craved her full attention, luring her eyes back, back, back. Its death was a nightmare, broken in the dark. It made her feel polluted.

'Yes.' Freya's eyes shifted to Solveig's tree. Below the barbed hollow earthen rooms, in a spacious, beautified warren. 'It means we're condemning them. Someone thinks our being here is dangerous and will bring something even more heinous to the huldra.'

She tugged Kira toward Solveig's tree. Inside, ghostly voices rose and clattered and clashed and fell. Kira's stomach did a strange little jump. 'Wait, what?' She stopped, digging in her moccasins. Gifted moccasins. Huldra moccasins. The snow was scattered with ash. 'We're going in?'

Freya let Kira go, ducking to enter the hollow. 'Yes.'

'But…' Kira's voice pitched more than she'd like. 'Won't they tear us apart?'

'Maybe.' Briefly, Freya blocked the glow and then vanished into the tree.

Damn. Clenching her fists, Kira bobbed on her toes. The stench of rot wafted over, mixed with burning wood. Suddenly, every shadow was loud.

Damn. Damn, damn, damn.

'And we're still going in.' Kira made it a statement, holding her breath and taking the plunge. The passage was earthy, steep, and narrow, slanting down in dizzying rounds. Freya was already out of sight. 'Does that not seem unwise to you?'

'If we stay out here, we'll look weak and guilty.' The voice came from a hairpin bend. 'Again, you think you know how things work, but you don't. The bird is a show of defiance, and we need to match it by going in and confronting the huldra. It's…' She trailed off.

Kira slipped, reaching out a hand, steadying herself on the wall. A crumb of earth trickled down, puttering into the candle dug in a dip in the floor. Every step felt precarious. 'A gauntlet?' she asked, inching on. God, how she hated this tree. She was Alice again, trailing the rabbit; one trip and she'd tumble away through the dark. Kira's stomach flipped and flumped, like a failed, flaccid cartwheel. The passage opened up. The fiery light dragged it out of the gloom, and with it bloomed the warring anger, bruising more with every bend. What a confrontation loomed.

'If it means you get the concept, sure.' Freya straightened to her normal height, stretching her shoulders and back.

'Is that specific to the raven?' Kira caught up to Freya as the dirt flattened out past Solveig's spare, refined nook, past Bea's, past Colette's. Weirdly, the most bedecked nook was Yvette's, with souvenirs and colourful cloths, carvings, instruments, tiny art. Ingrid had said Yvette collects on her travels. 'The gauntlet, I mean. Defiance?'

'No.' Sardonically, Freya glanced back. 'It's specific to a crucified bird.'

A foot from the communal room, Kira stopped. Her dread took off like a rocket: this was where the voices raged, dampened by the earth but no less hot. A fire's warmth curled from the doorway. Soon, they'd go to war. 'Why?' Kira asked, scrounging for time. The hatches of her apprehension didn't want to batten; they clanged in the wind and moaned.

'Because'—Freya's face was set like fired metal, her eyes adrift, or afraid—'death equals death.'

Death equals death. In the communal room, no one confessed to the raven, but more stood behind it than Kira would have expected; for the last day or two, she had felt accepted, or at least not out on her ear.

Yvette's scar writhed as she spoke in disgust, condemning the killing of the bird. Solveig concurred, as well as some of the girls, but they were by far the few. Some, like Anne and Elsie, wanted Kira and Freya gone tonight, and lashed them with sharpened tongues. Others said the morning would do; others said Kira and Freya weren't a threat, but perhaps shouldn't linger long.

In the end, it made no difference. She and Freya were leaving tomorrow anyway. Stalking out through the curtain, Freya fumed that that was enough.

The hostility, though. The hostility, if not outright hatred, that jaded colourless faces, bitter and afraid in the dim-lit room, it made her understand, with a clunk in her chest, what it must feel like to be huldra.

From that, Kira had understood why they wanted her gone.

Still. Rolling over under Taika's blankets, Kira stares through the moss-packed wood. She curls her toes, grimaces, and clamps her thighs tight. The clearing is quiet now, returned to the stillness of the rolling night, but the skydd feels more vulnerable than ever. She'll be in a sorry state to leave without sleep, but every time she shuts her eyes, another thought bats them open.

Ingrid, on the first day, full of wicked glee when Kira had returned from Nova Vanca, saying she could stay if she paid. The payment, no more than outside tales.

The meal that night was brought in by the hunters. It lodged in her mind as a waystone; she realised then, if she wanted to live, that vegetarianism was out. The subsequent, sickened fight with herself, caught between loathing and her squalling stomach. It brought back being here with Callum, multiplied to the skies.

The way she'd eaten with the others underground, cast looks but nothing else. The way Solveig showed her, to no small amusement, how the huldra get washed and dried. Kira had felt like one of the tiny girls, who saw her as entertainment, rather than anything sinister, wrong. Kira hadn't thought she'd be a pariah.

Pariah. Martyr. Human. Not.

Stop. Rolling over the other way, Kira thumps and settles and sighs. It's been only two days; nothing can be set in stone in two days, especially not when the women tend to spend their time apart. It's a maze, in the treetops and beneath the roots; how could any group feeling be certain?

It can't. It couldn't, rather; now, her rose-tinted spectacles are cracked. Kira toys with the fraying edge of a blanket. She needs to be more careful, more aware, less naïve. More paranoid, maybe, so the next time people take her in, feed her, give her dead men's clothes, let her join their late night fires, and allot her village upkeep tasks, she'll be ready for a change in the tides.

Although Freya got it just as wrong. She thought they'd be amusement and missed the rising waves.

'You're sighing loud enough to reawaken that nachtkrapp.'

The web of branches moves aside. Kira's body jerks as much as her heart, and she lurches to ninety degrees.

'Relax.' Bent almost double, Ingrid flaps a loose hand. 'Can I come in?' She enters the skydd. 'Too late. Now, if you're not asleep, which you're not, because I heard you from over there'—she waves vaguely at her own skydd, one thick branch along—'I have something to say.' Replacing the web, she crosses her legs and settles by Kira's feet. 'I'm coming.'

Kira blinks at the girl in front of her. Her pulse is slowing from a gallop to a trot, but the shock fused her brain. 'What?'

Ingrid levels her violet, bone-sharp gaze. 'Are all outsiders really this slow?' A shiver rattles through the folds of her nightclothes. 'Brrr.' She tucks her legs into the blankets. 'Tomorrow, when you leave, I'm coming too. Did you get it that time?' She dips her chin with a crafty wink. 'Or do you need a bit of persuasion?'

Kira's chest flutters, but she ignores it. Ingrid's been dropping the same kind of comments since the first moment she pounced.

'No?' Ingrid shrugs off the hint of allure. 'Never mind.'

Kira watches her in silence. Despite the teasing, Ingrid is as serious as she ever seems to get, scrunching her face appraisingly and sizing up the skydd. 'How?'

Ingrid scrubs a hand over her hair, short and rough from a mirrorless hacking. 'How what?' she asks, rotating her fingers encouragingly. 'How can I persuade you? If you like, I'll give a demonstration.'

Ingrid's attention flits away, and her words don't lure, flat without their rich, sensuous ooze. With her nightdress billowing over her tail, she could be any teenage girl: bolshy and rumpled, one cheek patterned from her bedclothes, perched on the end of a bunk in a dorm, or drinking cheap vodka at a sleepover. In any other world, she would be. But this is Whiteland, and in Whiteland, she's abhorred.

'How,' Kira asks, above a hiccup of impatience, 'can you come with us? You're…' Her eyes travel down Ingrid's nightdress and linger.

Ingrid very clearly pretends not to see. 'Oh, I don't know.' She lifts an eyebrow, toying with Kira's old clothes. 'I guess I thought I'd walk.'

Kira keeps her eyes on the nightdress, to the left of Ingrid's broad hips.

Slyly, Ingrid smiles. 'Oh, that.' Equally slowly, she looks up. Her violet eyes glint like glass. 'Why didn't you say? I'll do what the others do when they travel. Wear a longer dress, move with ladylike grace, and not let anyone get too close. If you and Freya are flaunting convention and dressing like men, no one'—she grins—'will look at me twice.'

Kira huffs. 'Or they'll look at you three times, for being so different from us.'

'No.' Ingrid curls her hand through the air, affecting an accent more like Solveig's. 'They'll think I'm conservative. Demure.'

Kira looks at her. A moment passes. Another. 'You're serious.' Slowly, she shakes her head. A heavy unease is starting to roost. 'But—'

'I really wouldn't tell me I'm too young.' Ingrid's grin becomes something darker.

'I won't.' Kira holds up her hands, then wishes she hadn't. Far too placatory, weak. 'I'm barely older than you. It's just'—she pulls a face—'why?'

In a passing shadow, the darkness clears. 'Oh, you think I want to get *out*?' Ingrid juts her neck forward, bugging her eyes. 'That I'll go big, bad huldra on you?' She sits back, smirking. 'Don't worry. I don't want to get out of Whiteland.'

Kira frowns. 'You don't?'

Ingrid bends toward a ruby-covered bird of Taika's, blinks fast, and bends back. 'Wow. Creepy things. No, I just want to leave *here*.' She swirls her hand around the skydd. 'Sixteen years of one village. They teach you to hunt from an early age, but that's the only upside.'

Kira wrangles her face into Freya's forced blankness. 'Really.'

'Really.' Ingrid snorts. 'I told you before: until they think you're "old enough," you can't even go on the curse-breaking trips.'

Kira opens her mouth.

'I know, I know, they aren't called that.' Ingrid waves the ever-flippant hand. 'Whatever fancy name they gave them, it's curse-breaking. Accept it, ladies, demons, beasts. And anyway, it's pointless.'

Kira's mouth curves into a smile she can't feel. 'So you're bored?'

'Like a bird that never flies.' Quivered by a shiver, Ingrid pulls Kira's blankets up to her chest. 'Think of it as a coming of age. And there's always strength in knowledgeable numbers.'

Something cold touches Kira's ankle. She forces herself not to draw away. It's a foot, not a tail. It is.

'You're not wrong.' Kira pulls in her legs to cross them. Ingrid's *not* wrong; there's strength in having another hunter, another person in tune with the land; just another *person*, if things go sour. Kira considers, as quick as she can. Ingrid gets the same treatment from Freya as she does: the implication that they're mildly insufferable but can be teased and mocked and borne. That's one positive.

Tick, tick, tick. Sharply aware of the passing seconds, Kira's mind dances faster. Positive number two: at the first sign of man-related trouble, she and Freya can carry on, as they would have all along. And anyway, they're searching for a witch, not a warlock. If a warlock existed, they'd know.

Tick, tick, tick. Ingrid's growing restless, digging around in Kira's old jeans. Can she control herself? If a man appears, can she leave him alone? Ingrid said she usually succumbs out of boredom, and it's only happened three times...

Three times. An unhappy mania babbles through Kira. She's weighing up deaths—no, *murders*—as if three times is okay. A charm. It's relative, but still.

Macy. Eva. Veronica. Their pallid faces fill Kira's mind. That was three.

Stop.

'Okay.' Kira lifts her hands again. Fiddling with her vest, Ingrid cocks her head. 'You can come. But don't lie. Just'—Kira shuts her eyes—'don't. If you're doing this to get out of Whiteland, we're leaving you behind.'

Be careful, careful, paranoid.

'I'm not.' Ingrid's cut-glass eyes meet hers. Nothing's grinning now. 'I want'—she flicks her tail—'to live.'

This feels like a tipping point, but for what, who knows. Commitment to the plan they don't really have? Immersion in this world, this life? Authority? Leadership? All and more?

Kira listens to the clack of Ingrid's teeth as their thinking quiet seeps. She never wanted to call any shots. She never wanted to lead. She never, ever welcomed that responsibility, and if that made her a sheep, okay. There were other ways to be a lion.

Now, there's only one.

When Ingrid has gone, Kira curls up and broods. *That,* she's good at; she deserves an award. Leading, though, spearheading a quest, for lack of a fancier name. Running in circles. Endless mishaps. Not even a smidge of intelligence, and certainly no clue. That's how this will go.

Great. Kira pulls the blankets up to her chin, trying to force herself to drift toward sleep. No plan, no brain, no clue, and now, there's a third musketeer. Ingrid is not a child to look after, but still; maybe saying yes was a mistake. Kira already has a little sister to save.

The brink of sleep cuts clean away, leaving her starkly awake. Kira stares through the birds until the gemstones blur. Maybe she should have said no, but she didn't. What can she do about that now? Leave Ingrid here?

No. The rejection is a fierce surge of feeling, tensing every limb. Instantly, Ingrid befriended her, even if her friendship is crooked, sharp, and like edging around a mine. She enjoyed her mocking role of teacher and haughtily sprinkled facts: *Ørenna,* Ingrid had told Kira, *is everything. It's becoming the* air when you perish, going back to where you came from, as peaceful, nay, serene as you could hope.

The Chlause, wow, you saw them? They're purebred evil, though I'm not sure how they breed. They were forcibly ejected from the meadowlands and sucked their exit out with them.

Of course I don't know how, I wasn't there. It was something to do with the Whispers. Did you know they used to be warlocks?

No. No, Kira hadn't known that.

Wow, you really do know nothing. Warlocks are rare, and they turn into Whispers, or, I don't know, die.

No, we hardly saw Taika. She was a scary witch, but we terrified her.

They can't leave Ingrid here. Kira shuts her eyes and tries to quash the guilt, that scraping, scouring feeling that she's done something wrong. Ingrid's just a girl who needs something new. Women her own age, a life beyond survival, shaken up by more than tales of Whiteland, of primal dancing by the fire at night. More than a future of trips to Skarrig, searching for what might not exist. She's hard and soft, just like Romy. And you can't help who you're born.

※

Masked by shadows, Freya sits. She was wrong.

Wrong doesn't cover it. It doesn't even start. She's never been more wrong, and so, in the roots of what was her tree, she watches Kira's skydd like a night bird. The only life she's seen is Ingrid, who's latched onto Kira like barbs on pollen. She won't have posed a threat, but the others…

Freya shakes her head against the tree. It was Taika's exposure to the Whispers, that's what Freya didn't consider. Before, Taika was hidden, so harbouring her wasn't a problem. Now, the Kyo are wrathful, the Whispers bay for blood, and humans know some if not all of what happened. It's no longer the huldra's sly little riddle, a dig against authority. It's out there, and they're worried.

Which makes them dangerous.

A yawn burbles up her throat. Gritting her teeth to swallow it whole, Freya pinches her blanketed hand. Morning won't be far away. As soon as it breaks, she'll whisk Kira off, and no one ever needs to know just how wrong she was. For now, all she can do is curse the day she started caring.

And stay awake. Freya hardens her jaw against another yawn, pinching so hard it hurts. The clearing is dark, but her eyes adjusted several hours ago. A dim light, the kind you only catch with the side of your eye, glows in one of the hollows. If she strains, she can hear the thud of a hammer; Bea must be awake again, inventing something new.

Freya scrapes her skull on the tree again. This time, it stings, and the sting wakes her up. Somewhere in the skydds come the strains of music, and the hollow knocking of wooden chimes. She tilts her head to listen. You wouldn't think there was danger. You wouldn't think that death equals death, but while the nachtkrapp has gone, the branch has left a shadow, a deep depression in the snow. She's only ever known Anneliese to receive that, and Anneliese truly did raise Hell.

Far away, something cries. It jolts Freya awake again, and she tenses her legs, ready to go. It's almost tempting to grab Kira now; this worry will make her old.

The something cries again, followed by a squeak, a flap, and a beating of wings. Freya relaxes, just enough to sit back among the roots. The drifting panpipes have stopped. The treetops sway. The chimes knock. The scent of pine is tart in the air. Someday, finally, she'll leave that smell behind.

With luck, she'll still be alive.

15

The lies

Kira wakes to an insistent tapping, uncut nails on her cheek. 'Nngh.' Batting the fingers blindly, she clumsily rolls away. Her voice is as clogged with sleep as her eyes. She'd been dreaming and may or may not have drooled. 'Just a few minutes, Mum.'

The nails rap her neck. 'You're funny. Joke later.'

Kira's sleepy velvet fug is fading. '*Nnngh*.' Scowling as deeply as her face will allow, Kira unglues her eyes. 'You're a killjoy, Freya.' She shakes her woolly head. Her lips are slow. Her mouth is fuzzy. 'What?'

'Shh.' On her knees, Freya leans in, close enough to kiss. Her voice hardly forms a breath in the morning. 'Wake up. We're leaving now.'

Rubbing her eyes clear with a knuckle, Kira fights their longing to close. Her eyelids are as heavy as iron. 'Why?' she slurs, with a petulant pout. 'You never said we'd leave with the morning chorus.' Suddenly, the white dawn's quiet is loud. 'There is no morning chorus.'

'*Shh.*' A backlit silhouette, she blocks the light, and her face is masked in gloom. 'We're leaving now, and we're leaving in silence.' She brushes Kira's lips with her fingertips. The surprise of it makes Kira shiver. 'If you like, we're going undercover. I'd have left in the dark if I thought it was safe.'

With her long hair trailing down Kira's arm, Freya rocks to sit back on her heels. The light shifts with her.

'That doesn't really help.' Slitting her eyes, Kira struggles upright. This land is far too goddamn *white*: outside, the trees glitter with snow. Every shade of green and brown is tipped with early frost. 'Why'—she rests on her elbows—'now?'

Freya flashes her eyebrows and loads her voice. 'Because, my dearest human, I don't think the pitchforks are too far away.'

The words chill her wool-wrapped skin. Kira's mind sharpens, rudely awake: ogres, fires, villages that somehow reproduce. Distantly, it blends with oddly pleased pride. Chasing people with pitchforks was something she'd had to explain.

'Has something happened?' Kira asks, throwing back the blankets, grasping in the tent-like space for her clothes. Victims' clothes all over Taika's skydd; God, Kira thinks herself awful for using them. 'Move.' She flaps a hand at Freya. 'I can't get dressed if you hover.'

Victims' trousers. A victim's shirt. Obediently, Freya backs off, and Kira swallows her self-disgust. When did she become so callous? Stored with all the things to reuse, chances are that even her blankets, womb-like, thick, and cosy, once belonged to someone dead.

Which makes everything in here loathsome. Dragging on her woollen coat, she follows Freya out. At least Erik's alive, and they're leaving; she need never see dead men's things, or anything linked to Taika, again.

You were the one, Ingrid had laughed, *who wanted to dress like a man.* She waved around the storeroom, deep underground, as Kira stood there in horror. Roots snaked through the walls like serpents. *Waste not, want not.* Kira leered at the stash. *It's no different to using animals.*

I prefer not to do that, either, Kira thought, but managed to hold it in. She didn't need any more mockery; explaining vegetarianism had uproariously been enough.

Thankfully, she hadn't had to respond. Ulrike, working with a jerkin, looked up. *There, you've got it wrong,* she said. Ulrike had grinned, like a wolf eyeing up a doe. *Men are the worst animals of all.*

Ingrid. Ingrid?

'We have to get Ingrid.' Kira cuts off whatever Freya had been saying. Replacing the branches in front of the skydd, she turns. 'She paid me a midnight visit.'

Her voice echoes in the still dawn. Freya winces. 'For the love of—will you shush?' Beside the ladder, she pauses, unfurling the kind of smile that says *well, what have we here?* 'Although…'

'Not that kind of visit.' Kira douses a rush of heat and the urge to elbow Freya's ribs. On an icy branch, it would end in disaster. 'She wants to come with us.'

Well-what-have-we-here turns into oh-my-God-it's-rabid. 'No.' With far too much easy grace, Freya starts down the ladder. 'No way. I wondered what she wanted when I saw her, but no.' The top of her shaking head disappears. 'No. No. Just no.'

Kira peers down the ladder. Her stomach lurches, and she looks back up, fixing on the light white sky. This high in the trees, the ground seems to pulse. 'What do you mean, you saw her?' She breathes through her vertigo, as sick as a drunken head. 'Were you not asleep? If neither of us'—she swallows—'have slept properly, this is going to be so much fun.'

Freya's scorn doesn't need to be spoken. It boils up the tree in a dragon's fire and chars Kira's chilly bones.

'What?' Kira dares a millisecond's look down the ladder. She was right; the dullest deadpan stare, probably meant to belittle her. 'What have I said now?'

Blinking in an equally belittling way, Freya carries on climbing down. 'I'm going to give you some advice.' Reaching the last, weather-worn rung, she hops lightly to the snow. 'Leave your head sometimes and listen when people speak. I was explaining that when you mentioned Ingrid.'

At the fork in the walkway to Ingrid's skydd, Kira pauses. 'Explaining what?'

'Exactly. Now stop yourself right there.' Freya's voice is as faint as an angel on her shoulder. 'Your bosom buddy is absolutely not coming too.'

Kira lifts her voice, just a little. 'Why not?' She sways, swoons, and rights herself on the behemothic branch. The lichen is sheeted with frost. 'I already told her she could, last night. All she wants is adventure.'

'Sure.' The voice from the snow turns from angel to devil. 'Adventure littered with bodies.'

Kira shakes her head, extends her arms, and picks her way forward. 'She said not.' Wobble, breathe, ground her feet. 'She said she doesn't want to get out.'

A soft noise floats up to her, a muffled, stifled snort. 'She'd call her mother a kraken if it'd help her plead her case. How many men has she told you she's killed?'

Kira stops again. 'Three.'

Suddenly, she feels stupid. Quiet wraps around them. It's the quiet of digesting news, of realisation and thought; it makes her feel far too exposed, in the treetops with nowhere to run.

'She lied.' Freya's own calling quiet doesn't sound like her. She could scoff, or sneer, but she chooses neither. Kira feels more stupid still. 'She's killed seven. Eight, with the man from the other day. The one who caused the fight. She propped him against a tree near here.'

Kira's insides grow cold. Colder than they were with the raven, colder than picking through dead men's clothes. 'Like the Kyo did,' she says, 'on the outside. At Romy's boyfriend's house.'

Like the Kyo made Kira's father do, but that, she doesn't say. It's too grisly, too much. Flat eyes, rictus faces, blue puppet limbs.

'Yes.' Freya's voice takes on an edge like slate. 'Exactly like that. She's in danger of becoming the next Anneliese. She's in danger of being the danger that the huldra pin on us.'

Kira takes a wavering step back. For once, she wasn't overthinking; all her worries last night were justified. 'Are you lying?'

'No.'

It's only a word, but it comes so fast. It still lacks scorn, and it feels like a hole in the head. 'And you didn't tell me before because?' Kira steps back again and again. This is why she needs to be paranoid, God. 'Because you saw I'd made a friend? Because you wanted to sit on your high horse, and laugh at the serf being duped?'

Foot by foot, she creeps back, watching Ingrid's skydd. Dried petals, pine cones, and two small nests weave in and out of the moss.

'Nothing so supercilious.' Freya's words are hardly a whisper; Kira strains to hear. 'I didn't think it was important. We were never going to be here long, and if Ingrid was with you, she wasn't wreaking havoc. Now, though'—Freya pauses, as if checking that their coasts are clear—'we should go. Before anybody wakes up.'

They're sharpening their cleavers and their knives…

Shankill Butchers. What a timely song. Softly, Kira descends the ladder, resisting gravity's pull. It's far too early for this; her mind and head and gut are spinning. Lies, deception, a possible witch hunt; all and more before breakfast.

And now they're going on an actual witch hunt.

What about second breakfast?

'Shut up.' With a scathing mutter, Kira lowers her shaking self to solid ground. Every time she's climbed it, the ladder's gotten worse.

'Rude.' Packed fat enough to burst the seams, Freya drags their ready satchels from her hollow. 'Time to go.'

She slings one to Kira. Kira misses, and it crunches onto the snow. 'Ouch.' She tightens her lips at the *thud*. 'We're not saying goodbye to Solveig?'

Freya makes the worlds-wide noise for *no*.

Scooping up the satchel, Kira follows her. 'Why?'

'You're full of riveting questions, aren't you?' Freya darts a hundred looks around, at the hollows, the fire's embers, the intricate, unruffled skydds. Her stride steps up to almost a lope. 'Pitchforks is your answer. I'm not risking any kind of conflict.'

'Even with Solveig?'

'Yes.' Veering left out of the clearing, Freya cuts a glance at Kira. 'I was wrong before about them. I don't belong with them anymore. I don't think like them anymore, and I can't pretend that I do. If something were to happen, I'm not sure I'd get us out.'

Her honesty is both welcome and not. Lifting her satchel so it doesn't bash her hip, Kira matches Freya's march. It shows trust. It shows humanity. It also shows the extent of their danger, and how much Freya was concerned.

'It's changed that much in a week?' Kira asks. Entering a sheltered grove, the snow grows deeper, and they slow to a crunching tramp.

'Mmhmm.' Freya hitches up her quiver and bow. 'Don't feel bad about Ingrid.' She squints at the sky. Fluffy snow is starting, bringing with it silence, like the forest is holding its breath. 'You will anyway, but you shouldn't. She's notorious. Reckless, and notorious, and besides, she lied to you.'

Kira holds out her hand. A snowflake drifts down to her mitten, lonesome and frail. 'I know.' Impossibly slowly, the flake dissolves. She watches it melt in her mitten's thick fur to nothing but sparkles and ice. 'As well as being a martyr, and now a pariah, you'll find I'm great at feeling guilty for the world.'

Freya catches her eye. 'Or three worlds.' Her eyes flit to the side. 'Maybe two.'

A laugh bursts out of Kira, so quick she didn't know it was coming. 'Yes, no, two. Definitely two. There's no way in hell I'm feeling sorry for the Chlause.'

The tension slides off Freya like water down a waterfall. 'They were that bad?' She trails sardonic fingers through the twigs of a branch. 'Who would ever have guessed?'

'Well, clearly not me.' Kira looks around. In brief snapshots such as these, the forest is stunning. Icicles scrape the ground like stalactites. Postcard-pretty, the snow falls soft, the fat, flimsy puffs of the first days of winter. Its tang is electric-fresh. 'How are we starting this hunt?'

'We're not.' Freya flicks a glistening icicle. The note rings crystalline, a clear soprano note that hangs in the air. 'Not witches, at least.'

The note vibrates through Kira's head. 'Come again?'

Freya ducks beneath the icicles. On the other side is a frozen pond, with pawprints in the rime. 'I was up all night, and I changed the plan. We're hunting a fossegrim.'

16

The mysteries we know

Nikoli is not a god, as the boy's awe suggested. He's a grizzly bear of a middle-aged healer.

From the name, Leon expected a hunchbacked villain, with a goatee sharper than his long, curved nails. Whyever that idea piped up, though, it couldn't have been more wrong. Nikoli is tall and wide, hairy and wild, and looks more like he'd be doing the damage than the nursing in the aftermath.

'I'm busy, Thom,' he'd called at first, before looking up from his workbench. 'Oh.'

Yes, *oh*. Very much *oh*. Leon goggled at the room, and goggles some more. The small, white-wood house had looked inconsequential, dwarfed by a large, ramshackle tavern and what Thom described as *the night lady inn*.

Inside, however, it's anything but. Strings of herbs hang from the ceiling, in faded purple, burgundy, green. Slivers of wood lie scattered on worktops, covered in etchings that seem to move; they're not quite writing and not quite pictures, in mounds, molehills, mountains slanting all around the room. The rose-dyed dusk lights the dusty windows, throwing clarity through the smoke. Not smoke, incense. Miasma? Mist? Despite its depth, its fragrance is light. It should make him cough, but it slips down his throat, in a fashion that's oddly relaxed. Is it gold, or tinted by the sun that doesn't shine?

Probably both. Leon breathes it in, its scent of grass, of eucalyptus and mint. Through the amber haze winds a spindle of a staircase. Beside it hangs a heavy drape, screening off the rest of the house. Does the rest of it look like this, this den? There are bowls of flowers, pots of powder, plates of petals and oil. Trinkets, dense creations of stone that sigh *curiosities*. It looks like the house of an oracle: a mysterious woman veiled by perfume, with the weirdest skimpy clothes; it doesn't seem right for the lair of this…

'Nikoli.' The man thrusts out a hearty hand, his black eyes shrewd and piqued. They flick between the boys.

'Leon.' Leon's mouth speaks for him. He shakes the man's hand. The fingers are puckered with scars.

'Leon?' In Nikoli's mouth it sounds foreign, a lie. The man's face cracks in two. 'Ha!' A single laugh storms out of his throat. It rumbles and is mighty. 'Thom! Who in the skies have you brought me? No—*what* is it you've brought me?' He heaves himself up and appraises Leon, a study so thorough it's physical. 'He's a strange one. And he has something.'

That word again: *something*. In Leon's mind, it turns muddy and rank. Something about him; something else.

An urge surges up from his gut to his throat before he can try to comprehend. Fires are lit on mountaintops. Warning bells peal. The punch of panic is visceral; he has to throw Nikoli off.

'I don't know who I am,' Leon says as calmly as he can. The man's black gaze travels back from Leon's navel to his face and thicket-like hair. Hovering and bobbing, Thom's mouth forms an "o." 'I mean, I don't remember. How did you know?'

Wow, how staged that sounds. Internally, Leon winces, fighting it from appearing on his face. *Oh, fancy that, how did you know?* It's more wooden than this house.

Nikoli lowers himself to the bench. 'Interesting,' he says, 'but that's not what I meant.'

Leaning forward, he brushes dried stems from a chair. They spill to the floor with a flat sigh. 'You're…' he stills. 'Did you come from Skarrig?'

Leon lets the word rattle round his mind. It clears away no cobwebs and spins like tumbleweed. 'No. I don't know where that is.'

Nikoli regards him. 'Thom,' he says, without looking away.

Reluctantly, Thom stops bobbing. 'Yes?'

Nikoli rests his elbows on his knees, and his chin on his burly hands. 'Go get to cooking. You're dancing like a fast walker stuck behind a snail, and it's starting to drive me mad.'

Thom half-bobs, catches himself, and stops. 'I—'

'Goodbye, Thom.' Nikoli's black eyes gain a glint of light. 'We're hungry, hungry men.'

Thom opens his mouth and shuts it. Without a word, he slopes away, weaving through the room to the drape.

'So.' Nikoli lifts his snarly brows, jerking his head at the dusty chair in a way that says *sit*. 'So-called-Leon. You know your name, and that's all. Correct?'

Gingerly, Leon takes the chair. Its three legs complain. 'Yes,' he says, as the tetchy wood teeters. 'I woke up today. In the water.'

If he hadn't been watching, he'd have missed the reaction. Minutely, Nikoli's eyes constrict, widen, and thin again. 'Which means?'

Gripping his seat, Leon hesitates. He'd been tuning Nikoli's thoughts to a buzz, background crickets on a soft summer night, but a moment's nosing, in caution's name?

A moment, only a moment. Leon cracks open the door.

…swum from Skarrig? Stupid. Wouldn't survive. Too far. The dese—no one lives there. Maybe they do, and he's escaped. I wouldn't stay, either. Thom thought to cook for him too? Get him a bed. Looks about…

Raising the crickets, Leon closes the crack. 'The first thing I remember is water, and it felt like waking up.' He holds his stomach, yearning to growl. The word *cook* must have hit home. 'Like I'd been knocked out and left there.'

Unmoving, Nikoli watches him. 'Why would someone knock you out?'

'I don't know.' Leon shifts, pressing his stomach tighter. The growl is fighting back. 'I don't know that, or how I didn't drown.' He shifts again. The chair groans. The noise is close to his earlier panic, boiling beneath the surface. It was easier when he tamped it down and focused on finding food. 'Seriously, that's all I have. I know it sounds like a lie, but it's not.' His white knuckles catch his eye. 'I've got dust in my nails from somewhere else. It scare—'

He snaps the sentence off. Fear isn't something he wants to admit, and certainly not to a stranger.

Behind the drape, a door creaks open. Two discordant pans clang. A high voice laughs.

'Ahh.' Unclasping his hands, Nikoli reclines. The workbench squeaks in protest. 'I don't think you're lying, so-called-Leon. Thom did something clever for once, in encouraging you here.' He drums his fingers on his beefy chest. 'Saying mysteries are my speciality is pompous, but I know them well. I solve them.'

Let's go, gang! A voice chimes in his head. In a second, the drawl is gone.

'Can you solve me?' Leon grips his chair tighter. The thought makes him jitter with tuning-fork hope. 'I don't know where I am, but it doesn't seem like waking up in rivers is normal.' His stomach punctuates this with a moan. Clapping his hand to it, Leon heats from head to chest. He shouldn't have held the hunger in; this is a revenge growl, the roar of a mother bear.

One second. Two. Three.

'Ha!' Nikoli's thunderous laugh storms out, and he claps his giant hands. They boom. 'I don't know about solving you, so-called-Leon, but I'll feed you. Thom!'

Beyond the drape, silence falls. 'Uh.' Thom's voice is hesitant, as though he senses a scolding. 'Yes?'

A teasing look tugs Nikoli's face. 'Tell me, Thom, loyal novice.' Resting his forearm on the bench, he strokes his thoughtful beard. 'Are you paying more attention to the food or the girl?'

The pause gathers an atmosphere, thickly grey with guilt. A smile stirs in Leon's chest and almost makes it out. One second. Two. Three.

'Um.' Thom's voice wobbles at the end. 'The food?'

Nikoli's teasing stretches into a snaggle-toothed grin. 'Now that'—he tips a swarthy finger at Leon—'sounds like a lie. Doesn't it?'

Feeling like a fish in a very big lake, Leon nods.

'Good lad. If Gretel's here, Thom,' Nikoli lifts his voice, 'she can season the potato cakes. And get her to tell you how she does it.'

Dull mutters. A spitting sizzle. The high laugh.

Nikoli huffs. 'I thought so. Word of warning.' Swivelling, he taps Leon's knee. 'Gretel can gossip from Ørenna to Urnäsch. By morning, all of Al-Sanit will know you're here.'

Pealing bells. Mountain fire. Leon's stirring smile snuffs out. 'What?'

'Ah, don't worry.' Nikoli covers Leon's knee with his hand and gives it a hard, warm pat. 'If you really don't remember anything, you've nothing to fear.' Bracing himself on his knees, he stands. 'It may be a storm, or it may be a sunset. In the meantime, come and meet cooking Gretel.' He steers Leon toward the drape. 'I'm hoping if she takes to you, I'll get my student back.'

17

The husk

He's been sitting like a lemon for quite a long time before he thinks he should probably move.

Not like a lemon; he *is* a lemon. Bitter, with a frown like he's drunk the juice.

Rubbing the gust-blown grit from his eyes, he smooths the frown from his face. He may be landed here, in barren, hilly valleys, but he will not go mad. He may be getting blasted with furious winds, dry enough to start a hundred fires, but he will not go mad. His cheek may be marked by the straw-like grass, and he may be faced with the strangest mushrooming trees he's ever seen, but—

He hasn't seen them; that's the point. Smacking his eyes clear again, he spits grit from his lips. His mind is blank, his memory's blank, and for a while, he was blank too. It was a long enough while to make him truly irate, until suddenly he knew: his name is Peder.

Except he's pretty sure it isn't because the word swam into his mind from nothing. Scratching his unknown stubble, he extends his aching, unknown legs. He may be going crazy, but he does know this: thoughts aren't isolated that way. They don't appear, clear and bubbling, exempt from static, background noise, and coloured association. No, this was a newsflash. Slapped on the inner lining of his brain, the letters were bold and brash: PEDER.

Which means what? Having explored his dusty stubble, he moves to knead his legs. While he sat like a lemon, he processed, and while he processed, he theorised. If *Peder* was rudely planted, then someone must have ploughed the ground, sown the seeds, and watered the baby shoots. While ploughing, that same someone took his memory. They scraped him out. They left a husk. They tried to remake him and dropped him here.

What a gorgeous choice they made. He lets his hands fall slack and sags. The landscape is parched. Not quite countryside and not quite desert, it's layers of beige, tired green, and wheat-pale yellow, sliced with rocky, sun-browned furrows. Clouds mist the sun, but they don't dim the heat, leaving the day looking sickly and weak. The most annoying thing, though, is where he's been put.

Once he realised, he thoroughly cursed the someone, and has plenty left to give. They've placed him at the top of a ridge overlooking a valley. A steep rocky scrabble is his only route down, unless he wants to jump off a ledge. Sure, he can see for miles; he can see *valleys* for miles and trees and sky. The location would be great if he were under attack, but he's not. He's alone, barring a mouse that scampered past, and even she looked at him with pity. What a joke. What a jolly good *lark*.

Which is why he's now irate. With his legs cramping, Peder stands, as graceless as a gazelle. Step one. He brushes down his trousers (rough and brown), brushes down his loose vest (rough and sandy brown), and scrunches his toes inside his boots (rough hide, the darkest brown yet). An animal tooth hangs around his neck, snug against a feather. A complete identity that isn't his.

Peder's identity. Or does Peder not exist?

Thrusting his hands in his baggy pockets, he starts down the hill. When it's not a ghastly slant, the bumpy slope is strewn with hillocks, and he sticks his eyes to the ground. At some point, he'll find someone, or something. There's undergrowth and sun and bugs; it can't be apocalyptic. He already found a mouse.

Besides, he isn't the only human. Someone's pulling his strings.

The arid air blows dust from the ground, shrouding him like mist. Stones jab his soles. The hot gale rolls. Sweat slips down his back and pools in his waistband. Windswept and alone, he scrambles down, down, down.

18

The hazards

On the edge of the forest, Vasi stops. 'This is as far as I'll take you.'
In front of them, the trees open. Not in dribs and drabs, but all at once, to hills that look like Devon. Copses and hollow ways, an outcrop of stones. Lime-green fields, lemon flowers, a shallow, rock-bottomed brook. Vaguely, Mathew nods. 'Okay.'

After a moment, Vasi turns. His look seems to wait for more, but that requires energy, and energy is something that Mathew doesn't have. It seeped out with his sweat and the loss of his life.

'Good,' the leshy says, with an odd amount of emphasis. Shifting his weighty look away, he clasps the staff with both hands. 'I ventured out especially to find you in the mountains, but from here, I believe you'll be fine. When Grey returns, I'll send him along. He'll sense any unknown hazards.'

Hazards. If his mind is a fish, the word is bait, and it pulls him up to the surface. 'Hazards?' Mathew repeats. His mouth feels foreign. 'Different from— from surviving outdoors? In a regular world, I mean. I can…' He's not making sense. The fish is wriggling, close to getting away.

Vasi's smile says he sees this but will act as if he's blind to it. 'Yes, there are different hazards,' he says. 'My best warning is to prepare to be surprised.' He waits.

Mathew forces the fish to bite again. 'By what?' he asks. Breathing in through his nose, and out through his mouth, he steps from the woods to the springtime grass and opens his arms to Devon.

Instantly, the air changes. A drier heat carried on a breeze, it's less humid than the cloying trees. Closing his eyes, Mathew lets it whip him.

'The odd troll,' Vasi says.

'What?' Mathew's mind sharpens fully. Dropping his arms, he spins back to Vasi. The leshy is as mild as ever.

'Trolls.' Vasi's eyes take on a faintly innocent look. 'They roam but favour this area. When you come upon human settlements, you can ask about anything else. I don't know where your search will take you, so I can't advise you further, but trolls, depending on their mood, are pleasant company.' Sagely, he meets Mathew's eyes, and holds them. 'More scintillating than you expect.'

Mathew stares and forces himself to stop. If he'd thought about troll-related expectations, *scintillating* wouldn't have featured. Even without the world's *Harry Potter* worship—Kira and Romy shrieking *ewww* each time Harry stuck his wand up the monster's nose—every child hits adulthood with the knowledge that trolls are dim. Slowly, Mathew lifts his hand, scratching a bite on his cheek. Does it come from Grimm? *The Billy Goats Gruff?* Either way, he never thought they'd be real.

'Okay.' Mathew says it again, because he should say *some*thing. 'I will keep that in mind.' He drags his gaze from the edge of the woods, where the stony trail peters out, and two ecosystems rub shoulders. Biologically, it's bizarre.

'Good,' Vasi says again. A smile twinkles through his eyes and leaves. 'The Night Hunter, however, is not scintillating, or pleasant. You don't want her company at all.' His knobbed hands tighten on his staff.

Mathew watches. 'Who is she?'

The hands rearrange themselves. 'That's far too long a story. Should she appear, all you can do is find a shelter, wait, and hope she passes by. Grey will sense her, if you're still alone; if you're with others, they should have wards.'

Mathew doesn't ask what wards are. If it isn't self-evident, he'll ask someone else, these mythical, all-knowing *others*.

'Other than that'—Vasi's eyes wrinkle in their folds of skin—'be aware, as you would in your own world. This part of Whiteland is relatively safe.' Ridges and valleys of inner amusement crack across his cheeks. 'Other areas, as I said, are where you might meet real danger, most of it stranger than not. Oh, and don't delve too far into holes or caves or other such things.' He raps his staff on the forest floor. It breaks a stick in two.

Rubbing his eyes, Mathew swallows his question. He doesn't need to know what waits in caves. Trolls are enough.

'And that,' Vasi says, 'I believe, is all.' Like a sunflower, he squints up at the sky, a smudged, wispy blue. 'Yes. When Grey arrives, let him lead you. He'll find the disturbances.'

Mathew frowns like kettlebells hang from his forehead. 'What disturbances?'

Vasi's amusement crinkles back into life. 'The ones Grey will lead you to. At one of them, no doubt, you will find your girls.'

The kettlebells drag on Mathew's face. 'A lot of this relies on a sentient wolf.'

'Yes.' Vasi speaks so fast, so abruptly deep, that he must have heard the thought. 'Consider this a teaching point: don't judge what you don't understand.'

Silence. For the first time in a while, it's a silence Mathew *feels*, as opposed to only knowing it's there. The warm, dry air rushes over the grass, like a hundred rustling skirts. Somewhere beneath it plinks the brook.

'I'm sorry.' Mathew dips his chastened head. 'But you have to apprecia—' He stops, his mouth still open, his tongue pressed to his palate. Is it the world? Is it him? Is his overloaded mind turning everything liquid, unreal…or is the leshy growing?

Christ on a bike. Mathew's mouth dries out, and he shuts it. Blurring at the edges, Vasi's getting bigger. His limbs warp and widen. His skull distends. His knuckles could be knots in bark, his fingers the twigs at the end of a branch. In an instant, his craggy face has weathered, to the coarse texture of a tree. He's melding with the forest itself.

Mathew's mouth searches the air for words. Shaded by the canopy of waxy leaves, Vasi steps back into the trees. His head sits among the green, his feet immersed in the soft, sweet earth. *Don't judge what you don't understand.*

'Exactly.' Vasi's log-like lips barely move. His expression is dappled with lemon and green. 'I feel my point is made.'

Rapid-fire, Mathew blinks. Christ. Mary, mother of God. The reminder winds him more than a punch: Vasi's not human.

'It—it is.' Mathew blinks again, and rubs his face, in jerky little spasms. 'Where, um—where do I go? Until Grey finds me?' He rubs his temple, his mouth, his jaw. Anything to stay his mind, aching to float to the moon. 'How do I know where I'm heading out here?'

With the creak of trees in wind, Vasi turns his rasping bulk. As he does, Mathew catches the edge of a smile, carved like a message in wood. 'There's no way you can,' Vasi says, throatier than before. 'You're too new to Whiteland. Head away from the trees, and Grey will hunt you.' He scrapes his way into the woods, mottled, cosmic, huge.

Mathew watches, his hand still pinching his jaw. 'Is that all the direction I get?' He blinks. For a second, he saw nothing but trees. 'No north or south?'

'It's all I can give.' Heavily, Vasi leaves the path. Leaves crunch. The canopy swishes. A bird *kraaas* in alarm. 'And when you find your daughters, get out for good. It won't be healthy to face what's coming.'

On instinct, Mathew glances away, as if what's coming is here right now. The soft hills list. There are molehills, tulips. 'What is it?' he asks, turning back. 'What's coming?'

It should be what's leaving. For an instant, Mathew feels two-dimensional, in a kinetic virtual reality world. The leshy and the sweeping oaks have gone. Unsteadily, he rotates. The hot breeze eddies around him. Bumpkin fields roll away. No woods. No mountains. Just countryside, in a peaceful déjà-vu of home.

Facing the way he was before, Mathew tightens the knotted coat at his waist. Walk away from the woods; Christ almighty. There aren't woods to walk away from.

Regardless, he sets the intent to walk, and moves his stupefied legs. Somehow, he has to meet Grey, find Romy, get them both out, and then—

Mathew stops. Something Vasi said slots into place, and greasily starts to whir. Romy?

Not just Romy. The machinery jabs his solar plexus, drawing a noose around his gut. Mathew pivots back fast enough for whiplash. 'Vasi!'

The bellow carries on and on and on. The grass sighs. His heart feels sick. He breath gets stuck. '*Vasi!*'

Mathew spins again. The woods stay gone. He heard the difference, but it didn't click; he was tangled in his own myopia, when goddamnit, he should have asked questions. Vasi didn't say *find your daughter*. What he said, as he slowly thudded away, was *daughters*.

'Vasi!' Mathew roars, his throat scoured raw. 'Where's Kira?'

19

The lost

On a horse behind Asgeir, Ella is dreamy. Oh, the sky is so light, alight, the rock and sway of the horse's back a dance beneath her hips. If she were tired, she'd fall asleep.

Ella hums. Maybe it's not a dance; maybe it's a boat, musical, lulling, and strong. It bears the sea's brunt with a debutante's flair. It takes her alone, with the wind in her hair. The wind, which lifts the heat, too sticky and mighty, not musical or dreamlike at all. She hums again, and tightens her arms, damp around Asgeir's waist. If it wasn't so hot, Ella wouldn't be here. She'd be floating, up to the clouds that aren't there. Up, up, up, to the sun she can't see, to the stars there should be, dancing and singing and ringing, alive.

Ella's dream slants as she feels the vibrations of Asgeir's voice rumble through him. 'You're making the same points,' he says. 'Which isn't going to work.'

A sigh. 'It should,' another voice lilts, the one from the head in the tent. 'The more I make the points, the more you accept them, without knowing what's going on.'

'In theory.' Asgeir's voice moves mountains and breaks through the earth. 'Unfortunately, you've told me your plan.'

Ella pushes her face into Asgeir's spine: stop, pretty, stop. She was dreaming. She was drifting, and she was hazy, but now she's falling, back to *here*. Warm body heat. A sour shirt on her nose. A gentle *hush-thud* of hooves through brittle grass. The bump of sacks they're carrying home, the bony horse's back, the swish of human legs against flanks.

The final voice clears its throat. Ella saw him earlier; a small man close to a rectangle, up-and-down and greying and stout, from his hair to his skin to the whites of his eyes. He snapped at her to stop her staring, and then he started to shout. 'Ayomi won't accept her.' He rasps like his body is filled with smoke. 'So none of it's of any import. If Asgeir won't give her up now, he'll have to when we get there.'

'I won't.' Asgeir's words snap off at the ends.

The head sighs the sigh of the wind. 'I told you, Dad. He's got a saviour complex. It's like he went looking for a damsel.'

'Yes.' Asgeir's back muscles ripple. Ella smiles at them. 'That's why I walk when I'm awake at night. Hoping for a girl who's forgotten who she is, so I can save, kidnap, and mould her into a grateful little wife.'

'Stop.' The smoky man sounds like he'd love, more than anything else, to shove his sons off their horses. Ella inhales, pressing her eyes and lips against Asgeir's sweaty shirt. She can smell his father's body-smoke, or the fire of the night before.

Fire. Maybe, if she thinks of fire, she'll dream again.

'You're acting like kids.' The smoky man clears his throat, and hacks, a *wheeck-puh*. 'Iolo, he won't change his mind 'til he's made to. Asgeir, you will be made to, and that's the only reason Ella's still with us. At the first sign of danger, I assure you, she's out.'

'On her ear.' The head is a cackling pixie. No, not a pixie, and nor is it a cackle.

Ella hums a wispy hum and laughs a wispy laugh. She's drifting again, finally, and nothing is as it seems. Swaying with the dance, she rocks in the boat.

When she floats back down, it's dark.

'It's an omen,' the head says, and now they're sat around a fire. Ella breathes in. Sparks, meaty stew, night, heady horse dung. The head's eyes are suns and moons, staring at the black. Her belly doesn't ache. Her fingers are greasy. A pot sits over the flames, scraped clean. 'The Night Hunter and a myrling. They're omens.'

'Omens don't exist.' Asgeir's face is stone in the fire's glow, but he is staring too. Beyond him, shaking droplets from his hands, the smoky man retakes his spot in the grass, like a deer watching a wolf. 'This is just what myrlings do.'

'Bloody things.' The smoky man flicks his fingers. Flecks of water land on Ella, and she cocks her head. Water?

Water. Through a row of acacias, a thin creek burbles. Ella's eyes sweep to trail it. Away, away, a glint beneath the stars. Away, away, into long, waving grass. Away, away to—

To a child outside the firelight, standing still and watching.

The child is pearly, sometimes dark. Sometimes see-through, sometimes girlish, sometimes blank. Eyes too big for her tiny face, then no face at all. Fingers little more than bones, ragdoll arms loose. Now she flickers, now she fades. Now her mouth is open.

Now, in silence, she starts to cry. Ice-blue tears glitter on her cheeks. Her black mouth stretches. In dark, watching silence, the child starts a bloody scream.

'No.' Lurching to its feet, the head scrambles for its tent. Ella blinks. Screaming in a forest, surrounded by snow. Screaming in a white room, with something in her head.

'Come on.' Standing, Asgeir takes her greasy hand. 'It won't go away until the morning.'

He pulls her after Iolo. Ella twists her neck to watch the girl, tripping in the grass. A mouth as wide as galaxies. Moon-eyes there, moon-eyes gone, and screaming, screaming, scared.

'Ella.' Roughly, Asgeir turns her around. 'Why are you watching it?' Looking down at Ella, his face stills. His grip on her arm slackens, and he straightens, his eyes dancing back to the girl. 'It doesn't bother you. At all.'

A heavy, swinging pendulum, Ella shakes her head. It's a girl. A lost girl.

'It sure scares me.' The smoky man takes the pot, squats by the creek, and douses the fire with water. 'Doesn't matter if it can't get in. I won't sleep, knowing it's there.'

'Me neither,' the head calls, muffled by cloth.

'Don't,' Asgeir says, 'go near it.' His jaw tightens, and he urges Ella toward a tent. Tied to an acacia, the horses pack together, still and wedged and silent as ghosts. 'It'll latch onto you and not let go. You might not be scared, but you should be.'

The tent is musty. Stuffy. Trapped. Softly obedient, thinking of stars, Ella curls up on the furs. 'What'—faintly, she works her lips—'does…'

'What does it want?' Asgeir stretches out beside her. 'Burial.' His gaze slides to the tent flap. Hazy slivers of moon shine through. 'Just stay here. When it starts to get light, it'll leave.'

Too hard to look natural, he closes his eyes. Slotting her hands beneath her cheek, Ella watches. 'Lost,' she whispers, and then, the words falling from the sky, through the musky tent to her lips, 'like me.'

20

The love

Kira wakes with a gasp. *Lost like me.*

Fumbling up to sitting, her head collides with the patchwork blankets making do as a tent. For a second, Freya's sleeping form is a stern, tangle-haired man, then the back of a retreating giant, then another man, grinning by a wall of garlands. Lavender, basil, rosemary. Kira can almost taste their scent.

Shock, panic, horror, hope. They swell in her lungs, and lunging forward, Kira scrambles from the tent. The branches bow as she bats the blankets, threatening Freya with a material grave. *Breathe.* She can't breathe. They're all here.

The blizzard barely lasted the morning, and the night is indigo. No moon, no stars. The brightest thing is snow, and staggering away, Kira rakes her fingers through her hair. *Breathe.* Her nails on her scalp are grounding. She tips her head back. Her view of the deep, sharp, boundless sky is free. They camped—if scraping bare a patch of earth, draping blankets over branches, and hoping for the best is camping—on the edge of a clearing. Freya thought it perfect. Kira thought it too exposed.

Now, she's grateful. Ringed with hemlock and piled with snow, it's open to the crisp, clear elements. Kira buries her nails in her scalp. *Breathe.* In through her nose, out through her mouth, but it all gets caught in her throat. Romy and Callum and Mathew and Jay. The four of them here, in Whiteland. Is that the best of epiphanies or close to the worst?

They're out of the clutches of the Chlause, but in Urnäsch they were together. Here, they're scattered, and the dreams are fading. Kira's lungs swell, so close to bursting, like balloons you know will pop. All she saw for Romy was a tent and a man. Jay was sat in a hovel. Callum was scaling a scrubby bluff. Her dad was yelling, *Where's Kira?*

Her dad. Her real dad, neither dead nor Freya's accomplice to murder. Tears scour the back of her mouth. Kira's lips start to tremble. Her dad the worst off of any of them, after a year as a puppet. He'll be worse off than she was when she blindly followed Anna; at least then, she had company, had made the choice to come, and possessed a vague idea of what was going on. Unless he was shouting *at* someone, her dad has none of that.

And back home, he's a killer.

This is a good thing. Kira stares at the sky until her eyes feel stripped, striving for anything left of the dreams. It means they don't need to get the door open.

It also means that someone else did.

It means they're all alive.

It means she has to travel a whole world to find them.

Yes, but it means they're *alive*.

Breathing out wetly, she swallows her tears. Romy and Callum and Mathew and Jay; they're here, alive, and that's the only thing that matters. Anything else is the Whispers's concern.

Light blooms in the tent. Blinking at the glare, Kira focuses slowly, sinking down from the sky. The cloth has become a pink-orange haven, a pulsing heart by the trees.

The blankets lift, and Freya emerges. 'I thought I could ignore your exodus, but now I'm wide awake.' Laying the lightstone on the ground, she tramps through Kira's boot prints. The gentle colour of the lightstone suffuses the snow, taken from a dead man who took it from a weaver. When Freya first produced it, Kira cupped its warmth, and marvelled at its peace. 'What's wrong?'

Kira opens her mouth, sniffs, and shuts it. 'Wrong isn't right.' She shakes her head and clears her throat. She sounds like she's been crying. 'I mean, obviously. But the others are in Whiteland.'

Traipsing through the deep snow, Freya stops. Blinks. Her eyes skip to the trees and back. 'All of them?' she asks. Her voice sounds carefully placed, like the last drop of water in a brimming cup. Equally carefully, she carries on tramping.

'All of them.' Kira folds her arms, clinging onto her ribs. 'Somehow, my dad's here too.' She holds herself like a boa constrictor. 'I don't…I haven't figured out how I feel.'

Reaching Kira's side, Freya mimics her pose. In the lightstone's glow, Kira sees the woman shiver. 'If it helps you work it out, you look less like you've had a breakthrough and more like you've seen a myrling.'

'No.' Kira's hand jerks up, an immediate veto. 'We are not mentioning myrlings. Not now, not ever. Between you and Ingrid, I've heard enough ghost stories to last me through to Ørenna.'

Freya gives a one-shouldered shrug. 'That's okay. Tomorrow's a moroaica. Now pray tell, half-human sister, how you know the Scooby gang have made it out of Urnäsch?'

What? Kira feels suspended in time or outside the universe. 'You were in the outside less than a week.'

Freya spreads her hands slowly, deliberately. 'I took to the culture. Are you going to answer? Because if it's true, it means a witch is no longer our fall-back, and that would be my ultimate favourite revelation.'

Her words echo, as stark and clear and bright as Karliquai's light. With a shiver, Kira eyes the bottomless night. Shadows, shadows everywhere. She wasn't afraid when she first woke up, but the thought of an abandoned child's ghost—a monkey on her back until she finds its body, bringing bedlam if she tries to refuse—is enough to make the darkness writhe.

'I dreamt it,' Kira says, heading back toward the lightstone. 'I saw—'

'You did *what?*' Contempt explodes from Freya, and she laughs. 'Oh, my—this was a *dream?*'

'No, no, listen!' Kira's hands fly up, and she spins. 'I've had dreams before that have meant something. I dreamt about Karliquai years ago, of the exact scene where we went to the Chlause, me and Romy and Callum. I dreamt about Taika's burrow as well.'

Freya scoffs. 'No, you didn't.' Lowering her voice from an exclamation, she joins Kira by the lightstone's heart in the snow. 'You just want to convince me. You want to convince yourself.'

Folding her arms again, Kira sticks out her chin. 'I was on a train,' she says, 'and I dreamt about a cave. I saw Taika, and…' her hard tone falters. 'Probably you, come to think of it, and some kind of bluish magic. On a wall.' She shifts her weight to one hip. 'You were holding Taika up. Sound familiar?'

'Yes, because I told you about it.' Scooping up the lightstone, Freya stoops to part the blankets. 'If you really are an odd little prophet, why didn't you say before?'

'Because it wasn't relevant.' Kira fights to make her voice even, less akin to a petulant child and more akin to its mum. 'And I remembered that example when you were somewhere else. You don't have to believe me, but like you said, it means we don't need to find a witch. You should'—she crawls in next to Freya—'be turning cartwheels to beat the circus.' On her knees, Kira stills. An acid, tart pain slices through her breath: Gramps. He said that all the time, and it welled up inside her, out before she could stop it.

The pain steals the wind from her billowing flag. Slowly, Kira drags her feet into the tent. Yes, her other dreams were real, but could this be wishful, wistful thinking? A heart-racing nightmare you wake from, gasping. Sure you see the spiders or the demons or the beast? They seem so very manifest, but when you wake up fully, blearily focus, and realise you've fled across the room, it's empty, safe, and foolish. If Kira goes off chasing the wrong wild geese, and the others are still in Urnäsch—

'Forget it.' Lying down with a jarring thud, Kira yanks up their blanket. The hot stone rocks between them. 'Go back to sleep.'

Out in the night, the fresh snow crunches. Kira jerks upright. 'What was that?'

Her eyes lock with Freya's. 'Something a lot more solid than a myrling.' Freya closes a hand around her bow, rooting in her satchel with the other. 'But better to face it out there than in here.'

Tossing Kira a crude, angry knife, Freya leaves the tent. Snow creaks, near and far. Kira's mind lags. A knife on her knee. Potential danger. They're not in Kansas anymore.

'Oh.' Faintly muffled, Freya's voice turns flat.

'What?' Awkwardly gripping the knife, like a child learning to use a fork, Kira quickly crawls outside.

'Oh.' Kira was expecting a mist beast, an outlaw, a bear; she was not, in any way, expecting Erik.

Warily, Freya lowers her bow. 'How did you find us?' she asks. 'If it's that easy, I need to do better.' Straightening, she looks him up and down. 'One day, old man, you and me should learn when our obligations are over.'

Sheltering his candle, Erik snuffs it out. His shaded eyes and lined face look tired; even his bearded mouth looks tired. 'I think all three of us need to learn that.'

Heat sweeps Kira's cheeks like a Venetian mask. Ducking away, she slings the knife back into the tent. Thank God for the indigo dark; last time she saw him, she didn't quite lie, but she did elude to his face. 'I'm sorry.' Kira crouches by the smouldering cinders of the fire. If he can't see her properly, he can't read her shame. 'I couldn't leave while the others were trapped.'

'I know.' The briskness of Erik's tone makes her look up. 'I didn't expect you to stay away. It was hardly a day before a man said they'd seen you or someone I assumed was you.'

With a sleepy crackle, the fire rekindles. Its heat isn't warming. Kira's lips are dry. 'Someone saw me?'

'A girl with a huldra, less her tail.' Erik moves his fingers, as if brushing this away. 'That's not why I came to find you.'

Freya flexes her fingers on her bow. 'Then why did you?' Kira shoots her a warning look. It misses. 'How did you?'

'Please.' Kira's voice comes out too loud. Sitting on the frozen earth, she arranges her mouth in a smile. 'Erik. You can sit. Are you hungry? Thirsty? For once, I can offer you something.'

'No, thank you.' Laboriously, Erik sits beside her, extending his gloves to the flames. A glance at Freya, more canny than chary. Then he focuses fully on Kira.

'Are you sure?' The smile is starting to feel like a grimace. The pouches beneath Erik's eyes are dark. She's never seen him so haggard.

'I'm sure.' His beard shifts into a smile that looks as pegged-on as hers. Inwardly, Kira starts. He's not only haggard, but he's brought nothing with him: no satchel, no snowshoes, no skis. Guilt aches like frostbite. He must have run out in a hurry. For her.

Erik looks up at Freya, watching the night with an arrow in her bow. It's as if she *wanted* something to shoot and is daring the dark to bring it. 'I found you because…' Erik hesitates. The fire pops. 'The huldra. Because of the huldra.'

'What?' Freya's head snaps round.

Kira's echo is a cry. 'The *huldra*? You went to the huldra?' She gapes at him. 'And you're not…'

'I was lucky.' Gruffly, Erik firmly shuts the door on her shock. Rubbing his gloves, he bends to the fire. 'I accept that. I must admit, I assumed that age—'

Freya shakes her head. 'No. No, no, no.'

Watching her, Erik's gloved fingers curl in. Slowly, he turns to ice. 'Never mind.' He looks away. His voice grows gruffer still, buried deep in his beard.

'Never mind?' Kira couldn't stop gaping if she tried. 'Erik, you could have died.'

'But I did not.' Erik fixes her with a look that says *let's not think about it*. 'I came across a woman with a scar, and—'

'Yvette.' Freya traces a phantom gash on her face.

'And I told her what I wanted before she could react.' Erik gives Freya the shortest of nods. 'She was alone, and she told me that as far as they knew, the pair of you had gone to find our fossegrim. She didn't look pleased to see me, but neither did she look a threat.'

He bows his head and fixes on the low-ebb fire.

Kira shifts. The earth has numbed the bones in her rear. How much has she shaken Erik's world? His sanity? His life?

'The question is,' Freya says, as hard as the ground, 'how did you find the huldra?'

Erik lifts his old, blue gaze to hers. The air between them seems to thaw. 'I didn't,' he says quietly. 'I headed to where I believed they lived but didn't need to reach them.' He turns his old, blue gaze to Kira. It's sad, and it's rueful, and it aches. It *knows*. 'I assumed you would have nowhere else to go.'

As the deep, cold night wears on, as they crowd the crackling fire, Kira wars with guilt and worry and love. Erik speaks. A trading party recently returned from Al-Sanit, and what they'd heard and what they'd seen, spread through Atikur like wind.

Disturbances, all over Whiteland. More than the Whispers or other wild forces; they're more like fleeing huldra. They shake your bones and break them. They shake and break the world.

There's lawlessness. Rebellion. Schism. Bands of men are splitting off. Anneliese's return, the flock of outsiders and Freya got minds churning, burning: another world exists, and they're only stopped from seeking it by spirits above the ice. There's plotting and planning, hushed but there. Or at least, that's how it was before Taika. Now, there's not quite chaos, not quite anarchy, not yet, but Whiteland is starting to roar.

Humans want answers. Monsters want bedlam.

And then there's the boy. A girl has been dancing through Al-Sanit, singing songs of the boy from the river. He's told no one who he is. He doesn't seem to know. He's being sheltered by a healer who sensed something strange and is rumoured to be learning the trade.

'Of course, that's not certain,' Erik says. Kira feels him watching her, but studying the scabbed scar on her palm, she can't look up. Not yet. 'He's been there a short time only, but rumours like to fly. This boy's appearance reminded me, very much, of yours.' He pauses, with the air of an unspoken question.

Kira tries to link her threaded thoughts. They feel like a loom attacked by a cat or a manic cop's wall. 'I was with a boy,' she whispers. Her heart is a cross between thunder and a bird, drumming its wings to get free. The dream. She doesn't dare believe it, doesn't dare meet his eyes, see the blue, and swell with hope, but the thought of this being real, of somehow knowing. Her body sways between hot and cold, and the bird batters its cage.

'How old is the boy?' Freya asks, on a knife edge, showing signs of unease. She crouches on the firelight's fringes, scanning the forest for signs of life. Or, as she put it, signs of death. 'Because you call Kira "girl," and if you didn't consider me abominable, I'd probably get the same. "Boy" could mean man to you, and you'll have raised her hopes for nothing.'

Unless it's Callum. Kira's hot-cold spikes. It shouldn't be; if her dreams were right, then he's alone, in the country. It has to be Jay. If it isn't—

'Young,' Erik says. 'A lot younger than both of you if what I've been told is correct. Young and quiet, but when he talks, I believe the girl said he has a mouth full of words.'

An odd sound breaks from Kira's throat, a gasp and a laugh and a cry. God, this is crazy. She's crazy.

'Jay.' The strangled name comes thick and strange. 'That's Jay. He's twelve, and he's smarter than the rest of the world.' Kira drags her eyes up to Erik's. He nods, but in it, there's trouble. 'Erik?' The bird flutters at the base of her neck, giddy at the thought of freedom. 'What is it?'

Planting his broad hands on the earth, Erik heaves himself to his feet. 'It's what it means,' he says quietly. 'You don't need me to tell you that. I'm glad I made the journey, but you must see how it leaves the future.' Securing his grey hat over his ears, he critically eyes the forest. 'It leaves it open to mayhem.'

'Wait.' In a clumsy hurry, Kira stands. 'You're leaving? We haven't—'

What? Caught up? It felt strange, out of place, to ask anything about Erik, and so she didn't, despite the niggle that she should; it would have felt like discussing the weather in a hurricane. Whiteland isn't much for small talk.

Still, though. He'll walk off into the night, and she'll seem self-centred. She should at least have asked about the wife who cried wolf and rightly predicted the storm.

'I left quickly.' Erik dips his bearded chin. It casts Kira back a year, his usual assent. 'I prefer to travel in daylight, but I need to get back. My wife is ill, and my daughters need me.'

Guilt upon guilt upon guilt. 'I'm sorry.' Kira makes herself hold his gaze, even as the snow wants to swallow her. He needs to know this: that she *is* sorry and grateful, beyond any human words. 'I'm sorry you had to leave them, and that you walked through the night to find me.'

Erik lifts his hand.

'No, let me.' Kira talks over it, holding up her own. 'Just…let me. Thank you will never be enough. You've stopped me trying to do things that would have probably been insane.'

'They were definitely insane,' Freya clarifies. 'And ludicrous, to boot.'

Kira shoots her a half-hearted *must-you?*

'I know there's not much I can do.' Kira turns back to Erik, averting her eyes. 'But while I'm here if there is—'

'Girl.'

'I know.' A small smile tweaks Kira's lips. 'I know it's not much use, but seriously. You've done far too much for me, and you need to know how much I appreciate it. How thoroughly stranded I'd be without it, and how much I wish I could pay you back.' Chewing her cheek, she bobs on her toes. 'I'd like to know why you did it. All of it.'

Kira's cheeks billow with heat, yet again, and she fixes her attention on a white, weedy sapling. Any minute now. Any minute now, Freya will speak, and scoff as she did at the dream.

Nothing. Kira slides her eyes to the side and down, but Freya simply stands. An owl hoots. The sleepy flames *whoosh*.

Lighting his candle in the fire, Erik sighs. 'It was right.' Wick alight, he straightens. A painful bone pops. 'And if I evade something that's right, it will never let me live.'

Like taking her freedom while the others were stuck. Like trying to get rid of Callum, both this year and last.

'All of it comes down to that.' Stepping around the fire, Erik touches Kira's cheek. 'That, and the hope that when you've all left, the worlds will settle.' He moves away, out of the light, into the forest's murk. 'I don't want the wreckage that this has brought and will bring while the worlds collide. Whatever may stop it is worth trying to achieve. Goodbye, Kira.' He lifts a hand. 'Ørenna.'

The licking, shuddering shadows consume him. The owl hoots. A bat flits. Soon, his crunching footfalls have been eaten by the trees.

Freya lets out a long, long sigh. 'I do believe,' she says, 'that the girl has magic powers.'

Woodenly, in the newly still dark, Kira toes snow onto the fire. 'I do believe,' she murmurs, 'that the girl was trying to tell you.'

'And the huldra was wrong.' Casting a last look around, Freya stoops into the tent. 'I don't understand it, other than thinking your world-mixing parentage has tinkered in your brain, but I suppose it could be useful.'

Wearily, Kira crawls in beside her. Suddenly, everything has caught up: last night's insomnia, the full day's trek, the wallop of the dream. The ballooning shock that the dream is real. 'It's sporadic,' she says, nestling her head into her coat's warm collar. 'I've had three in three years.'

'But two in two weeks.'

Kira pushes out her lips. 'True.' Slotting her hands beneath her cheek, she blinks at Freya through the gloom. 'I thought you didn't believe me.'

Gathering the bear's share of the blanket, Freya gives a horizontal shrug. 'That was before. What matters is what we do now.'

Kira yawns. The lightstone's heat is intoxicating. 'You said we'd reach the fossegrim tomorrow?'

'I did.' Freya balls herself up like a foetus, wild-eyed, child-like, harmless. 'We can go from there to Al-Sanit. It's a trade hub, not far up the river. From the fossegrim, it'll take a few days, as opposed to…' her eyes lift, and she shrugs. 'Well, I'd guess a few days either way. From here, though, it's trees, snow, a wasted trip, and zero information.'

Kira wriggles into the tired ground. 'Even if—' she yawns again and smiles. Her lips make a *tuh* sound. 'Sorry. Even if the fossegrim tells us nothing, what else is good about going from there? I'm really'—a third yawn stretches the corners of her mouth—'angling for less winter.'

Freya shifts her head on her knuckles. 'We're just asking about the others?' she asks, as if dancing on the brink of danger. 'No more witch talk?'

Kira shakes her woolly head. 'No more witch talk.'

Freya smiles. For once, there seems to be nothing behind it. 'Then we'll travel on from there.' She winks. 'As far as I know, it's balmy.'

21

A hush upon the snow

Erik is far from the huldra when the girl steps out in front.

'Hello.' Striding forward, round faced and bitter, she reaches out her hand. 'Goodbye.'

His hat is yanked from his head. His hairs splice and leave his scalp. The fresh candle he's holding gutters.

Startled, Erik stumbles round. The girl is stalking off along the path he's just forged. A sky-black pelt encircles her arms. Below a sky-black dress flicks a tail.

Huldra. His feet grow roots. His lips grow numb. Rocks replace his innards. He thought the danger had passed; he's not far from Haavö, yet here the girl is, appearing from nothing and leaving the same. Her feet are hardly a hush on the snow; if she wanted, he'd be dead.

This is how they snare men. This is why so few survive.

Yet he did. Erik watches her leave him alive, a spectre with his hat in a fist. As soon as she's gone, before he can breathe, he turns and does the one thing he keeps reserved for truthful fear. With his candle in his shaking fist, Erik Mathieson runs.

22

And so he tricks

The morning is stark and the snow ever deeper. Kira's shins are sodden and numb as they tramp downhill, sloping to where the gorge meets the river. It's the forest's last hurrah.

'It sounds like there should be a rhyme,' Kira had said when Freya mapped out their directions. 'Where the gorge meets the river, there he stays. Sat behind a waterfall...'

'There he plays.' To Kira's surprise, Freya finished it. 'It'd work, bar the fact the Fossegrimmen are a race. This one's just the closest; they're all over Whiteland.' Freya had paused, then, thoughtful, 'I suppose you could have a verse for each.'

The idle possibilities pirouette in Kira's mind. They distract her from the snow, from the thick, scrubby bracken, from the stumpy press of the pines. The more they walk, the more the trees jostle. The more the trees jostle, shoulder to shoulder, the deeper the drifts of snow. She can practically feel her leg muscles growing, from her feet to the tops of her thighs.

'Shh.' Slightly in front, Freya holds out an arm, although Kira hadn't been speaking. Drawing an arrow, she crouches low.

Kira stills, raising her wary hackles. 'Wh—'

'*Shh.*' Softly, Freya sidesteps behind a thicket and a weedy, simpering sapling.

Pulling a petty face at her back, Kira follows. The snow squeaks. Her lips wince. She misses her moccasins; she felt like a ghost. She shouldn't have swapped them out for warmth.

In a whisper of wood, Freya nocks her arrow.

Kira lists to the left, unnaturally slow, holding her breath to peer past—

'No.' With a startled hiss, Kira grabs her arm. Freya's head whips round. The minute movement is sharp, her widened eyes conveying both *shut up* and *what the hell?* 'You are not'—Kira tightens her fist—'shooting foxes.'

Freya lifts her lip, like she's smelled something vile. *Let*, she mouths, *go.* She turns back to the thicket, cut from stone.

Doggedly holding fast, Kira teeters, tipping through the air. '*No.*'

Freya's side profile grows tight. Her eyes dart to Kira, to the clearing, to the bow, quivering out of position. 'We need,' she says, in a lockjawed breath, 'to bring the fossegrim something. A gift.'

Kira crushes her arm. 'Find something else.'

Freya hisses through her teeth. 'I've seen nothing else.'

'Well, we're not there yet.' Kira's legs tremble. Her fingers are cramping, awkward and iron. Her twisted sides complain.

Freya's lips curl. Her bow is truly quivering now, the strain of it tugging at strings in her face. Her cheeks are almost as red as her scar.

'Fine.' Abruptly, she drops her stance. 'It's on you to find something, though. I won't help.' She makes to get up.

Kira grabs her. 'Wait.'

In mid-air, Freya stops. 'Why?'

Kira says nothing.

With a slow mix of a sigh and an *ugh*, Freya lowers herself back down. 'You know, I'm not going to wrestle them to death.'

Kira shoots her their habitual look, the one that says *can you not?* 'Watch.' She steeples her mittened hands in the snow. The crouch is starting to throb. 'Be human.'

Through the thorns, in an untouched patch of white, two baby foxes roll. White-socked and rusty, one's back is streaked grey. Black rims the smaller one's eye, and they bicker, their fur hushing soft on the snow. Kira doesn't smile; it's too pure for that. All she does is watch.

They chitter and squeak. They grunt in their throats. Like play-fighting boys, the foxes tumble: over and over, up and bouncing, pouncing at the other's snout. Head over heels and back over head, spraying puffs of powder. Sock-deep, belly-deep, a scuffle and a plunge, and unaware they almost died.

Kira watches until, with a piping yip, one lumbers off into the bushes. The other bounds after him, nipping at his tail, and with a rustling of undergrowth, a squeak, and a snuffle, the trees settle silently still.

Kira glances at Freya, her lips apart. 'That,' she says, 'just lightened the world.'

Staring after the cubs, Freya huffs. 'Okay.' The sneer has lessened, if not quite gone. Quietly, she stands. 'Babies are off the menu. But we do need to bring the fossegrim something.'

Kira lingers on the patch of snow, churned and patterned by paws. 'I know.' Softly, she straightens, backing away from the thicket. The magic has gone, but the feeling remains: innocence, beauty, hope, as bright as a butterfly landing on your leg or a deer by the side of the road. There's a way out of all of this. 'I just wanted you to see things as more than they seem.'

Ducking through a cluster of fluffy-snowed spruce trees, they trudge on through the drifts. After a moment, Freya huffs again. 'I've been trying to do the same for you.'

Kira's mind can't find a response to this, and then, the moment has passed. In tramping quiet, she tunes her senses. As though it listened to the foxes, the forest is peaceful, awaking from slumber and coming to life. The more it slopes down, the more it lifts: the smells, the sounds, the air. The video-game sharpness lurks, if she looks, though it stopped feeling strange long ago. Brighter than a photo with too much exposure, it was giddy, sparkling, metallic on her tongue. It was nothing compared to the Chlause but a beast on her back nonetheless.

Atikur's weight. Atikur's presence. Slanting down to the river, now the menace is lifting up.

The barometer's changing. The storm clouds scatter. In the distance twitter unknown birds, scrapping in bushes and trees. Not quite bleak, nowhere near normal, but when the forest is twinned with fear, flight, death, any shift should be hailed and blessed.

'Ah.' Freya stops. The word drags on, between a sigh and frustration. 'Water.'

Kira stops beside her. Through the trees comes the sound of running water, and beyond it…she strains to listen. Beyond it, oh-so-faint, drifts music. 'Isn't this what we want?'

'Yes.' Freya turns in a steady circle, notching an arrow. 'And thanks to you, we're giftless.' She drops her voice dozens of decibels. 'At this point, anything has to do.'

Kira watches her slip into stealth mode.

Stealth mode? With a blink, her mind slides out of focus. Stealth mode, like a video game? Who did she get that phrase from? Callum? No, he sees games through the eyes of a grandma, bemoaning the fact that kids these days no longer play outside. *Go climb a tree,* he'd muttered, when Jay slammed his fist on his desk. It was hard enough to rock both the Casbah and the Richter. *Take a bike and ramble through hedgerows, and I don't know, pick fruit. When I was twelve...*

Eva. Eva's the gamer. Feet kicked up on the arm of the couch, controller gripped knuckle-white-tight. She trills out updates regardless of whether anyone's there or cares.

Trilled. The change slithers in, leaving acid in its wake. Kira kicks its slimy groin. No.

Stealth mode, that was the point. She forces herself to focus on Freya. She really does change when she hunts; languid and natural one minute, lithe and alert the next. Freya treads with the forest, becoming its eyes. Its eyes, its ears, its mind, its heart, the smooth, slick blood through its veins.

Above them shrieks a shrill *whoo-WHOO.*

Freya jerks her bow up, fires into the canopy, and steps toward a bird that hits the ground with a *whump.*

A rope knots in Kira's belly. Averting her eyes, she clears her throat. The gift is bigger than a nachtkrapp but mercifully not a Hyrcinian bird: its blue-black breast puffs out like a pigeon, its beak the same silver flash as its wings. Uneasy nausea burbles through Kira. She can block her eyes, but not her ears. As Freya starts to harvest it, Kira shuts her eyes. Snow scrapes. The arrow squelches. Her grimace hurts her face.

'Done.' The bird's body bumps against Freya's legs, matte and lifeless, dull. 'Come on, snowflake. Time to go.'

They walk. Kira keeps her eyes averted, dogged and ill. They worm through a knot of graceful trees, slender, swaying branches held like dancers. The forest is changing, and fast. Snow drips, wet in her ears, slushy under her feet. The air feels like early spring, when the sun is being brave.

The bird bumps against Freya's calf. It hauls Kira back, and she pulls a face. 'Can you not do that?'

Freya glances over at her. There's no fake innocence, in *do what, this?* There's no apology either. 'I can.'

She makes no move to stop. The bird's skull knocks against a gnarled old tree. It rots Kira's gut. 'Thanks.'

'You're welcome.'

Kira vividly imagines knocking *her* against a tree. 'You can take the woman from the huldra,' she mutters, 'but you can't take the huldra from the woman. Great.'

Freya swings the bird. 'Pardon me?'

Kira shuts her eyes. Instantly, she trips in the deep, snowy sludge, and watches her boots instead. 'Never mind.' She nods in the offering's vague direction. 'Will that be enough?'

Freya shrugs. 'Perhaps. If we still knew absolutely nothing, then no. He prefers larger things, from what I've been told, but when he's not our next-to-only hope, we should get by with this. And if he rejects it'—she gives the bird a shake—'then I've caught us our next meal.'

Kira holds up a hand beside her face. The mitten blocks her view and is weirdly satisfying, in a schoolyard-feud kind of way.

Freya snorts but says nothing. The bird bumps on.

The snow has really started to drip. Degree by degree, the air warms up, wet drops denting the ground like snout-holes. Kira shifts inside her coat. Heat wafts from her armpits, sticking to her skin. It's a gradual change, but the trees are shrinking, growing richer, broader, less ominous and harsh. Fewer pines and more variation, playing nicely with others that sprout alongside. Red berries on one tree, resembling a rowan. A few new shoots, a few bright blooms. Kira pushes through a tangle of dancers, and then—

And then. She stops with a jerk. The woods open up, the music swoops, and before them sits a lake.

Kira stares. It's as though, up to here, the forest was a wall, with a crack to let life leak through. To the right crawls the gorge, steeply curving, traveling sheer and bleak. To the left, a tributary trickles away. On its bank the pines falter, and the meadowlands begin.

Kira flashes hot and cold and weak. Flash: the church. Flash: the fire man. The meadowlands and Urnäsch.

No. She struggles back to the here, the now. The lands that used to be Urnäsch, before the Whispers tore them out. Now, the meadows are safe. They're green. They're quaint and sound like Kent. No Chlause.

'The fossegrim lives on the island.' Freya waves across the lake. Slowly, Kira turns from the meadows. The lake starts where her toes end. One more unseen step, and the water would have had her. A trickle trundles toward the gorge, as clear as the rocks in its belly, and the rest…

Jade doesn't do it justice. Neither does turquoise, aquamarine, anything under the sun; it's deep and vibrant and solid in colour, two hundred feet wide and triple that in length. On the far side, the forest climbs. It's much the same as here, growing greener, fatter, lusher, the more the trees trail to the left.

And the *island*. Starting to sweat, Kira squints at it. This place is such an oasis; twice the size of the one in the river, the island is grassy, rimmed with rocks. Trees grow dense, as rich as the lake. Ferns sprout on the fringes.

Kira's narrowed eyes stretch so fast the tiny muscles strain. Oh, oh, oh. From the top of the trees, at the island's sensuous heart, pours a waterfall.

'Compliment him on it.' Freya sounds like she's smiling. 'The waterfall, I mean. It might take the edge off appearing with a scrap.'

On the edge of Kira's vision, Freya holds up the bird. Kira ignores them both. The waterfall sparkles, mesmerising, gushing from the leaves and glimmering, shimmering, over the rocks to the lake.

'How?' Kira whispers, turning to Freya. Her mind is suddenly light and faint. 'How does it work? I know you said he's a water creature, but I thought…'

'That he lived in a puddle?' Pulling her satchel over her head, Freya lowers it to the grass.

Grass, Kira marvels. They've hit *grass*. 'No. I just wasn't expecting this.'

She casts a look across the lake. The music swells, a lonely fiddle, caught between an Irish ballad and a Scandinavian lament. High seas, rocky outcrops. Mournful crows in winter skies.

'He has some hold over water.' Freya lays down her bow and arrows and shrugs her heavy coat to the grass. 'Not huge but enough for decoration. Take off your bag and coat.'

Far away and wistful, Kira blinks at her. 'Why?'

'Because.' Freya empties her pockets—water container, twin of the knife she insists Kira carry—and snicks off her boots. 'We don't have to swim, but so the story goes, the lake's the water of dreams. If you call to him, there are stepping-stones.'

Dimly, something registers. Swimming means water, and water means a bath.

'I'll swim.' Kira strips to her trousers and shirt as Freya walks into the lake. When Kira relinquished her outside clothes, she'd considered keeping her bra, until Freya pointed out that blending in matters far more than support. Dropping Callum's phone in her boots, Kira pats her pockets. Ready. The phone is a sure sign she's a stranger, but it's all that's left of any of them. It links her back to home.

'Mmm.' Spreading her arms, Freya turns in the water. 'Behold. The stuff of dreams.'

Dipping a toe, Kira's eyes grow wide. 'Oh.' As quick as she can on the slick stones, she sloshes into the lake. For some reason, she'd still thought the water would be cold. '*Oh.*'

It's not a lake. It's a lush lagoon. It enfolds her ankles, her legs, her waist, and calls to her like a craving. It's humid, and velvety, and billows through her clothes. Kira sighs from her throat to her toes.

'I'd have made a special trip for this if you had told me it was here.' Kira dips beneath the surface. Oh, her body is hardly hers; it's mermaid-like and lithe and free. Cleaning her hair, her skin, her mind, Kira comes up new and fresh and buoyed and something close to happy.

'Doesn't compare to heated containers.' Wringing out her hair, Freya winks at Kira. 'Shivering underground is the crème de la crème of couture.'

Kira slaps back her sopping hair. 'Oh, aren't we funny.' Touching her palms to the gentle water, she turns and turns and turns. Blue-green ripples rock the lake, so many tiny whispers.

'I try.' Smoothly, Freya bows. Wading toward their things, she lifts the dead bird high. Kira averts her eyes again. The fossegrim had better accept it; she's not eating that for tea.

But watching Freya strike out for the island, a curious thought occurs. 'Freya,' she says, sliding into a breaststroke, 'how do you know how to swim?'

Freya's one-armed gait is clumsy but strong. Already, she's gliding ahead. 'I learned.'

'Well, yes.' Kira juts her head above the surface, tilted like a dog. 'But if you've never been here before, and you rarely leave the forest?'

Treading water, Freya breathes in bursts. 'Hidden pools,' she says, staccato. Switching bird-bearing arms, she swims on. 'Not many, but if you know how to find them, they're often as warm as this.' She growls in her throat, switching arms again. 'Ørenna, swimming's the worst.'

'Agreed.' Already, Kira's muscles burn. Gritting her teeth, she fights the shake.

'Actually'—Freya sounds like she's being bulldozed or minced—'we have a tale about a girl who lost her heart to a pool.'

Distractions. Thank you, Freya. Quite apart from Kira's cramping weakness, the dead, flopping bird is unnerving and lewd.

'You have a tale for everything.' Kira spits water from her lower lip. 'Actually, so do we.' Pausing, she treads the bottomless water. Her pulse beats her temple. Her breath is a heart-attack-worthy wheeze. When was the last time she swam? Year Ten? 'What is it? An elk warns her not to look in the water, but she does, drops her heart, and is doomed?'

Almost to the island, Freya laughs. 'Pretty much. She has to stare at the pool forever, hoping her heart comes back.'

Breathing deep, Kira strikes out. God, her breaststroke is awful. She feels like a wonky frog. 'Are there elk here?'

'Mm.' Freya's tone could go both ways. Laying the bird on the pinkish stones, she hauls herself to shore.

With a calm, sedate façade, Kira follows. Swimming should really have stayed in the past. Her limbs are feeble and jittery, and barely stopping her arms from buckling, she crawls up onto the rocks. Fun.

As if mocking her, the fiddle swells, jaunty, fast, and sharp. 'That,' Freya says, wringing out her hair, 'was less orgasmic than I'd hoped.' She flips her head upside down, musses her hair, and flips it back. It makes her look different: younger or wilder. No knife or bow or snark with her man's clothes stuck to her skin. It's like she's lost her shell.

Kira looks away. 'Agreed.' She crosses her legs on the smooth, warm pebbles, squeezing her hair and clothes. From here, her fatigue isn't obvious. Her knees can shake. Her head can flutter. She'll take the stepping stones back; she can say she wants the experience, and Freya's scorn be damned.

'Ah.' Emptying her lungs, Freya stretches, fills them, and stoops to pick up the bird. 'We might as well get this over with.'

The music hits a discordant ache. A melody lacking a start or an end, it soars and slows and flies and flows, both hopeful and yearning, alive and morose. It's easy to imagine, like Callum and the Havsrå, how it steals you, breathes for you, and leaves you lost.

'You say that like it's a bad thing.' Shaking free, Kira lugs her limbs into life. She feels like a trapeze artist, miles above the circus. 'I thought he was meant to help?' Breathless, she falls into step beside Freya, clambering up from the shore to the trees. Weeds sprout between the rocks. The rocks themselves are hot. On her bare toes, they feel like summer and beach holidays to France.

'He is.' Freya looks around. Her face is tapered, like someone who listens with every pore. 'He's also meant to be cryptic. Where's the music coming from?'

Kira opens her mouth and shuts it. She would have said *straight ahead*, but no. It's left and right and behind them, through and around this deep, deep green.

'Um.' She tilts her head. The fiddle is clear but all-encompassing, melding with the rush of the waterfall until the two are one and the same. She rolls her head on her neck: jungle trees, blue sky, Freya looking miffed. The sweet fiddle rises. The fairy song to their fairy glade, it's everywhere. 'Can he work the land as well as the water?'

Freya shakes her head, then stops. 'Not as far as I'm aware?'

'Okay.' Scrunching her toes in the mulchy earth, Kira rocks into the trees. Her lack of nerves is freeing, and she'll ride it like a wave. 'Then regardless, we'll find him. The island's only small.'

It is but how it stretches. The deep, leafy canopy hangs balmy and fragrant, beautifully welcome after days of cold. Blue mushrooms sprout on trunks. Pink hibiscus bobs on a branch. Violets shy beneath their feet, pansies pale on bushes and the knee-length, swishing grass. The sinless songs of birds chirp, mingled with the water and the devastating song. It's wrong. It's right. It's skewed. It's perfect, loud and fresh and rich.

Kira breathes, tasting every scent. Rose. Butter. Garlic. Reddish and golden, a hummingbird darts, vibrating past her ear. A flashing blue kingfisher bobs from a branch. She traces its dive through the crowded woodland. Plunking into water, it surfaces, whirs and skims past the waterfall.

'Aha.' Freya's voice is soft. Kira's eyebrows mimic it. The pool the kingfisher chose is small, circled by the broad-leafed, jade-green trees that make the island so vivid. The water crashes. The fiddle soothes it, harmonious, deafening, plucking at her chest.

Bingo. Soft on the leaves, Kira stops on the bank. Perhaps, without the bird, they'd have crept on by; the glade, the grove, the oasis gives the feel of secret places, of Freya's hidden pools and girls who tend to lose their hearts.

'And now,' Freya murmurs, 'we wait.'

Barefoot, Freya walks to the edge of the pool. Kira joins her, tucking her hair behind her ears. In the humid heat, it's curling. 'Wow.'

Looking up, up, up, her lungs pinch in. The waterfall, a glittering, cold cascade, spilling from the top of the tallest tree. It's as bright as rain when the sun is out. It hits the pool in pearlescent sprays, and it roars.

Until it stops.

Kira double takes. Her right ear dims and rings, so abruptly she wonders if she might have gone deaf. The waterfall gushes and rushes, but the music and the thunder cut off. Dead.

'A more beautiful gift could not be bestowed.' A male voice floats from behind the water. 'Who are my radiant females?'

For the first time, nerves snake in. She could be looking in a funhouse mirror: she's a warped, crazed version of herself, hunting for answers from…what?

'So,' Freya murmurs, leaning in. 'He's a charmer.'

Kira doesn't laugh. 'We're Kira.' She digs her toes into the just-rained bank. 'And—'

'Freya.' Freya's nails latch onto her arm. Kira glances down. Her fingers are white.

'And Freya.' A butterfly flits across the surface of the pool. Faintly, behind the hushed falls, a human shadow stirs. Kira swallows. 'We—I, I'd like to ask you some…questions.'

God. It sounds like a police interview, and a bad one. She'd meant to sound confident, but it came out more embarrassingly than if she'd shown her nerves.

Beside her, Freya shifts. 'She means—'

'You require my knowledge.' The shadow steps into the waterfall. His fiddle hangs from one hand, his bow from another, as rough as if whittled from bark. Light brown hair rests dry upon his shoulders. His thin face is angled, his bare chest pale. His veiny, naked feet are mottled, his moss-green trousers tight to his legs. An eerie kind of beautiful, his skin almost glows.

'We brought you this.' Crouching with her hunter's grace, Freya lays the bird on the edge of the pool. 'It's not much, but I wasn't allowed to kill foxes.'

The fossegrim laughs. Goosebumps skim across Kira's skin. The sound is the tinkle of music boxes, chiming in upstairs rooms at night. He may look more or less human, but he's not.

'Compassion is a virtue,' he says, and smiles. His mouth is ripe with tiny fangs. 'A virtue I can forgive. Please bring it to me.'

He steps from the tumble of water to the pool. His grey eyes, spring-snow slush, snag Kira.

'You'—the eyes pulse, and flick to the bird—'being the one with the questions.'

Kira's stomach writhes. It backs into her spine, away from her front. No, no, no, no.

'Kira.' Freya folds her arms. Peaked between expectant and curious, her eyebrows sleekly arch.

A second passes. Two. Holding his fiddle, the fossegrim waits.

Damnit. Damnit all to Hell and back. Jerkily, Kira bends for the bird. Her blind fingers brush a cold wing, and she flinches. The writhing in her stomach curls in on itself. Faecal matter. Wafting meat. Breathing through her mouth, she tweaks a scaly leg, and lifts.

Gross. Gross, gross, gross, gross, ethically *gross*. Forcing herself to keep the bird by her side, she wades through the hot-spring water. Beneath her feet, the pebbles are cool.

'Thank you, dear,' the fossegrim says. Four eyes dance across her as she hands him the bird. 'If you would hold these.' He offers Kira the fiddle and bow.

Irritation rankles. She's not a performing monkey, and she's certainly not a—

Seizing the bird in clawed hands, the fossgrim lifts the corpse to his fangs and tears off a chunk of flesh.

Oh, God.

A noise of repulsion sounds behind them, quickly cut in two. Kira's stomach pumps, sour with acid, surging up her throat. She drags her giddy gaze away. Focus on the swallowtail butterfly, skirting the fossegrim's legs; on the yellow, perching bird, making an indistinct cheep; on anything but the loud, wet ripping.

Smack. Rip. Crunch. Kira shrivels. The crunch is the worst; it brings to mind the stalk of monsters, stepping on a battlefield's bones.

'Meagre in form, but not in body.' With a light bounce, the fossegrim crouches, washing his hands of matted feathers, blood, and a pink, glistening sliver of flesh. When he stands, his lips are an ugly ochre. 'Thank you, both. What do you want to know?' He whips his fiddle back from Kira, so fast she hardly sees it go. The bow nicks her damp side. 'Let me play, dears. In more than one sense.'

The second the bow encounters the strings, music pools from the fiddle. It draws Kira's eyes and her ears and she softens. A pool is the only way she can think of it: rippling away like moonlight or curtains of the aurora. It's no longer a lament but a melody, exhilarating and sweet; fruity, as if you could squeeze sticky juice from its core.

'You,' the fossegrim pipes, 'are untypical folk.' Over the song, his voice is a mewl. The waterfall stays silent. 'You're interested neither in life nor death. Neither in prosperity nor poverty nor how a journey pans out. You've been touched by alien things.' His limber body curls. The water parts around his shins. 'You *are* alien things.'

Kira shifts between her feet. 'We are,' she says tentatively. Freya claimed that honesty works best; he may be tricksy, but he doesn't like tricks. 'I'm an outsider, and I'm trying to find someone.'

The fossegrim's grey eyes fix upon her. A click of his teeth displays their stains. 'A someone?'

Kira stops her fidgeting fingers. 'Four someones, actually.' Her eyes stray to his swaying legs. They look ready to leap to the music, capering like a child. 'I know where one is, vaguely. I was told you—'

'Know things. See things. Find things.' The fossegrim slows the song to three-four, bowing with its swanning dance. 'I do. But it's dreamlike, dear. I think you know.' He waltzes toward her with a closed-lip smile. Kira quashes a shudder. He's shown no hint of a threat, but still. 'Tell me what they look like. Tell me who they are. Tell me something tied tight to their bones, that the strongest witch couldn't free. You've both touched magic as well, I see.'

He waltzes through the water to Freya. Her outline is rigid, watchful on the shore. 'You especially,' he calls to her, before whirling and dancing away. 'Come down, dear. The water's warm.'

Freya's eyes slide to Kira's. *Be careful,* her expression says, in her odd lips, her white eyes, obvious if you know that that's never how she looks. Slowly, Freya obeys.

'Come, come, come,' the fossegrim cries. The fiddle trills and lulls and croons, rich and Arabian, off key and sultry, conjuring camels and sand. 'Ask what you will! The window will close, the water will run, and you'll fly back from whence you've come.' Bending at the waist, he grins, teeth and blood and spray. 'You won't be seeking someones for fun.'

'No.' Kira lifts her hands and lowers them. Funhouse. Fairy. Trickster. 'One of them is my sister.'

Step by slow, sloshing step, Freya quietly reaches her side. Kira quells the urge to grab her arm. *Tell me something tied tight to their bones.*

'Romy.' Kira twists her fingers and makes herself stop. 'That's her. My sister. She's seventeen, and looks like me but taller, and…' her eyes drift up. Why is it easy to picture your family but hard to put them into words? 'And curvier.' Her lips wince as though she's doing Romy a disservice. 'She has longer hair too. Much longer.'

'They're Anneliese's daughters,' Freya supplies. If a person really could darken, outside of a literary cliché, Freya would be winning prize after prize. She's a cloud in a storm or a scar.

'Oh?' The fossegrim draws out a long, haunted note. 'Now that is useful. That cannot be dislodged.' Half-spinning on his heels, he cocks his elfin head to the side. 'You make an interesting pair, you both. One fleeing her heritage to end up more tangled, and one who began by chasing where she came from, who realises now her best hope is flight. I see these sparks inside you, pretty, pretty things.'

He sweeps back into the Arabian dance. Despite the muggy heat, Kira's body grows stiff. Something about the fossegrim is raw. He sands off the edges of the humdrum world, and she's balanced on the edge of a void, a maw. Seduction. Danger. Games.

'Romy.' Kira's words sound faintly strangled. She should step closer to Freya, to make them both feel safe, but she can't. 'Is that enough? For Romy?'

Bowing his head, the fossegrim plays. 'It is,' he says, trailing off to a hum. 'She's somewhere where the sun burns. She dreams of stars, of dancing lights. Oh!' Sharply, he bends. The water splashes fiddle and bow. 'And she is not herself.'

Swooping them up, he blackens the song to a carnal sigh.

'What?' Kira jerks through the water. 'What does that mean, she's not herself?'

Snapping out a hand, Freya grabs her wrist. 'What Kira means—'

'What I mean'—Kira shakes Freya off—'is where does the sun burn?'

Dum. Dum. Dum. Dum. Her heart is suddenly everywhere, chest, ears, neck.

'Patience, pretty thing,' the fossegrim sings. Kicking through the water, he smiles like there's a bird snared in his fangs. 'She's traveling. On horseback with three men, two beautiful, glorious men. She saw a myrling and didn't understand.' The fiddle pitches to a point. 'Who's next?'

Kira's mind is starting to spiral. Briefly, she longs for Callum's phone. She can only hope that between them, she and Freya remember enough.

'My dad.' Kira rubs her damp forehead, aligning the cogs of her brain. Spiralling, turning frantic inside. What if she runs out of time? 'He's…he's human. Fully human. The Kyo took him over with a witch called Taika. They made him kill his parents. I think he's here.'

'He is, and he's travelled with Vasi.' The fossegrim's music misses a note, discordant among the birds. Mildly surprised, he almost sounds pleased. 'He's stronger than Romy and tied to Anneliese.'

Kira swallows. They should all be tied to Anna, but at least her dad *is* here. 'Who's Vasi?'

'A leshy.' The fossegrim whirls away. Water droplets dance in his wake. 'A wizened, ancient leshy. And the others?'

Kira opens her mouth, but Freya's nails dig sharp, shocking through her skin. One glance at the woman is enough: *don't push it.*

'Callum,' she says instead. 'Callum Reeve. We travelled through Whiteland together, a year ago. I saw him walking somewhere. Somewhere windy, hot…' She shifts in the water. Her trousers float. A rough pebble grazes her foot's hard skin. What's intrinsic to people here, or at least, what counts in the fossegrim's mind? Memories? Anecdotes? Character traits?

'His mother,' Freya whispers in barely a breath.

Kira seizes on this with a fervour. 'Yes. Callum's mother is a watcher.' She flashes Freya a quick-lipped *thank you*. 'He…he loves music but is basically tone-deaf. He loves the wild but hates the cold. He really, really loves animals but has some crazy idea that admitting it is girly.'

Jay told her that; as she pauses, she remembers. Callum kept dreaming of kittens.

'Go on.' With his back to them, the fossegrim hunches, playing softly on.

Something twinges, deep, deep inside, where she always pictured the most intense emotions to hide. Kira's eyes slide down to the water. 'He said,' she tells the pool, each word like a rock, 'that he loves me.'

Unwillingly, her eyes slide up. 'Ah,' the fossegrim says in a long, throaty rasp. Turning, he grins at her. His tarnished teeth glint red. 'Not tied tight enough, my dear.'

The words are a punch. They wind her, chop her, jab her in the solar plexus. Kira's hand strays to her stomach. Of course that's not tied tight enough; why would it be? It was a response to something she blurted out, a polite response, a to-hell-with-it-we're-not-getting-out-of-this response. She knew she shouldn't have said anything, either then or now. She lifted stupidly girlish hopes and all they've done is burn.

If the waterfall could swallow her, she'd worship at its feet.

'It's not enough,' the fossegrim taunts. Faintly, the water starts running again, a rush with the sound turned down. 'Men are always the hardest. So finicky, so full of flight. But hush, little baby, don't you cry. Maybe you'll find him before you die.'

'Stop.' Freya's voice is harsh, strangled. Kira's bones grind in her fist. 'Just stop it. This isn't help. This is poking and prying, and there's no need.'

Splashing away, the fossegrim spins. Keening close to a high, frenetic crescendo, the music skips and screeches, trills and wails, screaming like the Kyo, luring like the Havsrå, a choir, nails on glass—

Dropping his hands, the fossegrim stops. The fiddle's jarring notes lose breath and hang like diamond dust. 'Okay,' he says, a man again. Teeth sheathed, mania curtained, shunted off the stage. 'Goodbye, my pretty things.'

'No!' Kira cries, as the pool starts to roil. Boiling from clarity to cyclonic rapids, it forces them back, back, back. 'I didn't—I need—'

'We're done, Kira.' Freya's voice is rough, dragging them around to stagger to the shore. 'You've got enough. Even if you haven't, he won't give you anymore.'

Kira wrenches at her. Thundering at their backs, slapping their thighs, the water spits them onto the grass. 'How can you know that?' Her voice catches, like skin and barbed wire. 'He's the only way we have of finding anything out, and we're leaving?' She tosses a raw look back at the fossegrim. He's motionless, expressionless. Around him, the water writhes. 'I got nothing about Callum and Jay. Nothing.'

'Kira.' Jerking an arm at the waterfall, Freya lifts into a shout. 'I'm not going to spell it out for you. Listen.'

Soaked, her head roaring, Kira makes herself listen. The waterfall. Freya, having to shout. Her heart sinks like a stone through a pool. When the fossegrim started to pay them attention, all the noise stopped.

'No,' she whispers, cut adrift. Her voice wilts, withers, and dies.

'Yes.' Dropping her arm, Freya walks away.

Water flicks her ankles. Hazy, sinking along with the stone, Kira glances down. The pool is creeping up the bank, spitting close to fire. A rocky lump lodges inside her. It wants her to go; it's warning her to go, yet it feels like she'll leave with less than she came. All she's gained is riddles and an aching sense of loss.

'Kira!' Freya shouts back. Distant over the waterfall, the vibrant trees are eating her, wrapping her up in flowers and ferns. 'Things to do, people to see. That, or the other way round.'

A droplet burns Kira's foot. Holding the rocky lump in place, she numbly starts to walk.

'You're being followed,' the fossegrim murmurs. His sly smile strokes her skull, curling ear to ear. Kira chills but doesn't stop. If she does, she might never get going again.

A trickster, that's what Freya called him. In the end, that's all Whiteland is. Tricksters, and those who watch you fall.

In the end, she'll be fooled by them all.

23

Bird and prey

Peder hasn't been walking long when he sees signs of life. Just long enough, in fact, to grow unnerved by his lack of memory. What does he *like*? What does he hate? Is he meant to be alone? Does he enjoy being alone? Who are his parents, his girlfriend, his boyfriend? He climbs a rocky ridge, and the cliffs break the land.

At first, they are all just dusty, jagged cliffs in an arid, windy landscape, jutting in dramatic blocks. They form canyons, ravines, passes, bluffs.

Then he sees the holes. Holes with ladders, holes without. Tiny at the barren heights, grander at the bases. The same pattern, over and over, stretching in an uneven crescent moon from the low hill on which he stands. He crested it, having tired of being hemmed in by steep valley walls, and there they were. He can't stop staring.

It's wrong. Peder scratches his hot, greasy hair, holding it out of his face. None of this is familiar; what does he do? If he walks on in, will they attack him? From here, the people in the valley are toy-sized; he could try and slip around without being seen. If he *were* seen, he's probably far enough away to be mistaken for one of them.

Is he one of them?

No. The idea feels as false as his name, as false as his clothes and the pendant at his navel. Maybe he should head down the canyon with his hands up and surrender.

Peder tugs on his hair like the roots are to blame for his amnesia. Why? Why would he do that? This is the most frustrating thing; *why* does he have images of these things? *Why* does he feel they might work?

'I'd stay still,' a woman's voice warns, pleasant and doughy and low. Fingers grab a fist of his hair. 'Who are you?'

The woman drags his head back. Liquid pain shoots through his neck, and he shouts. 'What the—'

The tip of a blade is pressed to his back. Snapping his mouth shut, he stiffens. 'I said'—the woman tightens her fist—'stay still. Who are you?'

Peder's hands lift, palms out. His empty mind must really believe in it. 'I'm not a threat,' he says slowly. 'You can put the knife down. I don't have anything with me.'

'That doesn't mean you're not a threat.' The blade presses through his shirt. The tip pricks his skin, and he flinches, his head fills with a sudden hot rush. Whoever he is, he'd wager he's never been held up like this. 'And it's not a knife.'

'That's not reassuring.'

The knife tip twists.

'Okay!' Blood dribbles down to his waistband, and he holds his hands higher. 'Sorry. I can't tell you more because I don't *know* any more.' He wets his dehydrated lips. 'If you're going to stick your non-knife in me, can I at least turn around?'

The fingernails scrape his scalp. 'Careful.' The woman yanks his head down. His neck spasms, and he hisses through his teeth.

'I just want to—ah.' The blade digs in deeper, heady and stinging. 'See who I'm defending myself to.'

A pause. Wind brushes the dry ground, sending gravel skimming. With it drifts the sound of hooves, shouting, metal on metal.

'Fine.' The death-grip fingers tear from his hair, latch onto his arm, and spin him. 'That's all you get.'

The blade depresses the shirt at his belly. As long as his forearm, it's envy-sharp, lashed to a whipping piece of wood, and thick as iron. A spear.

'Okay.' Peder lifts his free hand. The woman is almost as tall as he is. Her hair is hacked short, her eyes the grey of snow clouds. Her stance snaps; she'd sooner kill him than tow him off alive. 'Completely understandable.'

He flicks his gaze right, left, around the scrubby hill. She's alone, but with a spear probing his gut; that's no comfort.

Abruptly, his senses click into place. Brown trousers, brown boots that mean more than business, a loose brown vest tucked in at the waist; he's seen it all before. 'You're dressed like me.'

The woman's eye sockets seem to shrink as though trusting him less by the second. Her eyes are so alive that he keeps coming back to them, slate-grey and sharper than the teeth around their necks. 'You sound surprised.'

Peder shifts on his toes. Before he's fully thought, or even tried to retreat, the spear whips up to prick his ribs.

'Jesus Christ!' He sucks in his stomach. 'I wasn't—I won't—okay, fine.' Slowly, he relaxes, smoothing whatever hideous thing his face has twisted into. Not a threat. Not a threat. 'Yes, I'm surprised. I have no fucking clue what's going on, and the first person I see wants to kill me.'

The woman's mouth pinches, thins, and settles. If she's a hovering goshawk, he's the rodent in the field. 'You're dressed like a snake, you're out in the open, and I don't recognise you. Forgive me for being prudent.' Her eyes snare the tooth of his pendant. 'Are you trying to tell me I'm wrong?'

Peder's mind skitters over her words and sticks. 'You're going to have to explain all that,' he says, more of a whip than the wind. He should be prudent too, but it's ludicrous. None of this makes enough sense for his brain to do anything more than boil, thrashing, scalded, and screaming in pain. 'Except, you know, not recognising me. That I can understand. But being dressed like a snake and out—'

'Shut up.' Too sharp for him to react, the woman retracts the spear, hauls him around, crushes his shoulder beneath her fingers, and jerks him into a march.

'Hey!' Peder yelps. Pricking the exact place it stung him before, the spear digs into his back. He winces. 'What are you doing? I told you, I'm not a threat.'

'There are seven skies of things about you that could be seen as threats.' The woman prods him onto a trickle of a path. Little more than loose dirt and fragments of rock, it cuts through the overgrown, ugly land. An edgy wire slices through him. The winding path rocks down, down, down. Down to civilisation.

Pinching his shoulder so tight it almost cramps, the woman manhandles him, past a parched, bleached tree in a tired riverbed. 'Like what?' he asks, scuffing the stones. God, his legs are tired. 'Do tell.'

Roughly, she steers him to the edge of a ridge. 'Voice. Clothes. Actions. Words.'

She pauses. For a hot, giddy moment, he thinks she'll throw him off the ridge; why get dirty when the rocks will shatter him? 'Is that all?' he asks, as she peers round his arm. Up close, she's acrid ash and dirt, the damp kind made for worms.

'No.' Reverting fast to her previous stance, she prods him into life. Over the ridge to a tinier path, teetering on a stony spine of land not meant for men. 'But I won't go on.' Down, down, down she urges him, out of the grassy wastes. The gully's so steep he feels like a mountain goat, dancing with death. 'Regardless, I can't leave you out here. Watch your feet!'

She wrenches him back from the edge of the path. Stones skate away from his boots, bouncing off the rocks and cracking like skulls in the gully's bony gut. The wire in his chest vibrates to a hum.

'I don't know this path,' he snaps, but his belly is hollow and sick. The path is skeletal, their bodies too large. One extra breath of the gusting wind could buffet them into the air. 'What do you expect me to do?'

'Watch where you're going and not be an idiot.' The path thins to a line. Skirting the drop, it's the thinnest trail of stones, clinging to the cliff for its life. 'Failing at both makes you more of a problem. You're not one of us.' Moving behind him fully, the woman tweaks the spear. He winces. 'You've no idea how to be.'

Around a tuning fork of a bend, he slaps the cliff for balance. Rock shards skitter. A bird of prey shrieks. The wind eddies around his boots, and the humming wire thrums.

'I told you.' Peder speaks through his teeth. 'I knew nothing. I still know nothing.'

Jon Snow.

'What?'

'Stop talking.' The spear jabs. Shot with a madcap longing to laugh, Peder shuts his mouth to hold it. This is ridiculous; fucking ridiculous.

He feels like he's thought that before.

24

A crucifix

Whoever he used to be, Leon thinks, he must have, must have, must have loathed being the centre of attention.

Nikoli was right: Gretel is a gossip to quell all gossips, and news of him had spread before the morning was awake. Now, days later, he's a dancing animal, or a prisoner on parade.

People gawk and then look away. People gawk, while pretending not to. Some people just gawk. Nikoli has no desire to pen him in and avoid it—in fact, he seems proud of his dancing pet—and so everyone has seen him, everyone knows, and everyone has an opinion as to how and why he's here.

'You'd think they have no lives,' Leon had said to Thom when the first day of people knocking on the door finally came to an end.

Pouring cups of a feeble, fruity spirit, the corners of Thom's mouth tugged down. 'Even in Al-Sanit,' Thom said, 'people don't pop up in the harbour. Everyone's going to think *whoa*.'

Leon wished they wouldn't. He wished they wouldn't so hard it hurt.

'The Yunavida range.' The old, arthritic woman stretches out her legs, veiny and mottled blue. Her wicker chair creaks.

'No.' Her daughter does the same. 'No, no. He wouldn't be alive.'

'Maybe it changed him.'

Massaging cream into the mother's fingers, Nikoli shakes his head. It says *ah, women*. It says *ah, gossip*. Sat on the splintering porch, Leon bristles. Why can't Nikoli tell them to stop?

'Skarrig.' The daughter nods at her mother, as sage as if she knows for sure. 'You get all kinds in Skarrig. They'll have messed with him and sent the evidence downriver.'

Charming. Two rotund weaver's lights sat in the shade, the women ponder and sweat. It smells. 'Most people think that,' Leon says. Clipping his impatience tight behind his words, he imagines clipping their flesh. Cleanly, not viciously. They're just too round.

'You really don't know?' The mother's voice is a horn, honking straight out of her stomach. 'That must drive you batty.'

Irritably, Leon shifts on the planks, watching Nikoli's hands. He's here to learn, to assist, and to make himself useful; to see if he can be the non-Gretel-loving second student. He's not here to be studied, like Nikoli's alchemical friends' specimens, festering in a pot.

'I don't remember anything,' Leon says, for what feels like the thousandth time. It might genuinely be the hundredth. 'I woke up in the Zaino and started from there.'

Except that's no longer true, not all of it. Silently, Leon hands Nikoli a cloth. It had begun with an image when he woke one morning, something he's neither seen, heard, nor plucked from other minds. Three figures with their backs to him, facing another with the weirdest of faces and a body as bulky as the women on the porch. It was dark, it was snowy. It was starry and cold. When he saw it, prone on a pallet in Nikoli's house with Thom asleep and snoring, he filled with a terror that could conquer panic with the toe of a baby's foot.

An image of a crucifix followed it, suspended bodies, a girl's cheeky kiss, and then gone. The next image was more of a scene: he was out with Nikoli again, visiting a patient again, alongside one of the alchemical friends. The patient was mourning his son, killed by a wraith in the Tomi desert—*he thought he'd be safe*, the man insisted, *as long as he mined on the edge*—and his mind was so heavily tangled, a low, mournful wail that punched holes in Leon's gut, that a devil swam up from the deep.

I used this when my daughter left. The alchemical friend had produced a coloured glass flask, stinking of the waste pits up in the hills. Leon was struck with a piercing flash of a girl with braids, wearing dungarees and slamming through a door, before his chest pinched with pain.

A man, leaving, slamming through a door. A woman with a scrunched-up face sinking into an armchair. A boy barely older than Leon is now, standing in the centre of a wood-walled room. He himself, crying by a dark cloud of dog, curled up on the rug. The older boy looked between the woman and the door, clenching his fists by his sides. Pain. Pain everywhere, in all of them. The same pain as the mourning man, as the friend with the wayward girl.

That was yesterday. Last night, he realised that he'd seen the girl before and not since he woke up in the Zaino.

'Leon?'

Leon blinks. He'd been staring through the old woman's swollen feet, and now the three of them are staring at him.

Nikoli plants a scolding expression on top of his normal humour. 'The lovely ladies were speaking to you.' He slips in a wink, so quick it could have been a twitch. 'And it's rude to stare.'

The wink would have been unnecessary; Nikoli's mind is rolling its eyes, *All he gets is stares. I'm surprised he's this polite*, and despite a flush of embarrassment, Leon has to fight down a smile. He hasn't yet dared to reveal his talent or his unfurling, incongruous past.

Not that there's much to unfurl. An eighth of a leaf at a time, perhaps, instead of a whole plant. The problem is that what he has is so *different*. Nudging nerves toward fear, it's foreign; none of it is from here.

'Sorry.' Adopting his most childlike voice, as Nikoli advised, he lowers an abashed face. 'I was memorising what Nikoli showed me. I didn't mean to stare.'

The lie works like a balm. The questions resume, questions he's learned to answer with his mind in the sky, and he lets it float freely up. The daughter's husband has joined the Stokers. A rebel group, they're angling for the land to go to humans, yet she's told everyone he's on a trip to "find himself." The mother is wondering if Nikoli has a woman; the answer is *yes, for every day of the week*. Outside the boxy property, a tidy girl passes, thinking of a woman just arrived from Bacaire, who told her of a strange man appearing from nowhere, the day before the—

Without a thought for privacy, Leon plunges in. She's walking on, will soon be gone, but a man appearing from nowhere? His heart balloons, bursting its banks. He never expected to be this hopeful, and he burrows deep, like a miner, a mole.

Ørenna. The tidy girl is a curious one, still musing about the man: dressed like one of the snakes from Bacaire, he had appeared above the vales, claiming not to know who he is. He's also claimed that his name isn't real, and the elders have locked him up.

The girl pictures rocky cells, high up in the air. Vultures picking bones clean and he himself, Leon. A generic, blurry man, and a boy, she thinks, as other rumours luridly swirl: bands of Moroaica, whispers of the huldra, torrid trouble under the earth that no one wants to—

'Leon.' This time, Nikoli's rebuke is sincere. 'You're clearly not listening, and you're clearly not studying. What's wrong with you?'

Leon's mind judders back. Back into his own thoughts, back into his body, on the porch, in the bug-riddled heat. Horse dung. Salt fish. The creaking chairs, singing, hammering, sweat. It feels like a slapping awakening, from a night-long fever sleep.

'What?' Leon blinks and blinks again. He shouldn't have drilled in that far; for several moments—minutes?—he became the girl. He knew her curiosity, her longing to travel. 'Sorry. I'm not...' an eye-blink, and he sees himself through Nikoli's eyes. Sickness-bright scleras, cheeks red and sheened. 'Feeling well. At all.'

The daughter tuts. 'Poor thing.'

'Poor *thing*.' Leaning forward, the old woman feels his forehead. Her tacky fingers smell of spices and cream. 'He's clammy.' She turns to Nikoli. 'The swelling sickness is doing the rounds. Is there something for that in your bag?'

But Nikoli is watching him, close and shrewd. 'Maybe,' he says. His voice is vague. His thoughts are sifting, shifting, sceptical.

Beyond the house, a woman screams.

Leon's sick head swoons. Oh, no. Oh, *no*.

'Nikoli!' The woman's yell splices the air. His name slides into a shriek. 'Nikoli, are you—*please*!' she screams. 'I saw you. It's Lykke and her head, and—*Nikoli!*'

The animal squeal tears the air apart. Bag in hand, Nikoli stands, barrelling toward the sound. The women follow in a sticky flurry, but freezing like a fever, Leon stays where he is. Freezing, frozen, and shattered. For a moment, he was the girl, Lykke. For a moment, Lykke was him.

Dread seeps sour through his frosty cracks. He can't have caused this, whatever this is. He was looking, listening. He had done it before. He can't have caused this. He can't.

The woman's screams become fevered sobs. 'Nikoli, she's—'

The sour taste turns into acid, scouring his throat. Leon's stomach *whumps*. Hot, blurred, and heavy, he slumps toward the steps, retches so his stomach clamps, and vomits. In the woman's thoughts, he captured a bloody, splitting forehead and a body skewed in the dust.

'Nikoli,' she screams. 'She's dead.'

25

As clear as day

Erik is tending the fire when his wife, Iris, jolts bolt upright.

'Oh, no.' She sounds alarmed and thick, as though she spoke before her throat was ready. With a soft gasp, Irene slips from Iris's knee to the furs on the floor. 'Oh, no. No, no.'

As smoothly as he can manage, Erik straightens. After his trek to find Kira, everything hurts; the cold crept into every crack of his being, scooping out his bones to make its brittle, frigid home. He wouldn't admit it to anyone else, but the journey was far too much.

'What's wrong?' He pushes from his weary lips, helping Irene to her feet. She could be Kira's younger sister.

Iris says nothing, staring through the wall with a face like disaster. 'Iris?' The muscles in Erik's forehead tug. 'Are you all right?'

Iris lifts a hand in a flutter. 'I am,' she whispers. The hand flutters back down. 'But something else…'

Erik's forehead struggles into a frown. 'Something else, what?'

Iris pivots her head toward the doorway. Through the grave curtain, the white day spills. 'Something else is not all right. I…' Her eyes widen so much it must pain her. 'Erik, there's a huldra.'

She lunges for the curtain so abruptly that no one has time to react. Her hip smashes the table. Her foot snags his loom, sending it toppling onto the furs, but she stumbles from the cave without a sound.

'Mamma?' Irene starts for the doorway.

Pressing her fingers, Erik holds her back. 'Stay here.'

The order is grim, and righting the loom, he starts to follow his wife.

'Why?' Irene asks. Her voice is plaintive. 'Is Mamma okay?'

Outside, Iris's voice pitches. It feels ominously akin to a scene he's lived, not once, or even twice, but several times. A sensation visits Iris, sometimes when she's lucid, like today, telling stories, and sometimes when she sleeps, or flits far away. When it visits, she has no choice but to follow; sometimes she's right, but often, she sees innocence as demons.

'Fine,' Erik replies, and steps out into the clearing. 'Just stay inside. Please. If your sister appears, persuade her too.'

In the village, the pale sky spits snow. His wife's arms are bare, and Erik's heart both loves and bleeds. *Oh, Iris.* After all his recent experiences, he both prays she's wrong, so he can rest, recover, regather his strength, and fears in a shadowed part of himself that this time, she's not. He can long for coincidence, but Whiteland is havoc.

'Can't you feel it?' Iris cries. Frantic in the centre of the clearing, she's trying to break a knot of people, tightly tied by the fire. 'It's rolling off her! Flying off her!' She grasps at forearms, shoulders, sleeves, fighting toward the middle. 'Why are you protecting her?'

'Erik, she's not huldra.' His grizzled brother, Wilem, has his back to the flames. One eye fixes on Erik, the other on whoever is locked in the knot. 'Please get Iris back inside. The girl wants food, nothing more.'

'She may not want more'—Iris heaves on Petra's boy's arm, feverish, scrabbling—'but she is. She *is* more.'

Stepping into the fire's aura, Erik takes her arms. 'Iris.'

'No!' Iris recoils, bumping into clustered bodies. 'Let me go!'

She battles his hands, but he urges her away. In the gaps between the villagers stands a girl, exhausted, gaunt, and cadaverous. Her face is dully void.

'She's one of the river people,' Erik murmurs, bending to Iris's ear. A familiar cloak cradles the girl, her braids in a familiar scarf. Wilem is right; whyever it is that she's traveling alone, there's not a chance she's huldra.

'She's more.' Iris shakes her head, so rough her teeth rattle. She's coughing and wheezing, blotchy, purple.

'She's not, Iris.' Tiredly, Erik steers her toward the cave. 'Look at her. That's all you need do. She's no more a huldra than you or our girls.'

Wrenching against him, Iris spits. 'She'll kill us!' Her voice grates up to a shriek, and she writhes. 'She'll kill us. Not just the men, but everyone. She'll tear everything apart and nothing is safe and you're *protecting* her, you're—'

With a sound like the bellow of a lynx in the night, Iris crumples, sags, and goes limp.

Time seems to warp, to slow. Iris's head lolls and snaps at her chest. Erik staggers. By the fire, the village stares. He gains a dizzy, distant quality.

And then his mind returns. 'Iris?' He wraps her in his arms before she slumps to the snow. Creaking to his knees, he holds her to his chest. 'Iris? Are you all right?'

'What happened?' The people are moving, living, breathing, untying themselves and hurrying close. Erik's ear starts to ring. He didn't see who spoke, who continues to speak; the people are breathing, but Iris is not.

'Iris?' He lowers his head to hers, but her eyes are open, bare. Dead.

Time crawls slower. His vision sparkles, too bright, unreal. '*Iris!*'

The shout doesn't sound like his. The clearing, Haavö, the world thins to nothing but noise. Every heartbeat thuds in his head. Iris. Empty. Dead. Her mouth slack, her lips wet, coated with the spit of her shrieking. She was screaming about the girl, and then…

As slow as dreams, Erik looks up. The flames of the fire lick the girl with light, and for a second, she meets his eyes. She is steady, cut sharp in his burgeoning horror, and in a breath, he knows Iris was right.

Is right. Was right. Everything warps and blurs but the girl. She's not huldra; not huldra, no, but dangerous, wicked, a thing of death and fire and the icy burn of magic, circling around her like the cloak that keeps her warm.

As slow as dreams, Erik blinks.

As clear as day, the girl by the fire is gone.

26

All he tried to teach

Vasi didn't reappear, and since then, Mathew has been alone. He was truly alone until Grey loped up, and he feels as though he still could be. Is a wild wolf company?

Grey turns amber eyes on Mathew, full of their typical reproach.

'Sorry.' Mathew shakes his head. Apparently, wild wolves count as company, but faced with the first hint of humanity he's seen since entering Whiteland, it feels as if they don't. He's been walking, worrying, sleeping rough, with a knife and a sentient torch, so to see a real camp, albeit abandoned…

Grey dips his muzzle to the trickling creek. Squatting, Mathew does the same. It's abominably hot here, dusty and blustery, so dry he's been chasing the shade. Up until recently, there was more than enough; cast by trees as tall as sycamores but with leaves like rounded ferns, there were glades with pools and patches of land where, for miles, the grasses, flowers, and bamboo stalks reached to the top of his head.

Since this morning, though, the wild has changed. It's barer. Rockier. Not quite desert, not quite Devon, and now, he's tackling a new type of territory, not dissimilar to the foothills of Spain. In any other world—in *the* world, Mathew's world—he'd think that's where he was.

But this is not the world, not his. His world does not have pools where lights skate and dance at night, like leviathan fireflies. His world does not have the plants he's been testing, gingerly daring to eat, or the coyote-ish animals hunted by Grey. His world does not have wood that turns violet when it burns.

Mathew's world does not have leshy, either, but that's already so long in the past. So long since this madcap experience began; so long since his solid, beachfront life was simple and complete.

'Come on,' Mathew sighs, before these thoughts smother him again. He looks to Grey. 'I assume we're heading for the signs of people.'

Grey's answer is a lift of his muzzle from the brook and a course set through the camp. Cinders by the slope of a low, rocky dell, the lingering scent of cooked meat. Singed branches, a spot cleared of pebbles where the pale grass is flattened. A smaller pile of ashes at the mouth of a cave, close to the nook where he spent last night, full of Vasi's warning not to venture in too far. Grey trots past it all and on to a curve in the valley where the land slopes up.

Mathew follows. He's surprised at how he's adapted to taking instruction from a wolf.

Gradually, the signs of people intensify. Animal tracks appear in the dust, mostly horses but sometimes smaller, enticing Grey to smell them to his wild heart's content. More abandoned makeshift shelters, littered with wrappings, tiny bones, scraps of unfinished food. At every new sighting, Mathew raises his guard. He's come to trust Grey far more than he had expected, and the wolf noses on with no apparent unease, but he has to remember: wolves are only beasts. He's being led to God-knows-where by an animal, and he has to stay alert.

Claws clicking, Grey scrabbles up almost vertically, through a gritty outcrop of boulders. Mathew clambers after him, panging bittersweet, in the way reserved for fathers. If Grey helped Kira, did she travel like this? Did she remember all he had tried to teach her, despite never being the outdoors type? Did Romy?

Jesus Christ on a hundred bikes. As Mathew straightens up, at the top of the outcrop, his thoughts scatter on the wind. Never mind signs of life; he's found the life itself.

It *is* Spain, or it looks like it. Mathew shades his eyes. Yellowed, drastic, rising and falling, like the cliff dwellings that charmed his sister when she took her kids to the States. Colorado? No. Texas? Maybe. Mathew drops his hand. A trail through the rocks slips down to the settlement. Meagre knots of grass sprout tufty, all the way to the towering caves. They look like slots for prehistoric graves.

Sedona. As Grey trots down, his nose to the ground, the trip to the States becomes clear. Montezuma Castle, near Sedona. Of course. For weeks, Nat raved about the rust-coloured, sandy ruins nestled in the rocks.

'Stop.' As Mathew sets one foot on the trail, a man melts out of the boulders. His greying hair scrapes his jaw, a fang hung around his neck. In his hands are a pair of knives. 'Who are you?'

Mathew's on-guard, preprepared tale clicks in. 'An outsider,' he says, without hesitation, even as the whole of his body grows taut. Vasi told him never to lie. 'I'm looking for my daughters. They're tangled up in something.' Without moving his eyes, he shifts his focus to Grey. The wolf's ears prick, but no more. 'I don't pretend to understand it. I'm here by accident, and I want to take them home.' This seemed the most harmless, innocuous story; the best way to present himself as not a foreign threat. It also sounds dreadfully naïve.

'An outsider.' The man tilts his knife blades up. His tone is flat, without inflection. Too flat, like a stretch of razed ground. 'That's not possible.'

Thank you, Vasi, for relaying to him the basics of Whiteland life. At the time, he felt childish, but the leshy had reason.

'It is possible.' Steadily, Mathew raises his hands. Better safe than dead. 'It's just rare. Look at me.' He makes a point of taking in each aspect of his clothes. Snow boots with dirty, tatty jeans, the awful brown jacket tied around his waist. A plaid shirt, something his father would wear. 'None of this exists here. According to Vasi, I'm a sign screaming stranger.' He takes the sleeves of his coat to untie them. 'I can show you some of—'

'You've encountered Vasi?' The man's voice is still as clipped as wings, but Mathew is almost sure that intrigue whisked across his lined, grey face. 'You're an outsider who has met Vasi and is travelling with'—his pale eyes land upon Grey and flicker—'one of Vasi's wolves.'

Grey ducks his snout and yips.

'I'm Dale Gonzàl, of Jurnado.' With a swift glint in the drained yellow sun, the man sheathes one of the knives in his belt, steps forward, and proffers a hand.

'Mathew.' Mathew offers his own hand, more than half-expecting a greeting Vasi didn't impart, but Dale only shakes it. 'Mathew McFadden. You know Vasi, then?'

'We all know of Vasi.' Turning to the rocky dip slashed through the land, Dale motions with one quick finger: *follow.* 'I personally have not met him, so it's something for him to have helped you. Snakes are the most likely to meet anything that comes from outside the vales. Maybe two I know have seen him, one from Jurnado and one from Bacaire.'

That is a lot of information. Mathew struggles for the words that seem to mean the most. To be fair, he must be confusing, too, and continues to be by existing. 'The snakes?'

Dale jerks a nod. 'Patrols. Of a kind. Rarely seen until they strike. Tell me'—he inclines his head to Grey, who has snuffled out in front—'what made you come this way? You could have walked to Ørenna and back and seen nobody, yet you're here. How long since you left Vasi?'

Mathew squints through the sunlight. 'Several days,' he says. 'Mostly of walking. Is that unusual?'

Dale's scarred fingers stray to the knife at his belt and tighten on the one in his hand. 'That depends on where you parted.'

Of course it does. Mathew quells the urge to feel like an imbecile. Now is not the time. 'A forest. He called it something like—'

'The Everland.'

Mathew's mouth stays open. 'Not—no.'

Dale's pale grey eyes stay fixed ahead, as if making out something in the distance. 'Everla.'

After a moment, Mathew nods. 'Maybe. Yes.' He toes aside a tiny skull, like nothing he's ever seen. The sparse ground is flattening. Too close for comfort, the cliff dwellings hulk. From the way Dale sticks to the beeline trail, this must be Jurnad.

The word trips in Mathew's mind. Not Jurnad; Jurnado. Beyond it, more hilly colonies unfurl, ridged, higgledy-piggledy areas linked by gullies and gorges and bridges. One wide road seems to lead straight through.

'Then I think,' Dale says, 'it's unusual.' His voice is careful. He doesn't look at Mathew. 'It means you are not a coincidence.'

He's working up to something. Mathew's seen it a hundred, a thousand times, when motorbike dealers are figuring out if he'll cheat them till the cows come home. It's a tone of voice. It's a dozen micro-expressions, glimmering into one.

'It's not coincidence.' Mathew skirts a dry patch of scrub, rustling as though something's slithering through. 'Vasi sent Grey with me to find "disturbances."' He indicates the nosing wolf. 'Christ, I don't know how he's doing it, but he's leading me to wherever something out of the ordinary's happened.' As though any of this is ordinary. 'It'll supposedly find my daughters.'

With another brusque jerk, Dale nods. Hot quiet flutters, barring the grating crunch of shoes on rock, Grey's wet panting, and the human sounds of Jurnado. Instructions. Creaking cart wheels. The weighty *thud* of crates on rock. The road through the cliffs, where it widens from the trail, is packed.

'He's found a disturbance.' Dale's voice is clipped again, but it's different. The ends of his words snap off too soon. 'But it's not your daughters or girls of any kind.' He pauses. It's that kind of hesitation where the words loop in your head. 'A snake from Bacaire found a man.'

This sounds underwhelming but seems to carry weight. Mathew tries to match Dale: flat, without inflection. 'I take it that it shouldn't have.'

'Not someone like that.' Dale shakes his head, as brisk as his nod. The ground flattens again. Jurnado floats closer. Mathew tries not to think about what that means. 'Those who travel far say they've heard nothing like him. He has no memories. The elders of Bacaire have shut him away in one of the higher cells. I don't think they've thought that he might be an outsider.'

'And based on me...'

'I think he could be.' Levelly, Dale meets his eyes. They're as razed as his voice, as carefully *nothing*. Unease stirs in Mathew. Whatever Dale's feeling, he's fighting it down. 'Do you have any leaning as to who he might be? I find it hard to believe you're not connected.'

Mathew's base instinct is to laugh. *The outside is huge*, he could scoff; *I've no idea*.

And yet, suddenly, he does. A man without his memory, suddenly appearing. He, Mathew, without his memory, for the last year of his life. The way all of this began. 'Is he young?'

Dale jerks his nod, and the thought unfolds. All of this began in a small Swiss village, with a night-time wander, Romy freezing, and a young man who brought her back from the woods.

'Then, yes,' Mathew says. The certainty surprises him: it's not a jigsaw but a melted image, with a swirl that's starting to clear. He tastes it, swallows it, and lets it digest as they cross the last bare, sweeping stretch toward Jurnado. Clamour, beasts, a working village. Working people, working lives. 'I know very well who he is.'

27

Burn.

'It's enough.'

They're walking again, always walking, although cleaner and warmer than they were in Atikur. Freya still has the edgy instinct to hide, and, barring the clothes, they both look like huldra. As diverse as Al-Sanit is, white skin, blue eyes, and pale hair is rare.

Freya's response to *do you know how we find the river people?* had been so simple, coupled with a shrug, that Kira felt she should have been able to work it out for herself. *Follow the river.*

Follow the river, follow the spiders, follow the branches that brush the ground. Once in a while, a sign would be nice or at least a wooden window with a vanishing motif.

'Explain it to me, then,' Kira said, idly nudging a pine cone from the bank to the water.

'A tributary,' Freya answered; she seemed not quite ready to travel the road by the main branch of the Zaino.

Kira had warmed to Freya after that. Well; not warmed. Thawed is better. Until then, an angry undercurrent still raged, but now, it's slowed to a stream.

Even more reason why their floundering is bad. They've had two days. Two days of brooding, tramping through the country, and the fossegrim's code is still uncracked. With the tributary opening like a serpent's mouth, their brooding has to end.

'We should have worked it out by now,' Kira insists, eyeing the clear, lazy blue like it bites. 'I know that's mostly my fault, but we're kind of short on time.'

'Kira.' Freya lifts her hair high and holds it. Her chest and face are heat-pink. The hair at the nape of her neck is dark, ringleted with sweat. 'I know this. We've both said this before. You may have been floating around in fairyland, but I've been thinking about it.' She lets her hair fall.

Kira fans her own neck. If Al-Sanit has hair ties, she'll trade both feet, all the food they've gathered, and her heart for one.

'Sorry,' Kira says and actually means it. 'I'm just…'

Freya stops. 'I know.' Crouching by the water, she splashes her face. 'The fossegrim said two things about Romy.'

Kira skims her toes through the glassy water. Here, it's beautifully, beautifully cool. 'The sun burns.'

'One.'

'And Romy's not herself.'

'Two.'

'*Ugh*.' Twisting with frustration, Kira kicks out. Rainbow droplets spray the air. '"Romy's not herself." None of us are ourselves here. Saying that could mean anything.'

'It could.' Rolling up the cuffs of her trousers, Freya sighs, and carries on. The day may be dripping into evening, but they're barefoot and on the unhappy side of warm.

Kira flaps her shirt, luring a breeze or even a gasp of air. The trees on both riverbanks give shade, but dipping into forest, after Atikur…

No. No, with bells on. No, with a whole damn marching band. Their days of river walking have been a retreat, a green, wooded serenity, the campsite in Provence she found boring as a child but would love to be bored by now. Burbling water, birdsong, the rich summer dryness that comes from nearing the equator.

Kira holds back a maudlin sigh, the one that Freya hates. 'So we're stuck.'

'No, my dear, we are not.' Rummaging in her satchel, Freya produces the waterskin. 'The sun burning is specific; it's either the Tomi desert or the grasslands. If she's with three men on horseback, it won't be the Tomi because there are never three idiots alive at once who'd choose to go travelling there. Also, they'd all be dead by now.'

Kira takes the waterskin. 'Thanks.' She drinks and wipes her tingling mouth. 'Pardon a stupid question, but what's in the Tomi?'

Freya links her middle finger and thumb. 'The To-*me*.' She enunciates. 'Not that it matters. Remember all the demons that chased you?'

Handing the waterskin back, Kira nods. Every muscle in her face wants to warp at her memory. 'It's not something you forget.'

Slowly, Freya opens her arms. 'Imagine the biggest, barest, uninhabited space you possibly can. Fill it with the demons from Monte Yuno, then fill the sky above it with lowly, punished spirits.'

She looks at Kira like she's waiting for *wow*, but a cool fizz spears Kira's chest. 'Like my mother.'

Freya pulls down her chin. 'Ah.' Apparently, that's the worlds-wide code for *oops*. 'I was mocking the Whispers, not the spirits.'

Kira looks at her. 'Okay,' she says and shoves it away. She can't think of Anna. Not now.

Freya's eyes linger. 'Okay.' It sounds like a word she's not sure about. 'Anyway, you see why I don't think Romy's likely to be in the desert. The grasslands, you know'—she swirls her hands—'Monte Yuno, the Yunavida range, that monster of dancing and joy, are the only other place where the visible, physical sun actually burns.'

Hope inches onto a ledge, daring to be brave. 'I remember.' Kira rubs her cheek. The grasslands gave her sunburn. 'I guess there won't be too many girls who popped straight out of the air.'

'Nope.' Freya ducks beneath a sprightly tree branch, stretching for the water. 'That's reserved for McFaddens.'

A smile starts in Kira but stops behind her lips. 'So we go there,' she says, 'and then figure out Dad. He was travelling with a…'

'A leshy.' Freya sounds impressed. 'A forest guardian. They form from a wronged tree, or something. We have one, but I've never seen him. Vasi's from the north.' She snorts. 'My, your dad will have a story and a half.'

Kira's eyes track a dragonfly, gold and iridescent. 'So he'll be easy to find?'

'I wouldn't say that.' Now, Freya sounds rueful, as though the thing that impressed her has sadly let her down. 'There's a lot to shift the world up there. But at least we know he's *up* there, as opposed to down here.'

Kira is quiet for a moment, two. The water runs in little splashes, plopping gently when a bird, a stone, a beetle plinks in. The air is smelling like evening now, that slight grainy pressure when the day winds down, when the scents of the land grow soft and swell. The clear, curving river colours, changing with the sky. The waifish blue is smeared with rose, with violet, with gold.

'And that's all we have.' Kira watches the ripples. 'On the outside, that's like saying we're in Chile, but hey, we know our long-lost loved ones are somewhere between Greenland and Iran.'

Crouching beside a shrub on the treeline, Freya doesn't look up. 'That means nothing to me, but I understand the concept. Where on the outside did I come out?'

'Switzerland.' Kira squats beside an adjacent tangle. Buttery berries sprout in swarms, and she opens her satchel. 'Somewhere between Greenland and Iran. You then went to the Netherlands, where you enjoyed a spate of murders, before returning to round us all up.'

'And what excellent sheep you were.' Freya catches her baiting eye. Weirdly, the ritual is comforting. 'Going back to that being all we have, you're wrong. Taika's not as clever as she thinks she is.'

With the bushes picked clean, they carry on. 'Taika died.'

'Yes'—Freya points a finger at Kira—'but I'm using her name as a placeholder for whoever reopened the door. I really hope it wasn't her because she'll be extraordinarily pissed off.'

Kira huffs. 'Then we'd have a pain for each of our arses.'

'Yes!' Clapping her hands, staccato, Freya laughs. 'That's the attitude you need in here. This is the worst, but let's glare at it and seize it by its malformed snout.' She mimes a vicious snatch-and-twist. 'Whoever reopened the door isn't our problem right now. We don't know who they are, where they are, or what they want and why, but we *do* know how to read what they've done.'

Kira dips into her satchel, then drops a berry in her mouth. They've rapidly become her favourite, close to basil and sour like lime, and she reaches for another. Understanding flickers on in Kira's mind. 'The others have been scattered.' Dropping the berry back in place, she slowly straightens up. Her mouth doesn't want to close. 'Jay with the river people; Romy in the grasslands. And "Taika," if we're using that name, must know I'm in the forest.'

'Precisely.' Freya beckons for a berry. Rolling her eyes, Kira closes the bag. 'And they've all been placed near people, so again, ta-ta to the Tomi.' She executes a one-handed flourish. 'The meadowlands are too close. Taika didn't place your father, but she led him back to Whiteland in the north. Meaning…'

'East or west.' Kira sparks with tiny pride. 'Wherever the desert isn't.'

'Precisely.' Freya flourishes again, ending with her fingers curling toward Kira, like a flower opening. 'And west gives us Skarrig or the valleys. There are mountains to the east, but as far as I'm aware, they're where happiness goes to die.'

Kira laughs. It's a proper laugh, one she feels, and the sound makes her grin. 'Isn't that just every other place around here?'

Freya pivots, walking backward. 'Yes, but those mountains are worse. They're empty, unclimbable, and largely undesirable.' She glances back, avoiding a log. 'Once we've got Romy, I'd go to Skarrig. It tends to stay put, which is helpful when the world likes to move around.'

Kira's whole forehead lifts. 'The world? I thought that was just the north.'

Freya spreads her hands. 'What can I say? It's a fickle, fickle land.'

Well, we know that, Kira almost says, when a man steps out of the trees.

Instantly, the words fall off her tongue. On the opposite bank, in the dusk-dark green, he stands, and he's naked.

Naked?

'What?' Cocking her head like a dog, Freya trails Kira's gaze. 'What is it?'

Beside the man, a woman steps out. Kira's lips part. Together, the couple are beautiful. Not just lovely, but spectacular, astonishing, their bronzed skin strong as they weave into a dance. The woman's hair swishes the tops of her thighs. The man's curls over his collarbone, and as another man appears, two women, two more, he fires Kira a wicked grin that turns her into snowmelt.

'What?' Freya repeats, impatient now, but Kira hardly hears her.

The man wants Kira, only her. Blooming up from nowhere, hot below her belly, it goes beyond desire; it's red and gold, animal, carnal, an intensity that draws her from the grass to the water. She has to reach him; she has to feel him flush against her, feel his smile on her neck, kissing, biting down. Hers.

The others dance, but he waits. He wants Kira, only her, and the knowledge is scorching, overwhelming as it sets her alight. His hands will take her, and they will be wild.

'Kira!' Someone shouts, intrusive and cruel. 'Kira, stop! They're Ellevolket!'

Behind her, water churns. The man holds his hand out, commanding and sly. She's almost crossed the river now; oh, she's almost there. She's a fire, an inferno. She wants to burn, needs to burn, needs to feel his fingers, trailing down her skin before they grip.

'Kira!'

Two hands shove her shoulders, and Kira crashes down.

Face first, she smacks into the river. Kira's bare belly slaps the surface, and she plummets underneath, water bubbling up her nose and surging down her throat. She can't breathe. She can't see. She's quenched. The dancers? The man? She's no longer burning, she needs to—

Her self returns with a slam.

'Run!'

Choking, Kira splashes back up. Freya is shouting, pleading, crazed, slapping Kira's hair from her face.

'*Run!*' Spinning her, Freya kicks her away. 'I'll go back for your bag. Get your clothes and run.' She jolts Kira roughly. 'Move!'

Blurry, Kira glances back. The dancers twine together like vines. The man, her man, is watching her. Any trace of a smile is gone.

Fear crashes through her chest. He's dark. He's a storm. He's a fire that sticks to your skin and blisters, and he turned her into a moth.

Kira's throat clogs up. The fear is a tsunami. Her head flashes hot, and she runs.

28

In spiderwebs

It's been a day for staring through walls. Truth be told, it has for many days now, but this evening, Carol wakes up.

A simple question does it: 'What do we have for tea?'

Julia, crawling up onto the couch, in the sparkly, holey leggings that Carol hasn't made her change. Julia, who'd plaited her own hair and left half of it tucked behind her ear. Julia, with chocolate stains around her mouth and anxious, urgent eyes. 'The clock says 8:37.'

8:37. Hungry twins and a restless dog, pacing the house and whining.

'Can you sign my agenda?' Julia rests her blonde head on Carol's shoulder. It's small and warm and snug. 'And Karl's? Monsieur Oberson put notes in them today. He said…'

Julia screws up her face. The scrunching crumples Carol's cardigan, like a fist in a soft glove puppet. Carol's lips are too dry, too rubbery to speak.

'He said'—Julia springs back up—'start as you continue. Something like that. He wasn't happy, though.' She sighs in a startlingly adult way and reaches for the remote. 'Not at all.'

The TV lights up. Julia clicks off the news without a word. She's probably as sick of it as Carol is, even if she doesn't really know what's going on. They're looking for the girls and looking for Callum, but Kira and Romy took everything with them. Carol has honestly said, several times by now, that she hasn't seen Callum in far too long, and she's worried. It's not like him; he's not much for keeping in touch, but he keeps in touch with her.

All this is true, and they'll see it in her face, in sacks beneath her eyes and the cracks of her mouth, every time they knock on the door. This isn't a manhunt, or a womanhunt, but it's so perplexing, magnetizing attention, that the police have spilled over it like ants.

Julia settles on a film. Something animated and bouncy and bright, about an inflatable white robot, and it's some time before Carol tunes back in and realises what it is. *Big Hero 6:* she's seen it dozens of times.

'What do you want to eat?' Carol asks, but the words are only air. Her face feels heavy. Her mouth is an anvil. Clearing her pinched throat, she tries again. 'What do you want for tea?'

Wriggling, Julia looks round and blinks. 'Anything.'

On top of the question being asked in the first place, this slides Carol back into her mind. She's a boat through the straits, imperfect but passing, and she forces herself to focus. Everyone needs feeding. Everyone needs her.

Everyone, including her sons.

'Potato gratin?' she asks. Julia's eyes brighten into streetlamps, and Carol fixes on this, on the excitement of a seven-year-old at the thought of her tea, to winch her body from the couch. She'd sunk into it, and the free air is weightless, casting her adrift in the sea.

'Potato gratin,' Carol repeats, barely moving her lips. The walk to the kitchen is foggy. 'If you—' speak louder. She lifts her musty, croaky voice, and dusts it off. 'If you bring me your agendas, I'll sign them now. And Karl.' She rubs her eyes, bleary, weary, twitching. 'Ask Karl to come here. You can both grate as much cheese as you like.'

The twins take the cheese to the television. Carol pictures shaking her head in amusement but doesn't quite get there. Let them; let them do whatever they like, for now. At the moment, they're all she has, but as soon as they're in bed, she'll kickstart anything that means that might stop being true.

Carol should have started the night she saw Freya. From the back, she'd thought the huldra was Romy; they're more or less the same height, the same build, the same hair. She felt so hopeful that her lungs all but stopped, until Freya spun around and said her sons were still in Urnäsch.

Kira got out; of course she did. Somehow, the girl who looks for monsters is never the one who gets hurt.

The door shut on the others. I think Kira. A flustered beat, and then, *Oh, I need to* go.

The huldra spun around again. She had looked so concerned, so sincerely frantic, that it was hard to think she was a killer. Something had gone wrong, and she was worried about it, haphazard as she shouted for Kira. And that was all Carol knew.

She had gone back inside, sat down on the sofa, and stared through the walls until dawn. She pretty much stared through the walls until now.

She's wasted so much time. Slicing onions and potatoes in the chalet's crowded kitchen, recycling and toys and pans run amok; an emotion strikes a match and flares: anger. Anger at the Kyo. Anger at the Chlause. Anger at Kira. Anger at herself for taking this long, with her sons still gone, to set her sights on the surface, fight off the seaweed, and kick her way up from the depths.

But she has, and she will. Once Karl and Julia are fed, in bed, and happy, she'll contact the Whispers.

It's almost twelve by the time she's alone. The twins will be hellions to get up for school, but as they lie all curled up on the couch in blankets, with old *Chucklevision* and cake in mugs, for the first time since Jay and Callum vanished, Carol feels close to being a mum.

She *feels*. That's the vital sign here: she feels something beyond a fug, beyond the sense that she'd skidded back in time, to the Glenfiddich days after Callum's dad left. She feels. Everyone needs her to feel.

Everyone needs her to act.

Quietly, Carol shuts her bedroom door and pauses. No whining dog; no sneaky whispers, snaking through the wall. Nothing. Carefully treading the floorboards, she lowers herself to her creaking bed. An in-breath; an out-breath. Linking her cold hands on her skirt, she lets her senses unseal.

Now, breathing evenly, she waits. A murmur should start where her head meets her spine. An inward expression of physical lips, it should whisper into her hair. It should rise like an ocean heard through a seashell, until the air sighs in a sifting breeze and the Whispers ripple through the exit.

The cuckoo clock chimes midnight. Clear-cut through the diamond in the shutters, the moon travels the sky. The dark wood chalet creaks and settles. Carol doesn't move. All she hears is a barking fox, and all she feels is her stiffening limbs and an unknown, unanticipated, comfortless void.

The analogy that fills her is a staircase. Carol expected to climb a complete set of stairs but finds one eroded away and trips. Her head and stomach swoon. Vertigo churns up gravity, and then, bemused, she sinks back to reality.

Usually, the Whispers approach her first, when they deign to approach her at all. She rarely contacts them; she rarely needs to, but whenever she has, they've slipped through. She's never been met with this nothing.

Perhaps she's not focused enough. Carol shifts, rolls her shoulders, and crosses her legs. God knows she's not been herself for days. She may not be reaching out correctly, so she's faced with a drape as opposed to a veil.

Sharpening every sense, she breathes. In, hold; out, hold. The wizened clock ticking tired time. The smell of the cedarwood candle, valiantly masking onions and cheese. The mirror, showing her puckered forehead and the upper left quarter of her unwashed hair. The cross-stitch mandala on the wall beside it, and her mother's indigo and swamp-green bedspread, bristly beneath her hands. The almond of the biberli cookies she shared with Karl, not quite freshened by toothpaste.

Slowly letting her eyelids droop, Carol loosens her body, reaches out, and sees her mind as an ocean.

The fox barks. Another answers. Cat claws scratch at the bedroom door, and Carol recrosses her legs. Her bare feet are chilled; she forgot to chop wood. Riding a shiver, she pushes out, out, out.

Out, out, out. Her mind is a muscle, stretched on the rack, close to the point of pain. Her limp hair sticks to her temples, mostly with grease but mingled with sweat. She's almost too alert, too—

The rush roars in like wind down a tunnel. *We are not your amusements to summon.*

On the bed, Carol sways. Her eyes fly open. The air is a throb, not a pulse. They're livid.

Yes.

The framed mandala bangs on the wall. Her dressing gown tumbles from its hook. On the shelf, her copper Artemus topples, crushing the flowerless orchid.

'I'm sorry.' Carol strains to keep her voice as even as her breath. With the shock of their entrance, that's not saying much. 'I needed to know what is happening. Other than fifteen words from the huldra, I've no idea what went wrong.'

The Whisper slices round her neck, an icy noose that chills. *Kira was pulled from Urnäsch*, it hisses. *Rosemarie and your sons were not. As far as we're aware, that's where they remain.*

Two fat fists clench Carol's lungs. 'How do we get them out?'

We don't. The Whisper scrapes down her side. Normally, it's fingertips; now, it's the tip of a nail.

Carol flinches before she can stop herself. 'What?' She forces her body to still. 'What do you mean we don't?'

Taika is dead, the Whisper says, *and she took one of us with her.*

Our concerns lie now with Whiteland. Another voice joins it, spiky on her cheek. *Its equanimity has been destroyed.*

The fat fists squeeze. Blood could spurt between their fingers, so hard is it to breathe. 'They can't stay with the Chlause.' The room is growing distant, grey. 'You said you'd get them out.'

We said we would try while we stopped the witch. The Whispers rake through her lank hair, yanking like a snaggletoothed comb. *And we did. We sent Freya to pull them out, and she did. Only Kira was quick enough.*

Bitterness spills like bile.

She's not to blame for your difficulties, Carol. A new voice nips between her toes, parting the bedspread's tassels. *Much as she's not to blame for ours.*

Unbelievable.

'Oh, that's right.' Roughly, Carol laughs. The sound barks crude in the moonlit room. 'For her, you're merciful. Why?' Her bile-filled voice pitches. 'Why hold her up above anyone else? The Kyo wanted revenge on her. That's why the last two weeks have happened. Last year, sure, blame Anneliese, but now?' She juts her neck out. Her hands jerk up, then back to the bed. 'I can blame her for my "difficulties," and you can blame her for yours. She went crusading and screwed us all.'

We blame only the Kyo, the new voice says, snaking sharply around her ankle. *Why would you understand?*

She would not.

You would not. The Whispers swell, and sigh. *You're not ingrained in the balance here. The Kyo will latch on like leeches to anything, or anyone, that may dredge them from under the ground. In the end, they inevitably lose.*

You're naïve, a low voice splinters off, *to blame one girl for it all.* This hiss is gentler, a breath in her ear, like a man well-versed in seduction. *If you're looking for someone to blame for Callum, blame Callum himself, not Kira. He was the one stupid enough to follow her into the dark.*

At this, Carol crumbles. She could take up the gauntlet, tinge herself with hysteria, but all her inner defences are gone. Hollowed. Scooped out and left to bleed. *He was the one stupid enough to follow her into the dark.*

'So it's hopeless,' she says. 'He and Jay are lost.'

The cuckoo clock ticks. Carol waits.

And waits. Around her, the room is quiet, empty. The stillness skulks through her, and coldly, she knows: the Whispers have left her alone. None of their ceremonial pomp, nothing that closes their words. Gone.

Just like Callum, and just like Jay.

Carefully, Carol doesn't move. She's fragile, suspended in a spider's web, caught in the air between billowing grief and curtain-dropping numbness. Shock. A thick, cut-throat dome lowers, blocking the outside world. What makes it worse is that her sons are alive.

They're not dead and never will be. They'll be stripped of themselves and forged in the fire. They'll be worse than shells, worse than cadavers, worse than ghosts. They'll be Chlause.

29

The darkness crows

She hadn't meant to kill the woman. At the time she decided to do it, she knew what she was doing, but she'd entered the village with nothing but truth. She'd barely eaten in days.

Inching into Haavö, so dizzy and light, had been a shameful last resort. Taika was starving. She was weak. She was more than sure that if she left it any longer, she'd fall asleep in the snow-bound cave and probably never wake up. She was doing what she had to and eating her pride.

But that woman, that damn woman. Somehow, the woman sensed her. She knew there was something awry in her village, something not fully human. Squalling and bawling her way to the fire, where Taika had been shivering, that woman—that damn woman—came perilously close to shouting it out.

Taika could have spelled her unconscious. The thought did occur, before she went too far, but it would only have caused a delay. Once the woman woke up and continued to shout, there'd have been a witch hunt.

And no one needs that.

Memory snatching. Taika could have caught the woman's mind and snared a few thoughts, but later on, it would have looked suspicious. As it stands, she's no more than a traveller. A young, flighty traveller, all the way from Hintab, who bought her food and fled when a woman had a fit. No one should suspect her. No one should think to, barring the husband who looked Taika in the eye. At the end of the day, though, who would believe him? He's grieving. She killed his wife.

Cloaked by lesser magic, Taika stops walking. She killed his wife. *She killed his wife.* The darkness that stoked her starts to subside, like blood draining away.

When did she start to toy with death? When did she start to throw it around? When did she start to think like this—so cunning, so callous, so cold?

When Taika started succumbing to witchcraft. When she was, if not exiled, strongly no longer welcome in Al-Sanit. When she chose to help the Kyo.

Taika shivers, although her magic is warm. When she chose to continue helping the Kyo, succumbing to more than witchcraft. Witchcraft made her both desired and undesirable; what shapes her is rage and revenge.

Cradling her bulky bundle, Taika holds it close. This is what happens when she thinks too much; Freya always warned her not to. Taika is a boat caught by rapids, or a woman lured by the alder tree men. Often, they're blind to disaster and powerless to stop as they tear to the end.

Touching a blueish, cloud-like mushroom, Taika shifts the heavy parcel's weight. At least she's got food. It should be enough to tide her over until she learns how to gather it herself. What's safe. What's not. Where's good. Where's not. She should have asked the huldra to teach her to hunt, but she never thought ahead that far. She couldn't face it. She never thought about leaving or of her job being done or of a time when she might want to stay a secret, untold even to them. She thought she grew up learning enough, but the forest is not like home.

And all the creatures run.

'Help me.'

The plea jolts through Taika's bones. Tripping, she lurches to stay upright, slapping a tree for balance. Her shoulder jars against the trunk. The bundle jabs her ribs. How? Warily, she looks around, trying not to seem wild. How—who—what—*how?* No one should be able to see her.

'Help.'

The withered plea comes again. Movement catches Taika's eye: curled at the base of a tree is a figure, rigid, frozen, blue. As Taika watches, it blurs, shudders, and flits translucent and back. A ghost.

Taika doesn't relax. As surely as creatures fear her, forest spirits flock like sheep, hoping for help, or release. To begin with, she listened. The more she listens, though, the more spirits appear, and the more she fears they'll expose her.

Taika's darkness snakes in cold, and she lets it. 'I can't.'

The figure flickers and moans.

'No.' Redistributing the weight in her arms, Taika holds herself higher, smooths her face, and sets off through the snow. 'Talk amongst yourselves. I've stopped listening to ghosts.'

The frozen figure is suddenly standing. Short black hair, frosted eyelashes, bruised skin, and cracking lips. The elongated, emaciated bones of the woman it was.

'I said that to get your attention,' it says. Its voice is undoubtedly human and curt, but the spirit itself is crooked. Crooked and distorting, contorting as she watches, the bones of its arms too thin. 'You're Taika.' Its neck pinches in. Its thigh pokes out in a way no human leg should. 'The witch.'

Taika slides coolness over her shock and ensures her face stays still. This woman is a spirit; she's bark without bite. Whatever she knows, from the look of her, she's the type who will only be seen by those already connected to death. From the look of her, she's an outsider, so she won't know that, regardless. She won't know who to look for if she wants an ear to bend. She poses no hint of a threat.

'Do you care?' Taika fixes her eyes on the woman's blackness.

The woman stares right back. 'I do. Anyone with sense would. And by responding, you've confirmed what I thought.' She spreads her arms, jolting, frayed. 'Goodbye, Taika.'

She fades.

'No.' Grasping her lingering death, Taika wrenches her back to the forest. The woman explodes with a black-white sharpness. Apparently, she does know what she is. 'You shouldn't have spoken. Your ploy was going to work.' Taika watches the warping woman settle back to her dysmorphic form. 'Did you love having the last word when you lived as well?'

The woman's broken mouth opens. One eye socket is caving in, but still, her face widens like she's made a grave mistake, and knows. 'You're not a k—'

'Too late.' Striking at her mind, Taika rips it to shreds. 'Goodbye, Lena.'

The darkness crows.

30

The name of skies

'What?' Freya cocks her head. Kira's face is suddenly emptier than a moroaica's head. Turning, she tracks the magpie-shiny, Nova-Vanca gaze. 'What is it?'

Nothing. The trees along the water are as bushy as ever. The pines gave way a while ago, to something as tall but wider, brighter. Freya sighs, a short huff. Kira's a girl to be distracted by anything, so it could be that, anything. A baby skunk, a pretty bee, a leaf. Whatever she sees herself bringing into art.

'Kira?' Scanning the trees, Freya gestures vaguely. 'What is it? Speak, please. Now.'

A noise rotates her back to Kira. For a second, Freya stares, in a dim, baffled blankness. Kira's eyes have hooded, and she's taking off her clothes.

The coat around her waist has gone. The satchel's gone. The trousers are on their way.

'Kira?' Freya's frown cuts tangible grooves in her face. What in the name of skies is she *doing*? 'I know it's hot, but it's nearly twilight. We kind of need to go.'

Kicking the trousers away from her, Kira's lips part. Freya frowns, deeper, until it strains. She knows that look. She's *felt* that look. It's a look of lust, where your face grows heavy, and all you do is burn. You're sexy. You're alight. You want to be ravaged or, in her case, ravage away.

It's not a look she'd ever associate with Kira. It triggers something, warm and raw, and for the first time in Freya's life, she fights it. Something's not right.

Lifting her shirt, Kira slips into the water. In a bloody rush, Freya knows.

No. Whipping around, she fills with a groan, a moan not of passion but of horror. How did she miss them? Entwined in their erotic dance, the ellepiger and the ellemaend, sensual in the sultry dusk. They lure from the shade of the alders—

Alder. That's what followed the pines, and by Ørenna, she should have known.

'Kira!' Throwing off her satchel, Freya lunges for the river. 'Kira, stop! They're Ellevolket!'

But of course Kira's captivated, on her way to being lost. Freya flounders toward her, slowed by the current, frantic and cursing and lucky, goddamn. If they'd both seen the dancers, then they'd both be entranced. They'd be danced into an ecstatic death, worn through and blistered by ferocious, hectic lust.

If she's not careful, they still could be. Freya keeps her head bowed as she splashes up to Kira, shirtless now and close to the man. His hand is outstretched. The other folk dance. Freya can't look at them or him, and his smile, destructively licking at the corners of her eyes. He's waiting. She's craving.

They can all go to Hell.

'Kira.' Seizing Kira's shoulders, Freya stops. Her head hurts. Her heart hammers. What a sign of her humanity; in the middle of a river, faced with the Ellevolket, she's pausing. 'You'll thank me later.'

With all her upper body, Freya shoves. Kira hits the water with a belly-flop plunk and sinks.

Unstable in the current, Freya rights herself, but a sharp thought burns like a spark: how does she break the fixation? Like the girl who lost her heart to the pool, can she do something wrong? Can she doom Kira to stare forever, pining for a spirit who'll never be hers?

Too late. Thrusting her arms into the river, Freya grasps for hair, breasts, whatever. She doesn't exactly have time to think.

As her fingers bash limbs, Kira thrashes back up. Freya grabs her arms, and holds her fast, peering at her face. No more magpie-shiny, Nova-Vanca, ravage-me-to-death. She's coughing. She's blinking, and rubbing her eyes, as pink as an afternoon nap.

'Run!' Exploding with relief, Freya shakes her. Kira teeters, her sopping hair plastered to her cheeks. Freya slaps it out of the way. They both need to run; with Kira's trance broken, the ellemaend is angry, stroking the edge of her mind. He seethes. He smoulders. He wants her, needs her, a gorgeous, furious love.

Freya's every movement slows. Why would she move Kira's hair? Why would she shake her back to her senses? Freya could add her own body to the dance. She could feel the seductive sway of her hips, skin-to-skin with his. She could feel the women behind her, caressing—

Tearing herself from the brink of desire, Freya cruelly pinches her hand. '*Run!*' Spinning Kira around, Freya kicks her shin. 'I'll go back for your bag. Get your clothes and run.'

Lunging for the bank, Freya dares a glance back. Jerking like a punch, Kira whips her head around and mercifully starts to move.

That'll do.

By the time she plunges back into Atikur, Kira is close behind. The forest is cold. Right now, it's a blessing. Freya's breath comes short. Her knife is out. Her bow dangles, clacking on her quiver. The satchels bump her sodden hips. Her trousers rub her thighs. Wet feet slap the earth behind her, slick on fallen leaves. Freya runs.

She runs until the river curves back into view. She runs until the pulsing of her body subsides, and then she rounds on Kira.

'When am I allowed to stop saving you?' Throwing down her burdens, Freya throws up her arms. Fury is filling the void lust left, and she fields it with both hands. 'If I hadn't come with you, you'd have died by now, enough to be a campfire song. "The Ballad of Kira the Witless."'

Kira's whole body trembles as she wrestles with her shirt. She shouldn't have taken it off and left it to float in the river.

'If you…' Kira's teeth chatter, and she stops.

'If, what?' Freya viciously folds her arms. 'Do go on. I'm riveted.'

※

Awkwardly, Kira starts on her trousers. 'If you don't want to save me'—she bites back a shiver—'try warning me instead.'

The shiver ripples through her regardless, so potent she almost falls. The forest is arctic, Kira's covered in goosebumps, and most of her is soaked.

'What?' Freya's laugh is loose, like an unhinged door.

Kira tries not to jitter too hard. Oh, God. Oh, God, oh, God, oh, God. 'I'm just saying'—tying her trousers, she stares at the ground—'maybe it would have been wise to, you know, mention the dancing sirens.' Shakily, she picks up her coat. 'All your tales of night-time terrors, and you leave out the ones that appear in the day?'

For a moment, Freya says nothing. 'You—' bending sharply, she swipes for her satchel. The tied boots collide with her thigh, and wild, she marches away. 'Did your mother never teach you,' she calls back roughly, 'not to gawk at naked men?'

Kira stares. Her head is reeling, her heart too slow, far too viscous a throb.

'No.' Gathering Freya's discarded weapons, Kira scoops up her bag and jogs through the trees. 'Shock, horror, she didn't! Believe it or not, but on the outside, men don't usually hang around naked. If they do, they don't have magical, come-hither summoning eyes. More often than not, they've got a bottle of vodka and a dodgy criminal record.'

'Ha, ha.'

Kira stamps up next to Freya. Thorns and twigs and roots rip everything they can and replace her shaking with anger. 'Go ahead,' she says. 'Mock, but you still should have warned me. What the hell kind of people were those?'

Freya's face could cut iron. 'Alder tree people. I'm sure you can guess what they do.'

'Yeah, now.'

'Well, good!'

On the forest's edge, Freya wheels around and batters Kira with a hug.

'Oof.' Kira's chin rebounds off Freya's shoulder. Crushing her once, Freya lets her go, with such a jolt that she staggers. 'What was that?'

'Mm.' Untying her boots, Freya rams them on and steps from the trees onto a path. 'Nothing.'

Staring again, Kira follows again. 'Nothing?' She gestures emptily, working her mouth like a fish. 'For the love of—when we find Callum, you'll be friends for life. I mean it.'

Beckoning for her quiver and bow, Freya points to the red on her cheek. 'Only if I get an apology for this.'

'If he gets an apology for murder.'

Freya smirks in a way that avoids her eyes. 'Attempted murder, please.'

'No.'

Freya huffs. Her face is smoothing, but her eyes stay crinkled, her gaze still a tad too far away. 'I suppose,' she says, 'we can both say sorry. It's probably only fair.'

Kira leaves it there, and in silence, they walk. It's a shaken silence, a too-calm silence, a silence more suited to a foreshadow than the madness of the aftermath. The fading day's heat wraps them up in its haze, bug-filled and muggy by the river. The stint in the trees lets the evening deepen. It's different from Nova Vanca and the sunset in the grasslands. Here, there's no sun, only colour, a painting, and one she'd love to paint. It's a wicked riot, a graphic fire, purpling the sky.

At the same time, it's peaceful. As the birds turn sleepy, and the water babbles, slowly, Kira settles. She's okay. She's alive. On a scale that spans demonic mountains, witnessing murder, and fleeing the Chlause, it ranks fairly low. If she had to, she'd put it somewhere around Romy's hospital attack.

Hugging her torso, Kira tries to shrink. She lost her inhibitions, stripped largely naked, and was giving herself to a man. Not only that, but he *wasn't* a man; when she glanced around, she saw him. His back was rotten through.

She lost her mind again. Freya saved her again.

'Thank you,' Kira says quietly. Avoiding seeing Freya's face, she looks across the water, widening and watercolour-vibrant. 'By now, you've earned your own campfire song. "The Huldra That Started to Care."'

She offers Freya a truce-forging smile. Freya offers her one that seems to accept, in a taunting, Freya-like way.

'Hmm.' Sliding on a theatrical mask, Freya taps her chin, and shrugs. 'I prefer "The Ballad of Kira the Witless." It's got a better ring.'

'True.' Kira huffs at her upcoming words. 'But it should be "The Ballad of Kira Scared Shitless." That's—'

She stops. Around a fish-hook bend in the water, both banks of trees halt. The river spreads into a waterfall, and in the centre...

Kira's lungs forget to breathe. Little more than droplets and light, a form shimmers over the water, and for a heartbeat, a skittish second, she'd swear on her life it's Lena.

There, then sparkling, glittering, gone. The waterfall sprays the dusk. Its thunder is soft, not the fossegrim's roar, and it sprinkles the image away. Shards of glass. Droplets and light.

Kira's face flickers with a tiny frown. She met Lena twice, three times, maybe; either she saw nothing, and the alder man's messing left an afterglow, or she saw something, and it wasn't what she thought. Who she thought.

Because she wouldn't see Lena. Why would she have seen Lena? Freya must not have seen Lena. If Freya had seen anything, everyone would have known. She shouts and shoves people underwater.

God. Kira's going mad. Rubbing her eyes for good measure, Kira quells her mind's delirious bounce, aligns her toes with the last of the bank, and peeps over the falls.

Maybe ten metres high, the water cascades, steaming into a cloudy pool that burbles into the river. Kira squints. Even in the sunset, it gleams a bright blue. It drags her back to standing in the forest with Callum, when it begged her to marvel, to stare. It holds Havsrå and the bishop-fish and memories.

Kira holds her breath and looks away. Although its pull is weaker than she remembers, the river still tugs, boring a hole into her chest. She rubs her snow-blind eyes again. Enough mind games for today, thank *you*.

'Freya,' Kira says, retreating from the edge. Across the pool runs a low wooden bridge, and on both sides, a dusty road. Inside her, something leaps. They're getting somewhere. 'Are you ready for the river road?'

'Pff.' Stepping up beside her, Freya sighs. 'I'll have to be. Remind me what we are?'

Kira starts to say *you know that,* then stops. Freya's fingers worry the bottom of her bow. Her eyes have glossed over with a glassy, staring distance, and her boots curl into the earth.

'Travelling sisters from Skarrig.' Lowering herself to the grassy mud, Kira slips from her rear to the topmost boulder. The rocks are damp but craggy and immense. 'I'll also remind you of the reasoning.'

Back on the bank, Freya huffs. 'Thanks.'

'People aren't likely to ask many questions if we say that's where we live.' Gingerly, Kira scrapes her way down to the next spray-wet rock. 'And I still believe we can pass for sisters. In some warped way, we are.'

'Mm-hmm.'

'We're looking for a boy who vanished from a hamlet.' Placing a hand on the cooling boulder, Kira wobbles across to the next. These boots grip like beasts. 'Why do we think he might be here?'

Behind her, Freya's bow clatters. Skin skims wet stone, followed by a curse that's probably colourful if Kira could tell what it meant.

'Don't know.' Freya's mutter is grazed with pain. 'I'm not sure we got that far, did we, before divine intervention butted in.'

'By that, you mean the magnanimous fish.' Kira's mind fills with the bright, bright memory. The fish Freya caught was of monstrous proportions, and after Kira had cooked it, they spent the night too full to even think of anything else.

'Okay.' Arms out, Kira takes the last level boulders and neatly joins the road. 'Then we've been journeying around, looking for this boy, and started hearing rumours. We volunteered to be the ones to find him because, quite frankly, we were bored.'

'Understandable.' Hesitant but nimble, Freya joins her in the dust.

Kira thinks of Ingrid. 'Yes. That should be enough, right? All the objections I had before you were answering with "Skarrig."'

What about the men's clothes?

Skarrig.

The auras we seem to give off?

Skarrig.

Why did the boy disappear in the first place?

I think you can figure that out on your own.

'Much like my love of this road, it'll have to be.' Freya nods at the sky and sets off. 'We shouldn't be around here after dark. We shouldn't be anywhere after dark, but at least inside, there'll be wards.' Freya walks a little faster.

Kira does the same. Her boots squelch, gathering sand. The air smells of hyacinths. The sky is violet. Up in the hills, snug around boulders, windows gleam with light. Wards.

Getting inside suddenly seems like all she'll ever need. Kira's boots scuff as she starts to stride. If they all go home—*when* they all go home—she'll live the simplest life she can. Getting a degree doesn't matter; it's futile. Fruitless. Give her a hut by the sea, a pug, and a demand for eerie paintings.

And Callum?

Not tied tight enough, my dear.

The words slither back to her, but she chops off their tails and dares, just *dares* their salamander brains to grow more. The fossegrim was smarmy and downright unpleasant, a madman, a trickster.

Oh, God. In the hot, deep dusk, Kira fills with snow. Her eyes grow wide and stick. She'd forgotten; how had she forgotten? The fossegrim said they were being followed.

And Freya doesn't know.

31

The things he knows

'Call me a paranoid miser'—Nikoli slams into the house, slams the door, and slams his weather-worn bag onto the table—'but I have a very distasteful niggle that you know what happened out there.'

Hours have passed. Hours since the screaming, hours since the blood and *Nikoli, she's dead.* Nikoli had stalked back out of the alley with a face like a tale meant to terrify kids, took a long look at Leon and ordered him home.

Ever since then, Leon's been sat here, on the old-man's three-legged chair. Around him, the sky grew steadily deeper. Outside, the furore grew louder, then quieter, then thinned to an eerie nothing-at-all. He's been sat, as wooden and stiff as the chair. His heart has not stopped drumming with the pace of a marching band. He's dead.

Leon has blocked out everyone's thoughts until now, but Nikoli's are roiling. They're the choppy purple waters of a nightmare, a fever. Dimly, Leon pushes them away. He killed a girl.

No, he might have killed a girl. Either way, he's never diving that deep again.

Either way. It sounds so heartless, but he can't think about it. He can't let himself. The hours of shellshock would become days, if that's not a foregone conclusion, and he'd never dislodge the sickly sheen, clammy on his skin like mist.

'Leon, I am *talking to you.*' Grasping Leon's shoulder, Nikoli yanks him to his feet. Leon's shoulder pops, and he flinches, startled. 'By the skies, this is enough. I took you in. I've vouched for you. I've stopped the elders banishing you and the mages from poking your brain. Granted, it hasn't been long, but the mood here is worse than the last Stoker raid and doing any of this is a risk.'

He looks at Leon like something's expected. Leon looks back, but blankly, muted. His thoughts won't translate into words, and his mouth couldn't move if he tried.

'Boy.' Nikoli lowers his pockmarked face to Leon's. His breath smells of bergamot, Nikoli's favourite leaf to chew. 'Tell me what happened,' he orders, his hands on Leon's shoulders. 'Anything. Anything you know. And if it isn't the truth, I'll rip the worlds open myself and leave you in Urnäsch.'

Crushing Leon's bones, Nikoli shakes him, hard. Leon's neck fires. His head snaps back. With it snaps his drifting stupor, and Nikoli's raging thoughts smack down.

No words. Not now. Just warped, blurry scenes, masks and flames, curtains of light that sweep the sky. A bug-eyed girl lying prone in the street, a wailing woman who looks just like her. Leon himself, waxy and ill—

With a roar of wind, of billowing fire, Leon's own mind explodes. The alchemist's wayward daughter, beneath a rippling, colourful sky. Again, staggering up a road, bawling at them to run. A bulky figure with a red-black face. Another dressed in flames, who smiled while he writhed, trapped within his skin. A raven-haired woman screaming *Chlause,* and all the horrors she—

Abruptly, Nikoli thrusts him backward. With a cry, Leon stumbles. His leg snags the chair, and it crashes down with him, the sharp corner flipping to jab him in the gut.

'Talk to me!' Nikoli roars. Spit flies from his mouth, and wrenching Leon up again, he slams him into the workbench. Runic stones tip off and smash. 'My friend's daughter is dead, and just before it happened, you looked like you'd seen a demon. I come back and you're puking like you've seen fifty demons, staring at me as if I'll have you spliced. What happened?' One calloused, swarthy hand encircles Leon's neck. It pushes and strangles, Leon cries out. 'If this is witchcraft…'

As madly as he can, Leon shakes his head. 'It's not,' he splutters. His throat is bulging. He's breathless, choking. 'I'm not a witch.'

'Damn straight.' Nikoli's fury could smoulder with heat. 'But you could be a warlock. That would explain why you were thrown away. Do you really not know who you are?'

'No!'

Nikoli jerks his neck. 'Don't *lie.*'

'I'm not!' Leon whines. His vision is red. Gasping, heaving, he battles to breathe. The bench digs into his pelvis. 'I don't know who I am, but I know I'm not a warlock.' Does he? 'All I remember—'

Oh, no.

'All you remember?' Nikoli hooks onto the words like a spear hooking a fish. Leon's stomach plummets through the earth. 'All you remember is what?'

Leon flounders.

'*Leon.*' Nikoli shoves him away, with the bellow of a taunted bull. Staggering, Leon flings out his arms. 'All you remember is *what?*'

'The Chlause!' Toppling onto a chair, Leon sits. 'I remember the…the…'

Poised like a boxer, Nikoli stills. His face flickers. 'The what?'

Leon swallows. His throat feels scraped and bruised and he shakes. 'The Chlause. In Urnäsch.'

Nikoli's ruddy cheeks go slack. His body sags as if it owes gravity a favour. His mind turns to ringing, and suddenly, Leon knows that everything he said was wrong. Inextricably, inexplicably wrong.

'You can't remember the Chlause.' Nikoli's voice is curdled butter. He steps toward Leon, slow on the floorboards, bloodshot eyes fixed hard on his face. 'It's not possible, and if you do…'

Shattered stones *skriiiik* beneath his heavy-heeled boots. Nikoli stops and looks down.

Leon scours his brain as fast as he can. The healer stands between him and the door. Where's Thom? In the kitchen?

'I think'—Nikoli kicks the shards aside—'you've had us on.'

Another step. With his heart whooping in his red-hot throat, Leon stays rooted. Thom can't be in the kitchen; he's bad at stealth and worse at staying quiet.

Go.

Electric-fast, Leon leaps up. Chucking the chair into Nikoli's path, he scarpers through the drape.

'Leon!'

The roar rattles Leon's ribs. His body flinching, Leon blunders through the kitchen, his panic soaring up to the sky. Sacks of grain trip him. He flails for balance, knocking pear compote crashing from the side.

'*Leon!*'

Whipping round, Leon kicks the sacks. They spill across the floor, and he spins again, slapping a hand to the splintering wall. It might slow Nikoli, just enough.

Just enough for what?

Run.

Hopping through the offerings of ripe fruit and bone, Leon barrels through the kitchen door. The evening alley is dark and deserted, barring a candle held by brackets on the walls. The alchemical flames flare midnight blue, but Leon pelts away toward the Zaino. He's beyond outstaying his welcome; if he lingers any longer, there'll be pitchforks.

Veering left, darting right, wriggling through a tiny space thinner than his shoulders. Nikoli's shouts ring out from the house. Hitting the road by the river, Leon runs.

Eyes stare from open taverns. Leon flies past them, gasping, gulping, hauling air up his throbbing throat. A stitch stabs his side, where the chair jabbed a bruise. More shouts clang off alley walls. Music lifts and fades like sirens. No plan, but he drives his legs toward the harbour. *Get away.* He has to get away.

…Nikoli's boy…

…there when Lykke died…

No one knows…

…running from?

People's thoughts are fragments as he hurtles along, his feet *whapping* far too loud. A mangy dog darts away from him, yelping. Find a boat? Sail off? No one would follow him, not at night. But then *he'd* be out at night, at the mercy of the dark, and he can't either sail or fight.

Find him…

…now, then leave…

…still has no more than half a clue…

Ørenna, they must know I'm a…

More thoughts, from down a backstreet, waft around the scent of a pepper-roast bird. The name is unpronounceable, but he learned to love it fast. Leon's stomach turns; he can see women eating it, hear one of them thinking it was worth what they traded, and they're almost out of range, he's almost past the harbour, when his fired feet tangle and trip. One of the bird-eating women is thinking of him.

The ground jars through him as he skids on his knees, skinning his grimy palms. Skewed in the dust, Leon stiffens and strains. He saw himself; he did. In the thoughts of the impatient girl demolishing her food; there he was, his head and hair and size if not his clothes. Lounging in a chair in a shadowed room. Worried in a doorway with a name attached: Jay.

Leon doesn't so much stand as grab the scruff of his neck, hoist himself high, and hurl his body down an alley. Voices holler from the river road, but here, no one knows. Not yet. Open windows are no more than curious, those that are among shut-up shops and the seedier evening haunts. In a tiny square, he pauses. The sea-shifter's sign creaks on a wall. Where are the women?

Leon picks a street at random. The women are back here somewhere, eating and drinking, caught in an ocean of noise. Again, he staggers, pauses, listens. Nothing. He dashes right, misjudges, catches his shoulder on a store-front sunshade, grunt-growls pain, and pelts on, on, on. It was him. It was him, and they're searching.

They must be here. Blindly, he barges past an empty cart, stopped by an open door. Light spills out. He picks up speed, frantic, burning, breathless. The women can't have gone. They're searching. They're here because of—

Pepper-roast curls up his nose. Leon slides to an ungainly halt, whirling. Close. Where?

Down a street to his right lies the marketplace, lined with blue-fire candles and stationed with iron-backed weavers. Beyond them, people gather, laughing at a show. The stage backs onto the rock-strewn hills. The smell is coming from there. And the minds?

Oh, there are so *many* now. Leon joins the shadows approaching the square, sifting through their heads. Thoughts of food, drink, the main actor's butt, how there are more weavers than normal, the depleted party that returned from the Tomi and the odd pair they brought with them, how her wife has really had too much applebalm…

Leon's head swivels round. There, at a table outside a shabby inn: two pale-haired women, one stiff and upright, squeezing the drink in her fist to death. The other fiddles with restless fingers, twisting her hair and looking, looking. Looking around for him.

As much as he wants to bolt to them, Leon makes himself stroll as if nothing is wrong. The weavers ignore him passing between them, a man and a woman with their cheeks tattooed. The protective flames flutter eerie, and then he's in among the crowd, so unobserved that any second he expects them all to turn. *Yes*, they'll cry, *we know what you did. We've been waiting for you, Leon, and you won't get away.*

Leon crams this down his throat. Squeezing past a sweaty man, shuffling through a throng, all heads turned to the stage. The women's minds are coming clear, and holding his breath, he listens and squeezes and follows.

Dum. Dum. Dum. With two rows of people left, Leon pauses. His heart is painful. His mouth is sand. The stitch in his side keeps cramping. Carefully, he reaches out to the women, staying on the fringes of their thoughts. If they're his escape, he can't risk hurting them; not unless they want to hurt him.

They don't. Hope swells inside him in a way that feels like tears. The women want to rescue him. They want to take him home.

Swallowing his heartbeat, Leon steps from the crowd, approaching the tavern from the side. His pulse is deafening. His flight made him sweat. Nobody pays him the slightest attention; they're either watching their plates or the performance, but even so, he feels exposed. Alone in the marketplace, causing an echo. About to get caught like prey.

'With the ellemaend, do you want to chance it?' The stiff, death-grip woman, her heart face set in uncomfortable ways, downs most of her drink in one. 'Really?'

The restless woman sighs. 'Do you really want to stay?' Leaning back in her chair, she flops her hands onto the arms. 'If you could look any more like you're sat on a spike, I'd honestly love to see it. I would.'

The stiff one throws the other woman such conscious disapproval that it radiates out from her mind. 'I'm glad you're no longer maudlin and dull, but I'd honestly love you to shut it. I would.'

The restless woman lifts and drops her fingers, drumming them on the chair. 'I just,' she says, drumming faster, 'want to find Jay and leave. All that boy you collared told us was that he's been apprenticed to Nikoli.'

Leon's heart jolts and chills. Nikoli. Nikoli and his rage.

Move.

'You scared him off too soon, so we need someone else.'

'In the morning.' The stiff woman's voice should be final. Between them flashes an image: her, grabbing a boy by his shirt, the tiny creature's tiptoes trailing on the ground.

Leon shifts foot to foot. They still haven't spotted him. Lurking by a potted tree, he shifts, foot to foot. Foot to foot, foot to foot. Any minute now he'll feel confident enough. Either that, or his heart will beat him up and leave him here as pulp.

'Why?' The restless woman pushes out her lips. One foot has started tapping. 'What custom exists in the morning but doesn't exist now?'

'Oh, *Kira*.' The other woman throws up her hands. The last of her crimson drink sloshes out of her cup. 'I have no idea. Being ostracised has restrictions. Can we not just leave it?' Shaking drops from her hands, she regards them with disgust. 'I thought you were past being dim.'

'I'm not dim.'

'Then listen to me.' The stiff woman holds up her hands like a picture. 'I. Am. Uncomfortable. I hate not knowing how we're meant to behave, and I want to stay beneath the waterline. For a thousand reasons, I refuse to do anything before the light of day.'

'But—'

'No.' This time, her voice *is* final. The restless woman's mind pictures a bear, pictures a stick, and lets it go. 'Does that not suit you madam? Madam, may I remind you, who neglected to tell me that someone'—she raps the table—'has been *following us*?'

The disgust maps her face like a plague. She looks away across the crowd. Her barbed gaze skims over him.

And then comes skipping back. 'Jay.'

32

You loved your games

Kira cuts a short, sharp look at Freya. 'What?'

'Jay.' Freya grabs her arm. 'Don't make a scene, but I've found him. Look.'

Kira looks. The marketplace, bathed in night. The audience, laughing. The blue flames, the boulders leading steeply to the hills. The boy standing half behind a bay tree.

Jay.

Kira's thoughts and mind and chest and lungs and world implode. 'Jay!'

'I said, don't make a scene.' Freya holds her in place with a hand that is a cold metal clamp.

Kira couldn't if she wanted to. It feels as though the earth is slipping, her feet neither linked to the stone slabs nor her back to the woven chair. Jay; it must be Jay. It can't not be Jay, but he's so far from her memory that she could be in a time warp or an alternate dimension layered thinly over hers. His thick brown hair is the same, sweaty with patches stuck to his face; his face itself is the same too, managing to be both red and pinched in, like he wants to fold small inside his clothes and fall through a crack in the stone.

Kira's throat catches. She's wildly out of breath and pleading, full of silent, reckless need; Jay is full of Callum too, in his hair, his eyebrows, his frantic, bark-brown eyes. He's Callum. He's Jay. He's Whiteland.

Jay fits. It jars Kira, tugs her down, back into the world. Burgundy tunic and waistcoat, loose blue trousers, and dusty shoes. He could be any other Whiteland boy.

'You know me.' Suddenly, Jay breaks from the crowd, jabbering as they clap. Onstage, the actors bow, the victorious man graciously swooping up the tailless huldra. 'I can hear it. In your heads.' He falters, then shakes his own smartly. 'Doesn't matter. You know about that too. I—'

He glances behind him. Kira trails his gaze. Over the applause floats another sound: shouting and the rumble of footsteps. Footsteps that sound an awful lot like they're giving angry chase.

'Right.' Kira's run-like-hell brain kicks into gear. It's had enough recent practice. 'I'm guessing we need to go.' She stands.

Freya looks at her. 'We do?'

'Yes.' Kira's hip bashes the table. Barging past the starburst of pain, she wraps fierce arms around Jay. *Jay.* 'You've no idea how good it is to see you, but what are we running from?'

Hurriedly, she scans the square: someone is talking to the weavers, waving and built like a bull.

'Um'—Jay scratches the back of his thistled head—'probably everyone now.' The words stumble over each other to get out. 'I screwed up, and then I screwed up again. If I'm the only…only thing you're…'

He tosses a hectic glance through the crowd. The bull and several others are charging through the crowd, forging the angry Red Sea. 'Can we leave?'

Kira keeps one eye on the man. 'Yes. Have you seen Romy? Or Callum?'

Jay's eyes flit to her and away. 'Who?'

'Kira.'

Ignoring Freya, Kira stares at Jay. 'What do you mean, who?' she asks. The world is slipping, slipping.

'Hello?' Freya urges.

Quickly, Kira looks to the bull and his cronies. They're still only searching; they haven't yet seen him. Unreality cloaks her like a shroud. 'Romy,' she says. 'My sister. And Callum. Your brother.'

'Okay, I'm done.' Downing Kira's red-honey wine, Freya slams the speckled cup on the table. 'My reluctance to leave doesn't stretch to being chased and certainly not by *that.*' She jerks her chin toward the men, hoists her bag from foot to back, and swings her bow around her body. 'Come on, ducklings. Mush.'

Kira knocks her hesitation loose. Grabbing her satchel, coat, and Jay, she hurries after Freya.

'I'd go back the way we came,' she calls, as quietly as she can. Through the mildly nosy tables, they slip past the tavern, into a candlelit passage. 'I know there's danger, and everything else, but Jay will hear it coming.'

'I know.' Freya stops at a spindly junction, three prongs of painted shops. 'Which way?'

Bobbing on his toes, Jay cranes his neck right. 'That way if you want to leave. If you want the elders or anything important…'

Wordless, Kira and Freya turn right. 'We want to get as far away from anyone as possible.' Kira brushes the hilt of the dagger at her waist. Using it would be abhorrent, but it makes her less little-girl-lost.

'And then, you explain what the hell is going on.' Freya flicks her knife to the right, to the left. Jay flaps a jumpy hand for right. 'What do you mean, who's Callum? Even I know who Callum is. The bastard left his mark on my— oh.'

Kira looks at her, sidelong, power walking on. 'Oh?' A frisson of unease slices flesh behind her ribs. That one word held too much understanding and too much soft apprehension. '"Oh" would refer to what, exactly?'

'Consider it becoming equal.' They pause on the river road's litter-strewn edge. In the sweeping dark, gilded with gold, the water shifts and sighs. 'You forgot the fossegrim's warning, and I forgot the rest of…well'—Freya peers around the corner—'the rest of Taika's plan.'

Tugging Jay down the road, the words barely dent. Behind them, muffled clamour brews, but beyond the port and into the night, the way is clear.

Enough. A group of men watch them pass. A girl closing the shutters of her house cricks her neck, but Kira is a whirlwind, a hurricane. They don't matter. None of it matters. All that matters is getting away, with Jay.

Wait.

Suddenly, Freya's words take root. 'What's the rest of Taika's plan?' Kira asks, slightly out of breath. They're not quite running; not yet.

'You won't like it.' Freya's face is ghostly in the candlelight from sconces stuck in the ground. Already, the blue-fire wards are scarce.

'When'—Kira throws a rough glance back—'have I ever liked any of this?' Tripping off balance, she looks ahead. Past boats of all sizes, shapes she should know, from her father's love of the sea. The port seems to curve along the shoreline forever.

'Mm.' Unconvinced, Freya's eyes rove the road. The last of the buildings are ramshackle huts, or stalls that brood in silence. From this point on, it's a ghost town.

'For God's sake, just tell me.' Kira looks back again. The shouts are fading; they've slipped away. Al-Sanit is soft, lit with blue and gold flames, by roads, in windows, and up in the hills, but none of them give chase. No torches. No fire. No mob. Freya must have been right; in a trade hub, everyone and no one stands out.

Not even lions in lambs' clothing, fleeing with a wanted boy.

'You really, really won't like it, though.' Freya's voice is grimly vague.

A soft noise catches in Jay's throat. '*Oh.*'

'Enough with the "Oh!"' Hauling Jay into shadows flanked by boulders and trees, Kira stops to round on them both. 'Tell me the rest of Taika's plan. My mistake was honest, and I admitted to being too upset to think straight. Right now, you're deliberately keeping this from me, and I swear to God, Freya, if you've deliberately kept it the whole time and didn't just forget…'

Kira flexes her fingers, hugs her body, and sets her eyes on the ground. She wants to know, but she doesn't. She really, really doesn't.

'Ahem.' Freya glances back along the road. With the bend, there's nothing to see, but she finds something fascinating and stares it half to death. 'Well.'

Scuffing the dusty ground, Jay sighs. 'Sorry.' He toes a stone toward Freya and doesn't look sorry at all.

Freya eyes him with the wariness of someone not big on kids. 'Why?'

Jay lifts deliberate eyes to Kira's. Kira's pulse steps up. 'Because'—he nods at Freya—'in her head, there are three of us. And a witch. The witch wanted to put us here and make us forget who we were.' Lifting his hands, he studies them. 'Completely. For good.'

Unreality. Kira blinks. 'What?' The world tilts further, further on its axis. The dust might well become sky. 'You—what?'

Dumbly, Kira looks between them. Jay, watching her, his bark-eyes flicking, like he's quickly skimming a book. Freya, whose wariness has warped into loathing, with a hint of disbelief. Jay, calmer out of certain claws. Freya, lined with night and gold.

Jay, whose expression is bare, and in it, Kira sees: she's a stranger.

Her jagged nails bruise her arms. 'Oh, my—oh, my *God.*' Open-mouthed, Kira turns to Freya. 'You…you didn't tell me? In all the time we've spent walking and talking and planning and trying to figure out what in God's name to do, you never thought to let me know what Taika wanted?'

Freya averts her ice-blue eyes. In the dark, they've paled to ash. 'It didn't,' she says tightly, 'seem relevant.' She keeps her gaze deflected, minding the road and the trail to the woods with unnatural resolve. 'And then, as I said, I forgot. A lot of things have happened.' Kira could laugh and scream and cry and sacrifice Freya to the Whispers. Again. 'I don't know which is worse.' Kira's exclamation is as hushed as she can make it. 'The fact you "forgot," or that before you forgot, you didn't think it was relevant. What about this isn't relevant?' She cuts a glance at Jay. Slowly forming fists, he stares through the river, lapping and black in the dark. 'We've been searching for people who've forgotten who we are. They've forgotten who *they* are, which is probably worse.'

And she is not herself.

'Jesus Christ.' Kira lifts her hands, half turning, scraping her hair behind her ears. The fossegrim now makes perfect sense. 'Jesus *Christ*, Freya.'

'I thought Taika was dead.' Freya's voice comes through her teeth.

'Of course.' Shaking her head, Kira runs her breathless hands down her face. 'Of course you did, Freya.'

'I saw her *die*.' Freya folds her arms. Her voice lifts, and she slaps it down, stepping close instead. 'Up until your saviour told us about Jay, we didn't even know they were here. I told you "Taika" was a placeholder.'

'Yes, but then we discovered they were here.' Kira's breath comes too shallow, too fast. Since they glimpsed human life, in the hills along the river, her hope had built and built and built, as frazzled as a panic attack. Now, she feels shredded. 'Was that not a trigger? Or is all this a game?'

Freya lifts her hands. 'No.'

'Well, it was!' Kira flings out her arms. 'You loved your games! "Hey, guys, let the girl get excited. It'll taste all the better when she gets shot down."'

'I'm not the Big Bad Wolf.'

'No.' Kira twists her mouth until it feels ugly and soaks it in contempt. 'You're the one who watches from a distance then skips off to tell her friends.'

'Shut up!' Jay claps his hands to his head and out. 'Can't you both just *stop?*' His voice echoes. The boulders ring.

The night falls flat around them, chirruping with crickets, and somewhere, the sound of a crowd.

'Thank you.' Legs splayed, Jay looks between them. Kira's angry, flittering heart hammers on. 'You two have got the best deal, you know. I'm the one with memory loss, and two other people are lost here too. It's terrifying.' Jerkily, he scratches his head. 'It's terrifying to wake up in the water and not know who you are. If this has happened to the others, we need to find them and explain.' Quickly, he licks his lips.

His dirty face looks small and young, and Kira flushes with shame. 'I'm sorry.'

He licks his lips again. 'Yeah, well. We need to go, and on the way'—his eyes cut to the corner—'you're explaining this to me too. I've got less than ten memories, and they're all messed up.' He nods at the tree-lined bend. 'Incoming.'

A shout echoes. Kira's head snaps round. 'Oh, my—not *again*.'

It's not one shout, but a louder one, travelling over the rest. The sound of a crowd is swelling; they're being followed after all.

'Okay.' Swinging around, her satchel bumping, Freya strides away. 'Move out.'

Jay follows her without a word. Dampened by the trees, the clamour floats on the water. Kira's insides groan. Not again, not *again*. 'You're right.' Hastily, she catches up to Jay. 'I'm sorry. We're sorry.'

Freya glances back.

'We are.' Kira shoots her an uncivil look Jay would hate if he wasn't so ready to bolt. 'This is all just…' she waves a hand.

Beside her, Jay walks faster. 'Insane?'

Kira speeds up. 'Pretty much.'

Faster. The first hamlet looms from the dark, three stark-white, tree-set houses. Faster. Faster, faster, faster.

'Can I ask you something?' Jay looks to Kira, heaving a hefty breath.

Tight legs burning, Kira sparks with satisfaction. In front of them, Freya's alone. 'Go ahead.'

Jay gulps again, close to wheezing. 'Jay doesn't sound like a Whiteland name.'

Faster, faster, faster. A sole dilapidated home trots past, deserted and disconcerting. Something in Kira kinks and aches. 'You're not a Whiteland boy,' she says, swiping at sweaty strands of hair, 'and I'm not a Whiteland girl. What Freya is, we'll come to later.'

Freya doesn't react. Behind them, the shouting starts to echo. Pitchforks. Torches. Death.

'Um.' Skirting round a wagon rut, Kira eyes the forest, lurking and murky and thickening fast. It must have somewhere they can hide. It must. 'At what point do we run?'

Freya slows. Glancing behind them, she glances at Kira. Her eyes are hard but alive. 'Now.'

33

And lies will part the clouds

Days dream past, and Ella floats. She floated while the horses trotted home. She floated when Asgeir helped her down and led her through people to a moon-sized tent. She floated when she joined them all, eating in a bigger tent, with pots in the fire and endless soup. Ella floated when she dreamt, and oh, how she dreamt, of spiralling through galaxies of pink and purple mist. She floated while the people stared; she floated while they argued; she floated while she helped feed horses and chickens and goats and three wizened pigs. She floated while she told children tales of her dreams. Each day, Ella floats a bit more.

They ask her questions, too many questions. Questions under the top-heavy trees, questions while she's foraging, questions in decorated tent after tent. She can't answer, yet they ask.

I saw Ella in the sky, she says, *and Ella came down into me.*

It's not enough. They ask her again, who she is, what she is, and sometimes, all she wants to say is, *No, I'm not human. I'm a sprout.*

Then it floats away.

'Listen.' Iolo lowers himself beside her. He's snatched two plates of egg and tomatoes, juicy, green, and fried with hot, spicy herbs. Ella stares through her single helping. She has a feeling she doesn't like eggs. 'They're talking about you again.' He nods across the tent.

Asgeir hunches beside two middle-aged women, in wrap-around dresses with black-rimmed eyes. Lightly, Ella blinks. 'He looks sad.'

Iolo bulldozes eggs like the world is ending. 'He looks like they're shoving a stick up his bum.' He swallows, loudly. 'Poor Asgeir. Anyway, they're quiet but not enough for these.' He taps his eagle ears. 'Hetti's meant to get back this morning. Can you see how worried they are? It's like they think she'll return with this woman and tell us all you're a demon.' He scrunches up his chewing face. 'I wouldn't want to be in charge of a village. It makes you too tense to eat breakfast.' He swallows again. His throat gambols.

Slowly, Ella places a tomato in her mouth. The sweet liquid spills hot over her tongue. 'You thought I was a demon,' she says and smiles, a tiny little whiskery thing. Another green tomato, scraped free of egg. 'Mmm. Mm. Who's Hetti?'

Iolo pops his buggy eyes at her. 'Who's Hetti?' His fork clangs onto his plate. 'You're really not here, are you? Ever? Hetti'—he scoops up some of her breakfast—'left a few days ago, to find Rana. The village. You know, in case that passed you by.' He wobbles his arms. 'Because of last year's story. Ella, come *on*.'

Ella lifts her eyes to his boyish face, slowly, slowly, slowly. Fuzzy hair tickles his spot-strewn chin, moth wings or baby birds.

'Okay.' Iolo lifts the fork, dripping with egg. 'It passed you by. You forgot. Whatever. Last year, some outsiders trundled past Rana, one stayed in their village, la-tee-dah, upshot, she looked like you. Hetti, you know Hetti.' He shovels more food from her plate to his. 'You helped her cook before she left, and now you're helping Sylvan. With me?'

Ella blinks at him. Sometimes, all he does is talk.

'Well, either way.' Iolo carries on regardless. 'Hetti's gone to Rana, to fetch whoever it was who dealt with whoever looked like you. Oh-ey.' He looks up, like a fox with a scent.

Slowly, slowly, slowly, Ella floats around to why, by which point he's left his food, clambered to his feet, and eagerly lolloped from the tent. The elders and Asgeir follow. Horsebeats?

Hoofbeats. The flat earth rumbles. Ella bites another tomato and gently stays where she is.

Bodies and brains and gossips are curious. The tent has half emptied, and it's close and soft, until the elders and Asgeir return. Smelling of air and reeking of horses, two strangers enter with them.

One. Maybe. Two women; one she thinks she might have known and one she's never seen. Dark skinned, eyebrows thick like beast hair, a chestnut plait falling over one shoulder. Faintly, Ella wonders how she rides in a frock.

'She hardly speaks,' the talon elder says, her middle-aged hair as black as her eyes and reaching to the bottom of her dress. Her, Ella does know; her hands have hooked nails. She asks questions, and the nails bite Ella's white skin and leave little petals of red. 'She walks around like a sleepwalker. Hetti's told you how she was found?'

'She has.' The new woman glances at Asgeir. 'Can I...?'

Like he wants to say no, Asgeir nods. Closing the short distance between them, he crouches in front of Ella, sighs, and lays her plate on the ground. 'Marya's going to talk to you.' His voice is low and gentle; since she's floated here, he's become softly lovely as well as a prettiness. 'Go with her. All right?'

He helps her up, and she lets him, resting her head on his shoulder. She's had enough tomato anyway.

'Talk to her alone.' Gently, Asgeir extricates himself, leading Ella over to the new, curvy woman. He eyes the others with a face like a wolf. 'She's better alone, and it's better for her.'

'Saviour complex,' Ella hears from outside.

'Iolo.' The talon elder jerks her neck. Her mouth is a sharp-clacking falcon beak. 'Behave or you're off patrol. I'll set you skinning with your father.'

Wordless hide boots scuff away. Marya's hand replaces Asgeir's, hot and rough, and Ella floats from the tent to the day.

It's a day she could sing for, sunny and hazy. It's a day she could swirl for, watching her dress, fluttering full through the air. Marya won't let her, though. Marya walks, and fast.

Faintly, Ella rankles, but then she starts to drift. She drifts through the village. She drifts past the horses. She drifts beneath the acacia, past the growing garden, and out into the grasslands. Still, Marya walks.

She walks for days, for weeks, for years. Finally, when she stops and turns, they're far enough into the open plains to see Ayomi as a whole. Every wagon, every tent, every hunch-backed tree. Every plot for the sun-baked animals. Ella rubs her whittling arms. The sun bakes her as well.

'This'll do.' Squinting around, Marya tugs Ella down, crossing her legs in the grass. 'Now I know for sure that no one can hear.'

The dry stalks of grass are long. They tickle Ella's nose, and abruptly, she sneezes.

Marya smiles a mother's smile. 'Health.'

Crossing her legs, Ella shuffles. 'Thank you.' The grass itches her thighs too, and she rearranges her dress. Airy, floaty, soft beneath her skin, tenting between her knees.

'You're welcome.' Marya's coarse, strangely clean hand touches her foot. 'Ella, can you look at me?'

Drifting, obedient, Ella looks.

Marya's smile is tinged with something keen and something sad. 'I'd like you to try,' she says, 'as hard as you can. I'd like you to try to talk to me.' She pauses. 'I think I can help, but it can't be one-sided.'

Ella squints through the sun. Marya wants what everyone wants, and Ella swims up to it. Breaking the sunny glass surface, she sighs. 'I saw Ella,' she says, 'in the sky.' Lifting a ladybug from her knee, she studies it on her finger.

Above the nail, Marya watches, bright and dark. 'You saw yourself?' She doesn't blink. 'In the sky?'

'No.' Ella sets the bug in the grass. It whirs off. 'I saw Ella, and Ella came down into me.'

She wishes the sky and the stars were here now. It was cool, then; now, the world is far too small, too hot.

'What does that mean?' Marya still doesn't blink. 'You've said the same to everyone. Exactly the same.' She brings her lips in to rub together, then out with a shake of her head. 'Do you have a sister, Ella? An older sister.'

Ella stares blandly through Marya's left breast.

Marya waits. The sun bakes. Something rustles through the grass. Eventually, she asks, 'Kira?'

An age passes. A heat-throbbing eon pulses after it, an era, a life.

'I don't know,' Ella whispers, in a butterfly voice. 'I don't know anything.'

Marya starts to sigh and stops. Trouble inks a map on her face. 'I know,' she says. 'That's the problem. But you look just like...' She stops. 'We're going back.'

In a blink, Marya's up on her feet, whisking her through the dry grass. Ella hardly feels her feet or her lips as she moves them. 'Why?'

Marya looks at her. Oh, there's inky trouble there and something twisty, like she's bitten through a bittersweet root. 'Because'—she squeezes Ella's fingerbones—'I don't need to talk to you. You're too close to Kira to be anything but sisters. What it means for you to be here I really dread to think.'

Floating, dreaming, drifting. In a hot swirl, they're outside the tents, back in the village, Asgeir beside her. Ella rests her head on his chest.

'You're sure?' He aims an arrow at Marya. 'You've barely looked at her. You walked more than said anything.'

'I'm sure. The girls are sisters.' Marya's trouble has become a map of the world, although which world, Ella doesn't know. 'Which means that Ella's an outsider.'

Poking his head through a cascade of leaves, Iolo waves a jaunty salute. Smiling, Ella waves back.

'Outsiders.' The stocky elder appears beside Marya, the one with dough for a face. Her bread cheeks knead. 'Ørenna. Why were they here last time? Do you know?'

The people surrounding them all shift, a thousand fish in the sea.

'Honestly, no.' With a rueful smile, Marya accepts the biting brew going round. 'Thank you. Kira lied at first, and I'm still not sure she then told all of the truth. She said she was looking for her mother and her sister, but we sent her off with a horse and never saw her again.' She draws in her beast-like eyebrows. 'Klaus is still sore about Maja.'

Asgeir's arm curves around Ella. His fingers brush her hip and tuck her in tight. 'How did they get here?' he asks, hard, warm on the top of her head. Lightly, Ella pats his chest.

Marya sips from the awful cup and pauses. 'Atikur.'

The crowd reverberates.

'Atikur.' The stocky elder growls a hum. 'Ay, ay, ay. It never rests. But there's no way she'—she dips her chin at Ella—'made her way here from there. Not like this.'

'No.' Hetti offers Asgeir a cup. Mute, he shakes his head. 'But there's a lot going on that we don't understand. All we hear are stories, from all over. Something's building.' She cradles the smoky mug. 'If outsiders are getting in, then…'

Shutting her eyes, Ella breathes Asgeir in and lets the voices fade. She is here; she is now. Sun heats her skin. Pink through her veined lids, it sends shooting star explosions across her mind. Somewhere, horseshit. Ella wrinkles her nose. It mingles with the morning drinks that taste like rotting sand. All the world turns into a bleary, blurry brown.

'Ella.' Big hands on her shoulders. Not clean like Marya's, but crusted with dirt. For a slow moment, Ella wants to kiss them. 'Are you okay with this? You can say no.'

Ella pushes her eyes up to Asgeir. 'Mmm?'

His hands squeeze. 'It won't be pleasant.'

The sun is higher than it used to be. Ella squints up at it until her eyes pop amber-gold.

'There's no point, Asgeir.' The talon fiend sighs, impatient and frustrated. 'She has no idea what's going on. She's probably forgotten who we are.'

Lies. The talon's lies part her clouds, and for a shadow of seconds, Ella sees.

'Asgeir.' Ella's voice is less soft than usual. It feels as though her throat has rung a jarring bell, and she butts Asgeir's arm away. 'Hetti.' Her gaze swoops to the woman with the ladle. 'Iolo.' To the tree and the head with extravagant ears. Iolo backs swiftly out of sight. 'Marya.' To the newcomer, smiling dryly. 'And you'—she levels her gaze at the talon fiend—'look like a really pissed off bird.'

'Ha!' The stocky elder erupts and covers her mouth with her hand. Asgeir snorts. The man beside him bites hard on his cheek.

'It may just be me, but I'd say she remembers us.' Marya looks to Ella with a light in her eyes. 'Whoever she is, she's in there somewhere.'

I am. Something hidden starts to howl. *I am, I am, I am.*

'Ella.' Stepping forward, Marya cups Ella's cheeks and shines the light up into her face. 'While you're lucid, will you let the weavers work?'

Ella blinks. Already, her mind feels pale. 'Work?' she manages, as light as a ghost.

'On you.' Marya presses her hot, hot cheeks. 'Asgeir's right: it won't be nice, and it might not help, but I think you should take it. It's the easiest option and the best.'

The clouds draw back across the sun. Deep in Ella's chest, the howling something wrenches, desperate and smothered and raw. *No,* it yells, *don't let me fade, don't let me lose me. NO—*

'Do it,' Ella chokes, on the last threads of *her*. 'Whatever. Find me. Hmmmm...'

The clouds grey and knit together. Her throat pushes out the hum, and as her lips vibrate, she shuts her eyes and smiles. Heat. Asgeir. Drift. She hums. *Let's become a carnival now Ragnarok is visceral.*

34

In rabbit holes

They put him in this godforsaken hole and left him. Just as well it doesn't get cold.

Peder's grousing thoughts are as dour as his cell. If it *was* cold, on the whims that bring people up here, they'd find him a wind-whipped sculpture. An ice sculpture, grisly and blue.

Better than being a sandman. He wipes his gritty face again, rough and chapping his lips. God*damn*. The only positive here is the view: the wind is worse at night, racing hot through the grasses and over the rocks, and when morning breaks, the dust lifting off the land is unearthly. Spectacular.

Before Peder fully wakes up, of course, and remembers he's stuck in a hole. What do we do with problems? Lock them up and give the key to a boy, a surly teen who won't open the door. Was there ever a worse plan?

They could have picked an even surlier guard, who'd have booted him over the edge. That would have been worse. Peder grumbles a sigh, stretching out on his belly. He's probably annoyed the lad to death. That would explain why the boy has stopped responding, stoically ignoring the charming commentary offered through the door.

Really, you can't call it a door. Also, there's no key, besides brute muscle, and some magic the lad's been learning. Peder found that out the hard way. Such fun.

He grumbles again. Such *fun*. The lad only deigned to tell him of the magic once Peder had spent a lifetime heaving and was quaking from foodless exertion.

The lad. Pissing the boy off with this is one consolation, but by this point, they're punishing each other. *Have my running commentary; ruin your limbs on a magic boulder; here, a condescending nickname; listen to me devouring your food.*

'That,' Peder mutters, 'is a nice boulder. I like that boulder.'

'Stop.' The lad's response is automatic, like a weary, long-married wife.

'Make me.' This is automatic too and fairly jocular. Shifting his painful pelvis, Peder folds his hands beneath his chin and peers over the lip of the hole. He's right at the top of these crow's-nest caves, a maze that thins to rabbit holes the higher up you go. They really do make you surly; in some places, still jabbed by that splendid spear, he had to crawl. In others, he had clambered through a shaft in the ceiling, and ever since, he's been stuck in this open cave.

Great. Fantastic. Utterly spiffing. This cave, mind you, that fits less than four of him side by side. He checked, both ways. It's an absolute terror when he wants to sleep, and the only way he can stand is if he hunches like a troll.

Now that was a sight. Emptily, Peder stares down at the settlement. Two days after he was hauled in, studied, met with blank looks and who-the-fuck-knows, guarded while those in charge conversed, and finally encouraged up here, he saw a troll. It was slow. It was gargantuan. It was built like rocks. He watched it lumber from the valley, and while he was grateful for his dizzying heights, he was also intrigued. It didn't come in to murder and menace. It looked like it wanted conversation.

Not that that helped at all. What do we do with problems of the kind we can't lock up? We fill their hides with arrows and chase them while they roar.

Peder felt a certain pity, as they ran it out of town. It didn't look dissimilar to some of the warriors, the great, leathery things he's seen stomping around. After a lifetime of dust and wind, they could be stitched from hide themselves. Yes, the troll was massive, and gruesomely naked, but you never know what someone's got on underneath.

Peder shuts his eyes. Oh my, he's going mad.

Today, though, there have been no trolls. He's seen plenty of horses, quite a few donkeys, and a very young couple sneaking secret kisses that will only be secret on the ground. The convoy from the Zaino rolled back in, with wagons of exotic food. It made his stomach beg to grow wings, nip down, and fetch it, but then, normal life resumed. He can't even hear the life from up here. All he has is the lad and the wind.

Not quite. A dark shape soars, and his tedium teeters. From time to time, he has Dog.

That was another dig at the lad. Very quickly, he learned that the teenager cringes when things are not called what they are. As a result, he has the sky-pit (his cell), the walking turnips (stubby donkeys that, when seen from above, remarkably resemble root vegetables), the waste-collector (the lad himself), and a peregrine falcon named Dog.

Sharply becoming a streamlined V, Dog plummets into the hills. Peder lifts his chin from his hands to applaud, and a few moments later, the falcon swoops in.

'Good job, Dog.' Peder nods at the peregrine. A smaller bird is gored on his talons, and shaking his feathers, Dog noisily, wetly tears it apart. 'I don't suppose you'd fly down again? You could catch me some of that convoy.'

Surprisingly, Dog doesn't answer. Leaving the fleshy bones of his meal, he cocks his grey head at Peder, spreads his fingered wings, and lifts off from the cave's edge with a piercing *pwee, tee-tee-tee.*

Alone. Well, the company was nice while it lasted. Once Dog's shadow has glided away, Peder rolls onto his back. Above him curls a dead spider, petrified in a crack in the stone. He hadn't considered it before, but Dog may be any number of birds; as Gaia told him when he saw them circling the cliffs, the peregrines often move in, and then there's no chasing them off. He assumed he'd be able to tell them apart, to know which was Dog and which weren't.

To be fair, though, he can't assume anything. He stares at the spider, at its dry, yellowed legs, at its crackling, bulbous core. How can he hope to tell birds apart when he can't even do it with his feelings? It's atrocious, but he can't tell which he has and which he only thinks he should. Does he love his mother? He feels like he does, but to think that he doesn't, because he really feels nothing, is cruel and strange. Is he scared of what these people might do? Maybe he should be, he probably should be, but no. He's not. He's got nothing to compare it to. No memories. No life.

'I'm naming this spider Antelope,' he says. 'By the way, it's dead.'

The lad sighs. Heavy and throaty, it must be for effect. 'And what's an antelope?'

Silence. Thumping his arms across his eyes, Peder groans. 'I have no idea.' He hadn't thought about that. Now, his mind tastes odd. 'Shut up, lad.'

Antelope has dimmed in the bleeding light by the time he hears anything more. Sleepy and bored, Peder doesn't move. He's grown numb from lying flat on his back, but he pricks his ears, as if he were a real dog, instead of a peregrine falcon.

The murmur of voices beyond his boulder. The grunt, scrape, and slap of bodies tackling the maze. Peder stares through the greying rock. Two? No. Three bodies, two voices. One voice is Gaia's, his original captor, and one belongs to an unknown man. The third body is also unknown; he's learned the sounds of his usual visitors. The way they breathe, the chafe of their clothes, how they move through the airy caves. He's had bugger all else to do.

Gaia is practised, smooth and lithe, with the sound of a snake through grass. The food goddess comes with little muffled oaths, little wet plops, and the chink of stone on stone. Messengers are usually light-footed children, with a love for a playful scrabble. The lad's fat master has a banged, bald head, bruised from overhanging rocks. These two with Gaia are strangers.

'How's he been?' Gaia asks, as the new man huffs and heaves through the final shaft. The third is a sigh, as soft as she is.

The lad clears his sullen throat. 'Annoying.'

As terse as her spear, Gaia laughs. 'I'm sure. Would you mind unlocking the door?'

Grudging clothes brush stone. At a ripple in the dry air, the boulder starts to crunch.

'Thank you,' Gaia says and almost sounds pleased. 'You're really getting quicker.'

The lad mutters something, muffled by his straining. The boulder grumbles, dull and tomb-like, grating against the wall. In the gap, a puffy face appears. The lad is red and blotchy, his muscled shoulders corded.

'Hey, old buddy, old pal.' Peder flops both arms back over his eyes, leaving a slitted chink. So far, these visits have amounted to nothing. 'Put your back into it. It'll make you a man. Turn your bones meaty so Dog can pick them clean.'

'Shut'—the lad's teeth grit,—'up.' He rests the boulder in its hacked-out slot and stretches out his limbs. 'If I'm getting quicker, do I get another task? He's going to drive me insane.'

Gaia's feet pad calmly into the sky-pit. 'Sadly, that's not my decision. I understand your pain, though, so feel free to suggest it to Magnus. Peder.' She nudges his boot. 'Get up. You've got guests.'

※

Far more out of breath than he'd like, Mathew joins Gaia in the cave. His legs are weak. His arms know they've worked. His mind…who knows.

He's had long enough, but he can't decide who he wants the captive to be. A stranger or the man who found Romy in the snow? Someone who leaves him back where he started or someone who confounds it more? Christ, it's already so wretched.

Without forcing tunnel vision, he might have just stopped. Not stopped for good, but stopped for a while, ignoring Grey and telling Dale he'll catch him up in a week. Mathew needs the rest. He does. But he didn't succumb, journeying through Jurnado and on to Bacaire, moment by moment and step by step and driving out the world. If he takes in much of anything, the disparity between here and home will make him scream for the hills.

So he's here. He's here, undecided, ducking into the cell, bending low so he doesn't scrape his neck. Carefully, he looks the young man over. Really, it could be anyone: muddy hair thick with grime, a beard growing dark. Dirty clothes, identical to Dale and Gaia's and a solid look, for a captive.

Mathew sighs a sigh that comes from his bones, as quietly as he can. Would he actually know if this is Callum? They only met for a handful of minutes, and then, they were focused on Romy. All he remembers is brown hair, a ski coat, and a handshake, satisfyingly strong. For Mathew, time has hardly passed, but for everyone else, it's been a year.

A *year*.

'Am I on display?' The young man asks, his sarcasm muffled by his arms. 'Because, believe it or not, I don't think I'm looking my best.'

Scottish. Here, of all places, somebody's Scottish, when all other accents are vague. Mathew's memory stirs. Was Callum Scottish? Or Irish? Or Welsh? He was something. Anna remarked upon it, how relieved she was that the one who had found Romy could speak English and explain.

'An answer would be nice.' Lifting his arms, the young man shifts, working them under his head. 'Please.'

Mathew stares at him and starts to blur. Under the dirt is the man who saved Romy.

Callum. Circles hang heavy under his eyes, but it's him. His matted hair has grown, and his face holds the purplish-pale hue of the almost ill, but it's him. The man who sat on the hotel couch, protected Kira, and toppled, accidentally, into an unholy mess.

Which means that this unholy mess is out of all control.

As if it wasn't already. Mathew feels sick and old and dead and also, far too alive. Turning, he smacks his head on the ceiling. '*Christ*.' He slaps his hands to his skull. 'Sorry. I just…'

Shouldering Dale out of the way, Mathew stumbles from the cave. The wall outside is cool, and he props himself against it. The back of his head is throbbing and hot. Gingerly, he prods the lump: egg-like. Consuming. Liquid pain. Internally juddering, he breathes.

'You know him.'

Mathew opens his eyes to Dale. Speaking lower than a whisper, the wiry man impedes his view of the cave. Minutely, Mathew nods.

Dale's face settles into its practised slate. 'And he doesn't know you?'

Painstakingly pushing off the rock, Mathew glances into the cell. Gaia watches Callum. Callum is scraping himself to sitting, his eyes thinned in the way that means he knows something's up.

Mathew's head throbs, inside and out. Rubbing his face, he thumps his shoulder back against the rock. The world is light, incorporeal, as if everything's whittled to tracing paper, and all that's left is his heart.

'It'—he rubs his mouth and sighs—'doesn't look like it.' The words are barely there. 'You said he doesn't know anyone, though. Anyone or anything.'

'He doesn't.' Dale's grey gaze slides to the boar-built boy. On the other side of the entrance, he's a tad too focused on full-body breathing. 'Gaia could lock him up again.'

'No.' At once, Mathew straightens. His voice slaps the walls, ringing through his head. 'Sorry.' He rubs his dry lips, his beard. 'Sorry. I'd like to talk to him. It's a shock, but I—yes.'

Giving the boy a parental eye, Dale turns back to Mathew. 'Who is he?'

His voice is air. Mathew reads his lips. 'A link,' he murmurs, as soft as he can. With his current exhaustion, it's easy. 'To my daughters. He may not be a link to finding them, but he's something. He's...' he pauses. The word tastes wrong. 'An outsider.'

For the first time, Dale shows an expression, one that can be pinned. Surprise.

Surprise and concern.

In the cell, Callum mutters to Gaia. Unsteadily, Mathew leans closer to Dale. 'Does that make him more of a problem?'

Shaking his head, Dale looks down. When he looks back up, the surprise, the concern, have both been scrubbed away. 'Not specifically. But with all the rumours and the real disturbances, he's another stone on the pile.'

Slowly, thinking, Mathew nods. By now, what Vasi meant by *disturbances* is clear: a boy with amnesia appearing in the river, is the one he's heard the most. It may be connected, but it's not much help if it doesn't find Kira and Romy. Callum may not be much help either, but Mathew can't just leave him here. He's a dad.

'He can come with me.' The decision is heavy. 'Whether he knows me or not.' Pushing off the wall again, Mathew tries to sound as though everything here is fine. 'Will you let him?'

'They'd better.' Folding his arms, the teenager finally abandons his no-I'm-not-listening slouch. 'If I have to spend any longer with him, he'll be screaming for Ørenna and learning how to fly.'

35

The bloody plan

It's been a day for staring through walls. Really, to be accurate, for staring through winter, waiting in the snow for the train.

After she had talked to the Whispers, Carol came undone. Unravelled, leaving nothing but rust. What can she do? What can she *do*? She hasn't given up, but she feels so helpless. Helpless, hopeless, and hapless, neither ornament nor use.

At least she hasn't run away. The whir of the train echoes further down the mountain, and she shifts weighty eyes to the old hotel.

Hazal left two days ago. Packing up her house, she disappeared. Carol had visited her in the aftermath, but other than a dull relaying that the Kyo had Talie, she got nothing from Hazal at all. That door, too, had been slammed shut, and then Hazal moved away.

How long before Urnäsch pulls her back?

Lally loved that. Buzzing with gossip, undercut with nosiness, running wires through every chalet. Disgust wicks through Carol's listlessness. Sympathy? No. Empathy? Less. Just whispers and looks and information that you know is being shared. The police had stopped poking around, once they saw there was nothing to poke, but the village kept Carol a pariah.

Maybe she should move. She and the twins could go back to Shetland, and it wouldn't be running. At least, it wouldn't be running from things she can't, and doesn't want to, escape. The twins are young enough to fit into a new school. Jay's disappearance could be kept a secret now that this mystery illness is wearing thin.

She has to do something. If she doesn't, the outside will grow fiercer than ever.

The train whirs its tame roar. Spattered with water, it rounds the corner, the speedy, white-blue space pod. She preferred the rustic reds, the cartoon aliens, the stars. This new model buddies with spaceships, leading the mountain to modernity like a ball and a screeching chain. Why does everything have to change?

Feeble snowflakes start to fall. Shiny in the grey day, the train door beeps. Caught behind the bigger children, Karl hops out, trailed by a laden-down Julia. She could let them walk up on their own—the house is about as close as it could be—but she can't stand the thought of feeling she's failed.

It's the main reason she hasn't hurtled to the forest, to plough her way into Whiteland: if she didn't come back, then everyone the children love will have left them. Coupled with, one: the fact that Lena died there, having entered in a similar vein; two: her boys being in Urnäsch, so the vein may well be bloodless; and three: the thought of it terrifying her, showing in colour how she's less than Lena, she's done nothing to act on the urge. Should she?

No. The seven-year-olds hugging her waist dictate that. She can't abandon them. She won't.

Up the iced stepping stones, though the winter days are warming. Carol dispatches Julia to fetch kindling, sets Karl the task of *quatres heures*, lays the fire, and forces her tablet to gather up emails.

There's cake. There's hot chocolate. There's wet, smoky pine, choking the lounge from the unseasoned wood. And there's an email from Clemence White.

The chocolate. The fire. The laughing twins, banging the windows open before the smoke alarm shrieks. It all fades out, until she and these five words are all that's left.

She hasn't heard from Clemence since she moved away from Shetland. With a finger that might not be her own, she closes her email and locks the device.

Clemence White, 15:36: *You need a bloody plan.*

36

The nebulae

They're inside her mind. They're inside all that makes up Ella, each star, every nebula, each planet, every world. They lay her on a bed haphazard with furs. They didn't speak, not to her. Marya took her hand, and then Asgeir and another weaver knelt by her sides.

They could be praying, Ella thought, before she felt them. They were shades behind a veil. They ghosted through, and then…

It burns. With a shriek, Ella bolts upright, pogo-ing off the bed. It burns, oh, it *burns*. The veil is razed. The shades are alight. They scorch her mind like wildfire.

'Ella.'

The shades push through the surface, and Ella's mind bursts. Her shriek becomes an agonised howl. Through the second layer, the third.

'Ella.' Marya and the stocky elder ease her back down. *No!* She wants to scream, but her mouth has splintered off. Her eyes bulge. Her back arches. Her spine pops. No, make them stop. She won't let them in; she can't.

'This won't work,' Asgeir, from far, far away. A wail sears its way out of Ella. 'Whoever's butchered her has done it too well. This will only make it worse.'

The shades burst another layer. Ella's back arches again, and she screams. She's on *fire*, in flames. Can't they see?

They don't care.

Another wail minces her throat. Tears scald her cheeks. The shades push down, grasping in the dark, panning for gold with bloodhound noses. Ella shakes, heaving, racked with pain. Whatever they're doing, it can't be worth this. They're stealing her stars, splitting skin from bone. She's going to wind up dead.

The next layer hurts more than anything else. It's hot glass; it's ripping muscle; it's amputation with a rusty saw. Ella screams, crimson, rotting, black.

The weaver sighs. 'It's working.'

<hr />

They're prepping to leave, in search of a boat, when Kira's eyes turn white.

'Holy—' Packing up the bags, Jay jumps to the skies. Kira's head snaps back. 'Freya!'

A chill whips through Freya, though she stands by the fire. Quickly, she douses the smouldering flames and drops to her knees. 'Kira?'

Slowly, Jay retreats, on his rear in the grass. 'Is she—is she okay?'

With a rasping gasp that must shred her organs, Kira bucks. Her head droops forward. Freya's chill seeps into her lungs and frosts.

'Kira?' She extends a tentative hand, a breath from Kira's cheek. 'What is it?'

Kira bucks again. Freya flinches.

'Nngh.' Kira's slack mouth lolls open. Her lower lip drools. Her eyes are forest-sky white.

Oh, shit.

'Get in her head.' Freya cricks her neck so fast that Jay inhales. 'Now!'

<hr />

'We've found something.'

Marya grips Ella's hand, grinding her bones. The girl has stopped screaming, but her silence is worse. Ella jolts on the bed, flopping, limp, letting out soft, slushy breaths. When the weavers pull back, how much will be left?

'Are you listening?' The older weaver's voice seems to echo through a mountain. 'There's a blonde woman, beside a river. Not the Zaino, but probably near. A little boy. A camp. We're inside someone close to Ella, really close. Through her eyes.'

Ella's body spasms. She hacks.

'Kira.' Marya grips the poor girl's hand to death. 'That's who was here before.'

'Could it be the mother?' Hetti asks in a hush. 'Either of the women?'

'Too young.' The weaver's voice is faint, fainter. Marya watches him, her heart thrumming. The man's dark skin pales, not in colour but solidity. He and Asgeir are almost ghosts. 'Both too young.'

He draws a rickety breath. The cool, juniper candles flicker. Outside the tent, horses whinny as though they know that something's wrong.

And it is. Ella whimpers. The bed starts to tremble. All of this is so, so wrong.

Pressing her kneecaps into the earth, Marya fights the urge to switch off. Ella needs her. Kira needs her. Ayomi needs her. Rana too and maybe the whole of Whiteland. Whatever this is, it's affecting them all.

'Asgeir, speak.' The weaver coughs. He's hard to see head-on, like a far-off star or a pale, dying friend. 'Need to get out. We can't—stay.' He heaves. 'For us or Ella.'

Soundless, Ella's chest jerks. Her back arches, clicking, popping. The furs shake as she crashes back down without so much as a sigh.

Pressing her kneecaps into the earth, Marya shuts her eyes.

'What do you mean, you can't?' Freya shouts, far hoarser than she'd like. 'When have you ever not been able to get in someone's head? You got me beaten with a stick of Hell.' She waves an arm. 'You got a girl *killed*.'

Kneeling on the grass by Kira, Jay folds in on himself. Freya sighs a frustrated growl. 'Okay.' She clenches her fists in the air. 'I'm sorry. That wasn't fair. But what's stopping you?'

Freya's fists start to hurt. She clenches them tighter. Anxiety blooms like a black, bruised rose. If she could, she'd beat it out of herself with her own stick of Hell, but she can't. Kira's ballad suggestion was right.

'Her thoughts are the same as her eyes,' Jay says. He's as dampened as morning mist, watching Kira with a wood-carved focus. 'That's what. I can't get past this…fog.'

He shakes his head, but not his focus. Freya shuffles closer to Kira, as though that will help anything. Kira hasn't moved. Not an inch; not a whisper. She sags on her knees, Callum's little box beside her, her head doll-limp and her open mouth wet. Her eyes have clouded into early Nova Vanca dusk.

'So there's nothing?' Freya fights the urge to push Kira in the river. Push them both in the river; then, there's a chance of the water shocking someone's mind into life.

'No.' Jay's mouth turns down. 'It's literally fog. I can't hear or see.'

Freya lets her head slump. Staring through her knees, she rubs the bone between her eyebrows. That means something, but—

Kira's breath sucks in in a guttural wheeze. With her head snapping up, Freya grabs her. 'Kira?' Freya shakes her shoulders. 'Kira!'

Puppet-like, Kira's head lifts. Recoiling, Freya lets her go. Those mist-white eyes are haunted.

'My name' —Kira's mouth works loosely—'is Ella.' Her words are made of rust and marbles. Freya's nails puncture her palms and bleed. 'I'm in the grasslands.' Kira wheezes again, from her lungs to her lips to the air. 'Ayomi.'

A cough wracks out of Kira. She topples forward.

'Kira!' Freya lunges to catch her.

'Nnnn.' Kira lolls toward the grass. Gritting her teeth, Freya heaves her back up. 'Not. Not Kira.'

Ørenna.

Freya's pulse has never whacked so fast, not even when the Whispers sent her running for the door. 'Not Kira?' She gasps, in a voice that's not her own. 'Who are you, then? Who's Ella?'

Wheezing, Kira slumps against her. The sides of her face are blue with veins, her lips drying and mauve. Her chest bucks. Her breath sounds like nails on iron.

'Who are you?' Freya's voice soars. The anxiety has lodged like a boulder, stuck in her vocal cords. 'Jay, I don't know—I don't know how to stop this.' Stopping herself from shaking Kira, she throws a raw look at his moon-eyed face. 'Are you sure you can't get in?'

Kira's chest bucks again. A wet burble thumps in her throat, and blood bubbles past her lips.

'No.' Freya's head rushes hot. Her chest floods cold. 'Kira!' Freya shakes her. '*Kira!*'

'Don't know Ella.' The weaver's voice is as faint as his form. Asgeir is more corporeal but barely; they've started to flicker, to shift. 'What's Ella been saying? Saw it in the stars?'

The name is wrong. Marya's heart and head and dread drum. It has a hundred implications, but if they've got through to Kira…

'Tell Kira her sister's with Marya,' she says. The words come out staccato and rough. Ella lies so limp, so lifeless. Her body hardly has the energy to twitch. 'Hopefully, she'll remember.'

※

'With.' Kira retches. 'Marya.'
Kira goes still.

※

Kira flickers on the edges of fire. Romy on her knees in the eye of the flames. Jay standing vacuous, Callum roaring, the tendons of his straining jaw fighting to burst out. Shadowy forms among papery trees. The Northern Lights. The labyrinth. The phoenix. The Chlause.

The sound is muted, so when everything stops, for a moment, Kira doesn't click. Then the afterglow registers, the quenching of the flames, quick like a pinched-out candle: in their place is the girl from Urnäsch. Jay's wayward daughter, Freya's teenage witch. Next to Romy, slumping to the ground, stands the unsteady force of Taika.

And then they're gone. Wraith-like, Kira lifts up or is unfocused here and sharpened elsewhere. She's outside the wreck of Karliquai, the Chlause's stolen effigy, and it's cracking, falling apart. The hill beneath her grumbles with thunder. The blue sky dips and flows, undulating, susurrating, every pretentious word she knows to describe what she can't comprehend.

The blue weakens. Beyond is white, ghosted with overlaid pine trees. Black and tracing paper that she learned in art at school.

A lucid dreamer, she turns. Urnäsch is crumpling. Paper tigers?

Paper worlds. Towed like a toy with a string in her spine, Kira skitters back, back, back.

Here, the world is whole. She falls to her knees, to the heels of her hands. Figures running off a road and running up a hill.

Could she make a deal with God? Paper Kira runs, a song in her head, in front of Romy, Callum, Jay. Real Kira can't feel the grass beneath her fingers. Touching Karliquai, Paper Kira disappears. Romy, Callum, Jay, stuck. The Chlause.

Dream heart hurts so much.

Yanked by her hair, Kira flies forward. It doesn't hurt. It should. She flies into dust and the Northern Lights. Fire. A teenage boy, disintegrating into light.

Forward, and she falls through the sky. No, not falling. She floats, looking down; looking down on the Chlause, crowded in the meadows below. Many more than she knew were here, ringed by forms that storm and swirl, physical then elemental, ringed by children, ringed by *humans*, facing a pine tree, shuddering sky—

Get OUT GET out GET out get OUT GET OUT getoutGETOUTOUTOUT—

Kira slams back into her body and vomits.

'Oh, oh, okay.' Hands wriggle under her head, lifting it as she retches. '*Now* can you get in her mind?'

GET OUT. Kira's thoughts ring. Vomit roils up her throat, splattering the grass. *GET. GETOUTGETOUT.*

'It's still messy,' a younger voice says. 'I couldn't really see what she was dreaming.'

It's hot. Water splashes and chortles. Too hot. Kira's breath tastes sour. Her heaving stomach pulses, and she pukes it up.

'Okay.' One hand holds back her hair, one supporting her chest. 'Okay, okay. Jay, I need more than that.'

'I don't have more.' The young voice sounds like a frown. 'It was…violent. She got thrown out, I think. I don't understand.'

'That makes two of us, then.' The older voice belongs to the hands. 'Are you done?' It lowers to her ear. 'Kira?'

Breathing hard, Kira's throb descends to a tremble. Spitting the bile from her lips, she nods.

No. The motion sends her seasick, teetering and drunk. Wetly, she inhales, spotted with black. The Earth rocks its boat. Hot tears trickle down her cheeks, and she whimpers.

'Okay. You're okay.' The hands fumble, raising her up. Kira's giddy back meets Freya's front. Black comes in waves. The boat keeps rocking. Her whimper becomes a moan.

'Kira.' Freya, the hands. Her arms. 'Focus, Kira. You're back. You're here.'

Kira shuts her eyes. So hot. Too hot. Freya's dizzy heart beats on her cheekbone. *Dum-dum-dum,* to the speed of *GET OUT.*

'Jay.' Freya's voice turns dark. 'Time to step up. You said Kira got thrown out. By what?'

Jay hmmms. 'The dream...?' He hedges, as though Freya might beat him up. 'I guess? I think you need to ask her. It really wasn't normal.' He swallows, loud. 'Has it happened before?'

'I have no idea.' Freya's sigh rattles sick through Kira. 'I'm not her mother or her keeper. Odd dreams, yes, because they told us about your delightful presence, but I think she'd have warned me of a problem with possession.'

Kira coughs. Scorched by acid, her throat sears. 'Maybe,' she manages hoarsely, 'I didn't think it was relevant.'

A single "ha!" bursts out of Freya. 'She lives!' She crows with a horrible clap.

Jolted, Kira inhales. 'Please'—spidery, jittery, she breathes—'Freya.'

Freya stills. 'Sorry. But without you, all I'd have would be a memory-deficient boy with a gift for psychic murder, a torn conscience over finishing your task, and an outsider body to bury.'

Far too many words. Kira scrunches her face and smooths it again. That just makes her headache worse.

'You have no idea,' Freya continues, 'how excellent this is. Now that you're back from the edge of the skies, all my problems are solved. Really.'

Far, far too many words. 'Bloody hell,' Kira groans. Unsticking her eyelids, she flails a hand in the air, finds the warm, grassy bank, and supports herself on a quavering arm. 'Shut up. You make my dream seem—*shit.*' Her eyes fly fully open. Jerking away from Freya, she tumbles to the bank, fixing Freya in her too-bright sights. 'Taika's alive.'

Freya's face full of triumph freezes. 'What?' Sinking slowly, she deflates. 'That—that is not helpful.'

Gingerly sitting back on her heels, Kira pushes back her hair. 'No.' She stares through the grass. 'No, it's not. She's the one who got the others out of

Urnäsch. Romy was in the fire, and Taika…' her head clears at a dizzying rate. 'Oh, *shit.*'

Turning her face an inch to the side, Freya gives her a thin-eyed look that knows it's not going to like what's coming. 'Oh, shit?'

Kira nods, breathes, wipes her mouth. 'Romy.' She clears her scoured throat. 'Romy was in the fire. How much do you think it took from her before she got pulled out? Taika—' Mouth open, she shakes her head. 'I thought Taika was *dead.* She must have opened the door again.'

'I could have told you that,' Jay says.

Silence. Merry water. A distant woodpecker. Kira's stunned gaze travels to Jay, who regards them as if they've made very odd choices.

'Well, chickie, you didn't.' Freya lifts her hands and drops them. 'Did you not think it was relevant?' Standing smoothly, she carries on packing up the camp.

Kira keeps her eyes on Jay. 'How did you know?' she asks, keeping her voice as still as her gaze. 'You said you saw Taika in other people's minds.'

'I did.' Jay fidgets with the hem of his waistcoat. 'I also saw her in my memory.'

'*What?*' Freya spins, a full-on, outraged huldra. 'Your memory?'

'My tiny bits of memory!' Jay's hands fly up, in a ma'am-please-don't-shoot way. 'Really, they're tiny. And they don't make sense.'

Rapidly, he lists them. Rapidly, Kira's nausea wraps around her intestines, coating her stomach like slime. They might not make sense to Jay, but they make sense to her: crucifixes in the church, killing him and Romy. The moment they faced the doll at Karliquai and fell into Urnäsch. Taika putting out a fire and starting one anew.

It's too much. It's all too much.

'I didn't tell you'—Jay balls his waistcoat in his fist—'because there's so much happening in our heads and in general. Also, when I told Nikoli'—he dips his eyes to his fabric-covered knuckles—'that's when things went bad. Mentioning the Chlause did something to him. I ran before I heard what.'

'That's because they're nightmares in costume.' Freya stamps back up to them. 'Can you stand?' She fires this at Kira. A satchel and coat loops over each arm, her bow and quiver on her back. 'Actually, you have to. I'll help you. Take this.' She tosses Kira's satchel to Jay.

It hits him in the gut. 'Oof.'

'Shut up.' Freya's glare could skin him alive. 'If Taika's out there, she's going to hate me. If she hates me, and she's still as strong as she was, she could be planning anything. We've been in Whiteland too long.'

Squatting, she flops Kira's arm around her shoulders. Kira's head swoons. Her stomach moans. 'What are you doing?'

'Helping.' Freya cups Kira's waist and braces. 'Let's find the stragglers and vamoose. Ready?'

'No?'

'Good.' Less gently than she could, Freya heaves Kira up to standing. 'Come on, Jay. Let's move.'

Kira's head turns woozy as they stumble off. 'What happened to me?' she manages, leaning into Freya. 'We were getting ready to leave, and then…'

'Another conundrum entirely.' Like hopefuls in a three-legged race, Freya guides Kira down the riverbank, back to where the channel meets the main hypnotic blue.

'We don't know.' Looking as trite as a twelve-year-old can, Jay bobs up beside them. What a rescue mission; it's even madder than before. 'Your eyes went white, and then I couldn't hear you. Your thoughts, I mean.'

Deliberately, Kira lifts her eyebrows.

'I know.' Jay's face flicker-winces. 'I've been trying to stay out. I have. It's just, you started thinking about everything that's happened, and I was there in scenes I don't remember. So I listened.' He lifts his shoulders up to his ears, setting his mouth like Jim from *The Office*. 'You know, in case it might help my memory.'

'And did it?' Kira asks.

'No.' Jay's nonchalance falters. 'Your brain literally clouded over. It went all white, the same as your eyes.'

'And something spoke from your mouth.' Freya's face gives nothing away.

Kira looks up at Freya from the side of her vision. 'That sounds…'

Like Romy in the hospital. Like Romy in the hotel, the very first morning. Like the horror films Romy used to watch.

'What did it say?' Kira sticks up a wall, as determined as Donald Trump. She can't think. Not about that. 'Or what was it?' Her skin shivers. 'I don't know which is worse.'

Freya grips her tighter. Here, they meet the trail they dashed up last night, and suddenly, it gets hairy. 'It was a who.' She grunts, slipping on mulch. 'She called herself Ella. She's up in the grasslands.'

'Ayomi,' Jay puts in.

'Yes.' Freya lifts Kira slightly. Her toes skim earth-set stone. 'She's with someone named Maria. However it happened, it's probably telling you where to find Romy.'

More riddles. Stumbling, her belly plunging, Kira clings to Freya. Ella. Maria. She doesn't know a—

Yes, she does. 'Marya?' she says, so sharply that Freya flinches against her. 'Not Maria, but Marya?'

Jay looks to Freya. 'Maybe?'

Freya's face is flushed. 'Yes, if it helps.' Navigating the crumbling slope, she talks in a hiss through her teeth. 'And Ella?'

'It might be who she thinks she is.' Jay sticks his hands in his pockets. 'I thought my name was Leon.'

Freya clears her bulging throat. 'True. Who's Marya?'

For a moment, Kira watches the woods and the winding, sunny trail. Tick, tick, tick goes her clockwork mind. A mouse, maybe, overwound and skittish, released to shin up the clock. This isn't a riddle; it's a message, and it's only meant for her.

'When I was following Mum,' she says quietly, 'I stayed in a village in the grasslands.' She tips her head. 'Well, "stayed" as in, I was there for a night. Marya looked after me.'

Kira's mind slips back. Marya and her soup and her herby poultice. Klaus and his rescue and the gift of his horse.

Freya curls her hand through the air. 'Okay, and they found her how?'

Kira stares through the track as it evens out, into spaced, dappled, pear-green trees. 'I've no idea, but it helps. We know where we're going, who we're looking for. And Ella...' she huffs, although it's far from funny. 'Taika's humour is twisted. There's a book Romy loved when she was little, and a film. *Ella Enchanted*. For a while, she wanted her name to be Ella because she thought Romy was weird, and Rosemarie was posh. I'd guess Leon is a similar thing.'

Reaching the bottom of the track, Freya pauses. She's pink and sweating, breathing in bursts, and extricating herself. Kira leans against a tree trunk. Her legs wobble but hold. At least she's no longer vomiting or seconds from passing out.

Lifting her hair, Freya fans her face. 'I wonder what Callum's been called.'

The pit of Kira's stomach bows. Suddenly, the tree's not safe at all. The bark is sticky with sick resin. The hazy light through the leaves makes her feel hungover. Thinking of Callum is a terrible plan.

Jay's eyes flit toward her, then away. Kira holds tight to the ridges of the bark until slivers get stuck in her nails. Romy lost her memory once; she can deal with that, work with it. Blood ties are something that can't be hacked apart. But Callum? The thought plagued her all through her watch last night, and she tried her hardest to kill it with fire. If Callum doesn't remember…

Not tied tight enough, my dear.

'Freya's right.' Breathing deeply, Kira pushes off the tree, diligently avoiding coming face to face with Jay. 'We've been in Whiteland far too long. Let's find the stragglers and get ourselves gone.'

Freya puffs out wearily. 'Yes.' Scanning the river road, she steps from the track. 'Before whoever wants you out does more than scream.'

37

The paper man

The departure from Bacaire was like walking to the gallows. Not that Peder thought he was heading to his death, but the road cleared for his passing, and the people lining it stared.

They must have made an unlikely crew. A notorious stranger, a weirdly dressed stranger, waltzing in with an notorious wolf, and the notorious wolf itself. Peder was glad when they left it behind.

He'd better not have swapped a pan for an oven and fifteen unknown Hells.

Although is fire any worse than death by boredom? The lad would talk about execution, and this is certainly better than that. Better journey with a stranger, and maybe discover who he is, than waste away in an open cave, with nobbut a boy through a boulder. Peder's only regret is leaving his Dogs. 'They were happy to see our backs,' he says, scrubbing the grime from his body; the water in his cell was rationed for drinking. The rock pool they found as the cliffs rose is beautiful. Grey has become a dog beside it, asleep on a sun-warmed stone. 'Weren't they?'

Waist deep in the water, Mathew looks up. 'Can you blame them?' Wringing out his socks, he flicks them onto a rock. 'One man with amnesia, who nobody can place. His accent is strange, and he unsettles everyone, but he's dressed like one of them. And one man'—the creases of his face pull tight—'who walks in with an infamous wolf belonging to an infamous leshy.'

Peder's eyebrow arches itself. 'A what?'

With a brief, taut humour, Mathew meets his eye. 'A leshy.' He assumes the blatant face of *yeah, I don't know either*. 'He described himself as a forest guardian. More or less a shapeshifting giant, who everyone seems to know. To respect.'

'Wonderful.' Submerging himself, Peder scrubs his hair heartily and bobs back up with a grin. As much as anything here can be perfect, this comes pretty damn close. 'And we're trailing this wolf to the end of the world.' He flicks the brief, taut humour back to Mathew.

'Yes.' Mathew returns to his washing.

Sitting back to tread water, Peder watches. Finished with his shirt, the man moves to his underpants, the creases in his face never gaining any slack. He's thinking hard, or worrying hard, or both: his expression is dislocated, far from his clothes. He's a man drifting out to sea.

But that doesn't mean he's allowed to lie.

The sulphur-scented water laps. Tiny mouse claws skitter on rock. Somewhere, a swarm of insects hums. Peder lets another roll of silence unfurl, then, 'Why did you ask me to come?'

The back of Mathew's neck tenses. One second, two, and then he looks up. 'I told you at the time,' he says. 'Sitting in a cell wouldn't help your memory. I thought travel might, and I'm grateful for the company.'

Peder's circling suspicion settles into stone. Not *what do you mean*; not a look of confusion; just a lack of inflection and a speech well-rehearsed.

'Yet you barely talk.' Submerged to his neck in the bliss, Peder's eyes stay on Mathew. 'Which is fortuitous, really, because it's given me a lot of time to wonder. When a whole community is wary enough to stick me in a cell and seal it with a weaver's protection, how does a stranger feel confident enough to take me away on his own?' Standing, he wades to the side of the pool. 'Unless there's more to you than an outsider who's lost his daughters, I'd say there's more to me.'

From the way Mathew stills, he must have stopped breathing. Peder watches him, clambering backward onto the rocks. Hot and harsh, they chafe his skin. Keeping his eyes on Mathew, he reaches for his clothes.

Grey snuffles in sleep. High above the cliffs, a peregrine dives. An indigo dragonfly skims across the pool, leaving tiny ripples in its wake.

'What do you mean?' Mathew asks. Each word is both too slow and too fast, as though he's tripping yet holding back.

Pulling on his trousers, Peder lies back. 'I mean'—and this is the suspicion, the cementing thought, the thing that's stuck in his chest—'that you know who I am. You stumble over my name, you frown at me when you think I'm not looking, and otherwise, why would you take the risk? In Bacaire, they had any number of theories as to what I could be involved in, which meant they wanted me locked away. Even what I might be a victim of, which was somehow worse, and meant they wouldn't touch me with those damn intrusive spears. You'—his heart starts to beat, beat, beat—'have none of that.'

In the pool, Mathew is very, very still. Staring through the steaming water, he doesn't so much as blink.

Liar. He's a goddamn liar.

'And'—Peder reaches for his dirt-free vest, as though his pulse isn't causing a ruckus—'out of all the people they could have brought to see me, why did they bring a stranger? An outsider, who, as it just so happened, was passing through?'

He pauses. Nothing. Mathew grips his shirt as though it's all that lets him live.

'Okay, yes, I'll go on.' Peder's voice grows louder and faster and thick, his unknown accent congealing. 'Why would that Jurnado man tell you about me? Why would he think to? Why would he, a snake, bring me to Bacaire? He'll have known they didn't like me being there. I can't see the elders advertising my presence, sending distress signals from the clifftops. You must have said something.' The words drop like stones in the water. 'Something to make them trust you. Something to make them trust you enough to mention me, and you know what this leads me to think?' He yanks on his boots with angry hands. 'I think you set me free for more than solitude and pity.'

He lets the last word spit and hang. His pulse is paper trapped in his chest, fragile, crumpled, old.

After a moment so long Peder could shatter and roar, Mathew moves. 'You're an outsider,' he sighs, dull and defeated. He's fragile, old, and crumpled too, as he wrings out his trousers and wades to the rocks. 'I met you briefly, once. You know my daughters.'

The words are dragging themselves out. Grey's ears prick up, one yellow eye slitting. Suddenly, everything is far too hot.

Heaving himself from the pool, Mathew rubs his chin and bows his head. 'Your real name is Callum.'

38

Where Hell flees and midnight devils howl

Carol's first thought is to feign innocence, or at least to buy time with naïveté. But if Clemence has contacted her, he'll have been following the news, seen Callum's name, seen the location, and will instantly know her naïveté is fake. She may have been naïve before, but she can't profess to it now.

With the twins satiated by their *quatres heures*, she sits down with the tablet and a feeling of shame. "Have we let ourselves down?"

The song shivers through her, rousing and bleak. It's something Callum whistled in the days before he vanished, and Carol shuts it away. She may have let everything spiral, but she needs to stay *here*. Present, prescient. She should have thought more, said more, done more, and maybe she did let her boys down, but maybe she can also change it.

Which starts by facing Clemence and telling him the truth.

I'm sorry, she types, finger by finger. It feels like pulling wisdom teeth when the anaesthetic didn't work. *I never thought it would get this bad. I suppose I was unconsciously relying on the idea that nothing in Whiteland would—*

No, no, no. Carol holds down *delete*. Even if she was convincing herself, the words are a forced cliché. A myriad of excuses. Instead, she puffs a short sigh and starts to type the truth.

He must have been waiting. Within four minutes, a reply comes back. Four minutes of making coffee she knows she shouldn't drink, not so late in the afternoon. Four minutes of fretting over why he got in touch even though the two of them never got on. In fact, he seemed glad to see the back of her. Being the only, lonely watcher in his hilltop cottage is a role that suits him to the ground.

So what does he want, unless he can help?

Setting down her tiny cup, Carol taps the message.

You're an eejit, Carol.

She rolls her eyes and almost relaxes. It's easy to hear him saying it, his island accent swallowing words like they're brawling in his throat.

We'll be clearing up your bloody mess 'til the cows and the sheep and the kraken come home.

All right, not quite so relaxed, but that's Clemence.

Maybe the giant squid, he continues, snapping. *Lord above. I'm getting hold of Beth. If you've got any brains left, think if you know how to contact any of the others.*

That's it. He's sour, condescending—among other things, he had taught Callum how to swear and how to curse with fingers, and then, whenever she confronted him, would lapse into incomprehensible dialect and feign not speaking "the south country hogwash"—but, if she's not mistaken, it sounds like he can help. Or at the very least, he might begrudgingly feel as though he has to try.

At this stage, any hope is worth Clemence White.

Biting back her hostility, bristling up from long-hidden depths, Carol types a quick reply: *What do you think we can do?*

A reply comes back within the minute. Julia patters in, enquiring about tea, and with a vague murmur Carol instantly forgets, she stares at the message. *Stop the noise.*

The watchers and the Whispers have silenced things before, but nothing as colossal as this. This is worldwide, worldswide, far more than the McFaddens's disappearance or the couple who chickened out of joining the Chlause. Fleeing from the desert, they ran back to Essaouira, running hell for all kinds of leather and howling of the midnight devils in the sands. This is more, even, than the disturbance that killed her dad, and at age fourteen, gave her his role. She's never been able to face details, but it was something to do with a warlock in Skarrig chiselling a hole out of Whiteland. The warlock rapidly became a Whisper, and apart from Anneliese and her family, everything since has been still.

Carol stares through the tablet. The strong smell of coffee curdles the air. In the lounge, the fire crackles. Karl's Tetris toy beeps its arcade jingle. To silence this, though? Without the Whispers?

Carol types one disconnected word: *How?*

At once, Clemence bitterly pounces on her flaws. *Don't ask dobbering questions*, he snarls, permanently angry even on a screen. *Get hold of whoever you can. If we've all silenced things by ourselves, we can bloody well do it together.*

Carol reads it again and again and slowly sits back in the kitchen chair. Okay. Clasping the coffee to her sternum, her mind starts to work. While Clemence may be less than savoury, a grouchy, white-haired man in waders who never leaves the island, he isn't often wrong. *We can bloody well do it together.*

Splitting the crosshairs in her brain, something clicks. Croatia.

With a caffeinated urgency, Carol's heart sparks, and she jerkily squeals back her chair. When she flew to Croatia for Callum, a watcher found them. A highly peeved watcher, whose details she surely, surely, *surely* must have kept. Swiftly, she quits the kitchen, thumping up the stairs. Somewhere, she'll have something. A phone number, an address, a full name; something she can use to trace the woman. Surely, she'll have thought it useful, reasoning that someday, she might need to be in touch. Few of them know each other; to meet another one, and then…

'Carol?' Karl calls as she slams her door open. 'What are you doing?'

'Looking for something.' Carol replies more to the room than him. Planting her hands on her hips, she regards the mess with dismay. She could have made a note and left it anywhere; at the time, she was more concerned with having Callum back alive.

If only she'd known it might be the key to helping him stay that way.

39

And so she sighs

*E**lla, we've found your sister,* they say, and their voices blend with the day. Each timbre has its own heat, gold to amber to a delicate rose. *This one is Hetti*, she thinks, so faintly as the lights and colours blend and swirl to white behind her eyes. Sister?

Sister is an image that doesn't float here. It doesn't sigh and drift on invisible winds, following a bird through mountain passes, sheer and peaked with snow. She can't have a sister; she barely *is* herself, so there can't be another. There's not enough air and dust in the world, not enough magnetised glimmers of stars to join and shape two wholes. If there was, they wouldn't have left her cold.

Can you hear me, Ella?

Yes. The long-haired pretty has a voice of embers, and within herself, she smiles. He walks on a path through the pass, looking up and calling, but so far below that she can't call back. She has no tongue. Her words become butterflies, pearly pink with opaque wings, flitting away and turning to snowflakes. They gently fall toward him, but she doesn't think they land.

She and the bird curve away.

40

Smiling, dark

Betrayal is a jaded, jagged thing. It twists a blade into your lungs, and then it seeps with poison.

She won't go any further. Two of them are here, bargaining for a boat, a tatty wreck that may or may not reach the grasslands.

May not be *able* to reach the grasslands; that's more accurate. Skulking behind a clump of strangling saplings, she smiles, dark. Freya and Kira have been trying to strike the bargain for a while. In time, she'll get a chance at them.

After that, as much as it's loathsome, she'll go back to Atikur. There'll be ways of finding Taika; maybe she can help wreak some kind of havoc before she bursts her banks. The death spell will have worked. If it didn't…

It did. She sets the thought on fire and sits back to watch it burn. It's as sure as her hatred of the women by the man's decrepit house, bargaining for his boat. Somewhere, Taika's alive. Those lying, bargaining bitches will know it too, right before she slits their throats.

The chaos hasn't ended. It's only just begun.

Finally—finally—the man breaks away. 'Where are you going?' Freya flings up her arms, spinning on her heels in the pebbles. 'You—*ugh*.'

To think she once envied Freya. Watching through the branches, she lets her mouth curl. Freya was cunning, ruthless, and lacking in mercy once she made the choice to break out. Now, she's a rodent, scurrying along in a weak outsider's wake. She sacrifices. She worries. She cares.

Just like Anneliese. They'd all heard how much Anneliese had changed when she came to surrender to the Whispers: she was older, faded, human, dim.

It seemed like rumour. It sounded cruel. It hadn't felt real, but now, with Freya, she's been brutally forced to wake up.

When she does burst her banks, she'll be vigilant. She'll stay cunning, ruthless, and lacking in mercy, and she'll shake the outside to its bones.

'Need a piss,' the man says shortly. Her lips curve into her hunter's smile, the one that starts her heart. He's heading right for her, this solitary fisherman, with his solitary hut and his poor-folk boat.

Oh, come closer. Do come closer. She hones her hunter's vision and slips around the saplings, calculating where the fool will end up. No one sees her. No one hears her as she stops beneath a willow, weeping its way to the ground. Crunching over the stones of his beach, the man is far from her usual, but at least he *is* a man. If he were anything else, even a woman, this wouldn't work nearly as well.

On the edge of the trees a short way ahead, the dowdy fisherman stops. Unbuttons his britches, sighs, and brazenly lets rip.

Closer. Soundless, creeping, closer still. Leaves shy away from her. Twigs don't crack. In her mind, she appears like a spirit of the forest, bright eyes first before a small, sly smile. Kira and Freya's voices are hushed. She steps as close as she dares to the man. 'Hello.'

Buttoning his trousers, the man looks up. His lewd eyes widen and drop to her breasts. She flicks her tail from under her dress and feels her pulse crow. 'Goodbye.'

41

Hello, goodbye

Leon, or Jay as Kira calls him, is failing at skimming stones when he starts hearing thoughts. New thoughts; not Kira's or Freya's. Those he's used to and dials down to a hum, unless they hold thoughts of him. The vulgar man he tuned out at once; this set of thoughts is different.

Hello.

Leon's hand halts in mid-air, the flat stone ready to fly. The ripples of the last two have not yet sunk. A flash of the fisherman standing by the trees. A flash of a plan, of Kira, Freya, bloody red and vicious. Back to the present.

Goodbye.

With a gargling shout, Leon reels back. Blood. Silver. Glee and death. Dropping his stone, he scrabbles to his feet. Why? Why did he agree to stay back? He should have stood up to them. He should have said no, you need me, I refuse to hide. He should have been there with them, using the skills that neither of them have, listening for threats like this.

'Kira!' Scrambling up the riverbank, Leon trips into a jog. A jog, then a run, then a sprint. 'There's a huldra!'

⚡

'Kira!'

Fast feet thud on the earthy track. Kira looks round. Jay's voice is cracked, hoarse in the way of desperation. 'Jay?' She frowns. 'Has something—'

'Huldra!' Bellowing, Jay erupts onto the beach. Stones skid and spray, and he doubles over. 'Huldra, in the…the…'

'He's gone.' Freya's voice is a breaking branch. Slipping her bow down her arm, she reaches for an arrow. 'The man.' She jerks her chin toward the woods. She's already edges and lines.

Tensing from the inside out, Kira looks to the trees. The man was only peeing; she'd kept half a repulsed eye on him, suppressing the urge to punch his randy, patronising face. She didn't want him jumping them, in any sense, or greedily waddling off to tell someone where they were. She'd thought it paranoid, but without so much as a rustle of leaves, he's completely disappeared.

And Jay is crying huldra.

'You heard *what*?' Freya cries, to something he gasped. 'And you couldn't have told us sooner?'

As her lungs start to swell, Kira's mind starts to whir. A hidden someone following them. A huldra in the woods. Slowly stepping toward the trees, she unsheathes her knife. Her senses taper to a fine-edged point. There's something lying on the ground.

Kira's insides still. Her feet step closer. In the place of the fisherman lies a hat, the grey winter earflaps splayed on the earth. She grips the hilt of her knife with a metal-like grip. Erik's; it's Erik's. He was wearing it the other night when he found them in the clearing. When he set off back in the dark, alone.

'Freya.' The word is bottomless. Her mind feels muted, as though her brain has clicked the safety on. 'That'—she nods to the hat—'is Erik's.'

Freya's boots chink on the pebbles. Slowly, she crouches, one hand on the ground. 'Are you sure?' She turns over the bulky wool. 'Because if it is—'

'Oh, it is.' Too fast for Kira to react, Ingrid steps from the woods and grabs Freya by the hair. Her dress is the black of two in the morning, her hands a viscous red. 'It's a token of my appreciation, Kira.' Snatching the bow, she yanks Freya backward, pressing a dripping dagger to her neck. 'For leaving me behind.'

Ingrid's hand flicks. Blood blooms on Freya's skin, and Freya grits her teeth. 'Bitch.'

'Maybe.' Ingrid dips her head, her lips to Freya's neck. Just above the crimson line. She smiles. 'But you should have known that already. Did you think sneaking off would work? Maybe it would have, by anyone else, but oh, you're so easy to follow.' She looks up again, her smile a slash. Her dark disbelief is more mocking than real. 'You never heard me. You never saw me. Kira I can understand, but you?'

She shakes both her head and Freya's. Freya's face distorts into hatred and scorn and a flash of something deeper. Fear. 'Stop playing, Ingrid.'

'No.' Ingrid twists the tip of the dagger. Flinching, Freya grits her teeth. 'Thank you, Kira, for the bond we shared and for telling me all your losses.' She grins, a stretched, monstrous thing. 'I really thought this would be harder.'

'Run, Jay,' Kira says softly. It's not her mouth speaking, and it's not her seeing this. Any of this. 'We'll find you later.'

'Oh, so you can handle me all on your own?' Ingrid cocks her head. 'Cute. It won't work, though. I'll kill you all regardless. Just look at my second gift.' She glances deliberately into the trees. 'If you've ever wondered what makes up a stomach, now's your chance to find out.'

'Jay.' Kira flexes her fingers on the knife. She can neither see nor hear him, which means he isn't fleeing, and he has a history of getting involved when he shouldn't.

'Jay's not listening.' Ingrid flicks her dagger. In an eye blink, it's horizontal, at the base of Freya's throat.

Kira's heart slides over several beats. For a fluttering second, she's back in her house, watching Freya do the same to her friends.

'Fitting, no?' Ingrid's look is pointed. 'Are you sure you want her to survive?'

Freya's gaze meets Kira's and holds it. In it, there's a message. In it, there's a choice. Kira's eyes fly wide. 'Freya, no!'

Freya snaps her head back. Her skull knocks Ingrid hard in the cheek, and savage, she kicks at her shin. Grunting, Ingrid staggers.

The dagger in Ingrid's hand jerks. Inhaling sharply, Freya crumbles and drops to the beach with a *thunk*, blood dripping onto the pebbles.

Oh, God. Kira's mind swoons and rushes. She can't move. Can't think. *Oh, God, oh, God, oh—*

Throwing her hands to her head, Ingrid shrieks.

'Kira.' Jay is a whisper, and Kira swings her gaze toward him, all horror and weakness and wildness and bile. Glistening and clammy, he stands stock still. His eyes are bolted to Ingrid. 'I…'

In a queasy haze, Kira sees. Ingrid screams again, a raw yell ripping its slow, whetted course. Her nails pierce her scalp. Veins bulge in her forehead and burst in her bugging eyes.

Kira blurs. The girl from Al-Sanit. Jay killed her by accident, holding her mind. He'll do the same to Ingrid.

He's already doing it.

Kira blurs, whirling, whacked by terror. Freya lies dying. Jay is killing.

Skin splitting, Ingrid keens. Kira swivels. 'Stop!'

Jay wavers, set to faint. *Why?* He mouths. His lips are blue.

'Because.' Kira wheels around again. 'We're not killers. We're—'

With a strangled shout, Ingrid slumps. Cracking to her knees, she clasps her head. At Kira's back, something thuds.

Jay. Kira spins, so fast she's growing dizzy. His eyes are closed, and he sprawls, but he's breathing. She could faint herself.

'Bad choice.' Hands close around her throat. 'Hello, Kira. I'm stronger than I look.'

Ingrid squeezes. Eyes widening, Kira chokes. Everything roars, everything's bright, and then it rushes clear. She either fights or dies.

Gripping the huldra's wrists, Kira wrenches. Knife in her fingers, in the way, doesn't matter. Ingrid jolts off balance. Her scarred hands loosen. Kira twists.

One knee to the huldra's stomach. Ingrid folds, gasping. With one hand, Kira grabs her arm. With the other, she punches.

When she pulls her hand back, the dagger comes too.

At first, Kira stares. It felt like her fist, but the blade is scarlet, and Ingrid inhales, a spasm in her throat. Soft blood wells from the slice in her chest. Slowly, slowly, Kira lets go.

The huldra slips to the beach. Her head smacks the stones. One twitch, two. Ingrid's eyelids shiver. Red lips. A splashing cough that burbles.

Nothing.

Kira's legs give out. *No.* She drops the knife. Her eyes strain. Her mouth falls slack. *No, no, no. That wasn't…she didn't…*

Kira lifts a shuddering hand to her mouth. Scarlet.

She did.

With a wail, she topples back and scrabbles away. Ingrid isn't moving. *Oh, God, she's not moving.* Blood drips down her black dress, dribbling onto the beach. Staining. Tainting. Leaking from her torso, pooling with the spit that clings to her open mouth.

Open mouth, open eyes. She's dead.

Because you killed her.

Kira's shaking hands lift. They have to do something, scrape her scalp, or clutch her face, but they're red, still red, and she stares at them in horror. She wanted to knock Ingrid out and run. A huldra would only get so far before running out of places to hide; she'd be hard pushed to cross the river, and even if she managed to, the plains would stop her short. That was the plan.

Rushed, yes; optimistic, yes; naïve, maybe; but it didn't mean murder.

They're all murderers now. Blind and wild, Kira breathes too fast. Ingrid. Freya. Jay. Many veils of misty gauze divide her from her mind. This can't have happened. It can't be real. Three bodies lying here, bodies on a beach. Dead, alive, somewhere between. One torn up in the woods.

If you've ever wondered what makes up a stomach, now's your chance to find out.

Freya draws a haggard breath.

Kira's hazy attention drifts toward her. Tiny workers beat hammers, behind and over her eyes. 'Freya,' she murmurs. Her mouth has turned to sand. 'Are you…'

Swallowing the rest, she drags herself over. Bloody handprints mar the stones. Kneeling next to Freya, Kira dully blocks them out. The world is quiet, far too quiet. On the outside, there would be screaming and sirens. Murder on someone's property? Havoc. There shouldn't be silence barring breaths and the river, gushing loftily on.

'Ingrid.' Freya coughs, and a gauzy veil lifts.

Shaking, Kira blinks. Shaking, shaking, shaking all over. She binds herself to the here and now: red on Freya's pale skin, her chin, her neck, her chest. Her colour sick and grey, her lungs shallow flutters. Her hand twitches in Kira's direction. Freya stares away at nothing, nowhere. Not even space, just blankness. Death.

'What can I do?' Kira blurts through a sob. So much blood. *So much blood.* God, she can't stop shaking. 'How can I…I…you can't die. No.' She scrapes both hands through her hair. 'You—you can't. But I don't know what to do, there's no one here, and even if there was, they wouldn't…'

Her words croak to nothing. Looking up, her hair stuck to her lips, her breath skips. 'Hold on.' She scrabbles to her feet, ungainly. Her body's never been so ungainly, so stubbornly awkward to move. She shoots a look to Jay: out, but colourful. 'Stay awake.' She stumbles off. 'At least, stay alive. I'm—I'll find you something.'

The hut. The little, ramshackle hut. Bloody, she slaps the fisherman's door, clawing around it and in. The tiny workers are in her heart, and her heart is up in her throat. The man must have medicine, whatever form it takes. They should have thought of medicine before they left the huldra. Why did they not—

Shut up. Too late.

Inside the hut, for a second, she's thrown. It could be the house of a man on the outside: out on an island or a cliff by the sea or a cottage on the breeze-blown moors. Dark, a little desolate, dusty and neglected, sparse and weary and forlorn.

Kira blinks. Medicine; that's why she's here. The man was human, and humans break.

Jittery and dazed, Kira scans the lonely room. A meagre table, three-legged chairs, cupboards smoothed with age. She veers toward them, slams them open. They smell like must and mould.

Her heart hiccups. She wants to moan. Mother Hubbard, looking in the cupboard. It's not bare, not exactly, but extremely sparse, as sparse as the rest of the hut. So sparse that she's coming to the cloying conclusion that the house is not a home.

Everything is fishing. Apart from vaguely familiar supplies, there are basic cooking pots, a knife, a spoon, and not enough food to fill a cat. But he *must* have something, he *must*, he—

Does. In the middle cupboard, in a wooden box, engraved with an elegant version of the sketchy Whiteland tree. Kira tugs it toward her, fumbles the latch, and shakily tries again. There are creams that smell flowery, needles and thread. Bottles of oil, strips of material, pouches of herbs.

That'll do. Cradling the box, Kira runs from the hut.

'Freya.' She drops to her flimsy knees. The stones jar her bones, but she kicks past the pain; Freya's open eyes barely see. '*Freya*.'

No better words spring into her mind. When you're here, and you're clueless, willing someone to live, the lines from films don't come. *Stay with me. You're okay.* Futile. Kira squeezes Freya's hand. The fingers chill her. 'Freya, *please*.'

Minutely, Freya rolls her eyes to look at Kira. 'Mm.'

It takes such an effort. Hot tears clog her throat. 'Okay.' With a sniff, Kira opens the box. 'I have…I don't know. What helps wounds here?'

Panic heats her, chokes her, eats her. Jesus Christ, she sounds like a child. Back home, she could muddle through, but here, she's useless.

'Okay,' Kira whispers, to calm herself. Clear the blood. Look at the damage. 'I'll clean it up. I'll be quick. Okay.'

Grabbing a strip of material, she stumbles to the river and back. Freya's throat wasn't slit. Thank God. Okay. Just her collarbone or the skin beneath. Swallowing, Kira presses down with the blood-drenched, trembling rag. Do people usually die this fast?

Maybe Ingrid did something to the dagger. Keeping pressure on the wound, Kira rifles through the box. Marya's poultice healed her head at the speed of a Turkish march. There must be something like that in here, but if she gets it wrong…

Freya's chest barely lifts. Her eyelids droop. Kira wars with hyper, hysterical despair. The brown, smeary bottles are blank. Unreadable symbols pattern the jars, as useful as Greek, or less. Kira picks them up and puts them back. Either she goes on instinct, or Freya sighs away.

Or both.

Desperation flares. Callum's words drift back, from the olive tree: *it was weird, how careful and reckless you could be, somehow both at once.*

Kira shuts her eyes. 'I'm sorry, Freya.' Grabbing the biggest, emptiest bottle, she removes the plunking stopper, and upends it over the blood.

For a moment, nothing happens. Then, all at once, it does.

Freya's eyes bulge. Her body bucks. Her head juts off the ground.

Oh, no. Kira's breath speeds up and judders. Slowly, Freya's lips stretch. A low, animal groan becomes a moan and then a scream.

Kira stares in horror. 'Oh, no.' Seizing another strip of material, she daubs at the glassy, iron-scented oil. 'No, no, no, I'm sorry, Freya, I didn't think, I didn't know.'

Freya's wail catches and roughens to a roar. Reeling in her limbs, she tips onto her side, stony and shaking like a fit. Kira covers her mouth with her terrified hands. The world spins away from her. The tiny workers hammer, a wallop in her heart and her head and her lungs. Hugging her torso, Freya groans from her gut. Throaty. Inhuman. Kira feels like a storm. A cyclone. A hurricane. What has she—

'Idiot.'

Reaching for the medicine box, Kira freezes. The word was spat, forced through a moan, but Freya has started to laugh.

'What?' Warily, Kira sits back on her heels. Freya rolls over onto her back, relaxing her hands on her stomach. Her humour comes in coughs. 'What are you…' Kira flounders. '*What?*'

Like a man who's been dragged from the edge of a cliff, Freya shakes her ash-grey head. 'You're an idiot.' She shakes and shakes. The pebbles clink. A cough and a laugh, a laugh and a cough. 'You're an idiot, but you're not. Look.'

She flops her arms to either side. Dumbly, Kira stares. Up and down and back again, her mind just wants to fall.

'The cut.' Viciously coughing, Freya wipes her mouth. When her hand comes away, it trembles. 'You beautiful imbecile. Look at the cut.'

Dragging her eyes down, Kira looks. The scarlet gash is oily with liquid. Hissing, the edges bubble into a ragged, lumpy scar.

Kira's heart slows and thumps. 'It's healing.' Tears block her voice. 'But you—'

'Screamed like the fires of Urnäsch were on me?' With a grisly grimace, Freya nods. Her pasty face folds in on itself, in sweat-sheened, ghoulish lines. 'That's what it felt like.' She pushes her shuddering torso upright. 'In a less dramatic way, it still does. You doused it in what we dubbed Firewater. Original name, I know, but when it makes you scream like the fires of Urnäsch…oh.'

She wobbles. Kira snatches her arms before she can fall.

'Thanks.' Long and steady, Freya breathes. In, hold. Out, hold. 'For anointing me thusly as well, I suppose. No sane person would have chosen it first, but under the circum…*ah*.'

Pain shrivels Freya's face and curls her in. Holding her tight, pulling her closer, Kira shuts her eyes. Ludicrous, madness, hideous. Hell. In, hold. Out, hold. Next, the sky will fall.

'Jesus.' Freya's voice suddenly lurches. 'You killed Ingrid.'

42

The stars that arc

Grey trots ahead through the dry, scrubby valley. The two of them are silent.

Since Callum challenged him, this is mostly how it's been. The young man doesn't take well to lies, or economy with the truth, and seems to suffer from the same minor shellshock that blew into Mathew at the meeting of the worlds. A few days of mutual brooding, and their company is complete.

Really, it's just as well. Mathew could slip off the edge of the world.

'All right.' A sunset silhouette, abruptly, Callum stops. Hands in pockets, he turns around with the ready, steady face of someone who's been waiting to speak for a while. 'I can't walk in silence forever. You're spiralling.'

Mathew carries on after Grey. 'I'm not.'

'Oh, yes. You are.' Clapping his shoulder, Callum pulls him around. The young man looks exasperated. 'Every time I talk to you, you "hmm" or stare at nothing or mutter a one-word answer. I know I was pissed, but I stopped being pissed, and it totally passed you by.' He pauses, letting Mathew go. 'There's a difference between processing and never speaking again.'

One second. Two. Five. Shrugging slowly, Mathew moves past him. The land is monotonous, yellowed hills and rocky gorges, red with the setting sun. They have no idea where they're going.

'Oh, come *on*, man.' Callum's voice rockets up, grinding like an engine in a too-low gear. 'You're really still denying it. Really? You're just—you're proving my point, Mathew. Spit it out, punch something, I don't care. But if you don't stop acting like a zombie, one of these long, very dull days, you'll become one.'

Toneless, lifeless, Mathew laughs. It's automatic and holds no humour. 'You've grown profound. I'm impressed.'

Callum laughs too, a sarcastic bark. 'You met me once. Jesus, stop digressing. I'm trying to make sure you don't eat yourself alive.' Jogging up to Mathew, he throws out his arms. 'What is it? Specifically, please, instead of *everything*.' He rotates, waving around them, at the crimson shadows sinking to violet, creeping down the valley. At the sheer walls on either side, broken up by cracks. At the violent sunset, greying to the gloaming.

Evening shouldn't fall this fast. Mathew walks through it, his legs like lead. It shouldn't, but does it matter?

No. Possibly. Probably.

No. Mathew follows Grey, and Callum goes quiet, not even a huff by his side. The grainy gloaming deepens. Soon, too soon, it's early night, sucked of warmth and colour. All it leaves are angles. Mathew walks on.

Of course, Callum is probably right; his imagery and his point. All these thoughts, and his warring insides, are eating each other alive. Why is he here, is this real, is it possible? Is he being tugged along on a string? Are his family waiting for him at home? Should he give in to weakness, admit defeat, and stumble sobbing for the hills? Should he stumble on behind the wolf, full of self-loathing, for the weakness, the defeat, and all that writhes and roars?

Callum waits until the desert-clear dark is full before he tackles Mathew again. 'Okay.' Holding up a hand, he turns, and stops. 'We're done for the day. You're worrying me, and I do not like how quickly it's gotten dark.' He lowers his voice, as though the night can hear him. 'I think we should stop, eat, and sleep. There'll be a cave around here somewhere.'

Mathew doesn't walk past him but neither does he speak. Inside, Callum twinges with more than unease; in such a strange, inhuman land, apparently so removed from their own, Mathew's heavy, staring vacancy seems all the more human. He's a desperate father looking for his daughters, and whatever he says, he's spiralling. Fast.

'Mathew.' Pushing his hands into his pockets, Callum squints at the rocks. The shadows could be caves, or they could just be cracks. The night is too deep to tell. 'You'll never find Kira and Romy if you don't at least rest.' He turns to scan the other side. Shingle skids beneath him. 'Ow.' Wavering, he frowns at it. 'Here's a thought. Let's try asking Grey to find shelter, give him a good old chal—'

Callum's gut bends like rubber. With a gasp, he jackknives, clutching his middle, and then, the feeling is gone.

Mathew smacks to his knees and retches. Up the tilting path, Grey stops.

As weak as though he's had the flu, shuddering, Callum straightens. 'What the hell was that?' He croaks. His voice feels faint and far away. 'Not that I've much to go on, but I've never—'

The valley tilts. Callum sways. Callum opens his arms for balance, but again, the feeling is gone.

'Christ,' Mathew moans, reaching for his head. 'Me neither. Even drunk.' Mathew retches, heaves, and slowly, as if the rocky ground is thawing spring ice on a pond, pushes back to sit on his heels. '*Christ.*'

Breathing less than steadily, Callum offers a hand. 'Agreed. At least it woke you up, though.' Bracing his flu-like limbs, he helps Mathew to his feet. 'Have you got the torch? If this isn't justification for using it, I really don't know what is.'

Grey yips. Callum's eyes cut to him, the sound jolting through the silence. The flat silence. The stifled silence. The silence before a storm, where birds, beasts, and leaves on trees hold their breath and wait.

Callum finds himself doing the same. Watching. Waiting. Listening as his pulse stutters up. The air doesn't move. No night birds call.

Where the peak of the valley meets the sky, Grey starts to growl.

It hums through Callum from his mind to his toes, trailing ice in its wake. It's nothing the wolf has summoned up before: it's a quavering rumble, not a whine, or a yowl, but a mix of them all, and a threat.

'Mathew.' Callum drags his voice lower than a breath. 'How are we doing on the torch?'

Slowly, Grey lifts his snout. The whine, the growl, the yowl strangles into a howl, and Callum stiffens. It doesn't just hum through him; it echoes, a thing of being abandoned and fear of cold nights and hopelessness that feel like an abyss.

'Oh, my…' Mathew doesn't finish. Retrieving the torch, he bungles it on.

The valley tilts around them, and the sky explodes with stars.

Gravity. Consciousness. A yawning black hole. Nausea turns him upside down, and Callum hits the ground. Mathew drops on top of him, all elbows, torch, and hips. Grey's howls echo off the valley walls, howls and howls and howls.

'We...' Mathew tries. The word sounds like a vortex has sucked it from the air. 'Need to...'

Move. Get up, run, run and hide, but holy Christ, they can't. Mathew's torso crushes Callum's shins. Callum sticks to the stony earth, and his eyes stick to the sky.

Stars flicker in. Stars flicker out. Sparking, arcing, they trail to the ground, cresting the hills and sighing from sight. They fill the dark for a handful of seconds, a spectacle eerie with the frozen howl. They burst and flare. They sprinkle, sparkle. Silver-white, they're quiet in the night, until the final pinpricks dance to life, float to the ground, and die.

Grey's howl dies with them, sliced off clean. Callum's bondage loosens like the ropes were real, and slumping, blinking hard, he stands, hauling Mathew up. His tailbone smarts. His spine is stiff. The fall must have jarred his neck, unless the starburst held them for hours.

Crouching for the torch, Mathew clicks it on. Off. On. 'Nothing.' He slaps it against his palm. 'Damnit.'

Callum breathes through a thrill of dread. At the valley's peak, Grey is a shadow, icy shades and lines. His silence is worse than the howl. Callum shivers. The night is growing cold. 'I'm guessing you've not seen that before.' He risks a glance at Mathew, still battering the torch. It's good to see the man alive, but damn, they need a plan.

'No.' Looking around them, Mathew shoves the torch away. 'If it's over...'

'If it's over, we can walk beside the walls.' Callum grabs the plan with both hands, scanning the empty sky. Now, there are no stars at all. 'Find a cave the old-fashioned way, like running our fingers over rocks. Whatever. Whatever the fuck just happened, at least, you know, we're fine.'

Mathew's eyes drift to Grey. 'I'm not sure we are.'

Callum trails his gaze. The wolf's tail has sunk, the black tip dipping, inching between his legs. His hackles stand stark against the sky.

'All the more reason to get out of the open.' Pushing down a pulse of dread, Callum strides across the valley. The rocky walls are uneven, winding, filled with ledges and jutting edges; somewhere, they'll find a nook. It's worked before, albeit in the day. A hollow beneath a ledge would do or a narrow gap between spines.

Hell, at this point, anything would do. Callum inches sideways, a scrutinising crab. Shards crunch beneath his boots. Come on. Come on, come on.

Grey's hollow howl splits the air. Chilled out of his body and back, Callum whips around. Across the thin valley, Mathew does the same, tripping on a prickly bush. Grey's howl echoes on, wretched and desperate, one long, cold lament. He skitters backward down the track. He jerks his snout toward the sky and howls and howls and howls.

Fear wires through Callum's veins. It heats his cheeks and cools his chest, bloody in the howling. The wolf is a frenzy, snarling and yelling, claws catching the stones. Do they run?

Framed against the sky, two silhouettes move. Callum's fear becomes a blaze. His muscles lose mass, and he staggers, thumping back against the rock. Cresting the hill from the direction of the stars, darkness slides from the shapes in sheets. Somehow, they're blacker than the night.

Until they start to stride, and he sees what they are. Callum's breath holds itself. A woman in silver-blue and a wolf, a wolf still blacker than the shadows. The shadows themselves wick out of its path. Dwarfing Grey, it almost dwarfs Callum, giant but sinuous, coarse but lithe. A spindly leash spills from the woman's hand. Together, they approach.

Half of Callum quails. The other half tenses his weak-willed muscles, poising him for flight. The woman walks with an upright spine, her limbs like willow, her dress like wind, catching on moonlight skin. Her braid trails the shingles behind her. Shaded eyes command hollow cheeks. Darkness billows from her ankles, and through her, Callum sees skies and galaxies, a dusted veil of stars.

Grey's howl pitches, piercing Callum's ears. His mind is both too fast and slow, like caffeine when you're exhausted. Does the woman know they're here? She must. Callum's eyes dart everywhere. Do they wait her out? Run? Grey stands his ground, his ears flattened back. Mathew is retreating, edging down the valley, beckoning for Callum to follow.

'Callum!' His arms gesture urgently. Callum just stares. His limbs have forgotten how to move. 'For Christ's sake!'

But something's saying not to. Something's saying *stop*. Something's holding Callum flush against the wall while the woman and the wolf draw close.

'Move, Callum!' Mathew shouts, slewing down the slope. Callum's fever gaze flicks to him. 'I don't think she'll be…*ah*!'

The word rebounds, and flies back into his lungs. Mathew's eyes turn manic. His mouth falls slack. His stumbling body lurches, stopping by a weather-bleached tree. The woman and her wolf stride on.

But something. The air shifts, honing, sharp, like winter skies giving in to snow. The smoky darkness arcs past Callum, and with a dizzying rush that swallows him whole, he realises where it's going. Mathew.

Callum's gut grows as giddy as his head. Mathew shouted. He drew attention to himself. Maybe if he hadn't, the woman and her wolf would have swept down the valley, and…

The darkness reaches Grey. The wolf crumples with a whine.

Oh, Christ. Mathew stands frozen, more corpse-like than ever, as the woman follows the wispy dark and strides down the path. From the back, she's not just stars but the cosmos.

A woman with stars in her back. A woman with stars in her back and a wolf and shadows that live and breathe. It's insane.

The insanity shakes Callum free. Mathew. He has to get to Mathew, and then they have to run.

Scalded by fear, Callum shoves off the wall. The woman is metres from Mathew now, her wolf loping lazy and aloof. Ten feet. Barrelling over the path, Callum skirts them, skidding on ruptured dirt and stubborn, grassy knots. Six feet. Five feet. Four.

He slams into Mathew with the force of a landslide and ricochets into the wall. His skull cracks. He bursts with pain, sliding down the rock to the ground. Mathew doesn't waver, a pillar or a tree. The empty darkness clouds his feet, a void that makes Callum feel ill. Breathing through the pain, he blinks his own void away and claws back up the wall. With shivering flanks, Grey lies limp. Two feet.

One. On a breath of wind, the woman stops.

At once, Mathew straightens and lightens into grace. Lifting his chin, he relaxes his shoulders. Something drops away from him, a shade of a shroud, and in silence, he walks toward her.

'Hey!' Too late, too stunned, Callum lunges. His fingers slide off Mathew's arm like water over glass. 'What the hell are you doing?'

He grabs for Mathew's shoulder, but he's less use than rain. The man steps past the black-hole wolf, up to the woman…and in.

The air beats once, like giant wings. It throbs through Callum's head and sickens.

The woman lifts her arms. She's melded her skin with Mathew's, a shadow of stars in a shimmering form, and although he should be doing something, tearing the man away, or *something*, the unreality of this rips Callum's resolve to shreds. In a horrifying way, it's beautiful.

In a beautiful way, Mathew's outline bleeds. His blurring edges drift from his body, tailing off through nebulae and seeping into the woman. Her spectral skin glows. The scale-like swathes of her dress are pearlescent, rainbows pale beside the wolf. Tilting its snout, the wolf howls in silence. Callum feels like he's caught a dream.

Callum stares. This can't—no. It's impossible, mad. How can a man be dissolving into shadows, to dust and threads of light? How can he blend with an apparition? Uncertain, Callum steps forward. An apparition, who's becoming human. Her stars fade. She lowers her arms.

Mathew disappears.

No.

Callum stares at the woman with fear in his throat. Corporeal, she watches him, impassive and infused with light, more human than ghost but more ghost than not. Normally, she'd be stunning. She'd leave men and woman awestruck in a way that would grasp their minds forever.

Callum's fear mounts to bloody-hell terror. Grey's not moving. Mathew's gone. The woman's wolf howls, and from far, far away, it starts to make a sound.

The woman smiles. Callum doesn't move. Pinioned by his terror, he couldn't if he tried. The howl echoes around them, settling in his bones, in his stomach. In his mind, forever.

The woman's smile wisps away, and then her lips are moving. The whisper travels skies and worlds and galaxies and reaches him softly. *We're sorry.*

The wolf's howl fades back to the dark. Leash in hand, as sad as loss, the woman looks past him and strides into night.

Callum doesn't turn to watch. Silvered where she stood is the sketch of a man.

The sketch, the outline, the shifts and blurs. He wouldn't call it ghostly; it's more of a sheen, heavy sprays of rain and the forms seen through it. For a brief moment, it takes shape.

Callum's heart catches. 'Mathew?' he manages, tripping forward. His feet are boulders. It was Mathew, it was. Mathew, in his odd clothes, with his coat around his waist. 'Are you…' he fumbles, 'here?'

A soft noise whines from Grey's still form. Callum glances at him.

'Yes.'

Callum looks back to Mathew with a start. He's as real as he should be, as if he never paled. No shimmering, no shifting. No misted hints of space.

'You were…' Callum peers through the warming night. No silvered outline; nothing. 'You know what?' Lifting his hands, he starts toward Grey. 'Never mind. If you're okay, that's fine. I'd say count our lucky stars'—the woman flits through his mind. Uneasily, he elbows her away—'and escape. What happened to you?'

He squats beside Grey. Mathew joins him, on the snuffling, twitching wolf's other side. As far as he can tell, Grey's breathing is normal, or what passes as normal for a human.

And when he wakes?

Quickly, Callum sits back. Those stern yellow eyes could open any time, and after being floored by an unearthly shade, the wolf isn't likely to assume that the first faces he sees will be friends.

As if thinking the same, Mathew stands. 'What happened to me?' He shakes his head, retreating to a smooth, flat stone. 'I don't know.'

'No.' Callum jumps in at once. 'No, there's no way you're giving me that.' His face puckers, and twists, into God knows what as he watches Grey start to stretch. He could be any other dog waking up. 'I just had to watch you vanish, so again: what the hell happened?'

Mathew doesn't so much frown as look slightly more confused. 'I suppose'—he glances up at a moth, fluttering past his head—'the woman made me stop, and then she made me start. Then she was gone, and you were in front of me, asking if I was here.' He watches the moth as it flits away, pursued by a bat. 'Did you see where she went?'

Toothy and cavernous, Grey yawns. Wriggling up to his haunches, the wolf shakes himself to his feet.

'No.' Pushing on his knees, Callum straightens. His face sets, so rigid it hurts. Something's not right. If this had happened to him, he wouldn't be sat there, quietly watching a bug. 'I didn't.'

Eyeing Mathew, Grey yips. It sounds a lot like *let's go*.

'I agree.' Nodding, Callum follows the wolf as he trots off up the valley. Right now, nothing seems more ideal than hurrying away. Tightly, he swallows. His mouth tastes odd. The silver man won't leave his mind.

'So the woman just vanished?' Mathew's heavy footfalls crunch behind him in the dirt. 'And the wolf?'

'Yep.' Callum loads his voice with a curt, healthy dose of *case closed*. 'I don't know where she went. I was busy making sure she hadn't turned you to stone or a second ginormous wolf.' Hands on thighs, he propels himself toward the top of the track. 'Frankly, I don't give a shit where she went, as long as she's not coming back. Whoa.'

At the valley's peak, Callum sways to a stop. The land has changed its face.

Vibrant moorland rolls away. Thick, grassy, bolshy hills, jumbled with bracken, dotted with purple heather, and sprinkled with yellow gorse. Different shades of stumpy bushes, slanting down to stumpy trees. A short line of standing stones perches in the distance, an indigo sky of stars winking overhead. Nearer curves a creek, winding off into hedgerows. Two misshapen lakes glint dark beneath a hillock. It's peaceful. It's wild. It's *known*.

A breeze flurries around his legs. Callum fights the urge to open his arms and let it beat him clean. The air is fresh and tart and perfumed. A hint of coconut. Something sweet. Compared to the harsh, arid valleys, this land holds a promise that calls them on.

'Oh, wow.' Catching up, Mathew stops, breathing hard. The breeze gets up to bluster. Callum's hair whips his face. As much as it may be an over-romantic, over-sentimental cliché, with all of this below them, they could be on top of the world.

'It's a change,' Callum calls above the wind, but there's more than that in Mathew.

Not the vacancy of the last few days or the drifting of the last few minutes; it's a sweeping energy charged by the night, by the gusting, electric air. He looks as though he's returned to life and possibly gone beyond. 'It's not so much that.' Mathew squints across the moor. Callum lifts an eyebrow, but it's false and wrong. 'It's more that this is home. It's so much like the outside.' He rubs a hand down his face, pausing at his chin. 'Exmoor or Dartmoor. We don't live far from Dartmoor.' Mathew sniffs hard, against the wind, and then he looks away. 'When your memory's back, you'll see what I mean.'

A shadow of his desolation returns. Callum can't blame him: a wandering journey in search of a mind sounds absurd, even to him. For a man who actually remembers his life, it must be preposterous. Impossible. Pain.

'We'll walk until it's light.' Drawing his pieces together, Mathew sets off after Grey. The wolf is grey and shaded, heading down the dirt path, a ghost on the night-struck moors. 'After what just happened, I'd prefer to keep moving.'

Even if he wasn't awake and electric, Callum wouldn't want to argue. He doesn't want to blink, let alone fall asleep, lest the woman comes back or worse.

Quicker than before, they keep pace with Grey. The wolf regards them with amusement, or approval, and trailing the dirt path down to the creek, they wind through the cool, heady night.

In the low, early morning mists, Mathew disappears.

43

All the time she waits

Carol's reasons for why she didn't think of this don't sound like reasons at all. They felt justified when she first worked through them, but now they're excuses or fibs.

One: the mess was ongoing. It threw them all out of rational whack, and the endgame was masked by death.

Two: even the Whispers were ignorant as to what was going on. No one could know it would get so big or so wildly out of control.

Three: it happened too fast to process.

Four: Carol was blind to the Urnäsch plan. She would never, ever, ever have thought that anyone, especially not her son, would dream up something so drastic. She would never have thought that she herself could drastically respond.

Five: the ongoing mess was also ballooning. She wouldn't have thought they could temper it, let alone tamp it down. Confidence in that regard was Clemence's domain.

Six: maybe if he hadn't piped up, it would never have occurred to anyone.

The list is self-gratifying and weak. Carol taps her restless fingers on the table, a habit of Callum's that drives her mad. She's done what she can to contact people; it's the waiting around that bites.

Oksana spoke eventually. She still resents the stir they caused but agreed to find Khalid. Who knows how easy that will be when he travels Morocco nomadically, but it's something. Clemence got hold of Beth, and now they have three out of four in London. The fourth is unlikely to come around; she's at odds with the whole idea of having to stay, having to play, and having to live as a watcher.

Carol can't blame her. Drumming on the table, she waits and waits and waits. At some point, Clemence will link them together, if Morocco and Australia agree. It feels like a global business deal, the types she has to manage when she temps at Nestlé. It drives her as mad as Callum's fidgeting, the navigation of the corporate world. They're blind to how the real world works, or that there's more than one.

But needs must. She's supposed to temp again in a week, maternity cover for ICOS. That whole sphere feels alien and very far away.

Refresh the tablet. Stare at her mail. Refresh. Stare. Sip tea, make more. Refresh. Tap on the table.

There. Her heart bounds up to her throat and sticks. She opens the message from Clemence at once.

Names, emails, locations, numbers. Ned, Jannali: Kosciusko, Australia. Carol: Lally, Switzerland. Clemence: Shetland, Scotland. Sabine, Khalid: Essaouira, Morocco. Oksana: Cavtat, Croatia. Beth, Nayab, Will: London, England.

This is it, Clemence says. *None of us is useful enough to know more. Apparently the Banff rangers manage things there but damned if we can get through. Otherwise, it's rumours of the Taiga and Peru. Bloody stupid not to have a way of being linked.* He leaves white space, and his scorn is glaring. *Now someone else can take over.*

Thank God. It's a knee-jerk thought, and Carol hardly feels bad. With correspondence came belligerence, and despite him stepping in to help her out, she'd like him to fall into the sea. At night. When the lighthouse keeper's having a snooze and the lamp for boats is dark.

Carol almost, almost smiles. It stirs, but stops at her breastbone before its feathers can lift.

Reply all. Quickly, she taps, before anyone else can step in to take the baton. It's her mess. It started here. She might have failed her sons before, but no way is she failing them now.

44

Spark.

Jay and Freya stick out their arms. Her look holds danger in every angle, but he grins, and says, 'Kelpie.'

'Keep doing that,' Freya snaps, 'and I'll skin you.' Returning her attention to Kira, hovering beside the squelching field, she waves a hand and concedes. 'But he's right. There could be a kelpie.'

Kira blinks. It feels like she's fighting through fog, although the dusk is no more than bruise bellied, overcast. 'Surely you can't be serious.' She makes to continue alongside the path, opposite farmland trees. The rutted, muddy ground is too narrow for three abreast, but Freya and Jay fling out their arms, in almost perfect time.

'Stop it, you…' gritting her teeth, Freya shuts her eyes and breathes. 'Never mind. Kira, I'm serious. We're near a marsh, and marshes have kelpies. Kelpies are—'

'I know what kelpies are.' Hoisting up her satchel, Kira shoulders past them, walking ahead alone. 'The same way you know about witches in hats. *Harry Potter*.'

Her eyes slide to the furrowed field, glistening with rain. Kelpies are probably a hundred times worse here, shrouded in mist and haunting light as they lure you out to drown. They're probably seductive in some crooked way. They'd probably eat you for breakfast and pick their teeth while your bones still breathe.

Either way, Kira won't chance it. And if she tramps on ahead, she can brood on her own.

'I promise you, Jay,' Freya starts in again, 'you will definitely come to some harm.'

As the rain-fresh farm path winds on, Kira tunes the two of them out. What began as an effort to lift her mood has become Jay's way to pass time. He loves it all the more when Freya gets annoyed.

On a surface level, it's funny. On a not-so-surface level, Kira's back on the beach with Ingrid, punching with more than a fist. She was on the beach when Jay woke up, fragile, weak, but mobile. She was on the beach when they left through the woods. She was on the beach when they joined a gaggle of misfits and sailed up the Zaino, such a short time after Ingrid attacked that she spent it numbed in a blur. She was there when they docked in the meadowlands, asked for Ayomi, and struck out alone. She's back there every time she sees Freya's angry scar.

'I'm scouting.' Freya barges past so abruptly Kira jumps. Dropping her satchel, she walks into a leafy copse and away. 'Take that.'

Taking "that" to mean the bag, Kira loops it over her shoulder.

Hands in his pockets, Jay steps up beside her. 'She's going hunting,' he explains. 'Because I'm driving her mad. But it's too good a game to stop.'

They forge their own way through the tepid copse. A nightingale sings, a tad too early. Kira pushes her humid hair from her face. The rain cooled nothing down.

'I'm sorry,' Jay says.

Mistily, crossing a gurgling brook, Kira looks a question at him.

Around the bend, Freya curses. Mud squelches. Leaves drip. Jay takes a breath, his eyes on the path. 'I'm sorry I'm not helping.'

His voice is small and childlike. Through her fog, Kira pangs. 'I don't…' her mouth winces. She tilts her head a millimetre. 'I don't think anything would. Not yet.' She breathes out, long and rushing. It sounds tired, even to her. 'I need to…'

She trails off. What? She needs to what?

'Deal with the fact that you've killed someone.' It's so matter-of-fact that Kira looks round. Jay's expression is so even. So Callum. There's no emphasis on "kill," as there is in her mind, a big red slash with klaxons. 'So do I.'

Kira opens her mouth and shuts it. Shrouded in her mist like the possible kelpie, she'd forgotten what he did in Al-Sanit. What he tried to do to Ingrid.

Dropping her eyes to the mud, Kira heats with shame. 'Now I should be sorry.' It makes it worse that he'll know she forgot. 'I—I don't have an excuse, other than guilt and self-pity. People tell me I wallow too much.'

Kira stretches her lips, a glum, wry thing, and looks out toward the fields. Drystone walls, hedgerows. Clusters of cottages, pinpricked lights, wildflowers, and sheep. Tunnels of trees that bow their heads, leaning in like lovers. In the distance, squat-looking, small-looking cows.

Twisting her fingers in her shirtsleeves, Kira blows out her cheeks. 'I don't—' her voice blurts out on its own. 'I don't know how you do it. You're amusing yourself by annoying Freya, you're as chirpy as ever, which is far chirpier than b*efore* you lost your memory, but you…' she twists her sleeves tighter. The words battle with her teeth, warring to stay inside. 'You killed someone. How do you do that? My sister's been the same, but everything gets to me. Everything, whether or not it's mine to feel bad for. Now that I genuinely have something to feel horrific about, and I…' Her throat closes. Ducking her head, she breathes through her mouth, anything to not sound like there are tears snorting in the wings. 'I feel'—she sniffs at her chest—'like I'm drowning. It's crazily heavy, and it's wrapped itself around me, and it makes me want to scream or curl up in a ball or both at once, until I just can't breathe.'

Kira grips her sleeves so hard it makes her finger joints hurt. This isn't the kind of thing to unload and certainly not to a twelve-year-old. It's the kind of thing she keeps inside and swallows until it dies.

'Don't be patronising or dumb.' Jay levels both at her with the same accusation. 'I'm not a little boy.'

Kira's shame flares hotter. God, if she could just burn or drown. 'I know. I'm—'

'Maybe now,' Jay lifts his voice over hers, 'you're the child. You think you're fine locking everything up, but I know you're not. That no one is. While you've been staring into space, I've been talking.'

Kira blinks again. For so few words, he dropped a startling amount of uneasy truth. 'Um. Talking to who?'

Jay tilts his head, lifts his eyebrows, and dulls his preteen gaze: *don't be dumb*.

Kira brushes aside a spiderweb. 'Freya?'

Jay shrugs. 'Not specifically, but she's the one who listened. She's talked to me as well. Did you know the huldra asked her to stay? They wanted her to help them travel for a cure, seeing as how she's human.'

Kira watches a cow lumber after its calf. What's the response to this? She's too full of fog. 'Why'd she say no?' she asks. 'Or did she say yes?'

Lighting up with mischief, Jay grins. His head bobs, side to side. 'You'd know if you'd been listening.'

Kira opens her mouth, but nothing comes out. Clearing her throat, she sighs. She drops her eyes. 'Point taken.'

'Good.' Glancing at Freya's bag, and ahead to Freya, Jay rubs his slender stomach. 'I'm hungry. Do you think'—he watches Freya vault a wall—'she'll notice if we steal her food?'

'She will.' Lifting her voice, Freya pivots in the field, crooking her finger at them. 'Speed up. It's getting dark too fast.'

Kira drags her eyes to the sky. 'It is?' The twilight has sunk to a cloudy night, the violet-blue horizon streaking away the day. 'I thought that was relatively normal.'

'Eh.' Freya moves her hand from side to side. 'It is if something's wrong. It might affect us, or it might not, but I refuse to meet my makers in a field.' She claps her hands. 'Quick-march.'

Disquiet slinks through Kira as she straddles the wall, slipping over the slick, thick stones.

'Oh-ho!' Jay lands with a squish in the tufty grass. 'If something's wrong, will you let us approach a house? People? A *bed*? Wow.' He's a bouncy mix of sarcastic and eager. 'The danger must be real.'

Readjusting the satchels, Kira glances at Freya, marching across the field. The mist. The Kyo. The Monte Yuno devils. The fossegrim, and, uncomfortably, the alluring ellemaend. 'If Freya's worried,' she says, speeding up, 'then the danger's very real.'

It's much the same as her dad and Romy; if he worried, then something was wrong.

'Okay.' Jay rubs his hands together. 'But are we going to the village? The people? The inside and the beds?' He waves a dirty hand at the cluster of cottages. Snug between two hills, were they snowbound, they'd be an old English postcard. Gingerbread houses, holly and ivy, cherubic kids at Christmas.

'Yes.' Freya flashes her eyebrows. 'Although it doesn't exactly fill me with joy.' Her fingers stray to the end of her bow, brush it, and move away. 'If I'm wrong, at least we can sleep in a barn. If I'm right, well. We don't die.'

That doesn't exactly spark joy either. Kira sweeps the land in a single look. A watchful look, an unwilling look. A peering-round-corners-don't-let-there-be-a-ghost look. Copses. Rutted paths. Fields with crops and fields without.

Twilight shading humpbacked fells. She kneads her sleeves between her fingers. During the day, there were woodpigeons, blackbirds, or facsimiles, but the dark sinks in silence. No more nightingales. No owls. No soft wind, no rustlings, no small night hunters, slinking out of sight. Kira's senses suddenly sharpen. There's nothing.

'What's around here?' she murmurs to Freya. Her voice is a ripple masking a riptide. 'Ambush-wise?'

Freya vaults another wall. 'Nothing, really.' Her boots hit the path with a *thump*. The perplexed hint of doubt in her tone draws Kira's shoulders up. 'That's why there are so many people. Without the Chlause, it's usually pretty safe. The kelpie's easily avoided. The Ellevolket are sunset people and maybe sunrise. I'm not sure, but either way, most of these'—she indicates the trees—'are either chestnut or oak.'

Kira climbs the wall beside Jay. 'So why are we heading to a village?'

Freya toes a conker the size of a tennis ball and tightens her mouth at the night. 'Because I'm not an authority. There could be any—'

Her eyes bulge out. Her cheeks puff, as if she's going to vomit, and she claps her hands to her stomach.

Kira chills and recoils on instinct. 'Freya?'

A jolt of electricity spears her in the neck. Kira flinches, inhaling, her hand flying up. The skin of her neck is hot. 'Wh—'

A second jolt slaps her skull like a headrush. Her legs fold, and she hits the ground, gasping into the dirt. Her mind buzzes red and black. Pain in her tongue, blood in her mouth. Her head too heavy, shocked by a socket—

Then it stops. Kira's eyes spark. Sweat breaks out in hot little pricks. She's sprawled on her forearms, breathing hard, nails digging down to the quick in the earth. The blood slams her temples, trying to get out.

Slowly, shuddering, Kira looks up. Through the curtained hair in front of her face, she sees Freya, towing Jay to his feet. Behind the clouds, light explodes.

'Yeah, now we *really* need to go.' Freya wraps an arm around Jay. 'Can you walk?' Her eyes meet Kira's, hummingbird-fast. 'You can. You're going to have to.'

Fixing on the dirt, breathing deep, Kira clings to the straps of the satchels and heaves her legs up. 'What—' she sways, in a genuine head rush. 'Whoa. What just happened? It...' Vigorous and giddy, hot and drunk, she blinks the fizzing black away. 'It didn't get you.'

'Not properly.' Glancing one-two-three between Kira, the path, and the star-split sky, Freya flickers with the look she wore when Ingrid held a knife to her throat. 'That's how I know we're screwed.'

She hauls Jay's reeling form away along the path. Her mouth bitter with blood, Kira staggers after them. 'What?' She catches weakly up. 'Screwed by what?'

'Ørenna.' Freya shakes her head, again, again. Around the edges, her face is clammy, her eyes rimmed with red. 'I didn't even *think* about her. In Atikur, we don't have to. Not along the Zaino either.'

Blurry, Kira squints at the outskirts of the village. Her head swoons. So close. 'Who?'

'The Night Hunter.' Freya lugs Jay toward a splintered gate. Beyond lies a paddock of restless cows, an odd-looking well, a barn. 'Probably. Actually, no.' Unlatching the gate, she hustles Jay through. 'I'll go with definitely.'

She holds the gate for Kira. Kira's legs tremble as she drives them through, but she can make it before she collapses. She can.

The sky's too black. The air is cooling. Kira stumbles through the tan, harrumphing cows. Another gate. A close-cropped field. Ahead, the barn door groans. A waft of straw and dung drifts out, farmyard beasts and feed. It's welcoming, familiar. Safe.

Blundering inside, she leans against the wall, slides down the wood, and fights the urge to faint. Safe.

The door scrapes closed again. Darkness settles soft. She shuts her eyes.

Safe.

'When you can,' Freya murmurs, 'find the lightstone.'

Kira blinks herself focused, awake. Dragging the satchel straps over her head, she crosses her cumbersome legs and rummages. With the blocking of the night, her headache fades, as does the frail nausea in her gut. 'The Night Hunter'—she retrieves the stone—'doesn't sound like too much fun.'

Freya laughs the laugh of the newly-out-of-danger. 'Yes. Well'—she lifts a hand and drops it—'I'd have told you about her, but she wasn't relevant.'

Kira snorts.

Something snorts back.

Boomeranging with cold, she looks up. All she can hear is their breathing. That, and the sighing peace of slumbering horses that fill the space. 'Oh. Right. Okay.'

As the lightstone spills its amber-rose, the glow lights up the barn. Tethered to wooden stakes, the horses ignore their lodgers, barring the bay that snorts near Jay.

'What'—Jay yawns a colossal yawn, and sleepily smacks his lips—'did you expect?' Sliding down to slump in the hay, he rests his head on the wall. 'Mm. Time to sleep.'

Kira huffs. Freya flaps a hand at him. 'Go ahead. We'll be here till morning.'

Jay wriggles himself comfortable. Kira's eyes wander back to the lightstone, like a moth to a gentle flame. They could be making camp; squatting on dry plains rather than straw, surrounded by their hobbled mounts. The smell of beast. The sound of sleep. Keeping watch for bandits in the old Wild West, crowding around a fire.

'You know.' Freya's voice is softer than Kira's ever heard it. 'I've never seen horses before.'

Kira rolls her tired head along the wall toward her. Freya stares at the rafters. Her face is hard to read. 'Really? Never?'

Slowly, slowly, Freya nods. 'Mm-hmm.' The corner of her mouth curves. 'Of all the things, right?'

Kira smiles, a tiny, private smile. 'I guess you wouldn't if you never left the forest.' She yawns, covering her mouth with her hand. The sleeping horses are lulling. 'You're right, though. Of all the things. You know about kelpies and the Night Hunter and the mythical Moroaica.'

'Which we never want to see.'

'Which we never want to see.' Kira gives a drowsy nod. 'You know about all of that, and you were supernatural yourself, but this is the first time you've seen something as natural as horses.'

Freya's laugh is more of a "huh" than a "ha." 'As you so called it, welcome to paradise. Supernatural doesn't mean much.'

A breathy snore drifts through the barn. Kira glances round. Mouth open, head against the stall, Jay sits fast asleep.

'Look.' Freya's voice holds a dry *how cute*. 'We've worn our baby out.'

Kira yawns and laughs, and it all mixes up into one big stretch. 'I'm not sure that's good.'

'Ah, we should be fine.' Sticking a hand into Kira's satchel, Freya tosses her a waterskin and tugs out a pouch. 'It's better that he sleeps.' She tilts her head thoughtfully, watching Jay snore. 'And now I know what parenting's like.'

She fills her mouth with roasted nuts. Kira pulls her chin down, lifts her eyebrows, and blinks at Freya. 'You've wondered?'

Holding out the pouch, Freya pauses. 'No.' Shrugging, she carries on crunching nuts. 'Unsatisfying food source?'

'No, thanks.' Kira digs around in her satchel. 'I'm really gunning for that weird bread.'

After several mouthfuls—spongy and briny and fairly like seaweed, it really is weird—she swallows. 'Do I want to know who, or what, we just ran from?'

'No.' Freya beckons for the hunk of bread. 'But I'm a lovely, lovely person, and I'll tell you anyway.'

45

And so he shimmers

'Mathew?'

They were weary, walking slowly, not really speaking, heads bowed through the clammy mist that clung to their waists. Callum had entered a type of daze, the kind where you plod like an automaton while your brain succumbs to exhaustion. Birds began to peep. Grey slunk off, presumably to hunt. On and on they walked.

Dawn crept in in pale hues, softly over the hills. The pastel mist muted the colour. Callum only noticed when the sun began to rise, and a bright beam struck him in the eye. It startled him back from robot to human.

That's when he noticed that Mathew was gone.

'Mathew!' he shouts, turning in a circle, scraping both hands across his head. How do you not notice when the man beside you vanishes? *How?* 'Jesus, Mathew. If you're back in your existential crisis and have curled up in a cave…'

It's not true. He knows it like he knows his name isn't Peder, a solid truth tied to his self. It's not true, and it's dramatic and insensitive, but hell, if he accepts it.

The night before slams back into his mind. Callum fists his hands in his hair and pulls. It hurts. Good. The pain means he's here, he's real. '*Mathew!*'

His voice falls flat. No echo, no answer. He grips the stile, staring around, putting his weight on the wood. He'd been about to climb it when he realised they weren't walking in single file.

Callum was alone. Fields, fields, trees, fields, picturesque in the early sun. Pretty rivers, hedgerows, hefty stone walls. The noise of animals, the noise of a bell. Cheeping baby birds. The mist lifted a while back into patchy, woollen clouds, so he can see all there is, all around.

And all there is, all around, is nothing.

'God*damnit*.' Slapping the stile, Callum turns away. What happened? Does the woman have a daytime counterpart, come to finish her night buddy's work? He saw Mathew's dusted outline before the man reappeared. Was he meant to vanish completely, and it took until now to work?

Shit. Shit, shit, shit. Climbing the fields, Callum climbs the stile, as if two feet will help him see. The milk has been well and truly spilled. Does he try and find Mathew? Assume he's been taken as the star woman's lover and is hopelessly gone for good? This was Mathew's course, Mathew's quest. Without Mathew, what does he *do?*

Callum sinks down to the dew-damp wall. The moisture seeps through his trousers. He could wander around, seek out people, try to discover what happened with the woman. He could, but then he runs the risk of a repeat of Bacaire. Strangers don't like him.

And he doesn't trust strangers. Callum stands again, scans the land again. Fields. Hills. Fluffy clouds. Seeing if Grey comes back might be better; they could carry on, to the other disturbances. If Mathew *is* gone for good, his daughters are the only links that Callum has to home.

That's assuming Grey comes back. If not, more milk spills, and he's well and truly f—

A yip. Sharply, Callum swivels, following the sound. He knows that yip. He knows it well.

The yip comes again. Callum shades his eyes. Loping down towards him, past dark, bushy trees, rusty, scattered brambles, and two stupid rabbits, is Grey.

Grey and someone else. Emerging from the shelterbelt, half a field behind, is a person. Mathew?

Callum's hope sparks and snuffs out. No, not Mathew. He drops his hand. It's either a woman or a long-haired man, which is really, truly great. The last time a woman found him, he wound up in a cell.

Listlessly, he watches as Grey lopes on. Over a wall. Startle a rabbit that actually understands peril. Yip. Lope. Through the last field.

The wolf has almost reached him when the woman calls. 'Callum?'

She left them sleeping in the barn. If a farmer finds them before she returns, at least they don't look dangerous; and if someone believes them a danger, well, they both know how to kill.

What a thought. Freya's lip crooks up, though she doesn't feel the fun. A trio of mismatched murderers, roaming the happy, shiny meadows. Oh, how she never thought she'd end up here.

Provider for outsiders! Freya's mind waves a flag. She should teach Kira how to hunt. She means to, but every time they need something, she frankly can't be bothered. She's been here twenty-five years; an outsider, used to safe little houses and shops of muck, won't learn very fast.

Also, it's an excuse to go out on her own. Which, after a restless night of animal smells, two snorers, and the horses' disconcerting size as they shifted in their stalls, is welcome. Beyond welcome. Freya washed in a stream that tumbled over rocks and made a note to drag Jay there later—unlucky for her and Kira, he's at the age where everything smells—and now she prowls the roaring, rolling fields.

At least Kira's unwound. When they first reached the huldra, she cringed at the thought of no privacy. *Oh, I have hairs on my legs!* Yes, Kira, don't we all. *Oh, I have all of my body parts!* Yes, Kira, don't we all.

A scurrying catches Freya's eye. Scampering around a rocky bluff are two, three stoats. Two tiny, one large. Dipping to a crouch, Freya smiles, wicked-soft. Perfect; the cuter the better, for the squeamish in their trio. She probably should get over taunting Kira, but why? It makes life less maudlin.

It also reminds her, a very good thing these days, that she hasn't lost all herself. She's caught herself slipping up and starting to open up. What's worse, she's caught herself not caring.

The stoats will see to that. Microscopically, Freya draws and nocks a newly-fletched arrow. Oblivious, their breakfast plays. Leaping, capering over the stones, springing through the grass. The poor little things should have stayed in bed.

Hardly breathing, Freya aims. One portion each; even more perfect if she shoots quickly enough. She should be able to. She was Yvette's begrudging pride.

Freya fires. The stoats scatter.

Dismayed, Freya stands. The arrow bounces off the rocks. Gone, just like that; back to bed with Mother, thanks for the look. How did they know she was *there*?

They can't have. They didn't. If they did, forget bed; she needs to go back to school.

She waits for a moment, but they don't come back. Oh, well. They were only small.

Shouldering her bow, Freya crosses the whispering field to the base of the bluff. The rock blunted her arrow; great. Tutting at it, she stands.

And comes face to face with a wolf.

Freya stills. As still as death; as still as the dawn. She saw wolves once, back in Atikur with Taika. Taika's magic hid them, so they stood in the dark and watched the pack pass through the snow. One pair of golden eyes briefly seemed to see them, but that was it; it was brief. The air moved around them, the pack brushed close, ghosted into the trees, and was gone.

This wolf is different. Sat on its haunches, it's far, far larger, the colour of yesterday's rainclouds. It sits, and it watches.

Now she knows what scared the stoats. Yellow eyes lock on hers. Freya still doesn't move.

With an odd little grumble, the wolf turns tail. Trotting past the rocks, along the edge of the bluff, it turns and looks back.

It wants her to follow. Of course it does. Freya watches it. It watches her. With another grumble, it starts down the shale. At the bottom, it looks up.

Fine. Replacing her arrow, one eye on the wolf, Freya navigates the rockface. The decline is sheer, but the wolf turns away, as if content it has what it wants. What fun. No breakfast and a sentient predator.

Halfway down the bluff, Freya pauses. Ørenna; she's starting to think like Kira. It sits in her uneasily, and she quickly carries on. At this rate, she'll end up in safe little houses, going to the shops for muck.

Hopping to the grass, Freya starts to stride. The wolf trots into a lazy run, across a stretch of empty fields. Wherever it's going, it'll spice things up.

The sun scuds across half the sky. As it dips, they come across Callum.

A blonde woman calling his name? Callum squints, both against the light and in the hopes of making her out before potential hell breaks loose. She could be Mathew's daughter, or it could be a trick. According to Mathew's story, enough of those have been trundling around.

'Callum?' The woman calls again. Quickly, Callum speeds through his options. One: run away. Two: trust Grey.

That's not a whole lot.

'Who are you?' he calls. Neither confirm nor deny; for now, that'll do. Grey trots up to him, circles, and stands erect by his side. His manner is undeservedly haughty, considering he failed to defend them from a ghost, and went on to misplace Mathew.

Grey swivels human eyes toward him. Slightly closed, sharp and seeing, they radiate disdain. Did he hear?

'Sorry,' Callum mutters, just in case. Returning his attention to the woman, he lifts his voice. 'Do I know you?'

She walks quickly, smoothly, a foot from the stile. On her back sits a bow. It draws Callum's eye and holds it fast. Weapon-wise, he's got nothing.

'Do you not?' She stops in front of him.

Callum climbs down, to the opposite side, a tad less king-of-the-castle. 'Should I?'

The woman tilts her eyes to the sky and shuts them. 'Okay.' The word is a reined-in sigh. 'This is pointless.' Her eyes snap open, as sharp as Grey's. She lifts her hands in a picture frame. 'Let's try another way. Do you, Callum, know who you are?'

She looks him up and down. A brusque, efficient inspection, it feels as though she's checking off points or mentally removing his clothes.

'Callum.' Whoever the woman is, she's right. This is pointless, and she knows him. She knows who he is.

She gives him a look that says *well, yes*. 'Care to add anything else?'

Her eyes slide to Grey, with what seems like interest, but also seems too forced. Callum bides his time, the only weapon he has. 'I knew I was'—he watches her closely—'before you called my name.'

For the shortest moment, the woman stills. In an eye blink, she looks up at him, and everything is impassive. 'How?'

He smooths his face to match hers, as far as he can. She knows him. She knows a lot. 'It's complicated.'

'Try me.'

Folding her arms, she rests her weight on one hip. Callum mirrors her inspection. Long, near-white hair. Rough, baggy trousers tucked in scuffed boots. An oversized, sack-like vest, escaping off one shoulder. Her curves stir something inside him, something yearning, something deep.

Instinct kicks back. He's the rabbit; she's the wolf. He's meant to stir, to yearn, to lust. He's meant to see her as alluring. Seductive. A hole to fall down and never climb back out.

Two women with wolves. Callum shakes himself free of her icy, glittering eyes. 'Sure.' He plants his hands on the glistening wall. 'But first, tell me who you are.'

'Freya.' The woman speaks at once. 'Your turn.'

Again, Callum studies her. Her accent isn't his, and it isn't Mathew's, but neither is it Gaia's or the lad's. It's lighter, more poetic, even as it cuts him up. He watches her watch him. If she wanted to drag him off to a sky-pit, there'd be an arrow at his throat. If she wanted to kill him, he'd be dead.

At the end of the too-short day, he doesn't really have a choice.

'I was taken from a cave by a man who knew me.' He speaks each word with pointed slowness, so she knows he's not easy prey. 'He didn't tell me for a while, and he doesn't know me well, but it was enough to get us started. Why did you expect me not to know who I am?'

Freya's eyes cut away, as though she's thinking fast. 'A man?' Just as fast, she scans the land. 'What happened to him?'

Callum's bursting huff shares more than he'd like. 'Believe me, I'd love if he popped up too.' He waves a hand around the field. 'There, by that tree or chilling in a ditch. It'd solve all my'—shut up—'problems.' He drops his hand and seals his lips. His heart has started to thrum.

Freya gives him a peculiar look. 'Okay,' she says, as if he's a horse she's not sure how to tame. 'Who was he?'

'Look.' Callum holds up his hands. God, he feels stupid. 'Let's make a deal. I'll tell you who he was, and whatever else, which I'll say now is sod all, if you tell me how you know me. And why Grey found you.'

He glances at the wolf. Waiting by the wall, Grey sits like a cat.

Freya's eyes dance over his. 'It's complicated.' With a smile less there than hinted at, she nods at Grey. 'Original name.'

Callum feigns ease. 'Not my choice. I believe he belongs to a giant.' He scours his draughty memory. 'A lech? Lachy? But that's irrelevant.'

Freya's smile slinks out from undercover. 'Round here, we don't say things aren't relevant.' Curiously, she regards him. 'Did you mean a leshy?'

Her gaze slides to Grey again. A second passes, two. Callum sees her register something. 'Vasi.' Slowly, she shifts her weight again. Equally slowly, she lifts her chin and forms a silent *oh*. 'Kira's father. The man was Kira's father.'

※

She scrutinised Callum for half a field before she decided she was sure. Now, standing in front of him, things wash through her like a lovey-dovey dawn.

Back in Taika's cave, before the Whispers' onslaught, she'd asked what had happened to Mathew. She got a three-word answer before the pain, and she never thought to remember it. At least, if Kira finds out, it shouldn't lead to more crucifixion. The fossegrim gave them the same.

'He was,' Callum says. His guard doesn't drop, not for a second. 'He still would be, if I knew...' he ducks his head and shakes it. 'Ah, no. Never mind.'

'What?' A second thought washes in, a lot nastier than the last. 'If you knew what?' She takes a wary step toward him. His gaze flicks back up. 'Where's Mathew?'

A metallic cloud drifts over the sun. In the shade, Freya sees a shimmer.

Oh, no. Oh, no, no, no.

The cloud drifts away. The shimmer winks out. 'Ahem.' Freya crafts her voice like careful clay. 'I'm going to be presumptuous and say you met a woman.'

Callum says nothing. Freya doesn't look at him. A second, darker cloud trails after the first, and for a few deepening heartbeats, the shimmer is defined: a silver tinge to daylight, like the sun or moon through dust.

'Last night,' she adds. She can't stop staring. *Oh, no, no, no.* 'I'm also going to say she had a wolf, and she did something to Mathew, and when she left, the world had changed.'

The clouds part. Freya butterfly-blinks and looks back to Callum. His forehead has wrinkled, his mouth partly open as he stares at the space beyond Grey.

'Callum,' she prompts. She wants to shake him or scream. 'Tell me what happened.'

Minutely, he shakes his head. His mouth stays open. 'I…' he shuts it. 'I thought we got away. I knew what I'd seen, but then he was fine. I mean'—his lips barely move—'I mean, he seemed fine. Jesus.' He lifts a hand and lowers it. The dust-light is there but faint. 'What is he?'

'Not a…' *great deal.* Freya stops the words before they march. 'Honestly, I don't really know.' She lets her eyes linger on Mathew or the sliver of stardust so far from a man. 'As much as it's bad for him, I have to say, I'm jealous.'

Callum looks at her as though she's grown a tail.

'Of you,' she clarifies. 'I'm jealous of you. Seeing the Night Hunter is rare, and people don't tend to survive. Come on.' Feeling rather idiotic, she beckons to the stardust. 'Kira and Jay were asleep when I left, but that was…' She squints at the clouding sky. Here again, time is different. 'A lengthy, indeterminate while ago. Kira worries for all three worlds, and as much as I love to mock her, she doesn't need to think I've split.'

Neatly spinning, Freya starts across the field. Grey trots past her, speeding up, up, up, his tail flying out behind him. In a matter of seconds, he's gone.

Dazedly, Callum appears by her side. 'Jay?' he asks, skirting a molehill. 'Mathew never mentioned a Jay.'

For a second, the words make zero sense. For a second, Mathew's glimmering shimmer had taken precedence.

But then, sinking through her, Freya's mind catches up. 'Oh.' Gravity drags her eyes closed, and her gut through the ground. 'Oh, this is going to be *so* much fun. You don't remember Jay?'

'Judging by the fact I asked—'

'Okay.' Freya tips her head back on her neck. 'I get it. Okay. Why this is falling to me, I don't know.' She shakes her head at the sky. *Why?* 'There are two things you need to know straight off before we get back to the others. One: Jay's your little brother. Two: Kira's…I don't know, your girlfriend. Your lady interest. She doesn't talk about her feelings.' Freya turns to squeeze through a gap in a hedge, already ravaged by Grey. 'Do you not know anything about yourself? No memories? Nothing?'

'Only what Mathew told me.' Callum lifts his shoulders and holds them there, palms up and out. 'I'm learning my lovely character, but my memories are even less than whatever the hell you'd call him up there.'

He wiggles his head around. If Mathew's there, he's returned to the air, but Freya knows what he means.

'You don't seem too different.' *You're pretty, for a monster.* She elbows this away. 'Which is something. Although, I wouldn't count your blessings. When we get back to the others, there'll probably be a storm.'

She stoops, ducking into the shelterbelt. Instantly, the world is dark and cool, wrapped in waxy foliage. It feels intimate. It *smells* intimate, all heady and close, rich and alive. She could push him against a tree, and see...

'I wasn't counting anything.' Callum shoves his hands in his pockets, bulling through webbed twigs and out the other side. 'In my living memory, I've been held at spearpoint, taken prisoner, kept in a sky-pit, rescued by the epitome of an existential crisis, half-abandoned by the existential crisis, and now'—he turns to walk backward—'I've got a mystery girlfriend and an unknown brother.'

'If it helps'—Freya plucks bits of twig from her hair—'Jay doesn't remember you either.'

Callum looks to the side and shrugs. 'Fair enough.' He looks back to her. 'And Kira?'

It both pleases and bothers Freya to pause. If she wanted, she could win him over. She could make him switch allegiances, unwittingly enough. She could summon her familiar, mischievous seduction, and have him; he's such a fine figure of a man.

Part of her wants to. Quite apart from anything else, since the ellemaend, she's been simmering.

As they climb the grassy knoll, Freya sighs. It's apathetic. It's an eye roll in a breath. 'Kira,' she says, 'knows everything.' She purses her lips. How tragically human. How *good*. 'Including who her father should be, so like I said, there'll be a storm. Right now, though, it's story time.' She flicks on her huldra smile, and watches Callum blink. Damn right. 'You show me yours, and I'll show you mine.'

He's *such* a pretty man.

46

Sea and gales

When Jay scrambles back into the hayloft, Kira thinks he's crying wolf. 'What?' She frowns at him, closing her satchel. Panting and freaked, he quakes on his knees. 'What do you mean, there's a wolf?'

Jay jerks a look back. 'I mean, there's a wolf.'

Kira follows his shaken gaze.

There's a wolf. Her head swoops and swoons and everything else that feels like falling. Below them, slinking into the barn, is a giant grey wolf.

'The window.' Snatching the satchels, Kira spins on her knees, crawling to the back of the hayloft. Grabbing the coats, Jay scrabbles to follow. If possessed Romy can jump from a window at night, into binbags with icy concrete below her, they can brave some straw and a field. It's an awful plan, but at least they won't die.

Not by being devoured.

It'll do. Sticking her head through the glassless gap, she drags the satchels around and shoves them. They *thump* into haybales. 'All right.' She ducks back in. 'Go.'

Jay gapes at her like she's gone mad. 'Are you—no! I'll break both legs!'

'You won't.' Thank God the horses are somewhere else. In the next field over, the cows are panicking, bellowing up a cacophony. 'Please, Jay.' She tosses a wild look back through the barn. 'Just go.'

'No.' Jay's face tenses. His neck cords, and he swallows. 'Not unless wolves climb ladders.'

Claws click. The hayloft shudders.

'Okay.' Thrusting his burden out of the window, Jay scrabbles round. Wriggling through feet first, he drops with a gasp and a *whump*. 'I'm fine!'

Before she can freeze, before she can panic, Kira follows. Freefall. Letting go, her stomach soars up to her clavicle. Her breath puffs back into her lungs. With a jarring, chin-snapping jolt, she lands in a spray of straw.

Her teeth will rattle around her skull for the next fifteen years. Breathless, bones clicking, she snatches up the satchels, slides down the haystack, and pelts for the gate. Dry earth puffs beneath Jay's heels. He doesn't stop for the latch, clambering up and over, feet catching Kira's arm as she scrambles in his wake. The wolf might not have attacked, but she wasn't going to chance it. Surely now, it'll leave them alone. There's a whole field of cows to play with.

Across a tiny field, around a thirsty hillock. Kira's lungs gasp for air. She's so done with running. Across a track, around a pond. Past a spread of blueberry bushes, away from the village, into a rut between hills. Can they stop?

Behind them, the ground thuds. With the muffled sound of a rug being beaten, the wolf cuts them off.

Jay lets out a throttled yell. Kira grabs for his shoulder, and they lurch to a stop. Her heart hammers. Her legs shake. Watching them carefully, the wolf dips its snout.

'What do we do?' Jay grabs Kira's arm. 'Kira, we—what do we do?'

Folding its legs beneath it, the wolf lies down.

Kira's face is too frozen to frown, but her mind goes ahead. She's had this happen before.

That's not—no. Images slot behind her eyes, of polar bears and ice, a tunnel of white, of Romy and Mum and Dad. Flying toward them all on a wolf.

There's no way in hell this wolf is the same. It can't be. She sifts through her memory, one big, bright blur that yanks all the strings in her chest. It's ludicrous, coincidence, uncanny; this can't be the wolf that took her over the ice. That wolf was huge and dark and human with probing yellow eyes.

'Kira.' Jay's voice wobbles down to a whisper.

'Mm?' Kira doesn't look round.

'They're the same.' Jay must have read her memories. Releasing his death grip on her arm, Jay slowly starts to retreat.

Kira angles her head toward him. 'Then why,' she murmurs, her eyes on the wolf, 'are you backing away?'

'Science.'

Yawning, the wolf pushes up to its haunches. Kira's muscles tense, but all it does is pad around to Jay and lazily cut in front. Jay stops. 'Huh.' He turns the other way. The same thing happens. Circling them, the wolf cocks its head, with a look that on a man would read *really?*

Kira sighs, caught between a laugh and despair and probably some of both. 'I think,' she says, 'it wants us to stay.'

Retreating behind the shelter of a hedge, she drops the satchels to the grass. Wide-eyed and boy-like, Jay plops beside her. 'I think,' he says, 'it does.'

Snacking on tiny blackberries, at first, Kira doesn't hear the voices.

Jay looks up. 'Freya's back.' Swiping purple lips with the back of his hand, his grimy face wrinkles. 'She's got someone with her.'

Kira glances at the wolf. It doesn't so much as prick its ears; is this what they've been waiting for?

Unfolding her arthritic legs, she struggles to her feet. The hedge is too high to see over, patterned with cloudy caterpillar webs she knows from springtime walks. Further down the slope, it breaks for a stile. Cautiously, Jay stands, and they listen.

'…heard something.'

'About time.'

Kira's lungs lace like a corset.

'Not'—Freya climbs the stile—'necessarily. Ah.' Noticing them, she slowly dismounts. Her face holds everything under the sun, and for once, she lets it stay. 'Wait.' Holding up a hand, she looks back through the gap. The wood creaks and stops. 'Kira…'

'You found Callum.' Kira's voice is as tight as her chest.

Freya tips her chin in a weighted nod. 'It's…complicated.'

'Don't.' Kira threads a smile together, with all she has and more. 'It's fine. No. It's good.'

'I'm not waiting for negotiations.' Callum clambers over the stile. 'Hi.'

A gale of emotion sends Kira out to sea and whips her smile away. A sense of unreality, déjà vu. Relief that he's okay, thinner, but alive. A longing to rush to hug him. An equal longing to burst into tears. Deafening apprehension over what happens next. Shock that he's here at all.

Kira forces her head above water. 'I guess you don't remember me.' Running a hand through her hair, she strengthens her spine and pours it into her voice. 'Really, I know by now that you don't, but I'm so, so glad you're alive.'

Formal. Stilted. Wrong, but there's nothing she can do. She stretches her face in an appropriate way. 'Has Freya told you what's happened?' she asks blandly. 'Where we're going?'

Clearly, she's told him something. His uncertainty is awkward, and it makes her want to shrink. 'Bits and pieces.' Moving his hands to his pockets, Callum's lips slide to the side. It's familiar, and it aches. 'I get the sense she's the type to pick and choose what she reveals.'

'Hey.' Freya shoots him a warning. 'I wouldn't.'

Jay winks. 'I would.'

Freya swats at him. Meeting Kira's eye, Callum smirks, just a little. Just a little, it loosens the corset; it's not the best reunion but he's here. He's okay. Three out of five of them are okay, and they're that much closer to the end.

'As a side note,' Freya remarks, throwing Callum her satchel, 'is no one going to mention the scheming sleeping wolf?'

Callum shrugs. 'Ah. I'm used to it.'

He meets Kira's eyes again. Tilting her head, she pretends to consider. 'Honestly, I'd forgotten.'

'And'—Jay's mouth is full of blackberries—'he's cool.'

Freya looks at them, each and every one. 'Wow.' In disbelief, she starts to laugh. It shakes her, and she shakes her head, again, again, again. 'What a search and rescue team. All I can say is watch out, Whiteland. We're coming for your blood.'

47

Light and glass

As the sun slants toward the horizon, Callum and Freya get shifty. Not a bit shifty or could-be-mistaken-for-something-else shifty; the edgy, avoiding eye contact, getting quieter and quieter type of shifty, which means there's something they're hiding, and something they want to stay hidden.

When it starts to crawl through her like spiders in her skin, Kira pulls Jay aside.

'No,' he says, before she can speak. 'I refuse to take sides.'

This seems like weirdly untruthful self-denial, but Kira lets it go. 'I'm not asking you to listen,' she says beneath her breath. Ahead, Freya walks on, one hand brushing the long grass and a clutch of rodents in the other. Callum is a shadow, off behind a tree. 'I just want to know what you think. Are they acting strange?'

Jay stretches, wide and with a noise of pleasure. 'Without listening'—he bats at a whining mosquito—'I can tell you they're trying really, really hard not to think about something.'

Curiosity sparks. Kira tries to tamp it down. It feels a tad like jealousy 'Does that not count as listening?'

'No.' Jay cuts his eyes to Callum, scratching his head and mooching toward them. 'It's observation.'

Kira elbows him. 'It's not.'

'It is.' With a smile squishing his cheeks up, Jay eyes grow bright. He's a perfect, *perfect* smug incarnation of his brother. 'I answered your question. You should love me forever.'

Kira huffs. 'Right.' She starts walking again. They've walked so long the land is familiar; they're coming to the border with the grasslands. More plains than meadows, more space than not, it triggers last year's urgency. Nostalgia. Hope that she can make it, even though she came too late.

Hope. That's the key.

Jay clears his throat. Kira glances at him. Eyebrows raised, chin dipped, he's expectant.

She rolls her eyes. 'Thank you.'

'You're welcome.'

'But.' Smiling at Callum as he catches them up, she bends down to whisper, flicking an invisible something from Jay's heathen hair. 'Whatever they're not telling us, I want them to say it themselves.'

Kira straightens. The crimson sunset is tinged with magenta, almost cloudily purple. Depending on the slant of the land, the Yunavida range rumbles low in the distance, like a predator biding its time.

Devils. Moaning. Broken bodies.

'Freya?' Kira calls. The little-girl pitch makes her wince, more than the memory of the mountain. 'I think we should stop soon.'

'No.'

Opening her mouth, Kira shuts it, and frowns. That was fast. 'No?'

A silhouette on the open plain, Freya doesn't turn. 'Forgive me if I don't repeat myself.'

Kira turns her frown to Callum. His perfectly practiced eyebrow is rising, the other perfectly still. *Is she always like this?* It asks her. She tilts her head, side to side. *Yeah, pretty much.*

Kira turns back to Freya. 'I forgive you, but I think you mean yes,' she says, as if talking to a wilful child. 'I've been to the grasslands. You haven't. There's not much there, which is fine during the day but leaves us exposed at night. I was told it's really not safe.'

Freya shoots her a look that says she's an idiot.

'Even less safe,' Kira coolly amends, 'than everywhere else, barring Atikur. At least Atikur has cover. Trees. Hollows, and—you know what?' She holds up her hands, abruptly determined. 'Say what you like, but I'm stopping. I refuse to be caught out like last night.'

Freya picks a pinch of grass and throws it. 'She doesn't walk every night.'

'And?' Kira spreads her arms. 'Do you know her plans? Have you got her calendar?'

'Her what?' Freya glances over her shoulder, as if she misheard.

Kira looks between them all, but no one else is helping. Jay's eyes are on Callum as though he's doing something dirty. Callum scratches the back of his head.

'Never mind.' Kira shakes her head, once, twice. Why is this so *hard?* 'It's not important. What is important'—she flicks her fingers, at the dusk growing warmer, the flora growing flatter, the fauna growing sparser, the grass growing higher and drier—'is not getting stuck out here. Also,' she adds, as a helpful afterthought, 'I'm starving.'

'I agree.' Callum nods. 'With both things.'

'Fine.' Flinging down her collection of dead things, Freya strides off. 'Start a fire. I'm going to find water.'

Freya veers toward an olive grove, peeking over the crest of a downhill slant. Kira stares after her. If Callum was Callum, he'd wink at her, mutter *female problems*, and step neatly aside in anticipation of a well-deserved slap. She'd know he was joking but defend Freya anyway.

That was another crude wake-up call, an embarrassment she did not need: on her second day with the huldra, she had to sidle up to Freya for all the world like a preteen girl. *Yeah, me too,* Freya had said, with a shrug; and so, she would conclude to Callum, no female problems here. Freya's period isn't due.

Assuming cycles work the same.

Whatever.

'Kira,' Jay says quietly, as Callum starts picking up kindling. 'I know you said not to listen, and I said I didn't want to.'

There's most definitely a "but." 'Yes?'

Kira drags her eyes away from Callum. Caught between normal and wolf-distressed, Jay picks at the skin around his nails. Her suspicion of the shiftiness snakes on back.

'I didn't mean to.' Unnervingly staring at nothing, Jay picks too hard. A drop of blood blossoms on his finger.

Feeling her face tighten with her chest, Kira closes her hand over his. 'And?'

'Well'—Jay licks his lips—'um. Well. I was thinking about food, wondering if Grey had caught anything.' He nods at the horizon's low, shabby tree line and the sedately trotting wolf. 'I'm kind of tired of tiny things, but when you said something like "I don't want to be caught like last night," I got this image from Callum. It was so crazy strong, like he'd jammed it in a box.' He mimes a pop. 'But then the box burst.'

A ribbon of worry swells, so fast it's hard to breathe. Kira's eyes cut to Callum. A greying shadow in the olive grove, his arms are full of wood, and suddenly, it's all too much.

'Callum.' In a quick-fire instant, Kira makes up her mind. Confrontation is the worst but so are secrets. 'What are you not telling us?'

On the edge of the trees, Callum stops. The back of his neck stiffens. He looks like a little kid spotted sneaking out.

Slowly, he turns toward her. 'I'm sorry.' He tucks the wood into his chest, for all the world like a child. 'Freya said you'd take it badly, so we said we'd wait. It was stupid. We were stupid. We couldn't figure out what to say, and now…' His breath sounds strange as he shifts his gaze to the grove. 'I'm sorry.'

In the trees behind him, something moves.

Kira's eyes slide over, but the shadows are bare. The light is grainy still, the purple-grey quality of budget cameras and not dim enough for sneaking up, but nonetheless, her wary gaze lingers. It was probably leaves. It might have been a bird, but it *could* have been a trick, illusions or secrets or lies.

'Why?' she asks. Her voice is tiny. Her skin feels too thin for her skull. 'Why are you sorry? About what?'

Callum's side-on grimace could win awards.

'What, Callum?' Looking him in the eye he won't turn, Kira lines her tone with cement. God, that ribbon goes way beyond worry. It's marching right toward dread. 'I swear, if you don't start talking, I'll put you in a pit myself.'

Her gaze skates to the trees again. That time, something moved. Something definitely moved. As though she's trying to focus on a star, the glimmer only catches her eye from the side, but it's there. Dust motes? Kira squints. No. It looks like a waterfall made of air, or filtered, tinted light.

That means literally nothing. It's her literary mind throwing words at reality, and Kira shifts her gaze elsewhere. A bowing branch. Its bulbous olives.

A tear in the evening? Stranger things have happened. Kira stares at the glint without staring, as though this will help her worry, her unease, her need to shout at Callum and hug him. Whatever it is, it has a form of sorts, glittery and sifting. It drifts back. It darkens. Shimmering into a deeper shade, it blurs at the edges and focuses. A sharpening photo. A figure?

Callum is speaking, but Kira is transfixed. Retreating toward a tree, the shape shimmers less. It *is* a shape, no doubt about it, coalescing from light to grey to a solid silhouette. Faintly, Kira steps toward it. Her mind and body separate, floating apart. She has a feeling.

A feeling of what, who knows, but a *feeling* forming tentacles in her gut. Sliming up, it lodges suckers in her throat, and she takes another step. No breath. No thoughts. She drifts, unreal. The shape doesn't move.

The trees are cool as she enters. She passes Callum, still speaking. Behind her, Jay responds. The feeling slithers behind her eyes, sticking to her temples. Swallowing, she turns her head.

The feeling roars and gusts away. Winded, Kira staggers.

'Ah…' her voice cracks. Her hand lifts, hovers, drops. The emptiness is brittle. 'Yu…'

The first time, her name is weak, a glass against a wall. The second time, it floats, and shatters all she thought she knew.

The third time, breaking and familiar, it's Dad.

48

Spectral tales

'Oh, Christ, Kira. *Kira.*'

Mathew's arms are around her, and he's cold and papery and as fragile as she feels, but his lips move against her hair and…

Oh, my God, he's here.

Not a ghost, not a puppet, hugging her, knowing her. *Knowing* her. The more-than-makings of his beard on her forehead. The familiar way she settles against him, against his belly and into his chest, from birthdays and GCSE results and the art show featuring *Karliquai* and finally passing her driving test and coming home from business trips and the morning after the night on Callum's couch, one of the final times she saw him.

'Dad.' Saying it feels foreign, croaked into his shirt. No smell, but he warms her, a solid cocoon, aching between her ribs. It's a hug, a warmth, an ache that only a father can bring. 'I thought you were dead.' She presses her palm to his shirt. '*We* thought you were dead.'

Kissing her hair, Mathew's lips curve up. 'From what I've heard, I've been worse,' he murmurs. His voice is steady, but his body is not. He holds her tighter. 'You have no idea how much I—how I hoped I'd find you, but I…' Now, nothing is steady. It feels like falling and smells like home. 'How did we get here?'

Pulling away, he clasps her arms. His finger pads are painful. The dusk and trees shadow his face, but his urgency fills the air between them, his burning, childlike need to know. It hurts her all the more.

'I don't know,' Kira whispers, as he lets her go. The contours of his face, his hair, his shoulders; he's *here*. 'It's just, there are too many things. And there's so much none of us knows, and the things we do know are crazy.'

Mathew laces his fingers with hers. Kira holds them with both hands. If the tiniest breeze picked up, she'd blow over. She's too shocked to cry, and it's now, as she stares, drifting into the sky, that her thoughts sigh into place.

'This.' Fresh, rushing shock slaps her back down to earth. 'It was this.'

Eyes stretching, her head snaps round. Callum stands closer than he did before, with the restless air of someone unsure. Shoulders rounding, he looks away. 'It was,' he says, to the root-buckled ground. 'Can you see how I didn't know how to…um.' He looks up at her, as though she might stab him. 'Break the, um, news?'

Barely tipping her head, Kira nods. Her thoughts are swirling, coming together, and suddenly, she knows.

'Oh.' It winds her again, pinching her chest, leaving her less than real. Kira grips Mathew's hand, so tight. Everything is bare as she looks at Callum, achingly raw. 'Last night?'

The grove hangs, hushed and waiting, the seconds you taste before something is announced. Urnäsch flits behind her eyes: the night beneath the olive tree, the two moons, the purple sky, the whispers in the dark.

Callum inclines his head with a sigh. 'It happened as I said.' He grimaces over Kira's head, the wince of the slightly at fault. 'Except Mathew was there, and I didn't hide. Neither of us knew we should.' He snorts, but it's dour. 'The bloody wolf just stood there, and then he collapsed.'

Kira swallows. It tastes sick, wrong. 'And you—you saw it all?'

Callum drags his eyes to hers, and that says enough. 'I tried to help,' he says quietly. 'I promise you, I did.'

Kira says nothing, only breathing, only staring through his cheek. This is the cruellest thing to have happened. She got her dad back, but he's not back at all.

'Kira.' Mathew squeezes her shoulder, tentative and slow. 'If you believe anything, believe this: I didn't feel it happen.'

It. What is it?

'We honestly thought we got away,' Callum says. His low voice comes from very far away.

Mathew draws her toward him, against his chest. 'We did,' he murmurs into her hair. 'It was only this morning that we realised we didn't.' For a second, he grips her far too tight. His torso stiffens. 'Or I didn't.'

Kira's eyes sink shut. She doesn't want to know. It might knock her out or make her scream and never, ever stop. 'What…' Dry-mouthed, fists clenched, she swallows. 'What happened this morning?'

Slowly, as if he's forcing himself, Mathew's body relaxes. 'Think of it'—his breath hiccups, and he steadies it—'as falling asleep.'

Keeping her eyes closed, Kira stiffens. 'Falling asleep,' she repeats. 'Really.'

'It's the best I can say.' He shakes his head, his mouth brushing over her hair. 'Falling asleep and staying at the point where you know you're going, but you're not quite gone. I was there until it began to get dark. Freya and Callum saw me briefly, but otherwise, no one could.' His heavy sigh gusts through her. 'Christ, it's been so hard to believe. Not just this but any of it. Much of the time, as Callum will testify, I've been convinced I'm going mad.'

Callum huffs, restrained and subdued. 'He has. Although so have the rest of us.'

'Excuse me.' Off to the left, undergrowth crackles. 'What happened to starting a fire?'

Kira unsticks her eyelids. The dark is bluish, out of focus. Freya stalks into the grove.

Callum clears his throat. 'It's out, Freya.' His eyes flick to Kira and away. 'She knows.'

Freya stops. Her hands tighten on her satchel strap. 'Ah.' Her gaze dances over to Mathew. 'In that case'—she bows her head toward Kira—'and bear in mind I hate apologies, I'm sorry I didn't tell you. I should have. Part of me didn't want to deal with your reaction, and part of me was selfish.' She peers out of the grove.

'Yes,' comes Jay's distant voice. 'I'm surprised too. I was trying to be a good person.'

Somehow, this splinters something. Ice, tension, horror, *some*thing, and Kira starts to breathe.

'It's okay,' she says, quiet and hoarse. The strangest thing is that it *is* okay. She's scrambled, giddy, fraught, and breathless, stunned and cut like diamond dust, but the reality is this: she thought her dad dead for a year, and then she thought him the Kyo's toy, and then, after the fossegrim, her thoughts seized up and stopped. His hand is on her shoulder, his front against her back. She can hear him breathing. His body is warm. Whatever else he is, he's with her. 'Now we just need Romy.'

They build a fire beside the grove. By the time they've eaten and all is told, the last of the light has sighed into night.

For a while, her dad was silent. Kira wasn't brave enough to break through to him and neither was anyone else. When Romy had found out everything at once, she got drunk with a little girl; Mathew wouldn't go quite that far, but she saw him sink into drink and despair after hardly a day without Anna. Now that Mathew knows what his girls have seen, what they've been through, what they've done…it steals her breath all over again. Would he hug her? Pity her? Abhor her? Leave her?

Eventually, he cleared his throat, got up, and walked away.

Kira had walked after him and came across him mostly by luck. She'd been starting to think she should return to the camp, the firelight long having vanished behind her, beyond the grove and Freya's eager stream, when she heard him call her name.

'Yes?' She turns, looking around, and there, hidden behind a sprawling acacia, a ghost beneath ghosting stars. 'Dad.' She rustles through the straw-like grass toward him, folding her arms tight. 'Hi.'

He stands still, watching the plains. 'You shouldn't be out here alone, Kira.'

A low wind blows in the distance. Hunching in, Kira steps up beside him. 'I think'—she sets her sights on her boots—'it's all gone far beyond that.'

Gingerly, she looks up at him. Wistfully, he looks down at her. Just a little, they smile. 'I think,' he says, 'you're right.'

Kira presses her lips in and along. 'Still good advice, though.' She holds herself tighter, gripping her ribs. The dry wind blows, almost here. The year between them opens its maw.

With a soft, daughter-sigh, Mathew shakes his head, as heavy as the weight of the worlds. 'You've grown up.'

It's so cliché that a smile stirs. 'These are your pearls of wisdom?' she murmurs, letting the smile emerge. '"Don't go out alone at night" and "you're a woman now"?' She nudges him gently, gently teasing. 'Come on, Dad.'

He gives her that wistful, faraway look. 'I guess we're beyond that too, are we?' He holds out a hand. Kira takes it, large and warm and calloused, and he tugs her in again, her back to his front. 'Still true, though.' His arms encircle her shoulders. 'I was with you a long time before you saw me. I hardly knew who you were.'

Kira's chest pangs and keeps on panging, echoing down to her core. 'Maybe'—she makes to pull away—'you don't want to.'

'Stop.' Mathew tenses his arms. Kira jolts and gasps. 'Shush. Don't move.'

A sudden sound peals, fluting through the night. It's spectral, unfamiliar: the downward trill of a bird of prey, a sliding soprano on a minor scale, panpipes. Is it real?

The goosebumps on her arms say yes. The sound electrifies her skin, wiring through her chest. Her front turns to ice.

'Dad.' Kira backs into him, as far as she can go. The fluting trill resonates, reverberates, and soars. In a blink, a fine mist glints from the air. A breath tinged golden, it washes the night, and as it drifts over, as it envelops them, Kira's throat burns white and cold.

She gasps. The ice slides into her lungs. The sun itself couldn't warm her, the mist a frosted, dampened cloak. A brain freeze slicing her eyes and beyond, it wracks her with a shudder. Mathew grunts and flinches. All Kira sees is gold.

Before any fear sets in, it's gone. The mist passes through. The trill, the scale, the pipes descend to one discordant descant. Slowly, Kira turns her head. In the grass to her left, there are dancers.

The song, the series of harmonies, are all that hang in the night. Opaque and faded, the dancers could be ghosts, hand in hand and twirling through the storm-still grass. Laughing women in billowing dresses, men in clothes like Callum's. Boys and men in clothes like Jay's. Smiles and pirouettes, innocent and playful. They capture Kira whole.

The harmonies last until the dancers wane. A hint of mist gathers at their edges, early morning light through dust. They whirl and swirl, eight or ten, spectral tales of a long-gone dance. The mist drifts across them. One by one, note by note, the voices peel away.

The soprano note is the last to linger. Eerie and cutting, it blends with bells, with windy, distant chimes, and then, on a mourning sigh, it dies.

The night pulses. Nothing moves. Then, calm and chirping, it gradually returns.

Mathew lets out a long, long breath. 'Out of all the things I've seen,' he says, 'that's the only one that's been stunning.'

Kira's chest moves, slow and soothed. Her lips tug into a melancholy smile. 'Sometime,' she whispers, 'I'll have to tell you about the Hyrcinian birds.'

'Do.' Unstable, Mathew loosens his arms. The wind flutters up again, softer than before. 'Everything else…' He stops. His tongue *tuhs* the top of his mouth. 'Everything else that's happened to you and Romy sounds horrific.'

Kira shakes the back of her head against him. 'It's not just us, though, is it?' she says. Her sweet, sharp melancholy is rapidly drowning her calm, and she swallows. 'You've had it the worst of us all.'

Somewhere, a barn owl screeches. A quieter creature cries beneath it, the panicked squeak of its prey.

'I'm your father,' Mathew says heavily. 'It's meant to be worse for me.'

'No.'

'Yes.' Suddenly firm, Mathew tightens his arms. 'When you're a parent, you'll understand. It's meant to be worse for me, but it hasn't been. I'm meant to protect you both, but I haven't. Everything you've told me, and anything you've left out, I was meant to be there for. I was meant to stop this from happening.'

He ducks his forehead to her hair. Kira shuts her eyes. Her breath is wet. 'You couldn't have.'

'I should have, though.' The words are ragged. 'I should have kept you safe.'

'How?' Kira's voice pitches, bitter and hoarse. The tears are coming; she can feel them, scraping and ready to roar. 'How, Dad? This is dealing with things that are way beyond us. It's Mum's world, not yours, and when she tried to protect us, it only got worse.' She twists her fingers into Mathew's sleeves. 'If she couldn't fix things, we didn't have a hope.'

Mathew holds her fingers still. 'At least you tried to.'

'And you died.' Setting her jaw, Kira shakes her head. Her lips push out and shiver. 'And all of this happened regardless.'

The barn owl screeches again, and she flinches. The squeaking is growing piteous, desperate, the sound of a creature that's trying to run but knows there's no way out. She tries not to listen. The night has settled to a tapestry heaviness, biting and sharp and immersive on the fringes of the trees. Beyond, there could be anything. The world could bring its worst.

It didn't, though; it brought its beauty. Fixing her mind on this, Kira breathes. She's not ready to scuttle back to the firelight. Back to Jay, inside her head. Back to Callum and his memory, or his lack thereof. Back to Freya, who's Freya, and went killing with her dad.

'It's okay, K.' Mathew holds her close, and it casts her back in time. Dad, banishing nightmares, sat on the edge of her bed. The time she biked uphill and couldn't breathe, and he had to massage her back and stop her soaring into panic. The two of them on hospital chairs, before this turned to shit.

'At least I've found you,' he says, as the tears start to slide. 'Okay? That's the first step. We'll find Romy too, and I'll look after you both. I can't change what you've seen, and done, but I'm here now. Okay?'

It hurts. 'How, Dad?' Kira shuts her eyes, her voice cracking in two. 'Something's happened to you that we barely understand. The outside is a shitshow, and apart from anything else, you only appear in the dark. God.' She shakes her head. Her laugh is ugly. 'Me and Romy, Dad, we're not your little daughters. Not anymore. We can't pick up where we left off, even if for you no time has passed.'

Kira sniffs, hard, her throat sore. Her head throbs. Her voice is thick and barely wants to work. 'So much has happened to us,' she whispers. Her fingertips are shaking. 'We had to grow up so fast, and now we're these adults, and we can't go back to being teenage girls. You wouldn't even recognise Romy.' She swallows the pressure in her chest, but it swells. 'I'm sorry, but things aren't the same.'

Louder still, the owl screeches. Wings beat among the trees. The piteous squeaking stops. The silence that falls is far too full and makes her think of death.

Finally, Mathew lets her go. 'I understand that.' He steps away. The cold space hurts even more. 'But Kira, I'm still your dad. You're making it sound like we're strangers.'

'Dad, no.' Kira turns, and buries her face in her hands. 'That's not—that's not what I'm saying. We're not strangers, of course we're not, but we're not your little girls. You can't…' She looks up and swipes her eyes, tilting her head to the sky. 'You can't swoop in to save us. You can't be the father who fixes things and shields what he can't fix. We've had to face the world ourselves. We may not have fixed things, but we've been our own shields.'

She makes herself look at him. His face is mostly unreadable, masked by the sky and the dark acacia, but everything about him is troubled and sad. A man fraying, with rumpled edges. Dropping her head to her hands again, Kira lets herself cry.

At some point, Mathew puts his arms around her. When she heaves her throbbing head up, eyes puffed, frail and hollow, a speck of light is approaching.

'Someone's coming.' She sniffs, nodding her head toward it. Her voice is muggy, and she wipes her damp, sticky, hot face. If she wasn't so hung out to dry, so wrung and wretched and wrenched, she'd be worried. Maybe afraid.

Mathew turns and tenses. 'So there is.'

Behind the light, the night is dark. They watch it bob in silence. The speck draws nearer, illumining a shadow, and as it grows bright, it grows soft. The lightstone.

At least it's one of them. Kira watches it dully. The quiet makes the soft glow creepy, as though they're waiting in dread for the danger to come. The ghost getting closer, the midnight marauder periodically blocking the light. In a film, she'd be the witless girl, the one who quakes at the end of the hall and waits for the shadow to pounce.

As it is, when the shadow transmutes into Freya, Kira feels nothing at all.

'I'm balancing the bonding time.' Freya's eyes snag on Kira's face and quickly slide away. 'You two have had a pretty good share. Now the memoryless bookends can try. Tell you what'—she tosses the lightstone from hand to hand—'we saw something nice for once.'

Freya goes on to describe the dancers, the melody, the mist. Kira tunes out and, lit by the stone and a handful of stars, the sliver of moon peeking over the hills, they gradually start to walk.

Kira can't remember ever feeling quite so much at once. She can't remember ever feeling quite so much in a *day*. Not when she found Callum in the club, was framed by Freya, and ran. Not even in the days that had followed or the days that followed those. It's horrible, terrible, wonderful, torn. She links her arm with Mathew's and tries a feeble smile.

Freya keeps talking. They all keep walking. The fire comes into view. Fraying less, just a little, Mathew smiles back.

49

And so she smiles

'Hey.' Callum's hasty warning makes her turn. Her shirt was close to meeting the stream, and she quickly yanks it down.

'Sorry.' Standing on the bank, he holds up his hands. 'I'm not trying to be intrusive, but I saw you come down here, and as privacy is rare, I came too.' He shrugs, not overly apologetic. 'I had something I wanted to ask, but it can wait until you're done.'

Waist deep in the water, Kira draws a circle in the air. He turns, and pulling off her shirt, she submerges herself to the collarbone. 'All right.' She wrings the grimy garment out. 'You can look. Ask away.'

At a measured, overly polite rate, Callum looks. 'Okay.' He lowers himself to the earthy bank. 'What I was wondering was…' He stops on a breath and lets it out.

Kira watches him from under her lashes, scrubbing at her shirt. If this is about the two of them, she's diving underwater, joining the Havsrå, and rescinding the light of day.

'Okay.' Callum lets out another gusty breath. Kira's heart thumps a little. 'I was wondering, I suppose, if Jay and I were close. As close as you can be, with the age gap. You know.' Extending the toe of his boot to the water, he flicks it up toward Kira. Spray speckles the stream two feet away, and he shrugs. 'Oops.'

Thank God. Thank God, thank God, thank God. Kira ducks into the water, hiding her smile of relief. One second. Two.

Controlled, she lifts up again. 'Do you really think that'll make me answer your questions?' She gestures to a pouch beside her boots. 'Chuck me that, please, and reassess your priorities.'

Callum bends sideways, reaching for it. 'My priorities are stellar.'

'Sure.' Catching the pouch, Kira tips a tropical-scented powder into her palm. 'If you're here, you might as well be useful. Catch.'

Callum watches the pouch land on the grass, making no move to retrieve it. 'What is it?'

Rubbing the peony powder into her hair, Kira starts on her arms. 'See for yourself.'

Callum's eyes widen. 'Okay, I'm in. I get the feeling I used to enjoy being clean.'

Kira wiggles her fingers. 'More or less.' She paddles from the path of a second spray of water. 'What a shame, you missed again.'

Turning her back, she rubs the powder, blossoming into oil in the stream, into her water-hidden body. She definitely used to enjoy being clean, although her baths were not so tepid. Neither were they outside, though, under morning blue, with warm, dry air, and tiny, skittering lizards on the rocks. That she could get used to.

'In answer to your question,' she calls, 'I'm not sure. I know you were very protective of Jay. Very older-brotherly, and your focus once he was drawn into this was to make sure he was safe.'

Water churns behind her, and faintly, she smiles. He wouldn't remember, but they've done this before. 'So we were close?' he asks.

Kira wiggles her hand again, side to side. 'You were brothers. I guess you're right: you were as close as the age gap allowed.' She watches a lizard slip into the water. She didn't know lizards could swim. 'In Urnäsch, when the Chlause did something and Jay collapsed, you roared and ran after him without a thought. I guess that says it all.'

Dipping underwater, clean enough to squeak, she sluices the oil from her hair and skin. It's bliss.

'I guess it does,' Callum says, when she's surfaced, smoothing back her wet hair and breathing in the air. 'Cheers. I mean. Yes.'

Throwing the pouch back to land, Callum imitates her scrubbing. His concentration says her answer hasn't really helped, but he's going to act as if it has.

Moving her hands through the silky water, Kira watches him. 'Is this because Freya left you to bond?' She slides her eyes away, thinking, scrunching her toes on the slippery stones. 'She left you to bond…'

'And we didn't. Yeah.' Head tilting, Callum flashes his eyebrows. His eyes stay fixed on his shirt. 'Total strangers. He looked at me weirdly, and I felt like he should really be at home with his mum. It sounds harsh, but there's just'—he shakes his head and looks up at her, his eyes bleak—'nothing.'

The words nip. Kira's mouth winces. Callum's face pulls in. 'Ah.'

'Nothing?' Flushed with heat, Kira pivots in the water. Here she is, yet again, not controlling her body, with yet another man in a stream. Perfect. 'Really. That's—that's interesting. Sad.'

Lizard claws on hot rocks. Somewhere, Jay giggling. High above the plains pipes a bird of prey.

'Kira.' Callum's voice lowers, softly slanting down. 'I wasn't—I wasn't trying to make a point with that. Believe me, if I want to say something, I might hedge, but I won't use digs and subtext.' The lazy stream swirls behind her. 'I guess you know that already.'

He puts a dripping hand on her arm. Kira tenses. 'Sorry.' He removes it.

Weighty inside her, something slumps. It's been less than a day, and she's failed. 'No.' Shutting her eyes, breathing out, she forces herself to turn. The water laps warm around her shoulders. 'I don't want that. No way.' She drags her lids open. The morning glints, sun off the stream.

Callum watches her warily, like he stroked an unfriendly cat. 'Want what?'

Kira's chest pangs and cracks. 'This!' She lifts her hands from the glugging water. Rainbow droplets shower them both. 'Your face, me acting pathetic, like I've been, I don't know, jilted. I don't want you tiptoeing around me, to think anything will set me off crying because oh, the guy doesn't want me anymore. We don't have that much history. It's fine.'

'It's not li-'

'Yes, it is like that.' She slices through Callum's perfunctory protest. 'You don't want me anymore because you can't. You don't know me, and I don't want this to get any more awkward because you think there's some kind of pressure. There's not. I don't expect a switch to flip and it all to be the same.'

Like Dad.

'Don't you hope for it, though?' Callum watches her closely. One eye narrowed more than the other, his head tipped slightly forward. 'There's nothing wrong with having feelings, Kira. Your face is good, but you're putting on a mask, the same as you are with Mathew. You're still hoping it can all return to whatever normal was.' He makes to put his hands in his pockets. 'Ah.' He snorts. 'Nudity. Damn.'

She shouldn't have gotten into this. Folding her arms, Kira ducks her head, squeezing her thighs together. She should not, under any circumstances, have gotten into this. Never mind a tepid bath; she needs a pool of ice, to shock her out of her shame.

'I guess,' she says tightly to the stream, 'I'll try harder.'

'You don't have to try harder.' Washing through the water, Callum grabs her arms. She starts, but he doesn't let go. 'That's not what I'm getting at. Not at all. Would it make you feel better to know it's shit for me too? I've lost so much.' He grips her. 'So much, all because of a pissed-off witch and a crazy cave of banshees. If we ever come across either, they're getting great big hunks of my mind.'

A small smile creeps onto Kira's face. They've done this before as well. 'I suppose,' she says, cocking her head, 'it saves them taking it.'

Callum blinks, blinks and scowls. It's so familiar, so *Callum*, that her humiliation lifts, enough for her smile to spread. Enough for it to spread and feel warm and true.

'Fine.' Callum drops his hands, hitting the water with a *plunk*. His exasperation is art. 'I'll stake them. I'll exorcise them. I'll—I'll shoot them in the heart and blame someone else.'

The words shock like a fuse. Bon Jovi?

No.

Yes. 'That,' Kira says, every inch of skin prickling, 'is most definitely a song. Not necessarily a song you like, but a song that everyone knows. On the outside.'

Callum spreads his arms. 'Then there's hope for me yet.' Turning, he wades toward the bank. 'Come on. Bath time's over. We've got one girl, several identities, and a corporeal presence to find.'

Slipping on the stones, Kira paddles in his wake. 'Hark at you, taking charge.' She pokes his pale back. 'Maybe there really is hope. Maybe'—she looks down as Callum climbs from the water—'you will shoot the Kyo in the heart. It'll make a nice change from punching people or whacking them with pokers.'

Yanking on his trousers, Callum snorts. 'Old me sounds like fun.' Squatting for his shirt, he tosses hers to her. 'Who did I punch?'

'A siren.' Shirt secured, Kira wades from the water. The fabric reaches her thighs, and they're all beyond the point now where female hair is an issue.

Just.

'A siren?' Tugging his lips down, Callum nods, impressed. 'Nice. What about the poker? Who did I whack?'

Kira opens her mouth. Her mind kicks in—bad idea—and she shuts it again with a pop. 'Um, long story. Very long story.' Unable to resist, though, she side-eyes him slyly. 'If someone in particular annoys me, I might just have to tell it.'

Callum's eyes dance to hers and linger. 'I see.' He grins, less slyly but just as pleased. 'Don't worry, I'll piss her off for you. I'm intrigued enough to poke that bear. Wait.' He stills, face working. 'That's the mark on her face.'

Oh, dear. Quickly, Kira finishes dressing, burying her smile in her chest. She shouldn't have gotten into this topic either. She certainly should not have said *that*.

'I said nothing.' Her cheeks squirm as she tries not to grin. 'I'm saying nothing. No comment.'

'It is!' Callum clicks his fingers. 'Oh, what ammunition. Thank you, Kira. Any other nuggets?' He spreads triumphant arms. 'Any other absolute gems?'

His trousers draw Kira's eyes. 'Well, your fly's undone.'

Winking at him, she scoots away. Maybe there's hope for them all.

50

In the snow

'She didn't want us in the house,' Karl says. His arm stretches far in front as that-damn-dog, oh-you-*beast* Diego tows them on. They took two leads, but it hasn't really helped. 'She's worse with lies than you are.'

Julia pouts with her lips and her face and her eyes. The movement scrunches her hat down her forehead, and she bats it back up with a glove. 'I can lie.'

Karl glances at her thoughtfully. 'Not very well, though.'

Picking up a tasty scent, Diego lumbers faster. Julia slips on the ice. 'Diego!'

Diego ignores her, nose to the ground. Rebalancing his moon boots, Karl returns to looking thoughtful. 'I think Carol knows about your thing.'

Julia's scowl deepens and deepens and deepens. It feels carved into her face, like the woodwork at school. 'Then she should ask me to help,' she mutters. Her Christmas scarf takes most of the words.

Above his snood, Karl blinks. 'Help what?'

Diego yanks on his double leads. Karl squawks. Julia shouts, but the dog hauls them faster, across the slippy car park toward the buvette. Bundled up in winter coats, people sit on benches, eating fondue and *pâtes à chalet*. Diego pines for scraps—understandably, really, Julia thinks; the *croûte aux fromages* looks amazing—and *harrumphs* when, between them, they lug him away.

'Pardon,' Karl mumbles to whoever's tutting. '*Je m'excuse.*'

Julia blows a raspberry, and for a tramping, stamping while, they're quiet. Diego tows them into the field, hefty with old, icy, shiny, mud-spattered snow. Suddenly, Karl swivels to gawk at her. 'Hey. Help with what?'

She'd forgotten about that. Julia sighs her best adult sigh, and haughtily covers it up. 'You said'—she casts him her best impatient adult expression—'that

Carol didn't want us in the house, so she made us walk Diego on our own. And we're normally not allowed.' She swirls her free hand through the air. 'So…'

Karl says nothing. Julia swirls her hand faster, boggling her eyes. 'So…'

Karl shrugs, hauling Diego toward the boards to Les Tenasses. Patchy with melting snow, they're deadly. 'So you want to help with her secret? Die*go*.' He hauls harder, and swapping beasty dog sides, Julia adds her strength to his. They're in danger of being carted off cross-country, through the snow to the chairlift or Karliquai.

'Yes.' Grunting, Julia heaves on her lead, and they wrangle Diego back to the boards. 'But it's not a secret. Not really. She thinks she's being sneaky when she's on her tablet, but like, we have ears? *Diego!*' Out of breath, she stops. Diego strains against them, and she glares at him. 'Maybe you've been watching TV or something. Or she does it at night. But she's talking to these people with things like mine, about…'

She covers her top lip with the bottom and pushes them into a kiss. It's not been easy, understanding what she's heard, and what she's seen in the tablet's notifications when she's been playing *Dragonvale*.

'About?' Karl boots an ice ball. It skitters into the dried-up rushes.

With her best adult patience, Julia doesn't snap. 'Making all this stuff stop? I guess. The, the,'—she flaps her free glove—'the stuff with the girls and Callum.'

Karl nods into his snood. 'It's on the train TV. With the police.'

'Yes!' she exclaims, then claps her hand to her mouth. 'Oops. Carol and these internet people want to make it stop.'

Diego looks back at them, straining, his hooded eyes sad. With twin sighs, they lengthen his leads. Karl lifts his shoulders to his ears. 'Ask her.'

Julia rolls her eyes until they feel strange. 'I can't do *that,* Karl. She thinks she's being sneaky, so she *wants* to be sneaky. She doesn't want us knowing what she's doing.' She speeds up, trotting behind Diego's fervent lope. 'So…'

This time, she hopes he'll answer with a plan. When he doesn't, Julia huffs and puffs and burrows into her huge, knitted scarf. She always thought it would be fun to walk Diego on their own, but she's wanted to go home since they got down to the garden. Her arms are the sausage strings from *Tom and Jerry*, and her legs, if she stopped moving, would carry on trotting without her. Karl keeps breathing as loud as the train, and they've still got the whole way back.

'We're never walking Diego again,' she mutters. 'Never, never, nev—'

'Sneaking.' Karl sweeps and lifts a finger, a weird gesture he saw in a film when a character has an idea. Julia glowers at it. Right now, it's his most annoying thing. 'That's what you need to do and do it better than Carol. If we both listen and find out how you can help with your, your thing'—he moves his hands, his soft excitement almost costing him the lead—'then you can join in when they do whatever.'

He beams. The snood slips below his chin, but for once, she doesn't giggle.

'Yes!' This time, she lets the exclamation ring. Two snooty ladies doing snooty *ski de fond* look over, grouchy, but well, she doesn't care. 'Because like Carol says all the time'—she turns the dial of her voice to a screech, slitting her eyes, wagging a finger, and sticking out her neck like a pecking hen—'these walls are made of paper!' For the last few words, Karl joins in. 'Jay, turn it *down*!'

Their peals of laughter echo out, clacking off the car park. After they subside, he sighs. 'Julia'—he shuffles his boots, looking down—'I really miss Jay.'

Julia's face droops. All at once, they're sober. 'Me too. I miss Callum.' Reaching the towering sign, chattering in French about the nature reserve, they turn without a word, directing Diego back along the boards. 'She's not being sneaky about that either.'

Like a robot, side to side to side, Karl shakes his head. She feels what he wants to say before he says it. Jay says it's because they're twins. 'Carol,' he says to his snood, 'has no idea where they are.'

The *croûte aux fromages* smells just as good as they wend their way back home.

51

Butterflies

The energy whistles. Something is afoot.

Coming, coming, coming, Ella hears. Other words too, but this is repeated, fluttering around on butterfly wings. Rumours; maybe they're rumours. The thought flits away before it can land, lighter than wings, lighter than leaves, and she blinks and sways and sways.

A hand in hers. Squeezing liquid pain again. Ella slips down a rung, back to Earth. She stands with a woman—with several, actually—but this is the one who stays with her, her and the man who never leaves. Sun and shade fight over them, a tree in a breeze. They stand and watch, and in the distance, someone, something, is coming.

Coming, coming, coming. Black dots before the sun. Murmurs around her. If Ella became the bird again, she could soar, up and across the grasslands. She could see the someone-something and carry on, away, through the wicked mountain that makes the children whisper. She'd soar, and she'd fly. She'd flee, too fast for them to clip her wings or catch her by the claw.

Out, out, out to the ice. She'd soar there too. Not dragging anyone, not this time, not running with wolves or waiting with wolves or whatever she did with her sister.

The rungs judder. Sister?

For an instant, Ella can't breathe, but then she's here, she's down. Dots. Sun. A hand. A second on her back. Black dots, one in front. A wolf?

A wolf. Ella's eyes burn. Her tears outdo the sun. The wolf runs. *Coming, coming, coming.*

Coming, coming, come.

Ayomi crests the skyline. Within herself, Kira balks. Finding Jay with no memory was bad enough. With Callum, she was kicked off a cliff with no preparation for landing. With her father, she suspected something, and after she'd been torn up, jumbled around, and restitched to become a patchwork, hotchpotch ragdoll, she had to reconcile the fact he's now…what?

Romy, though. Every step is worse than the one before. She's about to see Romy, and if everything they think is true, Taika has wrecked her mind. Her mind fully returned to her only three days before it died.

So Kira walks through the long grass, sweating like a beast, full of dread and hope the closer they get. Nerve-racking feels wrong. Daunting doesn't do it justice. She has a trampoline inside her, a child on a sugar rush, and a looming, chuckling clown informing her with a gleeful scream that they all float down here. She's a circus.

'A pretty awful circus,' Jay mutters. Without a second thought, Kira shoots him a glower. Normally, she cuts him slack, but this is far too personal.

And how is he so *chirpy*? The boy blasting Bring Me the Horizon is nowhere to be seen.

Conspiratorially, Jay leans in. 'Do you want to know a secret?'

Kira lifts her hair and fans her neck. How does Freya cope with her mane? She rarely even grumbles. 'I want'—she lets her hair flop, wiping her forehead—'you to stay out of my mind.'

Jay puts on a wide *don't look at me!* face, turning his hands palms up. 'I try. You know I try. It's not my fault you're so loud.' He bobs up and down as they slog through the scrub. 'And you didn't answer the question.'

Kira shuts her eyes briefly. He's twelve. He's twelve. Ahead of them, Callum idly irks Freya. Grey is a shade in the grass. 'Do I want to know a secret?' She says with a sigh, stepping a little in front. 'About what?'

Jay bounces up to her side. 'Why I'm chirpy.' He pauses, his eyes glued to her cheek. 'It's because I like it here.'

Kira hears the words, but they don't sound real. He can't have said he likes it here. He can't.

Slowly, she lets her eyes slide to his face. Far too unnerving for a round-faced boy and especially this boy, he says, 'It's true.'

'We've got a probing party.' Callum's concern, mixed with amusement, draws her focus away, but Jay's honesty sits uneasily. It's a conker, shifting as she squints across the plains, at the two riders cantering toward them. 'Whiteland's mistress? Is this good or bad?'

Freya hitches up her bow. 'Normal. It means they've heard we're on our way.'

The spiny conker grows and rolls. 'They're expecting us?' Kira asks, too high. She tugs on its ballooning string. 'Well, that sounds really fun. I'd go for blaming those people earlier. We shouldn't have asked them the way.'

Freya waves a hand, but her face is that careful shade of blank. 'We needed to,' she says. 'And being expected isn't bad. They've probably known for a long time, actually, with the amount we've needed directions. That wolf...' She touches her fingers to her bow. 'Whatever. Party time.'

Kira's eyes go to Callum's. *Probing party time*, she can hear him saying, and his intentional eyebrows confirm it. If the situation wasn't what it is, she'd consider saying it herself.

As it is, she turns her attention to Grey. No longer slinking, subtle and stealthy, he stops, large and poised. She'll be wistful when he leaves, as presumably will he. There's something magical, mystical, about a journey with an animal, especially a wild one she knows. Whiteland really is so much more alive.

For a flicker of a flicker, she understands Jay.

'Is him standing there'—Callum drops back to whisper—'really the best idea?' He nods at Grey. The wolf bows his head, his hindquarters strong. 'He looks like a raging bull.'

Kira elbows him. 'Shush. He helped me before.' She watches the thunderous distance close. The riders continue, kicking up dust. Although the bull mars her mysticism, he isn't wrong. 'And he's been helping Dad for a while. I'd say we trust his judgment.'

'Speaking of.' Callum dips his voice further, dim beneath the hooves and the rumble of the ground. 'Do you know how you're going to explain your dad? If it ends up getting that far.'

The riders reach Grey, and the wolf wheels around, loping beside them back across the plain. Beyond growls the Yunavida range.

No.

'You said it already.' Kira presses her lips in and along. 'It might not get that far.'

Skidding around them, Grey yips and comes to a halt by Jay. The riders don't slow before they gallop to a stop. Imposing and dusty, they rear back, skitter back, and sit up straight in their saddles. Kira grabs Callum's arm. Daunting, nerve-racking, a conker, a circus. It's all of these and fear.

Callum cuts a quick glance at her. With a shiver of embarrassment, she lets him go, mouthing a sheepish, *Sorry*.

Callum rolls his eyes. 'Stop.' He replaces her hand. Grey yips again, more impatient than playful. The front rider shifts.

'You're coming for Ella.' It isn't a question. The bony woman appraises them. Her black hair is an ocean, her black-rimmed eyes small and sharp. A heavy stone owns one earlobe. Her eyes snag on Kira. 'You.' She jerks her arrowhead chin in a nod. 'You're Ella's sister.' She glances at Freya, dagger-sharp. 'That one, we saw through you.'

'"That one,"' Freya says at once, in a very restrained snap, 'has a name.'

The woman doesn't look at her again. 'Everyone has a name,' she says tersely. 'You won't be here long enough for them to matter, and not all of you are coming in.'

She appraises them again, like pigs at a market. That, or kids caught misbehaving put before the headmistress.

'We've come to get my sister.' Letting Callum go, she steps forward. She doesn't need to protest, not really, but she hasn't travelled three worlds to be treated like a child. 'We're not a band of rebels or any kind of threat.' Chin up, she plants her legs. 'We'll come in, find her, and leave.'

'You won't.' The woman's voice mirrors her chin. The second rider, a ruddy-haired teen, shifts on his magpie horse. 'Stories of you have carried, whether or not you're a rebel band. The truth is ambiguous, but I won't take the chance. Outsiders, witches, murderers, thieves. The disturbances existing at all are enough without us letting them in.'

The second rider clears his throat. 'Ella's fine, though,' he says. 'Why can't they come in, get her, and leave?'

'Iolo, you're here because of Asgeir.' The woman's look slices him up. 'Not to be heard.' She whips the dagger around again. 'Two of you can come with us, not the wolf. You,'—she jerks her chin at Kira—'and another.'

Now they're being picked for teams, and she's become the captain. Kira forces her eyes to meet the woman's and her mouth not to curl. 'I don't suppose you've got a preference?'

The woman looks at Freya. Kira waits until her gaze returns and folds her arms. 'Callum.'

And Dad. Kira tries to project some kind of message, entreating him to come too. The sunlight shouldn't fall yet; at least, it shouldn't fall before she can explain him and avoid being run out of town. Failing that, if all kinds of hell break loose, his shimmering form can hide.

Callum steps up beside her. 'Ready for duty.' His tone is spiced with a dash of sarcasm. 'Believe me, I'm the better choice. Far less volatile.'

The woman considers him. Her eyes flick up and down, up and down his body, until, with a nod, she says, 'Fine.'

Freya groans. 'Kira, you imbecile.'

Crooking a curt finger, the woman turns her horse. The peeved-looking Iolo follows.

'Keep an eye on Jay,' Kira says. Mouthing another apology at Callum, she sets off in their wake.

'There's no need!' Freya cries. 'We've got a bloody wolf!'

Kira fixes on Iolo's horse's tail and doesn't look away. The tail flicks a swarm of flies. She was making a point, and she'll stick to her point. A nomadic grasslands village can't be worse than crawling to the huldra.

Can't it? Kira's thinking like she knows it all, but oh, she really doesn't. She spent one night with nice people over a year ago. Daubing them all with one broad brush is dim. Daft. Dumb. It's the same as lumping the Welsh foothills with inner city Leeds.

Which she's not going to do. Kira squints past the riders. The woman is stiff and full of hubris, Iolo slumped and easy. It's hard, though, not to see this village as Marya's; as far as she remembers, they look pretty much the same. Crops crowding bowing trees, the supple sound of water. Horses in a paddock. Smaller creatures snuffling, chatting, indistinct.

Clustered tents and clustered people, facing them and waiting.

'Hey.' Callum elbows her. His voice is low, but she starts nonetheless. 'I don't believe you heard a jot of what I just said.'

Her eyes on Ayomi, Kira scratches her arm. 'Sorry.' She forces herself to stop. 'I don't believe I did.'

'Understandable.' Callum digs his hands in his pockets. It seems matter-of-fact, but looking at him sidelong, Kira knows it's not. He's too angled. Good, but a mask.

She tries for a smile she doesn't feel. 'Still, it's rude. What did you say?'

Callum snorts. 'I said'—he bumps her again—'that you've got no need to be sorry. Sitting around while others do things doesn't feel very me.' He tips his head, eyes narrowed, as if seeking disapproval. 'And, if we're being honest, I'd rather come with you than sit awkwardly with Jay.'

Kira bumps him back. 'I'm sure Freya would too.'

He snorts again. 'Freya's still taking baby steps away from being a huldra. I'—he prods his chest—'hit huldra with pokers.'

Eyeing him, Kira tries for dryness. 'You weren't so pleased at the time.'

'Maybe not, but our fate is almost upon us.' He nods at Ayomi. 'Someone's got to lighten the load before we start to crack.'

Fate is what it feels like as Ayomi rolls closer, and suddenly, they arrive. Enough people gather in the shade of the trees that the village could be here as a whole: each task left undone, each gaping tent vacated. Children ogle, whisper, grin, from toddlers to dirty boys, to girls about Jay's age, with hair brushed finely and black around their eyes. Women whose earrings drag them down, men with pierced noses. Men with broken backs, women with commanding postures, teenage boys with sweat-soaked chests, hefty tools in hand. Anyone and everyone.

Someone steps forward.

'Kira,' he says, in a placid bass voice. Bearded and broader with hair to his shoulders, he's otherwise the spit of Iolo. Nodding to his brother, he levels Kira a sombre, steady severity. 'Ella's not herself. You need to be aware.'

The fossegrim told me, Kira thinks but doesn't say. The less she reveals, the better; it was advice she received a year ago, and it seems to serve her well.

'What does that mean?' she asks instead. She can't help but be aware of everybody listening: every shut mouth and every open ear is a weight upon the air. Kira tries not to look like her breathing is a shudder. 'Not herself as you know her or'—she curls her fingers, searching—'not herself as you think she should be?'

Stepping close enough that their sides brush, Callum touches the small of her back. It's light. It feels natural. It goes some way to calm her and make her strong.

'Both.' The man looks to the bony woman, returning horseless from the paddock. 'Thank you. I'll take her in to Marya.' He nods to Kira. 'I'm Asgeir.' Again, to Callum. 'Come with me.'

The throng doesn't part. Kira forges a hot, sweaty path after Asgeir before it can swallow him up. Marya. They're really here; she's really doing this. Kira's heart is less in her throat and more around her throat and squeezing. Emerging from the crowd, a hundred thoughts batter her. What if Ella's not Romy? What if she is, but she's been taken by another woman of the Kyo? What if Romy's so far gone that nothing can bring her back?

A cold touch sinks through her shoulder. By the entrance to a small, patterned tent, Kira swivels. Callum is still battling bodies. She turns again. Asgeir lifts the tent flap, his expression as expertly smooth as Freya's.

The cold chills her again, a squeeze of both shoulders. This time, Kira understands. 'Thank you,' she whispers, as the parched heat returns, and love for her father swells. With Callum forging an exit beside her, she enters the sinewy tent.

It takes several black-spotted seconds, but once her eyes adjust, her heart leaves her throat and plummets through the dirt. On the floor beside Marya, hugging her legs, huddles Romy.

Romy but not. Not the Romy she knows, the Romy she knew, when Romy was still in the grip of her demons. Tanned and freckled, this Romy shrivels. Kira's mind shrivels with her. Her sister's face has been scourged of makeup, although her nose-piercing and round, black ear-stretchers stay. Staring at her, Kira just about forgets to breathe. Somehow, these things, these so very Romy things, only make her look more withered. A shell. A shadow. Her sun-bleached hair has been intricately braided, looped and pinned in a way she would hate. Riding up her thighs, clutched to her chest, her dusky dress is thin. Her angular feet dwarf her calves. Romy's pale eyes dwarf her face.

Oh, God. Kira's body turns to wood. Romy, in the hospital bed. Romy, so lacklustre she couldn't handle food. Romy, haggard and dragging their father. None of those Romys are equal to this one.

'Kira.' Marya stands. Her stocky cheeks and stocky frame haven't aged an hour. Lines etch her face in a throwback to Anna. 'Kira…'

What else is there to say? Kira's lips are dry. She no longer has the saliva to swallow. Unsteadily, in jolts and jerks, as though moved by an amateur puppeteer, Kira crouches before her sister. 'Romy?' Cautiously, she shifts to her knees, and extends a hand. The word, the name, doesn't want to come out. She works her too-large lips. 'Ella?'

A sleepwalker, lifeless, Romy stares through nothing. Kira takes her hand. Her feather-like fingers are cold. 'Ella?' she repeats. The name tastes as strange as *Dad*. As weighty as a bobblehead, she looks to Marya. 'How long has she been like this?'

'Mmm.' Romy hums and rocks back once.

Kira's breath rocks too. Oh, God, her *sister*. Fighting the need to grab her, hold her, Kira moves her shaking hands to Romy's cheeks.

'Romy?' she manages hoarsely. Makeup free, Romy's drawn with chalk, breath medicinal, thin lips chapped. She doesn't want to scare her, but it's a chore to keep quiet, to keep her voice soothing and slow. 'Ella? Can you hear me? God.' She drops her hands and swallows a shout. Everything quavers. 'What's *happened* to her?'

'I found her like this,' Asgeir says from behind. 'Searching for you made her worse.'

'Which shouldn't be surprising.' The harsh cut to Marya's tone is underlined with blame. 'Her mind had clearly been meddled with, and knowing this, the weavers went too far. Now, no one can reach her.' The blame singes. 'Not for long.'

Romy blinks, languorous. Kira wants to scream. She wants to, needs to, ruin, burn, the same crashing chaos as she felt at Karliquai. Shuffling around, she pulls Romy to her. *Oh, God. Oh, God, oh, God.*

'Kira.' By the tent flap, Callum's face is hard. 'Let's get her out and back to the others. If they can't reach her, they can't help her, and they don't want us here anyway.'

Kira links her arms tight about Romy's ravaged shoulders. 'In a minute, okay?' she whispers into her sister's dusty hair.

'Kira.' Callum squats beside them. 'I think it should be now, before anything happens.' He holds out a hand. 'Let me help.'

Sucking in a breath that bucks her spine against Kira, Romy stiffens and starts to scream.

'Jay.' Callum jogs toward them. Wild-eyed and urgent, he scrubs a hand across his head. 'Sorry. Leon. You need to come back with me. Romy's—oh, Jesus, I have no idea.' He stops, half turning, his mouth open, his hands up and out. 'You just—let's go.'

'Wait.' Freya's voice pops and sparks with disbelief. 'What's going on? What happened to the quota of two?' She grabs Callum's shoulder. '*Wait.*'

Like swatting a bug, he shrugs her off. 'It can't wait,' he snaps, marching off back toward Ayomi. 'You try and come too, I don't care. By this point, they're throwing us out regardless. *Shit.*' His foot hits a rock, and he stumbles. 'Where's Grey?'

'He ran off.' Leon points to the mountains. 'Freya said he's probably not coming back. What's happened?'

'I don't know. Get in my head.'

Callum breaks into a jog again, and Leon does the same. Beside them, Freya roils with confused irritation. Slipping into her mind has turned into a habit, largely because of the game he played with her, but Callum's mind feels like unlocking a door...

And then being slapped in the face. Leon catches himself before he trips, but Callum's head is havoc. Red. Disaster. Worse. The girl he saw in the fire screaming, the whites of her eyes shiny and popped. Her nails pierce her legs, and blood crescents bloom. She's screaming at him, at Callum, screeching, so raw it must be shredding her throat. Kira attempting to rock her, calm her. Romy lashing out, and Kira falling back. A man restraining, people shouting, barging in, barging out, blurring together in Callum's shock, and all the time that *scream*.

Leon backpedals out, as fast as he can, swooning back down to himself. The scene replays, over and over. Slamming the door on Callum's mind, Leon shakes his head so hard it turns hot and makes a noise. This is bad. This is extremely bad. Is it worse than Nikoli and Al-Sanit?

Maybe. Yes. On the outskirts of Ayomi, he can hear the commotion. It smells like horror and fear.

'What?' Breathless, Freya shouts. The village isn't screaming, now, but bitter voices rage. 'What is it, Jay?'

Leon ignores her. His ears ring. The image of Romy has scorched his brain, more animal than human and completely terrified. He knows what Callum wants, what Kira must have asked for. But Ørenna, he doesn't want to be in Romy's head.

Ayomi's minds are colourful, shrieking through the day. He couldn't stay out if he tried.

...did he do to...

...girl has finally gone...

...wouldn't mind a piece of that new...

ROMY. OH, MY GOD. I LOVE YOU. I'M SORRY PLEASE BE—

Shouldering past the man from Callum's mind, head bowed, Leon pushes his way into the tent.

One side of her face enflamed, Kira kneels beside a pallet. Emptily, Romy lies on her back, loose and staring at the walls. The marks on the fabric are the same as Nikoli's, giving a healer strength. A woman massages Romy's temples. For a moment, he's back in Al-Sanit: easing panicked minds, travelling the river, lulling babies, setting breaks. For a moment, Leon longs for it.

But then Kira sees him. 'Oh.' Standing, she wraps him in a quick-relief hug. 'Thank you. I—I'm sorry.' Crushing him half to suffocation, she jerkily lets him go. He doesn't need to see her mind; her face says she hates this. 'I know it seems like I'm using you, but she saw Callum and started—'

'I know.' Leon plucks at his lip. Callum has stayed outside. 'I saw it in his head. What do you want, me to listen to her?' He moves his fingers to scratch his cheek. Romy is crazily different from the girl he saw in Kira's mind, more like the dead things she thinks of as the Kyo. It feels mean, but lying there, she's nothing but disturbing.

'If you wouldn't mind...' Kira tails away. She's fidgeting, restless, and it makes this worse, the amount she doesn't want to ask. She knows he'd mind. She knows, but she's consciously asking him anyway, and for that, he can't say no. With his guts knotting, Leon side-eyes the healer. The balance between listening and screwing up is light.

'If that's all it is.' Leon shuts his eyes. He can't look at Romy, lying there dead. Inch by careful, guarded inch, he opens the dark, rotten door to her mind.

Nothing happens. Leon blinks. Romy stares at the walls, vacant but breathing. A further inch, then a foot, and there: a hum. A soft tune, lilting, fluting on a breeze. Stars.

Leon starts to float.

Up from his body and away, into blackness, both sparking with the night sky and diving into water. Down, down, deep to an oily, inky pool, one that sucks the air from you and never shows the surface. Oh, how it hums, and oh, how it keens, and it sings, and it echoes, so mournful, lost, and *hunting wolves above tonight, are we dead when we have died—*

With a violent wrench, Leon yanks himself back, so rough that he staggers and falls. 'Nope.' He scrambles up at once. 'No. I can't stay there. No way. There's nothing about Callum, and—no.'

He shakes his head again, again. His heart is one horrendous jitter. 'There's…' Ørenna, it's drumming so fast. He feels like he might throw up or pass out. Throw up then pass out. Kira reaches for him. He backs away. 'There's nothing there at all.'

52

Afterglow

There's nothing there at all. The words appear in front of Kira, scrawled in angry bold; in her younger sister's mind, there's nothing.

Kira looks at Romy, calm, but hollow. At Marya, very still, her hand on Romy's cheek. At Jay, who she screamed and begged to bring here, a boy with crooked, uncommon talents. A boy who shakes, his warped face damp, his wet mouth fish-like, poised with one leg turned to the door as though he's ready to run. Run from Romy. Run from *nothing*.

Kira's the one who runs. Something inside her drops and shatters, and winded, she whirls and staggers from the tent. Everyone is tainted, everyone is lost, and while normally she overthinks, this time she was right. Memoryless, Callum's still Callum. Bodiless, Mathew still loves her and knows her. But memoryless *and* mindless, Romy is…

Nothing.

'Hey, hey, hey!' Callum snatches her wrist as she stumbles away, the clamour ringing and blurry. Crushed and stretched and strangled by a gulf that might consume her, Kira fights her arm free and flees. 'What's—Kira!'

Nowhere to go, no one she knows. Her dad can't appear yet. Blindly, Kira runs, lurching through the village, pushing at anything blocking her path, heading for nowhere but *out*. Out to tall grass, a tree, whatever, where she can fall down and scream.

'Kira!' A hand yanks and spins her. A cloud of hair and fruit enfolds her, hers and someone else's. 'What's going on?' Freya grips her shoulders, scrutinising her face. 'What's wrong with Romy? Come here.' Pulling her into a quick, fierce hug, she shoves her out again. 'I'm coming back.' She whirls away. 'Take care of her.'

Someone else approaches. Wrapping Kira up, the someone holds her, and floating far, far from her body, Kira shudders and lets them. The world has turned to haze, a daze. Romy's not herself? Romy's not anyone. *Kira's* not herself, right here, right now, a dreamer besieged by smears of action who can't lift her feet from the ground. Kira sags against the someone's chest, breathing into a vest that smells of sweat and Callum's skin. Her lungs wage war, working far too fast. Callum murmurs something, warm on her ear, *in* and *out* and numbers, rubbing her back, up and down, and screeching to a violin crescendo, her horror starts to slide.

It feels like a rollercoaster cruising back to base. Sounds return, shouting, uproar, but normal life as well. The breeze ripples tent flaps. Horses' hooves, background sheep, kitchen-metal clangs. There's sun on her scalp, soft ground below her boots, her damp palms limp by her side. Callum's chin scratches her temple, and watery, slowly, she links her hands around his back. Horror slumps rapidly into exhaustion, as if everything speeding around has settled and fainted under her skin. In, out. She can just about breathe.

With that comes mortification.

'I'm sorry.' Pulling away, Kira rakes a hand through hair as unpleasant as her palms. Heat floods her wavering body. 'You didn't have to—' She flicks her fingers. A basket of tiny, mottled eggs sits in a wagon, and she fixes on it. Breathe in. Breathe out. 'You know.'

'I do.' In the corner of her eye, she sees Callum shift his weight, looking back toward the village. Standing on the outskirts, by hutches of squeaking birds, they're more or less by themselves. 'I also know you love to apologise, but don't. I heard what Jay said, and after the screaming…' His face compresses and tightens. 'Besides which, I fully thought you'd blame me for something. "What the hell have you done to my sister," or the like.'

Kira looks up at him. 'What? You wouldn't.' She fills her tone with *Callum, that's obvious* and paints it on her face. 'I know you wouldn't do that. Ever.'

'In a situation like that'—Callum wags a distracted finger—'you'd be forgiven for changing your mind.' His gaze slides to the village again. Freya is hurrying a harried, striding beeline past the tents. 'Either way, we're even.'

Shooing a chicken scratching the dirt, Freya stalks to a stop beside them. Her arms-folded, mouth-ready forward lean stops Kira from speaking. Freya's ready to burst.

'Are you okay?' Freya looks Kira up and down and doesn't wait for a response. 'Good. I'm not surprised you reacted like that. I remember Romy. I've *been* Romy.' She shakes her head again, again. 'For once, I don't feel like being harsh, but that's not Romy.'

Pity, it sits in the corners of Freya's mouth, in the downward curve of her eyebrows. Coming from her, it's even worse.

'It's not.' Twisting her fingers, Kira takes a breath. 'But it…it makes a sad amount of sense. The woman from the Kyo possessed her and left her with amnesia. Callum's mum forced her memory back. Taika took it away again and, according to Jay and my dream thing'—she turns her linked hands out—'something happened in Urnäsch. If the weavers have messed with her too, it's a cocktail of mind control. There were bound'—she drops her eyes and her voice—'bound to be consequences.' Kira bites both sides of her cheeks, hard. The horror coats her stomach, but she won't break down again. She won't.

'Two things.' Callum lifts a finger, cutting off whatever Freya was starting to say. 'Sorry.' He almost sounds it. 'One, my mother forcing Romy's memory. Two, and forgive me the stupid question, but how can you have been Romy?'

Freya's gaze lingers on Kira. 'Very long story that shouldn't be told. What I was going to say'—she steps closer—'was that maybe that's why Romy's scared of Callum. She remembers him from Urnäsch.'

Light blooms in Kira's mind. 'From when they put her in the fire.' She winces at herself. How cold. How heartless.

'Romy has linked the two.' Solidly, Freya holds Kira's eyes. 'And Marya just told me that when Romy saw us coming, she started to cry. So maybe she's still in there. Maybe'—she touches Kira's hand, just a graze—'we can still get her back.'

A startled cry goes up from Ayomi. Freya glances over her shoulder. Kira tracks the sound. Masked by milling bodies, someone is shouting.

'…*telling* you,' the voice yells. It sounds like a woman or a very young boy, galloping up to hysteria. 'I saw something. It was there, by the tree, and…'

Kira's chest plummets. Callum and Freya exchange a look.

'I think we've outstayed our welcome.' Freya starts back toward the crowd, a step in front of Kira.

Somebody gasps. Someone else cries out, and as she elbows through, Kira sees. In the murky shade of an old-man tree, her dad is taking shape.

'What's he doing?' Freya hisses, grabbing Kira's arm.

'No idea.' Pushing into Romy's tent, Kira drops to her knees. In silence, Marya stands and leaves. 'Romy. Ella. You have to get up.' She takes Romy's hand, limp on the pallet, and grips as hard as she dares. 'Romy, please. We need to go.' An urgent look flung outside. All over again, it's a fracas. She digs in her nails. 'Romy, *please.*'

Unbelievably, Romy smiles. It unfurls across her face like the languid Cheshire Cat, and with an airy hum, she starts to sing. 'I hope the wilderness will call…'

Let's become a carnival now Ragnarok is visceral. Kira's chest leapfrogs with hope.

Barrelling in, Jay slams it down.

'We really, really, seriously need to leave.' His colour has returned, and he's flushed, out of breath. 'There are all kinds of thoughts about witches and Skarrig, which seems to be an outcast place where all the bad things go—'

'Skarrig!' Freya barges in, grabs his shoulders, and forcefully kisses his head. 'You're an accidental genius. Kira, listen to me.' She crouches. 'Like this, we can't take her with us.' Freya presses her palms together, quickly glancing at Romy, still smiling, still singing, eerie and slow. 'We just can't. But what we can do is go to Skarrig and come back.'

'Hunting wolves above tonight…' Romy continues.

'Which does what for us?' Kira squashes Romy's hand, shaking, harder. Her sister's serenity doesn't stir.

'Jay's right.' Freya flips a hand at him. Neatly, he steps aside, and half a second later, Asgeir enters. 'It's a place for weird things and outcasts. It's also where the huldra often go when they're looking for a way to be human. A type of cure. It's full of witches and weavers, people who don't know what they are or have screwed up in some way. We might be able to help her there.' She cuts a glance at Jay. 'We might be able to help everyone.'

'I'll look after Romy.' Asgeir turns his back, head down. The air around them pulses. 'She'll be safer here than travelling with you. She wanders when she's mobile. When she's not, she does that.' He lifts his chin slightly. Romy still sings.

'How will she possibly be safe here?' Kira's head whirls. Outside, the noise is burgeoning, hammering. She doesn't want to hear what they've got to say. 'Maybe she was before, but…' she shakes her head, lips parted. 'We've caused *bedlam*.'

'He's a weaver.' Jay watches Asgeir in fascination, his voice full of untimely awe. 'He's protecting the tent.'

Light shifts like the moon through water. The air throbs.

'Kira,' Freya urges, 'listen to us. We'll come back for her.'

'What if they don't let us?' Kira looks frantically between her sister, Asgeir, her sister, Freya, the shadow appearing by the flaps of the tent. 'Could you blame them if they didn't? She was right, the woman. The one who didn't want us here.'

'Come back on your own, with whatever you've found, and we'll let you take her away.' The stout shadow enters, exchanging a pinched-in look with Asgeir. To Kira's surprise, her voice is soft. Kira had screamed at her when she wanted to go for Jay. 'Just you, Kira.'

Another shadow steps in. The first rider, the bony woman. 'I'd advise you to leave,' she says, taking in the tent with her bird-bright eyes. 'Asgeir can protect your sister in here, but once you're outside, he can't protect you.'

Her tone warns of *won't*. It tosses Kira back to the torches, to her flight through the forest, and as the uproar billows, raging like war, she kisses Romy's forehead, grabs her things, and gets to her feet.

'Thank you,' Kira says. The stout woman nods.

'She'll be okay,' the bony woman adds with a tight semblance of a smile.

Kira turns to Asgeir. 'I owe you so much,' she says quickly. 'But why?' Her throat constricts. 'Why do you want to help her?'

Asgeir's eyes stay shut, but his lips twitch up. 'I've got a saviour complex.'

'Okay, let's go.' Taking her arm, Freya filches Jay and yanks them both away.

Blinking in the sunlight, Kira shakes her off. Mathew? She shoulders through the people clumped around a tree, the tree where he appeared. Not there. The villagers have given it a six-foot berth.

'Kira!' Callum's shout sounds from somewhere to the left. Spinning on the balls of her feet, Kira sees him, a head above the crowd and beckoning.

'This way.' Latching onto Freya and Jay, Kira bows her head and wriggles and bumps through the throng. Just let them go unnoticed. Just a bit longer.

Keep the village scared by Mathew, calling the weavers, blaming Monte Yuno, whatever. Kira weaves her way faster, tripping, clumsy. Just a bit longer.

Out of the crowd, into the air. Behind two twin tents and there.

'Marya collared me.' Hopping from his box, Callum comes toward them, into the shade of another gnarled tree. 'Told me to watch out for you. God knows what Mathew thinks he's doing.'

Déjà vu swoops in on wingbeats. From the way Marya eyes her, the woman sees it too.

'They won't be pleased, but they can blame me.' Beneath the tree, Marya holds the reins of two horses. A hint of mischief nips at the heels of her concern. 'This time, Kira, I expect the return of both horses and riders. I'll be waiting, just to make sure.' She smiles, but it doesn't linger. 'You should go. Hopefully you know that in Rana, we wouldn't treat you like this. Suspicion and superstition don't always look the same.'

Kira takes the proffered reins. 'Marya.'

'You also know I don't like too many thank yous.' Marya considers them all in a way that clearly says *hush*. 'Do you know where you're going?'

Kira falters.

Freya steps in. 'Skarrig.'

Marya tilts her head. It's a moment, a shout-filled, dust-filled moment, before she speaks. Something in her eyes has changed. 'Then thank me by bringing back new ingredients.' She offers the second set of reigns to Freya. 'Not many people have been to Skarrig, so there could be any number of things. Now go.'

She moves off, in the opposite direction to the din. 'Thank you,' Kira says, hopefully quiet enough to be accepted. Callum bows his head. Jay and Freya look the horses up and down and find them wanting.

Lifting a tent flap, Marya turns. 'I'll let that pass,' she says. The hint of mischief nips again and settles. 'I'm sure Asgeir has said this already, but I'll add to it: we'll take care of your sister.' She moves her head in a question. 'Romy?'

Kira nods and lifts her lips. It's the best smile she has.

'Romy.' Marya nods too. 'We'll keep trying for ways to help her. Iolo's keen to go trading again, so maybe he'll find something helpful. Good luck.' She enters the tent. 'Be careful.' The thick flap falls shut.

Rubbing her eyes, Kira holds her hand there. They owe so many people. After one second, two, all she can spare, she sighs and looks to Freya. 'Can you ride?'

Freya shrugs a conscious shoulder. 'No.' Dipping around the twin tents, she returns with Callum's wooden box. 'But I'm a quick learner.' She pogoes onto the earthy horse, wriggling into position. This time, there are no blankets. 'Can you?'

'After a fashion.' Wearily pilfering the box, Kira propels herself onto her stallion, glossy and russet and raring to go. 'Are you going to be all right?'

Freya's lips crook up. 'Shout me instructions. If I don't ride, we'll be here forever. Is either man likely to take my place?'

'No, and they'd like to get gone.' Callum motions for Jay to jump up behind Kira. 'I'll risk the rider who can't ride. How are we picking up Mathew?'

Suddenly, guilt is all-consuming. 'I—don't know.' Kira glances around. The fact that she hadn't thought about it makes her want to cry. 'Dad?'

The touch of cold chills her thigh. She looks down, and there, in the shadow of the twisted tree: the ghost of her father.

Kira. She sees him mouth her name. With a gesture toward the grasslands, he steps into the sun and is gone. All that's left is afterglow.

Beyond tents and trees, someone screams.

And Kira understands.

'We're leaving him behind.' The words strain her throat like tears, and she digs the horse with her heels. Freya looks at her, questioning. Jay's arms are a boa about her waist. 'But we're coming back for them both.'

Kira flicks the reins, and then they're off. The tears scratch their way out. The air dashes them back. Directionless, yes; hopeless, maybe; but although her insides ache like a wound, with the wind whipping through her hair, Ayomi fading, and not everything lost, she allows her hope to bloom.

53

All the worlds that fall apart

She's been slipping away for ages, eras, but something is going on.

Talie shifts what little is left of herself, what little is left of her mind. Swirling in ever-fading circles, it's ever ready to fade for good, but inside her, there's light. A lightness. Something she can cling to as the worlds fall apart.

In the cold, stone forever, the women start to move. Pale, paling, paled, becoming the air or the walls or drifting up. Up toward the gemstone ceiling. This is it.

Talie tries to tame the thought, but it snarls and sighs away. It? She tries again. The women have talked. *It.* What?

It scuttles back when she starts to drift: Taika. Taika, the little witch, and something that needs to be stopped.

Drifting up toward the snow, she clings to herself for what light life she has left. Below her, the cavern is swallowed by the dark. Around her, wisps of women lift, ghosting dreams of grey. Taika and something that needs to be stopped.

Before the worlds all fall apart.

54

Revelation, golden art

Skarrig begins where the mountains stop.

On horseback they stand at the lip of a cliff. A cape jutting above the lake, it watches. No, it's an old, haggard sentinel, the stark version of Karliquai, looking over the water to the mist and rock beyond. It feels as though they've hit the edge of the world.

The grey-bellied sky is a bruise. The lake chops its stony shores, caught between glass and liquid metal, smashing with spray that echoes through the air, ricocheting like thunder. If there were birds, they'd be cawing crows, vultures over skeletal trees, scrawny gulls balanced on the splintered bones of ships.

But that's fanciful; a Peder Balke painting or her mother's favourite, *Wanderer Above the Sea of Fog*. Kira slits her eyes against the wind, turning to Freya and Callum. Callum is angled away, arms loose, far more relaxed than he was when they started, what feels like so long ago.

Freya's different. Watching the lake, truly watching, she's something close to sad. Her eyes thin, her face distant, as if searching for someone she loves to come home. It's a vulnerable melancholy Kira shouldn't see, and unsettled, she looks away. Kira can imagine the thoughts that must be running riot; she has plenty of them herself. That age-old cliché, true nonetheless, of *how did we end up here?*

'Ready?' Kira murmurs to Jay. He nods against her spine, and carefully tugging the stallion's reins, they clip back along the rock. Hopefully, Freya will follow, and Kira will have broken nothing.

The path of sorts to the shore is steep. Not just steep, but a biting, stony thread, the kind that exists to repel all travellers. Jay's arms will be printed on her stomach by the end, but for Kira, nothing will ever compare to the flight through Monte Yuno. They had followed the line of its range at a distance, as it grew less imposing and petered out to a chilled, barren waste where the world lies jagged; but the sight of it was more than enough. Of all the things that plagued her dreams, the demons had been the worst.

Hoofbeats clop behind her, cautious and light. Kira doesn't glance back in case her balance slips. Freya was a quick learner, although really, she didn't have much of a choice; it took long enough to ride here, so the walk would have been ghastly. As for what they do now that they've arrived…

Kira holds tight to the reins. It's as much control as she has over this, any of it, and she damn well won't let go. On one side, the land falls sheer to the water. On the other lies blackened, weathered rock. Goats on a cliff face.

She pushes this away. What they do next can wait, for flat land and whoever—or whatever—will be waiting when they get there.

'Can you hear anyone?' Kira asks, calling on a whim above the wind. Her skin is as smoothed and salt-spattered as the stones.

Jay shakes his head again, and they lapse back to silence. He's tired; they all are. Whatever the end is, she wishes it would come, although what's going to happen when it does? Out of Whiteland to brave the chaos? Maybe Skarrig can help there too. Maybe they can change their faces or how they appear to others. Maybe they can be their own versions of Freya and kindle brand-new lives.

That's crazy. A pebble, two pebbles skim away toward the water, nudged by the stallion's hooves. Kira summons her mind to the present. Focus on one thing at a time: reaching the shore, not too far ahead. Finding out how to navigate Skarrig, seeing as it's not a community as such. Finding help for Romy. Finding help for everyone. Then, she can fret about getting out and handling the mess the way they should have in the first place; or, at the very least, thinking the supernatural through before fleeing into its arms.

More forcefully, Kira shoves at her thoughts. She panicked over this in the labyrinth and wound up trapped in a church with a perverted façade of Callum. Freya had warned of Skarrig's reputation; one of the travellers they asked for directions did the same. She needs to focus, and stopping the horse on the shore, barely steadier than the trail, she mindfully makes it stay.

'No idea,' Freya says, once she and Callum have caught up. It's tempting to turn his phone on, to take a photo for posterity; riding behind an ex-huldra, forehead drawn down, holding her tight for support. There are so many reasons why she won't, but the thought makes Kira smile. Maybe she'll paint it. She'll return to art and paint everything, the photo album they'll never have and no one will ever believe.

'I say left.' Callum grips Freya's waist, swivels, and uses her anchor to drop to the ground. 'And that we go on foot. Fuck me.' Screwing up his face, he stretches his legs. Kira looks pointedly between him and Jay. 'Oh, come on.' He huffs through his nose, a derisive, scornful puff. 'I've been cursing horses in my head for hours.'

'Even so.' Kira waits for Jay to dismount, before holding the reins in one hand and slipping to the shore. 'Although you're not wrong.' Grimacing, she straightens her legs. They seem to creak, and then to groan, a tense spasm of her thighs. 'I feel like a cowboy.'

Callum snorts through a groan, popping his back. 'We'll find you a lasso. She's the Comanche.' Relaxing, he nods at Freya. 'Aggressive *and* in possession of a bow.'

'I have no idea what you're talking about.' Freya slides from the earthy horse, wincing on impact. 'But I will shoot you.'

Jay starts to laugh. Shaking his head, Callum turns away, his face distorted by a muted amusement wrangling to get out.

'Left it is,' Kira says. A smile wrangles her too, and she aims it at Freya as sweetly as she can. 'Keep in mind that if you shoot us, your journey will have been for naught.'

'But I'll no longer be the victim of your ridicule.' Freya enunciates each word like the point of a wire, leading her mare after Callum and Jay across the black beach. 'Plus'—she flashes Kira a dead, humourless grin—'I enjoy shooting things.'

A shiver scuttles through Kira, despite her lack of fear. 'Okay,' she concedes, looking down. 'You win. You can still be exceedingly creepy.'

'Good.' Freya's grin holds. 'Here, it might even help.'

Whatever "here" turns out to be. Keeping to the innermost edge of the shore, where the spitting spray just falls short, they face nothing but this most desolate of coasts. If they have to search the lakefront, they'll walk until the end of days; it may be the mist, but from these dark stones, there is no other side.

A quiet age passes. The horses clip and clop in silence, unnaturally, eerily quiet. Picking her way over slippery rocks, Kira shivers. The choppy lake slaps the shore. The wind moans through them, sprinkled with rain, into every thin layer of clothing. Kira wipes her face. Her skin is ice. They'll have to dole out the blankets and coats and hope there's enough to go around.

Abruptly, Jay stops. 'I hear someone.'

Shifting his wind-blown balance, he stares off, thinning his eyes to listen. Kira scans the emptiness uneasily. No lake birds. No people. Just cliffs and aching, yawning caves, the whittled beach that curves away. Her horse scrapes a hoof and whickers. Freya's does the same.

With a jolt, Jay's eyes fly wide. 'She's—'

Out of the cliff steps a black-haired woman. A swooning chill seeps through Kira; she didn't come from a crag or a hollow. She came from nothing at all.

Fixing Jay with eyes as black as the shore, she says, 'You're in my mind.'

She walks back from whence she came, meets the stone, and vanishes. The world seems to bend.

For a moment, there is silence. A bright, stunned silence. Kira's lungs can't decide if they're breathing or screaming. Is she running for the hills or made of stone? She doesn't dare blink.

'Well.' With a stiff laugh, Freya shakes her head, and it breaks the cold-cut spell. 'Taika should have come here.' She nods at the rockface. 'She did that with her lair. The two of them could have been friends, instead of one pulling jump-scares from inside a cliff and the other pissing off the Whispers. Although'—her eyes narrow and flick to Jay—'Taika can't read minds.'

Blinking feels like waking up. Kira presses her palm to her drizzle-wet horse, to ground her, keep her sane. Callum is glazed, almost dazed. Jay's face is an oddity.

'Wow.' Jay pivots, his expression morphing, from aghast at the woman's appearance to revelation, golden art. Lightening, he lights up, and beams. 'No one else could—she's the only one who's ever done it back. Ever.' He laughs, a single sound of surprise. 'I want her to appear again.'

The innocent longing sends a pang through Kira, but before it can cement, Jay stills. His expression morphs again, listening, attuned, and suddenly, she hears it too: *something*.

Something. As undefinable as the meadowlands's song, it sounds like someone knocking on bone with a hollow tool that echoes. Painful but not, unpleasant but not, rising in intensity until it is methodical, prodding uneasy areas that sounds don't usually reach. Scanning the cliff face, trying not to see, Kira grips the stallion's reins. The horses stand very, very still.

Gradually, the tone of the deep sound lifts. It's an alpine horn, church bells, a gong.

'I can see her,' Jay murmurs. Tight to the horse, Kira looks to him. He was still before, but now, it's wrong. He could be on another plane.

Edgy, Callum breaks his trance with an odd, grunting jerk. 'Um.' He flexes his fingers and frowns. 'Who?'

Jay nods at the barren cliff. 'The lady. She's standing next to Freya.'

'What?' Freya snaps her head around.

The wind moans. The beach is bare. Water sprays off the rocks. 'She's smiling.' Jay cocks his head, beguiled. 'She's not happy.'

Chills fizz through Kira's chest and wrap around her heart. Jay's Romy a year ago. He's Romy now. The vacancy in his eyes is alarming, and turning, he smoothly walks through the cliff.

Freya throws up her hands. 'Oh, now that's perfect.'

Just as abruptly, Jay walks back out. 'She wants us to follow,' he says, before melding with the craggy rock and vanishing from view.

Kira stares. She feels like she's somehow become a spectator, a member of the audience waiting for curtains; what, in the name of all that's unholy, is *happening*?

'Of course she does.' Shaking his head, Callum mutters into his chest. 'The invisible woman wants us all to merrily trip through a cliff. Why would she not?' He huffs, a disbelieving sound, and limply flips his hands. 'Who cares about normality, when you can disappear?'

'I'm pretty sure we blew raspberries at normality weeks ago.' Dropping the horse's reins, Kira pries herself away, toward the gloomy, looming rock. Her heart thumps. She's a tightrope walker. 'This isn't any stranger than anything else. What's a merry jaunt through stone?'

Touching the cliff face, Kira inhales. The one time she musters bravado, and it instantly shows her up; as stark as the rock appears, it's less solid than sand. Her hand disappears, then her elbow, then her arm. Listing forward, her mind going wild, she submerges herself to the shoulder.

No. What? No. Leaning back, Kira breathes. The rest of her arm is stuck in a mould. It's creepy. It's crazy. She wiggles her toes, scraping the stone. It's beyond crazy; it's awful.

'Fuck it.' Striding up beside her, Callum pushes through the wall.

Kira stares at the space where his shadow should be. Blank, rough blackness, and a heavy, church quiet. Her thoughts set off on a rampage, dragging her fleshy heart to her mouth. Is the woman still here? Is she dangerous? Did she lead Jay through? Did she lead Jay on? Was she there at all?

Fuck it. Sometimes, overthinking does more harm than good. Locking her limbs, Kira shuts her eyes and steps on into the cliff.

It's a rain of sand, and then it's over. She blinks, once, twice, again.

She'd half-assumed she'd find a cave, but no. Kira stares. Before her lies an amphitheatre, hacked out of stone. The dimming sky above forms a perfect, greying sphere, and while it looks real enough, it could easily not be. Massaging her arms, Kira feels herself quail. It's not exactly Gringotts or Diagon Alley, but it's something.

That word again: something. The hacked-out cleft is a dip in the rocks, the centrepiece of which is a fire. Stones range around it, some claimed, most not. Low and slow it burns, neither religious nor ritualistic, offering the appearance of a companion. The sweet scent of smoke and of rain. The space is deserted.

If anything, that gives it more power. Echoing, ringing with footsteps, as if no one is in control and as if that's how it belongs. Kira folds her arms and holds herself. It's a quarry, a holy place, a whole little world. It overawes her and welcomes her in. No judging, no stares, no looks. No one cares.

But on the flipside of that is being lost and alone and unsure of why they're here. Now, she's more unsure than ever.

Head tilted down, she steps up to Callum. Hands in his pockets, his feet are planted, and he squints at the far-off rocks. Jay and the woman are nowhere.

'Tell me.' Joining her without a sound, Freya butts Kira's elbow. 'What's everyday life on the outside?'

Kira feels like she's floating. 'All you'd get would be bruises.'

Nodding once and once again, Freya surveys the quarry. 'And if, suddenly, you get the urge to follow a wolf?'

'It'd go *Three Little Pigs* on you.'

'Which means?'

'You're food.'

'Fair enough.'

'The outside sounds like somewhere we should really get back to.' Callum drapes his arm over Kira's shoulder. Hazily, Kira pushes it off. 'Shall we start, I don't know'—he gestures—'eavesdropping? Ingratiating ourselves?'

'You two do that.' Freya carries on scanning the rocky murk. 'I'll see if I can track down Jay. This is not the best place to scarper, especially not with invisible women who lure you through cliffs with a song.'

Adjusting her bow and touching her knife pocket, Freya walks away. Kira tracks her path to a chiselled passage. You wouldn't know it was there—you wouldn't know any of them were there, in the gaps between gargantuan boulders or slashed through the slate itself—were it not for the people using them. Not many, and largely alone, only entering to leave by another crack or to speak to someone by the fire, and for a while, Kira watches. Still, no one questions them, standing here, blank. This is a place of shadows and silence, for secrets and keeping themselves to themselves.

Faintly curious, Kira turns. 'Oh.' Her mouth glues in an "o." 'Um. Callum. Look.'

The cliff they passed through doesn't exist. The black rocks waterfall over each other, cut with dark fissures and coarsely shrinking, tapering down to the shore. Grey in the bruising dusk, the lake chops away. The sun isn't setting; it hasn't for days. Like ink saturating a pool, the sky sinks into night.

'If that's a disguise'—Callum nods at the lake—'what's happened to everywhere else?'

Kira shivers and shrugs. 'There's a lot of magic here.' Another shiver tingles, and she turns to the fire. The wind is lower here, more a breath of cold than the gusts from the shore, but as night falls, it bites. She left her coat on the horse's back. 'I can feel it in my stomach.'

Callum nods. 'Me too.'

Kira looks at him, surprised.

'You know'—Callum voice is almost defensive—'if that's what the sickness is. Just a bit, like I'm hungry and dehydrated, and it's starting to make me feel strange.' He lifts both eyebrows in her direction. 'Is it science, or is it magic?'

Absently, Kira tuts at him. 'I reckon its magic.' Scanning the echoing space, she fixes on the fire. The flames are the only source of light, barring two separate shadows cupping glows in the rocks. 'How shall we start ingratiating?'

Callum doesn't hesitate. 'The fountain of heat.' He nods at the fire. Two men sit beside it, silent and apart. One looks into the flames, intent, intense, his arms on his knees. The other has his eyes shut, sitting on the ground, propping his back on a rock. 'While we're here, we might as well sit and get warm. Drop in an innocent question.' Removing his hands from his pockets, he heads toward the fire. His back straightens. His shoulders lift. He doesn't stride, but his self-assured manner makes him look like someone else.

Fiddling with her shirt hem, Kira makes herself stop. If Callum can wear a mask, so can she. She's practiced often enough. 'Like what?'

Her arms feel odd. Her fingers want to twist. Do people always walk like this, with their hands by their sides?

'Like "Hi, we're new here, where's the food?"' Scratching his head, Callum picks a stone, not far from the man and his flames. On puppet-like legs, Kira follows. As much as they need information and help, Skarrig's reputation sets her on edge. Simply being here would set her on edge, surrounded by a tangible tang of magic and the feeling of the edge of the world. Witches. Creatures. Spirits. Havsrå, skulking in caves on the shore. People who don't know what they are. It's a rough, raw danger, and it wicks off in waves.

Aware of every movement, Kira takes the stone beside him. 'I'm not sure that'll get you very far.' God almighty, she's forgotten how to sit. Awkwardly, she tucks one foot behind the other.

'What?' Callum murmurs, for all the world innocent, one eye on the fire. 'It's an in.'

'It is, but not a very good one.' She gives him the tiniest of teasing smiles. 'Even when you've changed, nothing changes.' Shifting the tiniest bit closer to him, she looks out to the darkening rocks. 'Jokes and food. The fundamentals of you.'

Linking his hands on his knees, Callum laughs, soft and low and something else, something close to longing. 'That's good to know.' He glances at her. 'When I get myself back, I'll be ready.'

'I found them.' Freya is suddenly there, taking the stone beside Kira. Kira's heart hops, but she quashes a flinch. 'Jay and the woman. She's visible again.'

Kira peers past her into the gloom. 'Where?'

'Over there.' Freya tips her chin to the left. The fire dances bright in her eyes. 'Behind a rock. They're sat on a rug. I don't know what they're talking about, but I made sure Jay was okay, and he saw me. He looked content enough.' She rubs her mottled hands together. 'If he's found someone like him, then good.'

'Ching Shih?' The voice is not one of theirs. Kira looks round; the fire-watcher has lifted his head, to study them instead. His face is craggy, older than her dad's, wild white hair electrocuted and straggling past his neck. Lit by the flames, his skin glows crimson, from years outside in an unjust climate as well as the flicker of the flames. His rugged clothes hang ragged. Barring the crystal about his neck, he could be a farmer or a fisherman.

Not that one excludes the other. Here, it certainly shouldn't, but to her outside mind, the two together don't fit.

'Sorry?' Hastily, Kira stops staring. 'Ching Shih?'

Turning a pendulum over in his hands, the man nods beyond Freya. 'The woman with the rug,' he says. 'I assume you mean Ching Shih. She's taken an interest in one of you?' His gaze slides shrewdly along, from Freya to Kira to Callum. 'That's more or less remarkable.'

Deliberately, Callum meets Kira's eyes. 'Why?' he asks, slowly shifting his gaze back to the man. His linked hands tighten, from loose to a knot.

The man turns the pendulum over and over, a smooth, pointed, pinkish stone hanging on a thong. 'She keeps to herself,' he says. His voice is a smoker's. 'Usually, we all do, but particularly her. She's notorious for solitude, even though she's almost always over there'—he lifts his head a little, a slight tilt left—'where it's as busy as this place gets. Any reason she might have latched on?'

He doesn't demand. He doesn't fix them with piercing eyes, full of distrust. He turns his pendulum, watches the flames, and wearily sounds as if he'd appreciate an untold tale.

Sofia's warning returns: don't reveal too much. Kira half watches him stare into the fire and tries to think on her feet. They came to the place of outcasts for help. If they don't reveal anything, they'll get nowhere, and after all, the uncanny was there to greet them at the door, or the cliff. Ching Shih sensed Jay's ability, making her more uncanny than him. Here, all of this is okay.

Kira nudges a red-hot, dying cinder. They're involved with the Chlause. They're involved with the Kyo. They're the catalyst for chaos all over Whiteland; that doesn't stand them in good stead.

'Le—I mean, Jay,' Callum says into the fire, 'hears thoughts. And sees minds.'

He straightens on the stone. A chill of worry is warmed by relief; the decision is out of her hands.

'Yes.' Kira speaks before she chickens out or overthinks. 'Ching—Ching Shih appeared and said he was in her mind, disappeared, reappeared so only Jay could see her and took him away.' Her eyes slide to the rocks. 'I guess they're still over there.'

The pendulum clinks. 'That doesn't surprise me.' The man's pinkish stone glows. For the first time, Kira notices his hand full of rings. 'She's naturally theatrical. Or rather, she floats around and does things that others find theatrical. I keep the fire'—the flames pop—'and she keeps this place disguised.'

'So she's a witch?' Freya doesn't sound especially easy or especially good at hiding it. Kira almost wants to hug her, a quick, panging urge. She'd forgotten that Freya recoils from magic. How much this must be taking a toll.

'Not specifically.' The man looks up from the fire. His wrinkled eyes are green. 'She doesn't know specifically either. Interesting about your friend, though.' He tugs on a tiny braid in his beard. 'We don't hear much about people like that. Are the rest of you that way inclined?'

'Making friends and spilling secrets.' A lilting voice comes quiet through the flames. Kira looks round, her breath catching: the dark-haired, vanishing woman, and between her and the sleeping man, a peaceful-looking Jay. 'That makes two of us this evening, Davide.'

Ching Shih steps through the fire, taking a seat beside Davide. The flames roar violet and settle like lambs. Half hidden by Callum, Kira studies her. She's hypnotising: black hair hacked off at her collarbone, a row of braids on one side and a thread of beads on the other. Her clothes are embroidered versions of Callum's. Reds and purples line the hems, curling across her chest and up and coiled around her thighs. Her wrists are looped with woven bracelets, copper rings trailing up one ear. She moves so gracefully, but looks so strong, so solid in every way, that it hurts.

Kira shifts closer to Callum, as close as she can without feeling needy. What is it, this hurt, this bone-deep cold? It's something, something like night in the daytime, keeping Ching Shih apart. A purpose in her still face. A sureness in her posture. Jay's right; there's a conscious, measured melancholy. An air of the wild, a longing for the plains, for horses to run with rather than wolves. Kira can't help but ache.

'Of course.' Davide looks at her, not a smile but a softening, less on guard. 'What else is there to do? I assume you've checked them all.'

Ching Shih smiles with her fleeting lips. 'What else is there to do?'

'And?' Davide rests his hand on her knee.

'And'—Ching Shih touches her hand to his, and then the contact ends—'they're looking for a lot.'

'We could,' Callum says dryly, 'tell you ourselves.'

Muted, Freya huffs. Kira nearly smiles herself.

Callum tugs down the corners of his mouth. 'You know, just thought I'd throw that out there.'

Ching Shih glances round. A second later, from the darkening rocks, a mournful sound unfurls.

It's both a song and not. For a heartbeat, Kira hears it as the noise from the shore, but it melts into music, and her chest swells up. It's a snapshot, a moment, that you don't forget; it sends creeping nails up her spine, while hot tears threaten her throat. Beautiful. Desolate. Haunting. It's the sound of Skarrig and more.

Near the top of the rocks, a silhouette plays the saw. Rising and hanging, to plunge and vibrate, the notes are a ghost's soft lament or the whistle of wind through rattling windows. Every hair on Kira's arms stands up. The wailing ghost himself could be expelling frozen breaths, quelling the fire into ash. The night hides the shadow, barring a clear-cut outline and the way the bow arcs against the sky. She's heard of it, in old books, in comments from her grandparents or on signs at county fairs; Kira never thought she'd hear it herself. She never thought it could be a moment to capture, like the dancing she saw with her dad; a moment separate from anything else, to pin down, to remember, that will move her, chill her, and swoop her back here in many years to come.

Beside the fire, no one speaks. Quietly, Callum moves his arm around her, and quietly, Kira leans in. For the moment, they are frozen. Set in stone, here, now.

With an ear-splitting sonic boom, the ground starts to shake.

55

Hot and bright and set on fire

9 p.m. Carol is at the helm of this, and now she's anxious, and now she sits and waits. They know how they're going to try, and what they're going to do, but whether it'll work… As restless as Callum again, irking herself by jigging her knee, Carol is anxious, and she sits and waits.

The twins are in bed. Finally, she whittled their sleep time back down in readiness for this, although from the purple bruised beneath their eyes, she should have done it sooner.

She should have. She should have done a lot of things, but guilt can hit her later. It's 8:54. A candle holder props her tablet up, and the kitchen holds its breath.

It's silent. Too silent. Carol taps her cup of tea. The cuckoo clock should be ticking, but she forgot to wind its weights. The fire grew too hot too soon. The red wood packed out far more heat than the new, smoky timber, so she let it die down hours ago. Diego snores away on the couch. The cats are nowhere to be seen. It's as if they sense a storm and have hidden; in a sense, they wouldn't be wrong. Animals sense all kinds of energy, and energy is what she relies on. The cats don't like it when she contacts the Whispers. When she's silenced things before, she hasn't seen the cats for days.

8:57. If it works, perhaps the Whispers will help her; they've been gone for every watcher since informing Nayab with a show of menace that the outside should handle its problems alone. If they do, then maybe—a very big maybe—she can ask one final thing. One final attempt on their part to find out what happened to her sons.

Unlikely, but Carol clings to it, as she should have clung to her sons. This, then that; then Callum will be cleared.

8:59. She unlocks the tablet and loads the group. Earbuds in. Ready.

9:00. Her nerves both ease and increase. Starting the call, she shuts her eyes, wipes her mind, and pictures the sky. An early spring dawn, no clouds. She and Lena had worked alone, but Beth and her father silenced together when the girls caused chaos in London. Others say the same, about smaller things. This is different; it's disconnected.

It's disconnected and huge.

One by one, they murmur that they're here. Jannali is last, two minutes late, and settling into a crackling silence, they spread their minds to the air.

※

In their bedroom, lights off, the twins hold their breath. One on one bed, one on the other, watching the digital clock.

At 9:06, Karl stage whispers, 'They must have started by now.' He scrunches his face in pantomime twists. 'Unless the time is wrong.'

'No way.' Vehement, Julia shakes her head. 'The thing said nine o'clock. Nine o'clock *today*.' Uncrossing her legs, stiff and tingly, she tiptoes to the door. Creaks it open, holds her breath again, and stills to listen.

'Anything?' Karl is bright and hopeful.

The landing is dark and useless. '*Nothing*.' Julia spins on her bare heels, huffing a vigorous puff. 'The message said nine, though.' She scowls at the door. 'I can't hear the TV either.'

Karl plucks at Callum's old ski-patterned bedclothes. 'If they're doing these…these…'

'Mind vibes,' Julia says, pompous and prompt. She came up with the name herself; it's cool, like *Scooby-Doo*. 'All linked up. That's what you heard?'

Karl nods in jerks so his chin knocks his chest. 'Maybe the mind vibes are quiet,' he says. Pausing on a downward jerk, he gives himself three chins. 'So there's nothing to actually listen to. We could go downstairs?'

Half sliding from the bed, he blinks at her. Pushing her lips out, Julia nods. It's not a bad idea, but it wasn't *her* idea. 'It might'—she stuffs her feet into her slippers—'be a thing you feel when you're closer.'

Cautiously, she creaks the door open. Pause, listen. Nothing.

'Come on.' Beckoning Karl, *Scooby-Doo*-style, she tiptoes toward the stairs. They've sneaked and eavesdropped enough lately to know where the landing creaks. Avoiding the path between bathroom and banister, Julia holds her breath a third time, lifts the beaded curtain, and replaces it behind Karl without a single sound. They should be spies. They should be *ninjas*, stealthy and unseen.

Light seeps under the kitchen door. Karl sits down, in the right angle at the bottom of the stairs, almost a ghost in the dark. Drawing her legs to her chest beside him, Julia summons her courage. She's not alone; her brother's here, breathing loud in her ear, the shiny elbows of his pyjamas chafing against her arm. She's got Carol in the kitchen, and they're doing something *good*. Not evil, not scary. They'll make the stories go away and find Callum and Jay.

Even so, the lounge is dark, except for ashy-red cinders. The moon stayed hidden, and so did the stars. The whole day was cloudy, wisping white outside the window, as though it would slither inside if it could.

Not helping. Resting her chin on her knees, Julia finds the familiar things. Television, sofa, book piles, paintings. Scratched-up candlewax, spilled on the table. These things are okay. Not evil, not scary. Not—

Inside her chest, something throbs. *Du-DUMDUMdum.*

Julia starts. It wasn't her heart. That's not where her heart sits, and anyway, it felt completely apart.

It throbs a second time, faster. She holds her breath yet again. It also wasn't her mind.

'What?' Karl hisses. She hardly hears him. It's coming a third time; she feels it brewing. *Dumdumdum* like a painless headache, it lifts through her chest to her neck to her shoulders, and when it hits her head, oh, she can feel.

She can *see*.

⁂

It's not enough. Carol tries to batten down her mounting frustration. The last thing to help would be breaking concentration, but damn, this is nigh-on impossible. The others are there, all connected, but their threads are frayed, the tin can telephone game she never liked. They're not strong enough.

Or not connected enough. Carol taps her mug. Her finger aches. Do there need to be more of them? Or, and this is what she fears, do they need to be together? The mystical and technology, devices and magic; one corrupts the other, and they're jarring. The combination unsettled her anyway, and this could be why; it just doesn't work.

When all is as it should be, the energy is palpable. Smallish ripples, setting small things right, not enough to be a butterfly, although a hurricane is what they're after. When all is as it should be, this energy webs her, setting her afloat in her springtime sky. The connections are feelings, like wires in her mind's eye, sparks to sever between Whiteland and here. Right now, she's blocked.

The unrest is there. The connections are there, but she can't reach through the veil to seize them. Her mind-hands are pinned to her sides. Frustration festers. It's too big, too involved. They're not—

A slash of light slices through her. Blossoming, blooming, it flares to a sunburst, and slapped by whiplash, Carol cries out. In her ears, other voices shout. The light is red-hot, molten-gold hot, as though the sky is branding her, and oh, good God, the *pain*. Her hands start to shake. She's staring at magma, an explosion, an eclipse. Carol can't hold onto the links, the connections. They're far too sharp, and they burn.

They *burn*. Carol's focus blows open, up, up, up. Her spine bucks back against her chair. It's a panorama of needlepoint clarity, and the needles dig in until she has to back out. She can't stay. It can't be done. Whatever this is, it's a warning.

As vivid as it slashed, the power surge dies. It leaves her frail, electrocuted, sickened, weak, but oh. *Oh.*

Hope rings where pain echoes, daring to believe. Her springtime sky is full of light. Carol tests it tentatively, but it holds, and hope fills her lungs with air. The unrest, the broken wires, become ties. The ties become solutions, sensations hewn from instinct and a hazy, inner knowing. The headphones buzz to static, and the voices start to speak. They're a map. They're a web.

And they tie.

✲

Karl sounds like he's speaking through water. Julia floats half below the surface, in that nice, soothing, bath time state where her body bobs and her hair streams but still, she can breathe. Karl's words get lost, but she's not trying to listen; the living room sparkles, as bright as summer or winter-blue sky and snow. It glitters in the dark and captivates.

All of her is streaming. From her bare toes to her kneecaps, from her elbows to her waist. From the blonde ends of her hair to her fingers, ink-stained on her legs. The hair on guard from her goosebumps streams, soaring and lifted like she's dropped in a dream, and among it all, there are lines.

Shattered-glass lines. Ice-on-a-pond lines. Jack Frost-on-the-window-lines. These are the lines that matter.

It's true, but why? No one knows why. Julia sits and listens to the throb in her chest. Her eyes are wide, and she smiles in the light, watching the lines in the front of her mind, where she normally goes when she's bored. Karl pinches her arm, but that's watery too. He sounds strangled. Maybe scared, but Karl, you shouldn't be. She's doing what she wanted; she's helping. She's hot and bright and set on fire.

Slowly, as the lines touch, the fire starts to fade.

※

Ending the call, Carol opens her eyes. It took a length of time suspended in space, but now, it's done. It's complete.

Slowly, she removes the earbuds, breathing deep and even. The end is always a sense of calm, of nestling into fresh bedding, along with the nagging sense of forgetting a task without knowing what it was. It's familiar. They've done it. They've silenced.

And relax. Sagging in her chair, Carol rubs her bleary eyes. In a while, an unpredictable while, they'll feel the effects of the silenced world, but for now, tea then bed. Talk about energy; whatever linked them all in the end stole every drop from her body.

Yawning, she stretches out her back, her arms, her legs, her cramping feet. This numbing, muscle-sapping fatigue could be from working with so many minds; she's never worked with one before, let alone ten. She had no way of knowing what it might cost, what its effects might be. Their communications have been brief and vague, the way every watcher talks about Whiteland. They never bond. They only spy.

Carol stretches again and stills.

Oh, no.

With a frisson through her chest, her fatigue is slapped away. Outside the door, there are whispers.

Quietly, without a screech, she pushes back her chair. It'll be Karl and Julia, miffed at their bedtime, planning mischief. Her core knows this as she moves to the door, but her watcher's mind is unsettled. There was nothing to overhear, so that's fine, but the slash of light, the sunburst, it was wild. A gold rush of strength, at odds with their control. They couldn't have found the ties without it, but something isn't right.

Carol's thoughts tick and whir. Something's not right, and the twins are outside.

The kitchen light illuminates them hunching by the stairs. Karl might have seen a spectre. Julia's aglow.

✧

'Did it work?' A grin splits Julia's cheeks all the way to her ears. In the doorway, Carol's face slowly loses its expression. 'All the lines? Did you fix them? I don't think *I* helped fix them, but I, I'—Julia scrambles up to her feet, bouncing—'I did something. I know I did. Didn't I? I did something?' She claps her hands. Her skin is fire. 'I did. I know I did.'

'Shut *up*, Julia,' Karl mutters, but the grin just won't go away. She helped it work. She did.

'Yes.' Carol grips the doorframe. Her lips hang apart. 'You. You were…'

Bobbing like a pogo stick, Julia nods, fire, fire, fire. 'I wanted to help, so I did,' she says, clasping her hot palms tight. 'It was amazing! There was so much light, and I saw the lines, and you were right, Karl, I had to be closer.'

'Karl.' Carol's voice is stern but quiet. 'Go to bed.'

Karl's eyes pop. 'What?'

Julia's perfect grin slips. Carol's eyes are pinned to her as though they're strangers. 'Now.'

'Why?' Karl's protest is a puppy-dog whine. For some reason, his justified outrage steals her grin even more. 'That's not fair. Julia should go too.'

'She will once I've talked to her.' Carol's eyes don't leave Julia's face. Stranger. Monster. God. 'It's okay, Karl. You're not in trouble.'

Julia would have hit the roof. Karl, though, has reached his not-calm limit, and sticking out his lower lip, he pushes to his feet.

With an ear-splitting sonic boom, the ground starts to shake.

56

Preaching to the lonely choir

In the snow above the Kyo, Taika lets the world go wild.

There was no great tremor when the women's freedom came; she finished the connections in the fire on the wall, felt the pressure build inside her, and as soon as she was fully focused, at the tipping point of her power's control, she let it loose. Once the gale had dulled to a storm, she left the cave and waited.

The magic was fiddly, but not enough to break her. The Kyo were imprisoned, not exiled like the Chlause. After stealing her way around the Whispers' witches' many spells, setting them all to catalyse at once, the releasing of itself was akin to pushing a snowball and watching it roll. Now, in the forest, she stands and watches the Kyo start to rise.

At first, they come in silence, ghosting through the trees. Maybe they're shocked or uncomprehending, but as more and more of them lift from the snow, greyish and haunted and weak and warped, the women return to life.

This is when the shrieking starts. How they thrive on striking fear, on crude intimidation. Enny, the foremost ghost, the speaker, rises in front of Taika, and with a mildly curious tilt to her head, breaks her mouth and screams.

Falling into madness, the other women follow. Translucent, flitting figures, they storm the darkened trees. Their cacophony is chaos, a cold born of pain and years of entrapment, and soon, the forest rings with it.

And still the women come.

Finally, Taika got what she wanted: no dread, no loss, no fear. Taika sets her face in ice, and lets the havoc feed her strength. The Kyo won't menace her; not anymore. She's done what she said she would, what no one else has tried, and she still has more to do.

In the distance, torches flash through the trees. Taika smiles inside, bitter and dark. They're scurrying out of their holes; good. The village will stare and run and feel terror, like nothing they've ever known. They'll smell the bloody magic, and then, they will die.

Screaming, fire, flitting forms. Magic chills Taika's fingers, coats her throat, and sends the blood to her heart. It's in her. It *is* her. Cloaked in the centre of the Kyo's exodus, she welcomes it like waves. The Whispers won't find her here. They shouldn't get into the snowbound cave, but if they do, she won't be waiting. Not again.

While the Kyo rage, she'll break through to Urnäsch. She'll loose the labyrinth. She'll preach to the souls of the lost church choir. She'll put the aurora back in the sky, and then, Ørenna will die.

57

Hurricanes

The rumble sends the fire spitting. The saw screeches once and stops. Callum grips Kira in a vice.

'What,' Freya asks, as the shaking subsides, 'in all Ørenna was that?'

Looking to the water, Ching Shih stands. 'The spirits are out.'

Kira follows her gaze. Over the surface of the lake dance lights, delicate fronds of mist. This far out, they're silver and formless. 'What do they mean?' Breaking from Callum's vice, she stands.

Ching Shih shuts her eyes.

'Nothing good.' As craggy as the cliffs, Davide nods at the water. 'Not when they're like that.' He drives himself to his feet and touches Ching Shih's wrist. 'What can you feel?'

Distant but distinct, a moan drifts toward them, a heartfelt, piercing keen. Hollow around the magic's nausea, Kira's stomach twists.

'Whatever it is, it's big.' Heavily, the sleeping man gets up. Everything about him droops.

'Big?' Kira glances at Freya. 'Like a huldra?'

Freya meets her eyes but doesn't see. The hunter has returned, and her mind is elsewhere, listening, focused, poised.

'No.' The sleeping man regards the spirits.

Their moan fills Kira with a yearning sadness, a seeping, dripping, unnatural knowledge that everything is lost. It's the bleak lake, the biting wind, the barren black cliffs. It's her, standing on the edge.

No. She spikes her palms with her nails: *unnatural*. The feeling is the spirits. She's not lost.

Not yet.

'A huldra wouldn't cause this.' A hunter himself, Davide scans the darkness. Footsteps echo. Shadows jump from rocks. Someone blows a horn. 'No. This is something else.'

'And if you don't know that,' the sleeping man says, 'or can't feel it now, start running.'

Shouldering a bulky fabric bag, he leaves the glow of the firelight, making for a gash in the towering rocks. Silent, Ching Shih follows.

'Why?' Kira asks, as the hollow sickness works its way through her chest. 'What? Run from what?'

'Just go.' Pushing his pendulum into his pocket, Davide follows the others.

That's not a plan. That's not anything. Kira pushes her hair back from her face and holds it over her head. The horn blows again. People shout. Something howls. The air smells of iron and tastes like dust.

'Come on.' Scooting around the fire, Jay waves toward the rocks. He's animated, shiny-eyed. 'We need to follow them.'

Callum's jaw works. His cheeks draw in. 'Why? What is this?'

'They don't know.' Snatching Kira's sleeve, Jay tugs her from the stone ring. 'They just know it's bad. Giant.' Halfway to the rocks, he stops. 'Whoa.'

Kira veers aside, sucking in her stomach, barely avoiding collision. In front of the passage, Ching Shih, Davide, and the sleeping man are static. 'Whoa?' She looks between them, her heart drumming faster, her gut an uneasy mess. 'What now?'

Freya steps past them and carries on walking. 'I think we should trust the natives. Move.'

Callum grabs Kira. Kira grabs Jay, hauling him out of his spell. As they reach Davide, watching and guarded, all sound in the cold, echoing, panicked space drops.

Silence. The eerie, waiting seconds throb, stealing Kira's breath, before a belt of wind lashes through the rocks. It carries a cry, a rushing groan, and then the air grows still.

Calm-before-the-storm still. Lull-between-the-battles-still. Kira grips Jay's sleeve. Somewhere, there's a butterfly. They must be close to the hurricane.

'Go.' Ching Shih's voice is an order. Bag bumping, the sleeping man takes off for the rocks. Sharing a look that can't be read, everything and nothing, open and masked, Davide and Ching Shih follow.

Freya is after them at once. Blurrily, Kira kicks herself into action. The hollowness bruises and makes her feel faint, but they have to run. There's a hurricane.

'Kira.' Jay's voice is a frown over the feet whacking stone.

'Yes.' Turning sideways, Kira scrapes into the passage. Her satchel thuds on the entrance, and she yanks it through. The strap tears with a *riiiik*.

'I don't know how to say it.' Batting her bag, Jay barrels in behind her. 'Just before the wind, I felt something.'

Ahead, Freya's bow clacks off the rocky walls. She curses. Kira lifts a hand to block its tip, at an angle now to jab her. 'What kind of something?' She calls back, unfocused.

'Like'—Jay's breath puffs the back of her neck—'when you think the ground's flat, but there's really a dip, and you trip. That feeling in your belly, where you start to fall.'

'That doesn't sound fun,' Callum says in a grunt, low from some way back. He's not wrong, and Kira stumbles on, her knees knocking every edge her elbows miss. This passage is a slashed, suffocating slit, deep and grey and dark. It's far too much like Monte Yuno, before all hell broke loose.

Beyond Freya, Ching Shih mutters something. Davide's coarse voice replies, and a small glow appears, throwing the rock into tiger silhouettes.

It's not Monte Yuno. It's the Kyo. Kira's chest pools cold at the memory as her clothes scrape rock, and she drags herself on. The draughty cavern, lit by candles, cupped in the women's hands. Enny, tugging her through a gap she thought would keep her trapped.

'Leon,' Callum says. Kira pools colder. He's been using the name since Ayomi, but it feels wrong. 'Do they know what this is yet? What's happening?'

'No.' Bashing into Kira's bag, Jay yelps, his palm skinning her back.

On instinct, Kira flinches. 'Ow!' Tripping, she slaps the wall for support. 'Jay, be careful.'

'Sorry!' A scrabbling. 'Sorry. Um.' His voice is growing shallow. 'No, they don't know what's happening. All kinds of things are going through their minds, especially that other man's, you know, but none of them are certain.'

Gruffly, the passage widens. Still thin and icy, it's a breath less crushing, less smothering, less heading-to-a-ghostly-grave. Vaguely, Kira notes that it shouldn't be this long.

'Taika.' Freya sounds incredulous, but sure.

The name jolts electric in Kira's chest. For a cold, cold second, she stops. 'What?'

'Taika.' Glancing back, Freya's eyes are phantoms. Her face is open, the rawness Kira felt when she first saw Mathew's shimmer. 'It has to be, doesn't it? Either her or the Whispers. I felt their effects before I was human, though, and no one reacted like this.'

Davide's glow veers left. Freya veers with it, her bruised bow clacking.

Kira rebounds off the rock as she follows. Their convoy is speeding up. 'What about when Taika got through to Urnäsch?' She rubs her hipbone, winded, wild. 'You were only just human then. Did you feel it?'

Ching Shih murmurs. At once, Jay speaks. 'There's been disorder, but nothing so strong,' he says. He could be automated or reading from a card. 'We weren't aware Urnäsch had been accessed.'

His monotone is unnerving enough, but the words cram fear into Kira's throat, constricting her windpipe to a straw. The tiger-shadows loom and laugh. The rock clatters, clothes scraping, the smell of urgency and sweat. No one needs to say it: whatever this is, it's bigger than Taika reaching the Chlause. Bigger than the Whispers. Bigger than them all.

Davide's glow veers again. Around the sharp-cut corner sits a square-cut opening, blasted with wind and night. The lake, its cruelty, its spirits, its light slaps the rocks at their feet. No time to hesitate. No time for anything. Swinging out after Freya, Kira hugs the wet wall, jumps to the path, and scrambles up through the pebbles to a windy, bitter bluff.

At the top, the men and Ching Shih go still. Kira staggers to join them, gasping, reeling and…her heart and her stomach and her mind and her sanity plummet down to the shore.

Her legs judder. Vertigo swoops. She wants to scream, needs to scream. Beside her, Freya stills. 'Ørenna.'

Her mother, the mountains, the Chlause, her house. Talie holds these things as tight as she can as she lifts from the snow and coalesces. Pine. Smoke. Fire. Ghosts. Breathing the air she can't taste, she draws her threads together. The women of the Kyo fly free and amok.

There's so much *noise*. The Kyo was madness and quiet and death, but among the trees, they flit and shriek. There are people too, terrorised, running.

It's a riot, a mob scene, fire and fear, and in the centre stands a black hole of a girl who must be the witch.

A thick dark cloak, an unsettling stillness, an air that makes Talie want to flee. She will flee, but she has to come back.

She clings to Taika's idea too, what the women spoke of her wanting to do. It can't happen. Because of her mother, the mountains, the Chlause, her house. Because of how she threw four people into Hell. This is her penance while she holds on to herself, the part of her that's still Talie.

In a way, Taika's timing is perfect. Any longer, and Talie would truly be one of them, but as it is, she has just enough left. Two, three forms flash past her, weaving and whirling in time with their screams. Fire burns, in human hands and fizzling out in the snow. Talie casts herself back to the echoing cavern, to the riffling breeze and the pool. Last time she saw them watching Kira… she was where?

The outskirts of a barren lake, cold and monstrous. There?

The Kyo screech. The forest rings. Taika watches, peaceful, cold. The lake wind whips through Talie, beckoning her close. There.

Tying all her threads to this, she lets her essence fade.

※

The bluff looks over the mouth of the Zaino and the gradual sweep into the meadows. Moorland stretches to a brighter type of life. Above it, the world is cracking.

The Northern Lights have burst the sky. Sheets of colour flicker, green, purple, rose. They ripple into blue day despite the leaden night, before settling back to darkness. Every shift, every colour makes Kira's head roar and crushes her lungs to dust. The clouds roil, churning, charging. Riders could be storming out, backed by fire with swords held high. The wild hunt. The end of things.

That's what this hurricane feels like: the end.

White breaks across the sky, a sheet lightning blaze. Kira's throat stops up. She swoons with horror, her eyes so wide they hurt. Dark figures amass on the meadows, there and then gone and then there again, gone. Caught among ghosts of buildings and masked by the straining night. The Northern Lights swell. Storm clouds curdle, as choppy as the lake. The figures beneath are lingering longer. Yawning, Kira's horror blooms and spreads like venom. Urnäsch.

The Chlause are coming.

The Chlause have come.

Kira's knees almost cave. Thunder booms, and she remembers, in a shock, in a scream, she dreamt this from the other side. Shadows of trees, a paling sky; she was there, flying backward, tugged and thrown around. She saw this coming.

Oh, God. Another blaze of lightning illuminates the Chlause, and Kira covers her mouth with her hands. They shake. The trees she dreamt were pines. Oh, God, oh, *God*. Not only will the Chlause break through here but all the way to Atikur, a dark line beyond the meadows, shrouded in mist. They'll implode the peace, the fields and farms, where people settled after they'd gone. They'll bring their fire, their shredded souls, and seek their crude revenge.

Thunder crashes. Kira's body flinches. The bass booms through her bones. More people are emerging now, from caves and cracks and air. Some human, some not, some elfin, some earthen, one with a fiddle like the fossegrim. Younger girls than Romy. Men as aged as the rocks themselves. They stand on the bluff, in the howling wind, and watch the worlds collide.

Collide and crack and crash, like immense tectonic plates. Kira keeps her hands pressed to her mouth, holding herself whole. The skyline is a coloured blur. Along the lake shore, creatures crawl, slithering, skittering forms. Crooked beasts, glinting shadows, elongated figures. Normally, she'd be terrified. Now, she hopes, in a vain, manic burst, that everything here survives.

Behind her, someone shouts, drowned out by the thunder. A sharp intake of breath, and then, 'Kira!' Callum yells, abrasive. 'Kira, move!'

A sheet of cold as cutting as lightning slices from her scalp to toes. Kira inhales, her body tensing, but the ice passes through and stops. On the sliver of cliff before her, almost nose to nose, stands a ghost.

A scream rushes up her throat.

'Kira.' The ghost lifts its withered hands. Kira's scream expires, whipped by the wind. The figure is pale, as gauzy as mist, the nightmare beyond it stark through its skin, but it's a woman. Familiar.

'Talie?' Kira whispers. A movement of her tongue more so than her lips, the word barely breathes. It's Talie, but not the Talie she met, the bolshy girl who lied. This Talie is nothing, emaciated. Her dress clings to prominent ankles, and while all kinds of life have been stretched out of her, her hair cascades in its wild raven curls.

'Kira,' Talie says, as the spirits moan, as the lake bellows, as the wind whips them all with spray, and Urnäsch shudders through, 'you need to listen.'

'Kira.' Callum's voice is urgent. He grabs her arm. Freya yanks him back.

Kira stares at Talie, through Talie. This isn't real. It can't be real. Kira fights to focus. 'Listen to—why?'

'Because you need to run.' Talie's words are both hurried and lazy, as though she's a dreamer not quite in control. 'All of you. If you can get out, you need to do it now.' She drifts forward. Kira stumbles back. Callum's hands catch her arms. 'Taika's freeing the Chlause. She's already freed the Kyo.'

Talie's head tilts, but she jerks it right. Her obsidian eyes stretch, too large in their jutting sockets. Kira backs into Callum. 'The Kyo?' she manages. 'The Kyo are free?'

'That's what we can see,' Jay says, in his monotone. Kira's eyes dart to him. Ching Shih is poised, gripping Davide, hissing something low. Spine straight, Jay watches. 'Above Atikur. It's the Kyo.'

The words shoot dread into Kira like lead.

Freya's hands float up and hover by her head. Her ashy face is stricken. 'Holy shit.'

'Kira.' Cold cuts Kira's arm. She jerks her head around again. Talie is even more stretched than before, more Kyo than woman. More dead. 'Go,' she insists, the word tied-up and garbled. 'You need to go and get out. After Urnäsch'—her neck slowly tilts—'Taika starts on the outside.'

A hunting horn rends the air. Wildly, Kira looks to the forest. The mass of grey above it, the mist. It's not mist.

Dread. Panic. Hollow horror. 'What does that mean?' Kira shouts above the wind, hoarse and high and cracking. The bluff beneath them shudders.

'Kira,' Callum says in her ear, but no more. His hands around her arms are iron. His voice is weightless, bleak, lost.

'All the worlds will open.' Talie's neck is tilting, tilting. 'Everyone who's everywhere. Every*thing* that's everywhere.'

Kira shakes her head again, again. 'I don't know what that means.'

'But *stop!*' Talie rights her neck with a violent crack. The words are a guttural yell. Hysteria looms, high and hot. Kira presses back into Callum. 'That's why you need to *run*, why I'm *telling* you, cut off the outside and save my mother. I'm *sorry*, Kira. I'm *sorry.*' Her jaw unhinges, hanging open.

Kira's jaw slams into terror. She's back in the Kyo when the women encroached, and she realised they were mad, all mad.

'Run!' Talie bellows. It ends in a screech. 'I'm nearly them.' Her skull distorts. She claws at it and howls. 'Taika. I need—to find Taika.'

'And do what?' Somehow, Freya's voice is level. Wind whipped, lungs shallow, Kira drags her eyes across. Freya watches Talie like she might throw up. 'Stop Taika opening the outside? How is she strong enough to do that?'

With a shriek, Talie flies forward, passing into Freya. Clutching her chest, Freya's eyes bulge.

'Just shut it. *Just shut it.*' Talie drifts back. With a gasp, Freya staggers and falls. 'If she can open it forever, she can shut it forever. I'll make her. Go!'

Talie's ghost disappears.

Bending, Callum hauls Freya up. Kira stares at them, and they stare back.

The enormity hits like a punch to the gut. *If she can open it forever, she can shut it forever.* It's in Freya's parting lips, in the way Callum leans back, turning his eyes to the forest. The Kyo possessed Romy. If Talie's joined the Kyo, she can possess Taika.

'Just like the Whispers.' Kira's voice drops to nothing. In the sky above Atikur, the grey mist swirls. The sky curdles, the clouds descending, grey-black and boiling as they suffocate the din. In their midst, the Northern Lights crash.

'She's right.' Holding her stomach, Freya wavers up to Kira. They can't see the Chlause as the rain starts to drive, but the chaos is building. Somewhere, beyond silhouettes, they're there. 'We have to go.'

Shaking her head, minutely, then faster, faster, Kira turns to the bluff. People panicked, others huddling. Closed eyes and moving lips, swilling lights, and pulsing air, as if anything witches or weavers or whoever can do will help them now. 'No.'

Freya crushes her arm. 'Yes, Kira. If we get trapped here…' She trails off, as if this is enough.

Teetering over mania, Kira shakes and shakes her fevered head. A web of light shoots up and quails. The man who cast it runs. 'We can't.'

'We have to.' Freya lurches to a shout. The rain drums down and stings. 'If Talie does this, and you know it's possible, we might be stuck here for good. For good, Kira, do you understand that? For good.' She pinches Kira's skin. 'And the Kyo and the Chlause are free.'

Watching the lake, Callum glances at them. 'As much as I don't like agreeing with Freya'—he jitters on his feet, glassy-eyed and stony—'she's right. We need to get out.'

'No!' Kira's hands fly up, and she steps away. Her voice pitches, harsh and hoarse, and she holds her elbows tight. 'What about Romy? What about Dad?'

The ground grinds and starts to split. Light flares beside them from the sleeping man, his face glittering gold.

'Kira.' Freya moves toward her. Kira jerks back.

'Oh, my—*stop!*' Freya's face contorts, ugly and huldra. Teeth bared, she snatches Kira's arm. 'Just stop! This is not the time to be a martyr. Your sister doesn't know you, and she barely has a mind. What she does have'—she yanks Kira toward her—'is people looking after her, one of which is Mathew. Yeah, he's your dad, but may I remind you, he only exists in the *dark*.'

'Let go.' Kira shakes her arm. Her voice judders in time with her bones, in time with the quaking bluff.

'No.' Painfully, Freya hangs on. 'I can't—I'm so sick of seeing you do this.' Her rain-drowned voice rockets up to a yell. 'I call you an imbecile, and my God, you are. You've tried to save them so many times. You've tried to save everyone, and you know what?' Viciously, she lets Kira go. 'You're allowed to save yourself.'

No. Yes. Kira's cold. She's on fire. Swallowing the ache in her throat, Kira scrapes her hands through her hair. The river mouth batters its banks. The savage air throbs, a bruise in a booming, thundering roar. Freya isn't wrong, but Romy, Dad, Anna, snared somewhere in the sky…

The storm rages. The meadows flash. Kira's breath rasps, wet and weak. God, how everything hurts. Such a short time ago, she was hopeful. She thought they'd all be fine, in one way or another, but now, she has to choose.

There's no time. Kira covers her burning face with her hands. The Kyo, free. The Chlause, out of exile. The doors to the outside shut for good. There's no time to choose, no time, no *time*.

At the back of her mind, something buzzes. Dropping her hands, Kira squints at the bluff, splintered through the rain. Light. People. Shadows. Metal. The buzz grows to a hum, to static white noise, roaring toward them, dizzying the air. Kira staggers. Callum's arms go out. In a sonic wave and a bellowing howl, the sound surges over their heads.

Wobbling, Freya rights herself. 'The Whispers.'

The howl fades back to a buzz. The Whispers. Kira's tears soak her cheeks as the rain soaks her bones. If they're involved, there *is* no time. No time to think, to choose. No *time*.

'I'm getting Jay.' Freya wheels around.

Kira's chest swells, so tight it might burst. Is that it? Is that the decision?

'Kira, you need to listen to her.' Lifting a hand, Callum shields his face. The rain drives in angry slants, and he braces himself on the rock. 'We haven't even started to look for help, and who's going to help after this? We're a part of it.'

He swipes his sopping hair from his face and grips her sodden shoulders. Weakly, Kira looks up at him, blinking, husky. 'People don't know that.'

Callum's Adam's apple bobs. 'Maybe not,' he says, 'but either way, they'll be focused on protecting themselves.' He ducks his head. Rain drips from his hair. 'Hell, Kira, we don't even know if there's any help to be found.' He looks up at her, pleading. His mouth is pained.

'There will not be any on the outside.' Callum cuts an urgent glance at Freya. Swallowed by the rain, she argues with Jay, her muffled words rising. 'Look.' He turns back, gripping Kira's shoulders, his voice more urgent than ever. 'Kira, I know it's a horrible choice, but on the outside, we have a chance. Romy and Mathew don't.'

Kira swallows the bubble at her lips. 'On the outside—'

The words wrap around her heart and squeeze it half to death. Kira's tears slip faster, salty on her lips, as a sob almost snaps her in two. Her chest heaves and racks. 'I only just...' Her voice is awful, jerky and thick and out of control. 'I only just got them back.'

'I know.' Callum props her up, peering down into her face. He blurs like sun on water. 'I know, but if they stay here, at least they'll be accepted. Marya said she'd keep trying to help, but if there *is* no help, and we all stay, we'll be lost, and always wonder what if we'd tried to get out when we could?'

His pleading intensity shames her. Shuddering, Kira shuts her eyes. With an *oh* like he doesn't know what to do, or what he's done, Callum pulls her to him. Her face mushes his wet shirt. It smells of rain. It tastes of rain. His fingers hold her shoulder blades. Callum wouldn't say please, but that's what he means. He wants to find his life.

'He won't come.' Boots thud on the trembling bluff. Pulling back, Kira wipes her eyes, breathing through her mouth. Marching toward them, Freya folds her arms. Beyond her, Jay is still.

'Come where?' Eyes narrowing, Callum turns. Slowly, his head lifts back. His mouth thins. He looks to Jay. It's a face that says he knows.

'Home!' Freya flings up her hands. She sounds close to tears herself, drenched and starting to drown. 'He says he feels at home in Whiteland. He wants to stay with Ching Shih, who he's known all of a minute, and worse, Ching Shih says she'll have him. He wants to find the others that she knows like them.' Clenching her fists, Freya spins. 'Shit!'

Her violence makes Kira flinch. Jay is a blur through tears in rain. Kira wipes her sore eyes, watching him stand, a mini, stubborn Callum. Her head is hot and so, so heavy. This is madness. Hellish madness. Romy and her dad can't come. Jay doesn't want to. Kira drags her puffed gaze to the lake, the sky, the fleeing creatures, people, spirits, Urnäsch taking shape amid the storm. Somewhere, the Whispers and the Kyo war.

And time is running out.

Ching Shih turns. Jay follows her without so much as a nod. The sleeping man's light consumes him. Across the lake, the spirits scatter, with a last unearthly keen.

'Okay.' Kira chokes on the word and instantly wants to tear her skin to strips. Blood. Flesh. Her mind scorches, screaming, red. 'Where do—' a real scream threatens, a firestorm of tears, and she balls her hands into fists. 'Let's go.'

Freya's mouth and eyes and shoulders sag. 'Thank God.' She looks to Callum. Statuesque, he watches Jay, stumbling into a sprint after Ching Shih and Davide. The three of them skid down the rock, away from the lake and are gone.

Ducking his chin, Callum shuts his eyes. The veins in his temples strain. For a moment, a stretched, domed moment, he stares through the ground. 'All right.' Looking up, he's as strangled as Kira. His eyes meet hers and swerve painfully away. 'What do we do?'

Freya looks to the water. 'I guess we run to the lake.'

58

Trust the dead

The women are wild. In the trees, through the trees, floating up above the trees. As Talie unravels, she watches Taika, standing on the edge between the forest and a gorge, and clutches at all her threads.

Cut off from the bedlam, it passes her by. Mist gathers in the treetops, tendrils snaking down to the snow. Something shrieks and growls and rumbles. The wind yowls, blending with screams and a growing, throbbing roar. Wings light up and fly away. The air blurs and sharpens.

Talie drifts toward Taika. Too close; fall back. Her control is frail. Wait a few moments, let it all swell.

The sky above the gorge detonates with the aurora. Taika tilts her head to watch, and Talie rushes in.

Taika's eyes fly wide, popping, straining, and she sucks a wired breath. Talie feels it in the lungs she's lost.

What are you doing? The witch's surprise is girlish, confused, but Talie ignores it. If Taika doesn't understand yet, she will.

Thinking as though the thoughts are her own, Talie flurries through them. Memories. Futures. Blue-line fire. Poisoned anger, oozing pus. Things suspended above the rest. A cold web. A matrix.

Something shoves the form she has left, like a grunting push in the back. Talie topples, losing her gauzy foothold. Her mind gasps. Her threads fray. She almost faints, almost falls, out of Taika and back to the forest, but she chose her moment well enough. The witch is brittle.

Stop! Taika tries, more hurt than a cry. Her second shove is more of a nudge. *The Kyo said—*

I'm not fully theirs. Talie gives herself this, and there, the web, cold and bright and clear: all that Taika started, in the cave beneath the snow.

For the witch who's managed all of this, you're hopelessly naïve. She ties the catalyst tight to her mind before Taika can throw her off. The witch is trying, layering images, bloody-faced Chlause, a river, a man. Talie sinks through the glinting magic. Nothing Taika does will work. Taika truly knows nothing if she can't pick up on a child of Urnäsch in her head. The Kyo knew it straight away. *Don't,* she lets the icy web enfold her, *trust the dead.*

Taika struggles, both to push Talie out and to carry on triggering the break. Talie latches onto the second at once. *They said they wouldn't touch me,* Taika says, her voice sliding up like the shrieks outside. *None of them.*

How convenient. Talie gives Taika a mental shove, the push in the back she received. Her lost lungs gasp. *They forgot to mention me, their newest little toy. You can guess who I am.* Another shove, spiteful. *You made the huldra threaten me. You made me send the girls to Urnäsch. You made,* she pictures the wind, and hurls it at Taika, *my mother into beaten-up blackmail.*

The wind is electric and fills Talie with life. The glinting magic sinks through her skin. It turns her to frost, cleansing and sharp. In her lost body, Talie breathes.

Pine. Snow. Burning. Taika's eyes, Talie's eyes, are beautifully clear. She feels feet in moccasins and unsteady hands. The weighty cloak that isn't warm. The aurora, causing the air to ripple. The white noise of the coming Whispers. The energy within her, shifting balance as Taika's control grows loose. Angrily, Talie smiles. She's more herself now than she's been since she died.

You should have protected yourself, Talie says. The energy builds and blossoms and blooms.

Somewhere in a shady corner, Taika whispers, *Don't.*

Too late. Build, blossom, bloom. It surges up, and it isn't wind. It's fire through a tunnel, an electrical storm, and if she didn't have control, she'd drown.

Thrusting back against it, Talie lets the storm go.

59

The little boat has left

'Carol?' Julia's voice pitches higher than Carol's ever heard it go. One of the twins has hold of her cardigan, trailing behind it as she hurries outside. Diego starts to bawl, but the sound cuts off. The cloudy night is still again, the wisps imbued with indigo-black. She can't see farther than halfway down the garden, but somewhere, something is wrong.

'Carol?' The knobbly hand tugs her sleeve. Karl.

Carol stands and listens, motionless. You could ring a bell, and the echo would resound off every nearby peak. The clarity is sharp.

Whiteland-sharp.

'Go back inside,' Carol orders, waving dimly into the chalet. The sharp, tart air lifts the hairs on her arms. 'Back to bed.'

'But Carol.' Julia's whine is drawn out.

'For God's sake!' Carol slaps the doorframe. Her shout resounds like the bell. Her face feels manic, and it wires through her voice, her head, her chest. 'The pair of you, go! Now!'

Julia's face turns pink, and she starts to sniffle, both lips wobbling and wet. Carol shuts her eyes. Four feet thump inside. The stairs quake. A door slams. A bed creaks twice.

It's not their fault. Breathing harder than she should, Carol opens her eyes, gripping the frame for support. None of this is their fault, but whatever just happened, it sickens her stomach and steals the ground. On a boat by a jetty, she's being set adrift.

Straightening and unstable, Carol rests her tailbone against the wood. Guilt seeps through her, oily and viscous, but she folds her arms against it. The twins will be fine. She'll apologise to them, no excuses, and treat them to Fun-Planet. They can bowl or spend hours in the arcade and have a milkshake and burger and chips. Then, she'll apologise again.

Carol tips the knob of her skull back, *thunking* against the wood. The upstairs is quiet; the twins are fine. This, though…the clouds curl in, silent and serene. The white cuts off her garden, creeping up the snow. The world could have fallen away.

For the first time, she truly gets the meaning of deathly quiet. The taste of metal mars her tongue, as sour and cold as a cent. The cloud snakes closer.

It's not natural. This clicks with the deepest sense of knowledge, filling with ice, freezing her chest, as she watches the world white out. Her back presses into the doorframe until she feels every bone in her spine. She's not imagining it; something is wrong. Anxiety laps around her, into the hole the moorings abandoned. Something is slithering out of Whiteland, like hot, bitter blood, seeping invisibly out of the trees and into the muffling cloud.

Her anxiety swells and flutes in her temples. So fast. Too fast. Not natural. Wrong. Tight. Warm. Far too warm. Her head rushes through a tunnel, drowning out her lungs. She's never had a panic attack, but—

Raging through the mountain, a second *boom* explodes.

Upstairs, Julia screams. 'Carol!'

The shockwave slams Carol into the ground. Ricocheting off the compact snow, her chin jars. Her shoulder pops. Her teeth clash and snap her tongue, filling her mouth with that hot, bitter blood. Black blooms in front of her eyes. The noise echoes round the mountains.

Shakily, her arm buckling, Carol lifts herself from the snow. Ice crystals line her lips. Something…

Her chest aches like fresh loss. She stills, probing, feeling for threads.

Nothing. Her little boat has left.

60

Ago.

They're pelting down the path when the earthquake hits. Kira goes sprawling, her face and palms plunging through specks of rock and grit. Her head smacks the ground, and her teeth clatter, but spitting out blood and stone, she scrambles up and runs.

No way is she stopping now. Gasping, rasping, she flings her arms out, slewing on the slippery pebbles. Her cheeks sting. Her ears ring. Her forehead smarts. Her palms are grazed, engrained with grey, but skidding to the bottom, her hip bashing rock as she spins, she squints through the rain. Run to the lake, and then what?

'Go!' Freya barrels into Kira's side. Callum trips, close behind. Storming thunder crashes. 'Jump! You—we have to jump!'

Kira's stomach churns as much as the lake. Jump into the seething water, choppy and frozen and frothy and wild, alive with unknown peril. Toward the centre, the remaining spirits glow and keen and dance. Their stretched faces freeze her mind. The lake whacks the rocks, needled with rain. Below the surface, silver light glides. Jump?

'Go!' Freya's yell rips into the air. With a last, lingering look back, at the chaos, the cataclysmic sky, she leaps from the slick rock and plunges like a stone.

Along the shore, something skitters. One of the crooked figures, its arms bent the way no human arms can go, all gristle and bristle and bone. Things too far away to distinguish slink and crawl from caves.

Kira quails into a shrivelled little stone. She shouldn't have stopped. She should have just jumped. Her tears have withered and dried, replaced by a washing, fevered wasteland, flaming terror that stops her thinking, believing this is real. That this is happening, all of this, and again, they're running away.

'Kira.' Callum shouts above the pounding rain. Hair and clothes plastered, he comes toward her, mouth open, eyes thin. *Please, please, please*, they say. *Let's go.* 'We've gotten this far.'

Callum's shoulders heave. Desperately, he throws a look at the water, too rough for Freya to leave ripples. Around at the approaching monsters. Up to the magic-strewn, panic-strewn bluff, and finally back to her. *Please, please, please*, he begs. *Let's go.*

The wind whips around her. Kira stares at him, his urgency, his burning need to live. Would Callum go without her? Should she go at all?

Romy. Mum. Dad. This was her Monte Yuno mantra, before the ice plains tore her down. She thought she could save them. Kira thought she could still save two of them, until less than an hour ago. Her sister and her father or herself?

'Kira!' Callum shouts. His voice almost breaks. 'Come on! We don't have—'

Time. Kira lets out a sob. 'I'm sorry,' she whispers. 'I'm so, so sorry.'

Closing her eyes, she grasps Callum's wrists, and tips toward the water.

They say that if you step out onto the air, at just the right place, you can walk to the other side.

Her dreamer's feet step out, and her dreamer's body falls.

Down, down, down. The wind howls past them, Talie and Taika sewn together. The magic is done, the two of them spent. She can feel herself fading, like falling asleep, a soft nothingness folding over her, succumbing to the air.

Taika might be screaming. Either way, it's too late. They fall through the clouds, through the rushing gorge, and Taika's life winks out.

Down, down, down. The water rushes past them. Frozen and thrashing, bubbling and smothering, it surges up Kira's nose and tosses them around. Her eyes fly open. The lake snatches Callum away as they sink, and she can only hope that now that they've tried, they make it out in time.

Down, down, down. Kira's head starts to pound, her eyes full of water, her bursting breath running out. She never could hold it for long.

Down. Faint and dizzy, her arms float up. The water roils less the lower she goes, calmer, colder, dark. Dark behind her eyes too, fading into grey. The water is empty. It turns her, whirls her. What did Callum say about the siren?

He had punched it in the face and swam to the surface.

The thought explodes like a blinding starburst, flaring, burning bright. If Kira doesn't do the same, she'll drown. If she doesn't start to swim, she'll drown. Her chest is shaking iron. Her cheeks puff up, ready to pop. Her heartbeat throbs in her eyeballs, in her neck, her breasts, her stomach, her feet. Her eyelids droop. If she doesn't move, she'll drown.

Go. Before she can split at her throbbing seams, Kira drags her anchored arms in, kicks, and starts to swim.

It's a slog. It's impossible. Kicking her weak, watery limbs, she struggles her bulging satchel over her head and lets it go. The lifted weight propels her up. She kicks, flailing, eyes bleary, swelling, straining, hot. Is the water getting lighter?

God, Ørenna, mother of Mary, it's so hard to not breathe. Kira's mind shuts down. Her blood *thuds*, claustrophobic. Kick with her legs, push with her arms. *Thud. Thud.* Gooey, slowing. Her lungs are ready to evacuate. She's trembling, floating outside her body, but there's no side to reach for. No rope to hold to. No one to save her except herself.

What a way to finally die.

No. Surging back to life, she kicks. Blood throbs hot, her eyes grow dark, and she kicks and panics, panics and kicks—

Her head erupts into open air. Gasping, Kira gulps, slapping the water with her palms. Opening her eyes, she treads feebly to float. The night sky hangs above her, hazy with a quarter moon. All else is blackened water. Lifting her chin against the waves, she tries to calm her heart. The shore. Wherever she is, it must have a shore. Did she make it out? Did the others?

Waves slap her bare arms, lapping at her lips. She spits. The water tangs of salt.

Kira's out, then. She must be. Faintly, she paddles, as her blood becomes steady, as the rushing in her ears subsides. Her limbs tremble. Her lungs wheeze, gulping and loud, right from her used-up core. Barring the *hush clap plop* of the water, her breath is the only sound. No thunder. No screaming. No fearsome rain.

But my God, she's cold. As her teeth start to clack, Kira slowly starts to swim. The gentle waves buffet her on. Her fingertips are numbing. Her sodden clothes drag. A shiver sets in and refuses to leave.

Something butts the toe of her boot. Kira blinks, fighting to stay alert. Her other boot scrapes something hard, something slimy, something very much like mossy rocks in the sea. Jittery with fatigue, she doesn't pause, doesn't think. Both boots collide with the smooth, slippery things. Stumbling, Kira splashes and splutters out salt, and then, she's half-swimming, half-walking.

The calm, inky water quickly recedes. The quiet night nips her neck, her shoulders, her waist, cooling her to way below zero. Wrapping her arms around herself, she tries to hold the tremors, but it's as vain as battling the tide. Her clothes are icy, stuck to her skin. Her feet are lumps. She trudges on.

The water swirls around Kira's knees. Dark and glinting, in and out. Kira blinks her flagging, leaden eyes, stripped from staying open in the merciless lake. In and out. In and out. Beneath it, there's sand, almost white in the moonlight. Swilling about her ankles, the waves eddy about her heels. Her boots leave deep, heavy imprints.

The tide sweeps in, teases her toes, and softly leaves her alone.

Vaguely, her cheeks return to stinging. Her palms prickle. The tremors rack her. Kira breathes in, through her nose, not her mouth. The briny water scours her nostrils. Swaying, Kira stops. Curled within the brine, fresh and sweeping, the air holds something else.

The sea.

With a billowing exhaustion, she sinks to her knees. The sea. The stars. The moon. The outside. Something twinges in her ribs and is gone, leaving in its hollow wake an ache like missing a friend. Dully, she hears someone crying.

Crying? The sound seeps through Kira's fug, sharpening her mind. Shuddering, blinking at the sand, she pushes her torso up.

Not yet. A headrush consumes her, and she overbalances. The glittering sand looms in her vision. Kira catches herself with one arm, her wrist jarring. Okay. Not yet. Breathe.

The crying carries on. It's not soft, relieved crying, or I-can't-believe-I'm-okay crying; it's the crying of someone who thinks they've lost everything and can't fight their way out of the pain.

Keeping her fingertips on the ground, Kira slowly sits back. One eye twitches. The world won't focus. Blinking hard again and again, she strains to see the night.

A beach. Mushy, pockmarked sand. This narrow ribbon links two low, grassy hills. Moonlight slides off the rocks by the shore, silvering the softening waves. Feet away, shoulders shaking, hunching over her thighs, Freya cries.

Kira's throat feels full of sand itself, scraped by a seashell. Resting her palms on her knees, she swallows. 'Freya?' The word is hoarse and chafes like a cough. 'Are you—are you okay?'

From the sighing sea comes a violent retch. Two thumps hit the sand. Spinning on her knees, Kira's head swoons dizzy, and she lands hard on her butt. Slumped in the breakwater is a body.

'Callum,' Kira croaks, blinking through the black. She tries again louder. 'Callum?'

Pushing up on his unsteady arms, Callum retches again, coughs, and spits. His head droops. His chest heaves. His hair hangs low and glistening. Panting, he looks up and squints at her. 'Aye.'

They made it. All of them. Wherever "it" is, they're here.

'Oof.' Wincing with every muscle in his face, Callum manoeuvres up to sitting. 'Do we know'—he stops, shuts his eyes, and breathes—'where we are?'

Kira shivers and holds herself close again. Everything is coated with sand. 'No.' She looks around, less bleary than before. Over the hills on either side, nothing is light, and all is nature, but right now, that's okay. Coming from the chaos, the horror, the flight, it's quiet and normal, soothing and open, the tamed outside. Life.

Callum breathes out, in a long, coarse, catching whoosh. 'Jesus Christ.' He plucks his vest away from his chest, shaking the waterlogged fabric. Droplets spatter his hands. 'I see Freya made it.' He stops mid-shake. Briefly, his eyes constrict. 'What's wrong with her?'

Kira glances round. Freya's hair hides her face. Her sobs are as silent as sobs ever are. 'I don't know. Should I go see?'

Shaking his head, Callum shuts his eyes, and tips his head to the sky. 'Leave her,' he says. He sounds more drained than she is. 'She doesn't seem the type to welcome anybody's comfort.'

Kira lets her eyes linger on Freya. Her chest pangs, just a little. 'Maybe you're right.' Bracing herself, she stands, like a child learning to walk. Feet.

Knees. Push. Torso. Sway, washed with black. Up. Teetering, Kira holds out an arm. Her cold, sandy fingers on her temple ground her.

'She probably felt the door close.' Sloshing through the shallows, Callum joins her on the beach. His lips are purpled. His beard is out of place on his pale, ill skin. 'If that's what it was.'

Rubbing her eyes, Kira glances at Freya. 'I guess.' She rubs her whole face, up and down, up and down. 'You mean the weird little flinch? Like something pinched you inside?'

Kira breathes into her palms. Salt. Sand. That bloody, staining taste of metal, the only thing left of Whiteland.

Lifting her head, she slops her wet hair back. About bloody time.

'Kira.' Callum's voice is strange.

Kira focuses on him. He's frowning at her, a thinking, searching frown, the way you look at someone you pass in the hallway but never see outside school. Kira turns her head a little, purposely stretching the word. 'Yes?'

He opens his mouth and shuts it. His eyebrows pull together. 'Kira.'

Disquiet stirs. 'I already said yes, Callum.' Warily, she scans his face. 'What is it? You look like you've never seen me other than in, I don't know, PE.'

Kira stretches her face in an appropriate way, but he doesn't so much as blink. No huff. No smile. Callum's cheeks work. His eyes thin and darken, as though he's sinking inside himself.

'Callum, please.' Uncertainly, Kira steps toward him. 'What's wrong? I thought we were done. I thought this was over.' She lifts a hand. Her tired heart thumps. 'Please don't say I missed something, and we're in for a brand-new Hell.'

Callum says nothing. Her heart thumps faster. Overworked emotion surges up, the kind you don't feel unless you're utterly exhausted. The lazy sea laps the shore.

Abruptly, the odd look lifts. 'Shit.' Callum's eyes widen. His face drops. Whatever he's trying to understand comes clear, and he stares. 'Oh, my—holy shit.'

Grabbing her wrists, he reels her in, and cracks her bones in a hug. A relieved hug. An I-can't-believe-you're-alive hug. Gripped to suffocation in his sodden arms, Kira's mind kaleidoscopes. He's gone mad. Their near drowning has addled his memory. He didn't truly register the fact they'd survived or really, who she was. Who he was.

Squashed against his salty vest, her heart skips a beat and leapfrogs onto the next. His brain. His memory.

Kira jerks back. Callum's hands fall away. Talie was dealing with Taika, and Whiteland slammed shut. Does that mean...

'You.' Pricked with hope, with doubt, Kira falters, half stepping back in the sand. What if she's wrong? His expression tells her nothing. It's a maelstrom, a flickering slideshow: shock, disbelief, confusion, epiphany, and everything in between. 'Callum.' His name comes out strangled. She bites her cheek hard. 'You need to say something.'

Watching her, Callum steps forward. 'I know.'

Cupping her face, he leans down and kisses her.

Kira's breath catches. His hands are warm. His lips are warmer. She wasn't wrong. *She wasn't wrong,* and sliding her hands around his neck, she crushes him to her like the world is ending and tearfully kisses him back.

Salt, the sea, they're soaking, but God, she doesn't care. Callum crushes her as tight as she crushes him. One of them is shaking. Kira can barely breathe. It's him, the him she thought she'd lost. The him she thought *he'd* lost.

'I'm so sorry,' he murmurs eventually. Slowly disentangling himself, he rests his forehead on hers. 'Shit.'

Inexplicably, he starts to laugh.

'What?' Kira pulls back against his arms, searching his down-turned face. 'What *now?*'

Trying and failing to stifle his grin, Callum shakes his head. 'Shetland.' Scrubbing a hand across his head, with a half-crazed huff, he reels her back in. 'You know, that's the daftest thing. After everything that's happened, it ends in fucking Shetland.'

It's as though they've reached the final frontier. The curtain drops, or a veil is lifted, and the opening credits roll. Closing her eyes, Kira slumps against him. 'Then'—she sighs, hugging him tighter, breathing him in, his salt, his skin—'we really did make it.'

Sand *thumps* behind them. 'Someone's coming.' Freya's harsh voice is wool thick.

Cooling and giddy, Kira turns. The sudden lack of body heat is airy and strange.

Callum huffs, surprised, almost pleased. 'Huh.'

Kira angles her head toward him but doesn't shift her eyes. Along the belt of sand tramps an elderly man. 'Huh?' she asks quietly, lifting her guard. Warped like a gnarled tree, the man stalks stoically, harangued by a limp and a cane. 'Why "huh"?'

Callum comes to stand beside her. 'Because,' he says thoughtfully, rocking on his heels, 'it's Clemence.'

This makes nothing clearer. 'Who?' Kira asks. The man limps on. Waders, a blue knit jumper, a green coat swarthy enough to repel the worst of Arctic blasts. His twisted face is far from welcoming but neither does he look a threat.

'The Shetland watcher.' Callum starts toward him. Less than convinced, Kira hugs her elbows and trails behind like a child. 'I knew him when we lived here. He taught me how to swear.' In front of Freya, he stops. 'Oh. The holiest of shit.'

Rigid arms by her sides, Freya says nothing. Her hair straggles, stuck to her cheeks. Bowing her head, she averts her eyes. Her face is puffed and stung.

'This whole time.' Callum stares at her as though she's come through a portal and morphed into a beast. 'You've been with Kira this whole time. You travelled with us, even after you...' He runs a hand down his beard, shaking his head, his mouth stuck open. 'Jesus.'

'He remembers, then.' Freya doesn't look up. She's taller than Kira, but now, she looks small. She sniffs and breathes out through her mouth. Kira takes her hand.

'Callum?' Clemence treks toward them, his cane thudding in the sand. A headlamp restrains his sheep-wool hair.

Callum blinks, still waylaid by Freya, and scratches his head. 'Um. Yes.'

'Ah know.' Clemence speaks in a bulldog bark. 'Wasnae gonna be anyone else, bu' still.' He tramps up to them and stops, spreading a large, gloved hand. 'The hell happened to ye? Yer mother's worried sick. More than sick. Actually scratch all tha'.' He stabs the sand with his weather-beaten cane. 'The hell's happened in general? I cannae feel...'

He narrows his cracked eyes over the ocean. Gentle in the night, it splashes.

Kira laces her gritty fingers with Freya's. 'Whiteland's been cut off,' she says. 'I guess you felt it go.'

'Go?' Chapped mouth slack, Clemence turns to goggle. The headlamp pierces her eyes, and she leans away, squinting. 'It exploded, lass. When it started, it was an earthquake, then another, an' now…' He shakes his shock-white head. 'Ye all need ta come wi' me, an' then ye need ter explain.'

Callum rests a hand on Kira's back. 'It's—'

'I don' give a flyin' fuck what i' is.' In the dark, the man's eyes well and truly flash. 'The others need ter know why they cannae feel the land.' He jerks his chin back up the hill. 'My cottage isnae far. My cats went feral, an' I felt somethin' happen, saw ye emerge, an' came straight down. Come on.'

Stabbing with his cane, Clemence trudges around. A cottage. Cats. Warmth. Sleep. Kira doesn't wait for a second thought, and tugs Freya to follow.

'Kira.' Behind her, Callum's voice is tangled. The heat from his hand and his body falls back. 'I left…'

He breaks off, as if he can't believe he was speaking. Tired, oh-so-very-tired, Kira stops and shuts her eyes. Please, no more problems. They've found cranky help, or cranky help has found them. Anything else can wait.

Reluctantly, she turns. Callum's expression cuts the thoughts from her head.

'Callum?' Kira's chest twists tight. On instinct, she steps back toward him. His face is hacked, his eyebrows hard. His eyes are far away, and the whites are filled with horror. 'Callum, what's wrong?'

But she knows. Suddenly, in a surge that makes the sand tilt, she knows.

Callum opens his mouth and shuts it. He swallows, so forcefully she hears, and he meets her frozen eyes. 'I left Jay.' His voice is church-quiet, but there's no God here. 'How did I leave Jay? And if I've…' his mouth hardens and creases at the corners. 'Jesus.' His eyes sink closed. 'If I've remembered everything, then he has too.'

The words Kira doesn't want to think billow up black. Freya grips her hand tighter. The world tilts, a spotting rush. Kira digs her heels into the sand. She might throw up. She might fall down. 'Which means, so has Romy.'

'Whatever ye've done,' Clemence growls, 'it's done.' His voice is unforgiving as he limps away toward a cold, mud-cracked path up the frost-sparkled hill. 'You said it yerself; the entrance is shut. Whiteland,' he glances back, 'is gone.'

A world away. A life ago. Gone. Squeezing Freya's hand until her own starts to hurt, Kira reaches for Callum with the other. Whatever they've done, it's done. Whiteland is gone, surrendered to havoc. Surrendered to the Chlause, the Kyo, the rebels, the Moroaica, the Night Hunter, the Tomi desert devils, and everything else that should have stayed scare tales. The worlds are shut.

And they chose to live. Washed by moonlight, choked by feeling, Kira lifts her chin, grips the hands in hers, and starts to walk. Whether or not it's selfish—whether or not there were better options, outcomes they didn't foresee—for Romy, Mathew, Anna, Jay, Lena, Talie, and everyone else, the three of them, here, on this beach, in Shetland, have to live.

Memento mori.

Epilogue

Whiteland, the present

At the top of the peak where they stood with Mathew, Vasi and Grey watch the bedlam unfold. It rages in the sky, the colour of ashes, and with a heavy, weather-beaten sigh, Vasi turns away. The Everla trees are his concern, and that is where he'll stay. They welcome him back with a rustle and a sigh, and he leaves the world behind.

Erik holds his daughters, huddled in his home.

Above the desert in between, Anna doesn't know.

Mathew clasps Romy to his chest in the tent, tighter, tighter, tighter still. Her spicy hair. Her familiar bones. Her fragile, curled-up warmth. The weavers throw everything they have at the wards, and in her father's arms, she smiles. 'Dad.'

On a rocky arch over Skarrig, Jay stands alone. Even more than he did before, he finally feels at home.

Switzerland, a few years later

Too small. Too warm. Sparks flicker behind Kira's eyes, and sleepless, she stares at the ceiling. It's dark, as black as black can be, and somewhere, there are whispers.

She's been hearing them for a while. At first, they could have been a draught or snow pattering onto the roof of the chalet. For a while, Kira thought they might be the fire, shifting soft in the dying grate. The more she wakes up, though, the more she's sure. The more the lasting heat becomes an unpleasant cocoon, the more her senses lift: there are voices. Voices that say nothing but are voices nonetheless.

Careful not to wake Callum, Kira inches up. A thrill of fear chills her, but she crawls to the end of the wolf-patterned bed and subtly slides to the floor. The wood is warm. Of course it is. She wouldn't be overheating if it wasn't, if the fire hadn't blared all afternoon, evening, and most of the night as a gesture to welcome them back. Kira was grateful at the time; returning wasn't easy. It still isn't easy, not after so long. Freya wouldn't come at all.

Both door and floor creak as she tries to leave the room. Kira stops like a burglar, up on her toes. She could shut this rickety door again and get back into bed. She could lie on Callum's chest so her ear is blocked and cover her head with the duvet; it might be stuffy torture, but the voices might drown.

She could. As catlike as she can, Kira steals onto the landing. The voices drift ahead of her, indistinct and breathy. She should ignore them. She should pretend she never got up and put them down to a dream, triggered by being back here. Back in the scent of pine, of woodsmoke, of cold, wild winter. She shouldn't follow. She shouldn't.

But she will.

The voices drift forward, fading, faint. Gently parting the clacking curtain, Kira tiptoes down the wooden stairs. The slumbering chalet is dark and still, cosy and homely and soft with breathing. Karl lolls on a blow-up bed in the kitchen, a tall, gangly lump on the floor. No one could blame him; the lounge is a furnace. By opting for Carol's floor, Julia's straw was definitely better. It was probably Ørenna not to share with her brother.

At the bottom of the stairs, Kira lets herself breathe. Mission burglar: one to her. In the lounge, nothing moves. Old, grouchy Nibbles sleeps on the couch. The setting moon lights up the curtain, brushing the window in haunted, pale shafts. The whispers dance like leaves in wind and flit toward the door.

She's a sleepwalker. A dreamer. An idiot, maybe. With the start of horror-film unease unfurling under her ribs, Kira follows. She shouldn't. She shouldn't, but her feet keep moving, curling on the thick pile rug. She's as hopeless as a horror film and numb to her mind.

As her fingers touch the door handle, Nibbles starts to yowl.

The sound is electrifying. Breathing in sharply, Kira chills with shock. Her hand flies up to hit her chest. The cat isn't loud, but plaintive, moaning, a rolling sound she's never heard that points to one thing: fear.

Cold pools through her, hollowing her stomach. Her fingers hover on the door handle. Beyond, the voices murmur. Now, she's between a rock and a hard place, or shadows and ghostly words. If she turns, something might be skulking, something that shouldn't be there. If she opens the door, she welcomes the night.

Kira's fingers hover. Nibbles keeps crying. The unease in her gut becomes solid and sick. It's been years. Years of safety, years of humdrum, years of no supernatural at all. The idea of seeing something here, now, is paralysing. Nervous dread seeps through her like water, filling every ounce of her skin. She should have stayed in bed.

She could still go back.

In a blink, the door is open. Her hand is on the handle, but she didn't feel it turn. The whispers float away from her. Pleading, Nibbles yowls.

The moonlit garden glitters. Watching it, Kira aches to leave. It's an ache that spreads through her bones, so cold, an intricate, integral need. She needs to leave the chalet, to journey through the winter night, down the icy road to the forest. That's what the voices want. That's what they hum and sigh and smile. Imploring. Beckoning. Begging. *Come.*

'Don't.' Callum's heat approaches behind her. His voice is low. Slowly, his hands take her arms. Kira blinks, too dazed to jump. Her bare feet had wandered out into the snow. 'I can hear them too. And look.'

Stepping back, her spine against his belly, Kira follows the dip of his head.

Her breath slides back into her throat. White knuckling on Callum's, Kira's fingers clench. 'Oh,' she whispers, in a soft little strangle. 'No. God. God, no.'

Come.

Nibbles yowls louder, moaning, pleading, panic. Callum's fingers pinch Kira's skin.

Come. The voices are insistent.

'What's going on?' Yawning, Karl shambles up beside them. The stairs creak, two sets of feet.

'You're letting all the cold in.' Carol wraps and ties her dressing gown. Julia's face ghosts up next to Kira's cheek. 'Why are we all here?'

Come.

Against her arm, Julia jerks. Carol looks up from her robe and stills.

Nibbles starts to screech. The voices dance and swirl and lift. Flush against Callum, Kira nods to her feet.

On the doorstep, in the untouched snow, is a symbol. A sketchy tree. Four lines for branches. One, a listing slash for the ground. Kira's world caves in.

Whiteland.

ABOUT THE AUTHOR

Rosie Cranie-Higgs is the author of the Whiteland series. She enjoys writing about darkness and ghosts.

Rosie grew up across Europe, and now lives in Malta with her family where she is currently working on her next novel.

Ingram Content Group UK Ltd.
Milton Keynes UK
UKHW010614020523
421079UK00019B/417/J